"Clever, honest, funny, and forever analytical. . . . Each new chapter brings a wise and tender look at single life, dating rituals, and marital unease. This is one of the most charming novels I've read in years, and I loved every last page."

—Jennifer Close, *New York Times* bestselling author of *Girls in White Dresses*

"Readers looking for some light escapism in the vein of *Love Actually*, with other rom-coms sprinkled liberally in the mix, will find that time with this novel passes at an easeful clip."

—*The Globe and Mail*

"An addictive, enthralling read, full of authentic, hopeful characters, each on a quest for their own version of true love. . . . They made me laugh, curse out loud, and cry. This is an impressive, ambitious debut novel about love, forgiveness, and acceptance that will undoubtedly warm your heart."

—Hannah Tunnicliffe, author of *The Colour of Tea*

"Heartbreaking and strikingly honest."

—*Quill & Quire*

"[An] intriguing and heartbreaking debut novel. . . . The novel carefully illustrates the power that each of us has to define who we are and who we can become."

—*Publishers Weekly*

"A living, whispering, shouting, beauty of a book that bypasses easy answers and cracks open the deepest, most contradictory longings in all of us. Stapley is an heir to the likes of Wolitzer and Atwood, with an eye that misses nothing in the way we love, hurt, leave, support, and sabotage each other and ourselves. This is vital and vibrant writing born of true insight into the human heart."

—Grace O'Connell, bestselling author of *Magnified World*

"Marissa Stapley searches through the layers women possess, how hard we work to hide the cracks, as we bury our secrets, pretend what's bad is good—and paper over the glaring flaws in our lives. . . . Stapley renders their awakening with grace and honesty."

—Randy Susan Meyers, bestselling author
of *The Comfort of Lies*

"An immensely readable novel, with smart, engaging characters who come to life on the page—the sort of characters you miss long after you've put the book down. You will see yourself in these women."

—Taylor Jenkins Reid, author of *Forever, Interrupted*

"Heartwarming and insightful, Marissa Stapley's unmissable debut is a sensitive, timely, and compassionate exploration of family, friendship, self-discovery, and the issue perhaps more at the crux of modern womanhood than any other—the struggle to keep hold of who you are while letting love in."

—Abigail Tarttelin, author of *Golden Boy*

"I found myself slipping away at every spare moment to turn the next page. Marissa Stapley has created an interconnected story of unique, believable, relatable women. I absolutely loved this book."

—Chantel Guertin, bestselling author
of *Stuck in Downward Dog*

Mating for Life

a novel

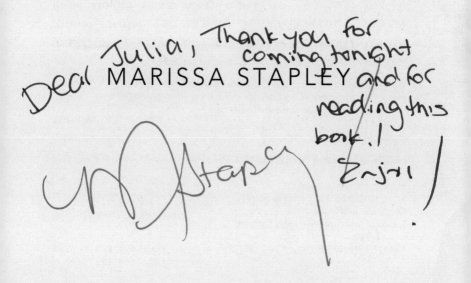

MARISSA STAPLEY

Dear Julia, Thank you for coming tonight and for reading this book.! Enjoy!

PUBLISHED BY SIMON & SCHUSTER
New York   London   Toronto   Sydney   New Delhi

Simon & Schuster Canada
An Imprint of Simon & Schuster, Inc.
166 King Street East, Suite 300
Toronto, Ontario M5A 1J3

This Simon & Schuster Canada edition June 2016

SIMON & SCHUSTER CANADA and colophon are registered trademarks
of Simon & Schuster, Inc.

For information about special discounts for bulk purchases,
please contact Simon & Schuster Special Sales at 1-800-268-3216
or CustomerService@simonandschuster.ca.

Design by Kyoko Watanabe

Library and Archives Canada Cataloguing in Publication

Stapley, Marissa, author
       Mating for life / Marissa Stapley.
Originally published: 2014.
Issued in print and electronic formats.
       I. Title.
PS8637.T358M38 2016   C813'.6   C2015-908148-3
                                               C2015-908149-1

Manufactured in the United States of America

10   9   8   7   6   5   4   3   2   1

ISBN 978-1-5011-3979-6
ISBN 978-1-4767-9748-9 (ebook)

For Joe, and for Maia and Joseph

You're just an empty cage, girl, if you kill the bird.

—TORI AMOS, "CRUCIFY"

Mating for Life

part one

All I really, really want our love to do is to bring out the best in me and in you.

—JONI MITCHELL, "ALL I WANT"

1

Snapping Turtle (*Chelydra serpentina*)

Unlike other turtles, the common snapping turtle cannot hide in its shell because its body is too big. These turtles snap as a defense mechanism, but aren't actually vicious. However, perhaps because of the misconception of aggression, snapping turtles are often targeted, and are endangered in North America. When mating, snapping turtles sometimes engage in an elaborate dancelike ritual in the water that involves eye contact but no touching. Snapping turtles have no defined mating season: they court and mate only when conditions are exactly right.

When Liane swam into the snapping turtle, she screamed. He didn't bite her, but clearly he wanted to. Then he was gone, dipping first his head and then his shell underwater. (She didn't *know* he was a he, but she assumed; there was something placidly male in his glare.)

She sensed the turtle was still there, somewhere below. She turned to float on her back, hearing her mother's voice in her memory as she did. "If you ever feel scared, *don't panic.* You'll drown," Helen had instructed from the edge of the floating dock while Liane paddled below. Liane's eldest sister, Fiona, had already been front-crawling to the middle of the lake, where Helen had placed a DIVER DOWN sign. Ilsa had been lying on the floating dock, too, but then she rolled off and swam, dolphinlike, toward Liane, grabbing her sister's ankle from beneath the waves. Liane had shouted and flailed. "Exactly! Thank you, Ilsa. That's a perfect example of what you don't do. Back float instead." Liane remembered her mother's red suit, brown skin, blond hair, and the way she talked to them as though they were already grown-ups. The swimming lessons were the one thing Helen insisted on during summers that spiraled out slowly, like the pucks of Bubble Tape gum they would buy at the marina for $1.25. The girls didn't even have to unpack their bags if they didn't want to. They were never asked to make their beds.

Now Liane looked up at the clouds and tried to fill her belly with air. But her breath was too shallow and she had to kick. Panic soon forced her to flip to her front and start to swim, fast, for the floating dock.

She wanted to go home, and it had only been one day.

Her plan: to swim and eat salads (mostly because she hated to cook, or couldn't cook; it was a chicken/egg situation she didn't care to analyze) and work on the final pages of her thesis. By the end of the week, when Liane's mother and sisters arrived for their annual early summer cottage weekend, she would have finished it. Then Adam would stop asking her *when* she was going to finish it and she would stop feeling guilty for not responding in a more appropriately proactive way to his father's offer of a job on the faculty at the university, as a teaching assistant, pending her thesis defense.

The other part of her plan, and one she hadn't told anyone about, involved the hope that by coming here alone, by treating this as a regular cottage and normal lake—and not the site of one of her life's greatest tragedies—she could erase the past and turn herself into a normal person. The kind of person Adam wanted her to be. The kind of person she didn't think she could be but knew she should at least *try* to be.

Liane ducked her head underwater—eyes closed, testing herself—and resurfaced with a gasp. In addition to the big fears, her week-alone-at-the-cottage plan hadn't accounted for her many small fears. (Turtles. Seaweed. Algae. Other things too embarrassing to mention. Like ants. Beetles. Walking into cobwebs.) All of these things seemed more frightening without company. (Currently: she could still sense the turtle near, perhaps now waiting at the base of the ladder to bite one of her toes.)

She went down again, and this time kept her eyes open. Then she surfaced, blinked the water from her eyes, and saw movement to her left. The turn of a page. There was a man sitting at the end of the dock at the cottage next door—it had been the Castersen place, but the Castersens had sold it, or were renting it out, or something. Liane couldn't remember but knew Helen had explained it last year when the new dock had appeared and, next, a pair of kayaks had replaced the motorized pontoon boat Mr. Castersen had once called his "Party Boat."

The unfamiliar man sitting on the dock reading looked up and Liane looked down, focusing again on her path through the water. But she should have waved. She was in cottage country. In cottage country, you were supposed to wave (even if you were swimming) and mouth, *Hello,* to people (regardless of whether you knew them). But she was too embarrassed. He had probably heard her screaming about the turtle. He had probably seen the awkward way she'd jumped off the dock, plugging her nose and splaying her legs. And either way, it was now too late because the man—who had copper-blond hair and a matching shadow of a beard—was reading his book again. She kept swimming and looked away from him, but looking away meant she had to look at the shed, so she closed her eyes and ducked under again.

"Why do you keep it?" she had asked Helen, years before, referring to the kayak that hulked in the shed just up from the water. "What am I going to do with it, throw it away?" Helen had asked. "I couldn't live with the idea of it in a garbage dump somewhere until the end of time. And it seems wrong to sell it. So we'll keep it. Maybe one day you'll take it out." "Never," said Liane. What a macabre idea. Horrible. Sometimes she wondered if Helen meant to be so insensitive. She tried to love her mother as she was, *did* love her as she was, but she also wished Helen was more like other mothers. Other mothers would never have left that particular kayak in the shed or suggested Liane go out on the lake in it, for example.

Liane climbed the ladder of the floating dock, wincing and curling her toes against the algae on the steps. Then she sat, hugging her knees to her chest and wishing for a towel. She squinted. The spine of the man's book was orange. A paperback. His head was bent and his shoulders were hunched and he was leaning forward a little. *As though he wants to actually get onto the page, or into it. As though he isn't just reading it but inhabiting it.* Or maybe he was just nearsighted. Still, Liane found herself thinking about a book she had read as a child, about a boy (or was it a girl?) who found a tree with a door in the trunk and when he (she?) opened it, there was another world that had always been there. Liane still asked Helen about it. "Maybe you imagined it," Helen said once. "You were very creative." But Liane still believed this book existed somewhere. She was certain her father had given it to her and had written an inscription on the inside cover she could no longer remember the words of but longed to read again.

She straightened her legs, shimmied forward, and slid into the water. The new dock, the one at the Castersens'/

Possibly Someone Else's Place Now, was closer than the other Castersen dock had been, and bigger. Its blond wood planks stretched out, around, and out again.

Closer now. A few more strokes and she would have a clear view. At the perfect moment, the man leaned back to stretch, tilting the book. She saw white, yellow, black writing.

Junkie by William Burroughs. Disappointing. *And* slightly alarming. Liane gulped air and dove, thinking about how Burroughs had shot his wife in the head. Accidentally. Who could possibly shoot someone in the head *accidentally*? A dozen worst-case scenarios surfaced. She was alone on an island with a man who appeared to want to inhabit a book written about rampant drug use by an "accidental" wife murderer.

Except, Liane reminded herself, they weren't actually alone on the island. It just felt like it because it was still late June and the lake was fairly quiet. The island had plenty of other cottages, most of them tucked behind trees above the granite. When the long weekend came, it would signal the true beginning of summer and the place would feel less isolated. The sound of motorized boats would cause Helen to shake her head and cluck like an irritated hen. She would start talking again about sending around a petition, but she wouldn't. Helen could now identify a lost cause when she saw one.

Liane had reached the ladder of the main dock. She put a foot on the first slimy ledge and pulled up, then took her towel from the closest Muskoka chair, stepped off the dock, and headed for the cottage without looking back at the man. When she was in the shade, she stood on the steps made of stones that had apparently been dragged out of the lake years before by Helen's father. This grandfather Liane had never met had purchased the property in the 1940s and bequeathed it to Helen—and not Helen's brother—when he died. Helen rarely said anything more about this, except that the brother (none of the girls had ever met him, either) had tried to fight Helen for it in court, saying it wasn't fair that she get such a valuable property when she already made such a good living from her music.

Water dripped down Liane's back. She flipped her head and wrapped the towel like a turban, then kept walking. At the door of the screened-in wraparound porch she dipped her feet into the bucket of lake water she had set outside for the purpose of not tracking sand (and bugs, and Lyme-disease-carrying ticks) around the cottage and dried them on the towel folded beside it. When Ilsa arrived at the end of the week, Liane knew, she would good-naturedly shun her younger sister's custom, saying she wasn't sticking *her* feet in dirty water everyone else had been sticking feet in, and that she definitely wasn't then wiping her feet off on a musty towel. ("You want Lyme disease? Take this towel to a lab and have it analyzed.") The sand underfoot would bother Liane, but not as much as it would bother Fiona. Liane would sweep but it would be Fiona who would eventually drag the old vacuum out of the closet and pull it around the main floor. Helen, of course, would have no part of any of it. "I vacuum when I'm about to leave," she would say. "You're wasting a valuable portion of your life by doing so now." "I'm wasting *something*," Fiona would say. "Probably the long-term health of my back. Tell me again why you don't get a new vacuum?" "Because that one still works!" And then somehow, Helen and Fiona would be arguing over an old vacuum versus a new one, landfill versus convenience, and Liane would either glance at Ilsa and roll her eyes or leave the room feeling guilty about causing the fight with her silly bucket of water.

Liane pushed open the screen door and let it bang shut behind her, the sound jarring in the quiet of the morning. From behind the screen she had a view of the dock and she saw the man look up from his book.

• • •

Liane napped. She made soup. She did the *Globe and Mail* crossword as a warm-up and then failed, as usual, at completing any of the crosswords in the *New York Times*. She stared at Sudoku boxes, but could make no sense of them. "Your brain just doesn't work that way," Adam had once said, meaning it to be an affectionate remark—but there was the superior undertone. He was one of those people whose brains worked *every* way. She had said this to him and heard the unintended resentment. *This must be what old married couples feel like. And we've only been together three years.*

She painted her nails with polish she found in Ilsa's room. (Dark red.) She found cream in a drawer in Helen's room and rubbed it all over her face, then broke out in red bumps from the essential oils. (This always happened, yet she always tried Helen's creams.) She iced the bumps. She removed the polish. Then she went up to the closet her father once used and opened it. But there was nothing in it but old jackets, none of them his. She stared into the closet until her breathing became slow and even. She wished that if she pulled aside the jackets, she would be standing before a whole new world, like Narnia. She pulled aside the jackets. This didn't happen. She felt childish and foolish, but also wistful.

What Liane did *not* do was work on her thesis. When she wasn't inside, she was on the dock. She and the neighbor— the Reading Man, as she now called him in her head—were now on cottage waving terms. He had finished *Junkie* and started on *The Sound and the Fury*. She had started bringing her textbooks and reference materials down to the dock. Lying parallel to him, also reading, felt strangely intimate.

Then, on Tuesday afternoon, it rained and she was forced inside, where the blinking light on her still-plugged-in laptop seemed to pulse with neglect. She forced herself to write two paragraphs. Then she reread the words on the screen. They no longer made any sense. She held her breath, and heard the clinking of dishes from the cottage next door.

Liane's thesis was called "The Evil Eye: Envy's Hidden Threat." Apparently it had the potential to be something of a sensation, even publishable, although Liane didn't understand how any of her findings could be a surprise to anyone. Perhaps it was because she had lived with them for so long that she was now like a woman shocked to find her husband of thirty-some years the center of attention at a dinner party due to the intrigue of his conversational paths.

"It's the way you present it," Tansy Miller, a brown-trouser-and-black-oxford-wearing academic, had explained to her when Adam's father, the dean, had arranged for Liane and Tansy to meet for coffee. It was Tansy whose teaching Liane would assist, *if* she ever finished her thesis. "It's your frankness. It's the fact that reading your work isn't boring and the students are bound to see it as such. You mention celebrities. They *love* celebrities." Tansy talked like she had once been a theater major, enunciating her words and using her hands. Liane liked her and wanted to work for her. This had done nothing to spur her into thesis-finishing action.

The problem was that Liane's work *had* become boring, at least to her. Adam had once said, "Well, of course it is, that's what happens, but you've found your niche and you need to stick with it now. You'll get out of the slump." Except she was afraid she wouldn't. Once, the folklore-related work of Alan Dundes, discovered by Liane during her undergrad years, had seemed to hold secrets. She had believed these secrets might even reveal an important *point* about humanity as a whole.

If she could just get back that fervor, maybe everything would be okay.

Now Liane took out a pen and started to make notes by hand, snapping the screen of her laptop shut. Her pen scratched against paper: *Envious gazes, Dundes has written, are driven by envious thoughts and have the potential to do actual physical damage. The evil eye is not a black-magic-related curse, as most people believe, but rather the embodiment of an envious glare—an instant curse that anyone is capable of, even without intent. It is the lack of intent that is the point: Can we control something we do not intend to do?* She paused and thought suddenly of William Burroughs. *It is as though everyone is in possession of a loaded gun he or she could accidentally set off at any moment,* she wrote.

Liane was not an envious person herself and did not believe she possessed anything in particular for others to be envious of (she considered herself average-looking, hated her reddish hair, was possibly of higher-than-average intelligence but not a genius, and wasn't rich). But envy, and its power to damage, was part of the myth of her childhood. Helen had been a popular folksinger who was now often featured in nostalgic documentaries; recently one of her songs had even been covered by a well-known alternative band. Liane had noticed as a child that Helen would never leave the house without first securing a necklace with an evil eye charm dangling from its chain around her neck. When Liane asked, Helen told her it was because, right around the time her first gold record was delivered (1969; Helen had only been twenty), her throat started to ache constantly. She went to see a shaman about it—"Why a shaman?" Fiona, who had been in the room at the time, had asked. "Why not a doctor?" But Helen had ignored her—and the shaman had told her that someone was doing black magic on her, possibly inadvertently and definitely due to envy. ("I was so young. It was unheard-of. Joni Mitchell didn't have her first gold record until the next year, and she was already twenty-seven.") If she didn't protect herself, the shaman told Helen, she could lose her voice forever.

Liane had pictured the shaman as a frightening character with a headdress made of dead animal skulls and felt foolish when, years later, it turned out he was an old friend of Helen's named Bob. Liane became afraid that her mother really would lose her voice. She had a recurring nightmare about walking in the forest on the island with Helen and a large black bird attacking her mother's throat. And as she grew older, she began to feel anxious every time she felt envious of anyone. She developed a fear of the damage she might unwittingly do to others if she ever allowed it to take hold—and so she tried to care as little as possible about what others had that she did not. (Once, as an awkward preteen, she had looked at Ilsa and thought, *Why can't I be that beautiful?* and then had run from the room and refused to make eye contact with her sister for the rest of the day.)

She put down her pen. *Fear.* This was part of her problem. She was afraid that if she completed the thesis and got the job helping Tansy teach classes about superstition and folklore, she'd eventually get a post teaching classes on superstition and folklore herself. (Wasn't that the entire point? Her *niche*, as Adam put it.) She was afraid she would then end up teaching the same thing over and over until one day she would look out at a class full of young people with futures ahead of them that were undetermined, all of these young bodies still possessing the freedom to walk out of the lecture hall and never come back if they didn't want to—

And she'd smite them all with an envious glare.

The fact that her childish fears still loomed large in her life was not the kind of thing she could discuss with Adam. Or anyone, really. She looked down at her wrist and fiddled with the red string that was there (she didn't practice kabbalah; the red string guarded against the evil eye and was less obvious than a necklace, so Liane wore it on the off chance that anyone ever became envious of her), then abandoned her work, even going so far as to shut down her laptop in an act that felt final, defiant. *It's only for now. I just need a break.*

She went outside and sat on the end of the dock. There was a slight chill in the air. Summer had not yet taken hold. The dock next door was empty, and no sounds were carried to her across the small expanse of water. She thought about what she might say, if she could work up the courage to talk to the Reading Man. *Hi,* would be a start. But, historically, she had never been able to do this.

Liane had been in grade six when she had her first irrational crush on a boy she didn't know. Boys she *did* know didn't interest her at all, but sometimes she'd see a boy walking down the street or working at a store and suddenly think, *That could be him, he could be The One.* She'd gift him with all sorts of characteristics he probably didn't have and lie in her bed at night dreaming up ideal meeting scenarios and perfect conversations. She would eventually feel like she knew the boy, even if she had just created an ideal version of him in her mind.

This was back when she still believed in The One, of course. Now she wasn't sure. But she was probably going to marry Adam anyway. "We should probably get married," he had said to her a few weeks before while they were out for dinner, eating at their regular table in the corner of a picket-fenced patio they liked to frequent. Liane had wished not to feel so disappointed. A different type of woman, the woman Adam perhaps thought she was, would have been thrilled. *So* practical, *yes,* why didn't they? They had made some rudimentary plans—nothing traditional, *obviously,* and not a destination wedding because it was overdone and presumptuous; how about cocktails? Adam even suggested screening their favorite movie for their friends. (It was a French noir film called *Breathless,* and it was his favorite, not hers. She didn't point this out.) Popcorn. Spiked Cokes. But wasn't that missing the point? The night was supposed to be about them. He had raised an eyebrow when she said this. *About* us? he had repeated. Liane hadn't told anyone yet that they were engaged, if they really were. But she knew that marrying Adam would mark some sort of shift into a life she had to stick with. It had never occurred to her that she might not want to. She had always been the type of person to stick with everything.

Back in grade six, Liane's routine was to cut through the parking lot of the plaza across from her school every afternoon, although it wasn't necessary for her to do so. Sometimes she would be with Ilsa, who was in eighth grade, but almost never with Fiona, who was in university by that point.

When she passed the window of the pet food store, Liane would strain to catch a glimpse of the boy who worked there, while trying not to look like she was looking. He was much older than she, probably sixteen. She was only eleven. This, combined with the fact that he worked at a pet food store and she didn't have any pets, meant meeting him was unlikely. But it didn't matter. Liane didn't know his name or anything about him other than the fact that he almost always wore a purple Barenaked Ladies hat.

She listened to the album *Gordon* over and over. When school let out for the summer, she walked by the pet food store at least twice a day. She made Ilsa go with her to three Barenaked Ladies concerts in the hopes that she'd see the boy. She never did.

"Why don't you go in and buy a can of dog food or something?" Ilsa had asked after finally refusing to attend another concert, or listen to the song "Brian Wilson," ever again. "He'll never know you don't have a dog." They were standing outside the store. "Do it! I'll wait here." But Liane shook her head, embarrassed. To Ilsa it would have been nothing to saunter in, grab a can of dog food, and ask dozens of questions about it with her hand on the boy's forearm. He probably would have asked Ilsa out, too. It didn't matter that Ilsa was thirteen. She looked sixteen and acted even older. But Ilsa would have said no. She would have been angry with the boy, even though he couldn't possibly have known that it was Liane, standing outside with red splotches on her pale, freckled cheeks, who had a crush on him.

"I can't," Liane had said. "I just can't. I can't talk to him. I'll *die*."

"No one has ever died from saying hello to their crush."

"*I might be the first.*"

Eventually he had stopped working at the pet food store. It was a while before Liane stopped thinking of him every time she heard that song. *Ring a bell and I'll salivate. How'd you like that? You can call me Pavlov's dog.*

Now Liane looked down at her empty hands. She was an engaged woman. Her days of girlish crushes were officially behind her. Whether she could bring herself to say hi to the Reading Man was of no consequence to anything.

She stood and walked back up to the cottage, entering the living room and standing before the built-in floor-to-ceiling bookshelf. Many of the books on it were hers, some were Helen's, a few were Ilsa's or Fiona's or Liane's father, Wesley's, and others had been left by cottage guests. Mysteries and romances and crossword puzzle volumes shared space with Vonnegut (Wesley's) and Plath (Helen's), a biography of Violet Trefusis (Ilsa's; she'd brought it to read the year before, sighed a lot, and left it on the shelf with a bookmark in the middle), Tolstoy (Liane and Ilsa shared the Tolstoy). The crosswords and Sudoku books were Fiona's. Liane remembered Fiona saying something about how doing these guarded against Alzheimer's disease. Everything Fiona did had a point.

Liane continued scanning the shelf, then picked up a book called *The Monsters of Templeton*. It was unfamiliar to her, probably left by one of Helen's friends. She took the book with her when she went upstairs to put on a bathing suit and a pair of denim shorts. With the book in her hands—it wasn't a textbook, not even a classic; there was no reason she *needed* to read it, but she had been drawn to it by the black-and-white leaves and shadowy figures on the cover, and this was something she had not allowed herself for a long, long time—she went back to the dock.

She stretched out her legs and started to read—pointlessly, simply for the pleasure of it, alone at the end of the dock, escaping from her own thoughts and memories into someone else's plotline. She read the first line of the book twice: "The day I returned to Templeton steeped in disgrace, the fifty-foot corpse of a monster surfaced in Lake Glimmerglass." She looked out at the water and thought of the snapping turtle.

At the end of the first chapter she heard the sound of footsteps on the dock next door. Instead of looking sideways, she looked up and around her, at trees and sky, then stretched and started reading again, feeling warm and indulgent. *This is what you're* supposed *to do at a cottage alone for a week.*

> I looked up and began to spin. The stars streaked circular
> above me, my body was wrapped in the warm black, my
> hands had disappeared, my stomach was no longer, I
> was only a head, a pair of eyes. As I touched the beast
> I remembered how, even on that long-ago night, I could
> feel a tremendous thing moving in the depths below me,
> something vast and white and singing.

She looked over at the man just as he looked up, his gaze moving away from his book and connecting with hers. And she wanted to say, *I just read something I thought was beautiful, and it made me feel less afraid. Do you want to hear it?* because she was sure at that moment that he would understand the joy of finding a book you've never read on your own shelf, falling into it quickly, and deciding to do nothing all day but read it. But instead she smiled at him (which was *something*, she told herself), trying not to squint too much in the sunlight. He smiled back, and they held on for an extra beat. Then they both looked out at the water and back down at their books.

By the end of the day, Liane had accomplished the following: she had read the entire novel, infused iced tea with the perfect amount of mint leaves and strawberry, given herself a pedicure using Himalayan sea salt as a scrub and kefir as a foot masque (the former was ingenious, the latter quite gross), and smiled at the Reading Man twice, both times because she had looked up from her book to find him watching her, his own book broken-spined in his lap, the pages blowing in the wind. Eventually he cleared his throat and said, "Hi," in a voice that sounded like it hadn't been used for a while, and she said, "Hi," in a voice that sounded the same.

She didn't die.

The next morning, Liane slid her laptop back into the bag she had brought it in. She took the cottage guest book out to the side porch with her coffee instead. She opened it and flipped backward in the book.

> *Thank you Helen for a wonderful week. We made the most of the weather and still enjoyed many long walks, warm fires and great food. We appreciate you being so generous in offering it to us for the week. Sincerely, The Smiths (Terri and Dave).*

Liane yawned and turned the page. She had no clue who Terri and Dave were, but they sounded boring. Perhaps they were friends from the village Helen now lived in. Helen had once said that most of the people who lived there were boring, but that she loved them for that because it made *her* feel more interesting.

On the next page she saw a familiar scrawl.

Your children are gorgeous, your cottage is magical and you, of course, are a queen of all things. Love, Edie.

Liane experienced a moment of surprise, because seeing Edie's writing made her realize how many years had passed since any of them had seen her.

Edie had *not* been boring. Liane had loved Edie. They all had—even Fiona, who had never liked any of Helen's friends but had spent more time with Edie as a young child than any of the girls, since Helen had toured more back then. There had been some sort of falling-out between Helen and Edie, though, and she had disappeared from their lives around the time Fiona graduated from high school. Liane remembered this because Edie had come to the graduation and Helen had refused to speak to her. Liane had never asked Helen what had happened, and now she wondered why not. They had called her "aunt"; she had been Helen's best friend.

Liane looked down at the writing and remembered the time Edie had taken her, Ilsa, and Fiona on an "expedition" to catch caterpillars, which she had somehow known would make cocoons in the jars, which would then turn into butterflies, which the girls would then release at dusk. "Why at dusk?" Liane had asked Edie. "You must always release butterflies at dusk," Edie had said, her voice full of the mysteries only a woman like her could fathom. She had long hair she braided around her head like a crown and she always wore swishy skirts and an anklet that tinkled when she walked.

Liane closed her eyes. She remembered more: Ilsa's jar

hadn't produced a cocoon. Her caterpillar had died. Later, Ilsa had told her she'd switched hers because she'd known something was wrong with Fiona's—and that Fiona would hate to fail at producing a butterfly. "But didn't *you* want one?" Liane had asked Ilsa. Ilsa had shrugged. "Not really. It felt wrong. And anyway, not as much as Fiona probably did." Liane felt like she was the only person who knew that Ilsa really did love Fiona. She thought perhaps she should tell Fiona about the butterfly, but also that it was too late. *My sisters don't like each other.* She realized this, also, as she continued to follow the loops of Edie's cursive script with her eyes, and thought about how strange it was that there were truths that could exist in families that everyone ignored, even though they were devastating.

Liane closed the book, stood, and went into the kitchen. She opened the cupboard closest to the stove and grabbed a box of spelt flakes and raisins. She scooped kefir onto the cereal. Then she saw her mobile phone sitting on the counter and brought it with her to the side porch. She thought about not calling Adam, but instead she did. She should have before now. It had been days. There were no missed calls, no texts from him, nothing.

"What are you doing?" he asked, as though they had talked a few moments ago.

"Eating breakfast."

"Ah, and you didn't want to dine alone."

"Well, no, not really. I just realized I hadn't called to tell you I arrived safely and thought you might . . ." She was about to say, *be worried,* but stopped, because it wouldn't have been true, and what Adam said next confirmed this.

"I figured I would have seen something on the news," he, ever the pragmatist, said. "I thought you were probably wrapped up in your work and I didn't want to bother you." Pause. "Getting a lot done?"

"Yes," Liane lied. "A ton."

"Good. As am I." There was another pause. Then: "I miss you," Adam said. "The bed feels even bigger without you." They'd just bought a king bed together, which seemed to have been or was *supposed* to have been symbolic of something, but in the end all it felt to Liane was vast. She couldn't imagine it feeling any bigger than it already did. In the night she was so far away from Adam she felt alone. When he moved, she couldn't feel anything. "I went out to that new restaurant on the corner with Jeff and Brynn," he said. "It was awful. You would have laughed. The waiter didn't even know what burrata was when we asked him."

"Well, why did you ask him if you already know what it is?"

He didn't say anything.

"I should probably get back to work," she said. "I miss you, too. See you next week."

She put down her phone and looked at her cereal. Outside, she could hear crickets and bullfrogs and a distant boat. The sound came closer and she found herself channeling Helen, clucking her tongue against her teeth.

She realized she wasn't hungry anymore. She left her cereal and went to the bookshelf, intent on finding another book to read because she already knew she was going to be taking another day off from her thesis. It would need to be the right book, one that would say something about her, just in case the Reading Man was checking out her book spines the way she was checking out his. (Halfway through the day before he had moved on to *Tropic of Cancer*, but then replaced it with *The Sound and the Fury* again. She wondered why.)

Tropic of Cancer was there, on the bottom shelf. Her father's, Liane remembered, picking it up and opening the cover, to where he had written his name: Wesley Robert. She remembered he had suggested she read it when she was only eight, the same year he had died. He had seemed strangely urgent about it, and now she supposed she knew why. "This is my favorite book," he had said. "I always wanted to share it with you." Liane was a good reader from a young age, and so she had tried because she adored her father. But eventually she had to concede defeat. "I'm sorry, Dad, but I have *no* idea what this book is supposed to be about." "That's okay, Li. It's probably a guy thing, anyway."

She flipped through the pages of the book. A passage was underlined. *"There are no more books to be written, thank God,"* she read aloud. Wesley had wanted to be a writer, to pen something similar to his favorite book, and there were times when he would not sleep, seemingly for weeks on end, emerging from the study only to ecstatically declare it was going well and pour more coffee or brandy. Then the crash would come and he would shred the pages while Helen begged him not to.

He seemed to give up in his final year, and Liane often wondered if that was why he had ended his life, or if the giving up had just been a symptom. But she would never know exactly why he had taken the kayak out onto the lake in late December, why he had weighted himself with rocks, why he had slid into the water to sink down, down, down into the icy depths. He hadn't left a note and it had taken her years to accept this. She had searched the cottage every summer. And she wasn't sure, as much as she loved and missed him, that she would ever be able to forgive him for not saying goodbye to her, for not leaving her fatherly instructions in some form. Instead, there was a boat in the shed and the feeling she got when she thought of him, one she had never been able to properly define: some combination of nostalgia, sadness, inadequacy, and disappointment. And the fear, of course. The Big Fear, that one day the darkness (more specifically, manic depression) would catch up with her, too. *My life right now doesn't feel happy enough to be able to avoid it.*

She picked up another book: Martha Gellhorn's memoir,

Travels with Myself and Another, about her marriage to Hemingway. It was Helen's, dog-eared and old. When Liane opened it, there were many passages underlined. One of them: *I knew enough to know that no woman should ever marry a man that hated his mother.* She went to replace the book on the shelf, and that was when she saw the ring. An engagement ring, unmistakably so. A solitaire on a white gold antique scroll band, just languishing on the shelf. *It must belong to one of Helen's friends.* Liane held it between her thumb and index finger and watched the stone catch the light prettily. She needed to text Helen and let her know it had been found so whoever had lost it could stop worrying.

But first Liane slid the ring onto her finger, forcing it slightly. Then she stared at it and tried to decide if it looked right or not.

It did not.

She pulled the ring but it stuck at her knuckle. She pulled again. Nothing.

And then there was a knock at the door.

Another knock; another futile pull at the ring.

At the door stood a man of about Helen's age. He had a gray beard, brown eyes. He held a burlap bag with handles and there were various forms of roughage poking out the top. "I'm Iain, the neighbor," he said, as though there were no other neighbors he could possibly have been.

"Hi, Iain, I'm Liane," she said, trying not to sound disappointed.

"Your mother told me." He seemed oddly nervous. "Anyway, I have a cottage up the road, and a big garden full of spring greens I can't possibly eat, so I let your mother know I'd drop some by for you and she thought it was a good idea."

"Thank you very much; I'll put them to good use. I love salads." He handed her the bag and they stood looking at each other.

"Would you like to come in for a coffee or tea?" Liane asked, because she felt certain he was waiting for some sort of offer, or at least that he didn't want to go. He seemed to be studying her carefully, taking in her face.

"Tea would be perfect."

She led him inside. In the kitchen, she poured water from the cooler into the rusty-topped kettle, making a mental note to get Helen a new one, even though she knew Helen would say that despite the rust it was a good kettle and there was no sense in throwing it away. She found herself sharing this with Iain, her observation about Helen and the kettle, and he said, "Absolutely, that's Helen to a tee, and then she'll either start using your new kettle as a planter or a watering can, or give it to someone else. Anything to save the old one from the landfill—because she doesn't believe they actually recycle anything, you know."

"Oh, yes, I know. Would you like to sit on the side porch?"

"Sure. You should wrap those greens in a towel and put them in the fridge, though. They're very delicate."

She examined him again. Well-groomed, face weathered in an appealing way, eyes crinkled at the sides. He was looking at her, too, with that same surprising intensity, as though he had met her somewhere before and was trying to place her. She felt self-conscious and lifted a hand to scratch a nonexistent itch on her face.

"Oh," he said.

"Oh?"

"You're wearing . . . an engagement ring."

"*Oh*. Right. Yes. It's . . ." The true explanation was too ridiculous, so she said the thing that made the most sense and was technically true. "I'm engaged. To my boyfriend, Adam. My fiancé. My fiancé, Adam." *Fiancé. My fiancé, Adam.* Did it or did it not fit?

No. It does not.

"Wow. Well. That's . . ." He cleared his throat. He was still looking at the ring. "Congratulations."

"Thank you." The kettle had started to screech. She opened the cupboard above the stove that held the spices and teas. "Green, mint, rooibos, chai, Earl Grey, English Breakfast, or something called Youthful Detox?" she asked.

"Oh, the detox, please. Perfect."

She put two bags in the chipped green pot, grabbed two mugs, and headed toward the porch.

"So," she said when they were seated across from each other on the black iron bistro set with the faded red and gold cushions. "Have you had a cottage here long?" Then she sipped the tea and grimaced. "Geez. This stuff is terrible."

"You get used to it. And I've been here since last summer. Two places down from here. I'm in the Bachmans' old place. They retired and moved to Mallorca."

Liane nodded as though she knew this. Then she leaned in, tried to be subtle. "What about the cottage on the other side of us? The one next door. The Castersen place. Did they sell, too?"

Iain shook his head. "They just started renting the place out. For this June and July, to the same people. The man there now is named Laurence Something-or-other. He's a writer. He's working on something. Although he told me he's a bit blocked, so he's been doing a lot of reading, trying to spur himself into action, I suppose. I brought him some greens last week and he told me a little about it. Apparently it's his third novel and he's afraid of having a midcareer slump."

"Oh. A writer?"

"I haven't heard of his books. He says he doesn't write sci-fi, but it sounds like it to me. His first book was short stories and his last book was . . . let me try to remember . . . something about the end of the world being in a hundred years and everyone knowing about it, the exact date of it and everything."

She looked down at the ring on her finger. "Well, I guess that doesn't have to be sci-fi. Maybe more just a study of human nature. It *is* pretty interesting. What would you do if you knew the world was going to end in a hundred years? Would that change anything for you?"

Iain looked thoughtful. "I really don't know. Selfishly, probably it would change nothing for me. But then again, for my daughters and sons it would. Not much point in having kids, right? Or more of them, in my one daughter's case. Maybe that would be liberating."

As he spoke, she wished for a moment that Iain was Helen's type. It would be nice to have someone like him around. "Liane's mother is a free spirit," Adam had once said to his own parents, employing his usual tact. "You know how it is in show business." "She's not in show business, she used to be a folksinger," Liane had said to him later. She wasn't sure why Adam's words had made her feel so angry. Maybe because he'd said what he'd said in the same way a person might say *Liane's mother is a mental patient.* But he was right, of course: the reality of this free-spiritedness was that Ilsa's father was an ex-lover of Helen's who lived in Paris and whom she had met while on tour; Wesley had stumbled into her life during a visit to an ashram in India (Fiona and Ilsa had stayed with Edie, and Helen had been away for weeks because she was experiencing some sort of career/existential crisis); and Fiona's father—well, no one was exactly certain who he was, least of all Helen.

She realized Iain appeared to be waiting for her to say something.

"Which could be good for people who didn't want to have kids at all," Liane said. "Then they could stop having to explain themselves. Liberating, I think that's exactly it. Because you feel this sense of obligation to procreate." She thought maybe she was now talking about herself, and hadn't meant to be. *Do I not want kids? Or do I just not want them with Adam?*

"True," Iain said. "It would be as good a reason as any. Better than the reasons most people come up with these days: 'I'm too selfish. I need more *me* time.' What else do you think might happen? A hundred years . . . would people riot, do everything and everyone in before the hundred-year mark hit, do you think?"

"Maybe. Or maybe not. Maybe nothing would change at all. Maybe we all think the world could end at any second anyway, so what would change in the knowing? Maybe it would be *nice* to know."

"Sounds like we're going to have to read this book," said Iain. Then he sipped his tea and said, "I'm afraid I don't have a creative bone in my body, and I don't understand the life of a writer. I wouldn't like to be alone as much as he is, I don't think. Although his wife and two girls join him on weekends."

Wife and two girls.

You're engaged, she told herself. *You're even wearing a ring.* She looked down at it again and a nervous giggle escaped from her lips. She covered her mouth. "Sorry," she said. "I'm feeling a bit weird. It turns out I'm not used to being alone, so I guess I wouldn't make a very good writer, either. I'm supposed to be working on my thesis, but I haven't gotten much done at all and I think I just . . . I'm feeling a little odd." She covered the ring with her other hand and looked up at Iain.

He had a concerned expression on his face. She felt guilty then for behaving so strangely in front of a person she didn't know. So she said, "Would you like to stay for lunch?" and then felt needy and embarrassed.

But he said, "Why don't I take you to the marina for fish and chips? I bet all you need is to reconnect with civilization for a bit and you'll be right as rain."

Right as rain. She found his presence comforting. She said, "I think you're on to something. I need to leave the island, just for a few hours. Do you have a boat?"

He nodded. "A small one, but yes," he said, as though ashamed of this fact.

Later that day, when she returned to the cottage, she didn't feel as alone. Lunch off the island and in Iain's company, their conversations about books, about the fact that he'd been a museum curator before retiring, his interest in her thesis, had officially broken the spell. (*Wife, girls.* That had helped, too. Although not in a good way.) She put away all the books she didn't need for research, ate all the greens in several giant salads, and finished the last page of her thesis by Friday morning.

Also: she went to the shed. She hesitated, then dragged the kayak out to the dock and spent a morning washing it carefully with lake water. She did not cottage-wave to the Reading Man during this time. She put on a life jacket. She wore it until the sun was about to set. Finally she got in the kayak and paddled away. The lake was like a garage-sale mirror, smooth but mottled. She stopped paddling, closed her eyes, and pictured the inside cover of that book she believed her father had given her. She remembered the orange of the endpapers, the vaguely musty scent trapped between the pages; he always shopped at secondhand bookstores. She saw the words,

To Liane, don't ever stop believing in the possibility of secret magical worlds. Love, Dad

She said aloud, "I'll try. Goodbye, Dad. I love you."

It didn't change anything, but it was something rather than nothing. A start, maybe.

2
Swan (*Cygnus*)

*Swans are famed for forming monogamous pair bonds, but
the idea that they mate for life may be a myth. While swan
"divorces" were thought to occasionally happen, mostly
due to nesting failure, scientists have now witnessed a high
enough number of swan partings to suggest that swans may
not be as loyal as originally thought.*

Something was going to happen. Looking back on
the day later, from the distance that would grow
between Fiona and everyone who mattered in her
life, she realized she had known this.

This coming Thing had woken her in the night and she
had taken one of her pills: they were hidden at the bottom
of her nearly empty makeup case. (Fiona only wore makeup
on special occasions. She prided herself on her barefaced
look.) Ativan, mostly. Some Xanax. She rationed the pills because she was not going to become one of those people who
thought no one could tell that she constantly seemed a little
too fast or a little too slow or a little too *happy*. Every time she
took a pill, she wished she had succeeded at making her life
perfect enough not to need them.

Next, Fiona looked in on the boys: Cole and Beckett, the
twins, had just turned fourteen, and Eliot, the baby (not a

baby anymore at all, she had to keep reminding herself), was eleven. Fiona and Tim's three sons were named after authors, even though she and Tim were not authors themselves, or even particularly voracious readers. Fiona had wanted a theme, that was all. Tim preferred the newspaper or weighty biographies, and Fiona kept up with her book club reading, or whatever Oprah was endorsing at the moment. But when Tim was away she read self-help books (most recently: *How to Stop Worrying and Start Living* by Dale Carnegie)—but *only* when Tim was away because the books embarrassed her. She didn't want her husband to think she needed *help*. (And anyway, she didn't *need* help. She just liked to have backup for the other twenty-eight to thirty days of the month she didn't allow herself to take pills.)

Lately, because of work demands, Tim had been away more than ever. She had grown used to it, and now found she was having trouble sleeping when he was home. When his cold feet sought hers, she rolled away. This bothered her, but she wasn't sure what to do about it. *It's probably normal.*

Fiona looked down at Eliot, her no-longer-baby, and felt a twinge. It had been a while since she had felt one of these. She had dispatched Tim to the hospital shortly after Eliot's birth, and once they had double-checked she could be firm when people asked if they were going to have any more children. She could smile and say, "Oh, Tim's been taken care of"—or, if she'd had a glass of wine, she might lower her voice to a mock-whisper and use the word *snipped.*

But even as the boys grew to impossible sizes (she now avoided looking at baby pictures of them because the idea that they had once been small and so entirely hers filled her with an ache), Fiona couldn't seem to let go of those night-time moments. If she leaned down to kiss their cheeks, Cole and Beckett would stir but Eliot wouldn't move. She could kiss him over and over, and often had. A secret: lately, when

Tim's being home caused her to be wakeful, she might climb into Eliot's bed to curl around him, feeling a sort of shame as she did so, but unable to stop herself from seeking this closeness. A few times Eliot had half woken, kissed the air beside her cheek, and said, "Love you, Mommy. Night," in the same way he had when he was five. (Each instance had caused the ache to become an exquisite starburst of pain and she had risen from the bed and returned to her room.)

On the night the Thing woke Fiona and she took a pill, she tried climbing into bed with Eliot but he squirmed away. So she went back to her room, where she hesitated, then slid her own now-cold feet toward her husband's calves. She was remembering nights, long past now, when they would both be awake, perhaps because one of the children had been up with a bad dream or he had been working late. On these nights, the moonlight would shine on their bedspread as they touched feet and talked about things that seemed special and secret because of the silence and darkness. But this night, Tim didn't respond to the invitation of her cold feet, and Fiona didn't roll toward him and rest her face against his shoulder the way she had before she grew used to him being away. She just closed her eyes and tried to breathe steadily, hoping she could trick herself into falling asleep.

The next morning, a mild headache was all that remained of her unrest the night before. The day ahead, a Friday, was a busy one. Fiona was going to her family cottage the following day, which meant flying with Ilsa, her middle sister—she lived in Rye, too, with her husband, who was Tim's business partner—from the White Plains airport to Toronto, then renting a car and driving north until the walls of rock appeared and she had to remind herself to focus on the road and not drift to the shoulder of childhood memory. The annual late

June cottage visit was the only time Fiona left the boys each year, and one of the few times she saw Helen. But this year she was feeling anxious about it for different reasons than normal. (The normal reasons: the undercurrent of animosity always at play between her and Ilsa; the sadness she sometimes felt because she thought she and Liane weren't as close as they could be or should be; and everything with Helen, all of it, nameless things, mother-daughter things that weighed on Fiona and forced her to strive harder in her own life to become bigger, and, perhaps most importantly, better than all of it.) This year, it wasn't all that, though. She simply didn't want to leave. She felt nervous. She felt like staying put, playing sick, crawling into bed, and waking up when the weekend was over and the threat had passed.

Something is going to happen.

For distraction, Fiona turned her attention to her list of things to do. Rita, the nanny-turned-housekeeper, would be around that weekend, but Fiona still wanted to prepare a few meals and label them with reheating instructions. (She would try to remember to write, *I'll miss you, Tim. See you in a few days,* at the end of the note she would leave on the counter.) And, importantly, she also had a cocktail party to finish preparing for. She always hosted one this time of year, inviting a few of Tim's colleagues and some key neighbors. She had said this once to Tim, and he had tilted his head and smiled and said, "*Key* neighbors? What, are you planning to launch me into a political career? Are we strategizing socially?"

Perhaps it was one of the good things about Tim that he didn't understand the importance of social strategy, that he wasn't aware of all she did to make sure things in their lives were just so. Didn't a good wife, a good homemaker, the kind of person *she* was, make it all look effortless?

When really it was all so contrived it was almost always at risk of breaking apart.

Fiona realized she had been holding on to the counter so tightly her knuckles had turned white. She released her grip. *Cocktail party.* Where was her list? It was always a challenge to manage hosting the cocktail party and departing for the cottage, but it was important to get it done before July, when everyone would be away and the regrets would outnumber the acceptances of her invitations, which were generally delivered in person or, at the very least, by telephone. And if she did it too early in June, there was too much of a risk for a cool or rainy evening.

Fiona found her list and then went to the front hall, where she stood, head bent, rifling through her purse, making sure she had keys, wallet, sunglasses. But when she heard footsteps on the porch, she paused. The mail carrier lifted her hand and waved through the beveled glass of the front door as she mounted the steps. Fiona waved back, zipped her handbag shut, and went out to the porch to fetch the mail. She was on her way out, yes, but she was still going to sort it, put aside what needed to be dealt with, recycle what needed to be recycled, and pass along what needed to be passed along. It wouldn't take long. The boys almost never got mail and anything to do with the household she handled herself.

Today: the regular assortment of flyers, a few bills, and a yellow envelope with wildflower seeds embedded in it that contained a thank-you card. She ran a thumb across the rough paper and found herself remembering the blue envelope that had arrived in the mail a few weeks before. It had been similar in texture: pockmarked, rough, and gritty, as though made from recycled material. It had arrived on a day similar to this one, when she had been on her way to do things that felt important, but had paused to deal with the mail. She hadn't recognized the handwriting and had taken the envelope up to her office (she had needed her letter opener; she had forgotten to take off her shoes), and realized almost too late: the letter wasn't addressed to her. She had stood at her desk, letter opener gripped like a weapon aimed at the heart of the envelope. A letter from Vienna. For Tim. Who did they know in Vienna? She had a sudden impulse to shred it. But, no. *You're being silly.*

Still, instead of putting it on Tim's desk, Fiona had tucked the letter beneath the blotter of her own desk.

And left it there. For two weeks.

Now she put the yellow envelope down on a side table. She'd give Tim the blue letter eventually. Really, there was no reason to be hiding it.

In the car, she turned down Parsons Street, toward Rye High School, where Beckett and Cole were each in a summer enrichment program, Beck for music and Cole for math. It must have been break time. She could see several students leaning against a wall of the school. And one of them was Beck, she realized. Her heart sped up. Lately, Beck had been different. He'd missed a few curfews, and was talking back to her and Tim. For a second, as she watched him now, she thought he was smoking. But it wasn't him. It was the boy standing a few feet away from him. The smoke hung in the air above Beck's head before floating away. Her son turned and slouched against the wall of the school, his back now to the boy who was smoking. She felt relieved. They weren't friends.

She kept watching her son, unable now to look away. He appeared, in that instant in the sunlight with its rays falling on hair so yellow-blond it looked like it couldn't possibly be natural (but Fiona knew that it was because it was the exact color her husband's had been before it turned gray), as though his skin were somehow too tight or too awkward to wear, but soon it wouldn't be and all traces of boyhood would be gone.

The driver behind her honked. She moved forward,

hoping Beck hadn't seen her. Although she had spent years preparing to let go, the fact that she couldn't stop the car, get out, and shout, *Beck! Hi!* when she saw her son at school made her sad. Being a parent had become to Fiona like falling in love with someone who would not exist from year to year. The helpless babies, the entrancing toddlers, the little boys who had filled her with a sense of everything—and then, these man-children. Eventually, men entire. Perhaps it would become easier when they *were* men, she thought. She caught a glimpse of herself in the rearview mirror and realized she was frowning, hard. She tried to relax the frown, but the furrows stayed where they were between her brows.

"Damn it." She had missed the turnoff that would have taken her to the commercial end of town, and ended up driving instead on the road by the water, her destination now behind her. She should have made a U-turn, and her GPS was frantically telling her to do so (even if she knew exactly where she was going, she always typed her destination into the GPS, because she liked following the directions, feeling a sense of accomplishment as she did), but instead she kept driving, turning her head to look out at the water, knowing she should be focusing on the road but unable to remember the last time she had driven along a road with no particular destination. Maybe never. The sun hit the waves, which smashed against the breakwater. "Make a U-turn," the GPS instructed. She turned it off. On the other side there was calm, and a pair of swans paddling together into the sun. She watched the swans until her chin was at her shoulder, then turned to face the road and redirected her car so that she was once again heading in the right direction.

Was Jane's comment at book club the night before still bothering her, was *that* why she was so out of sorts? "But haven't you ever wished for a little girl?" Jane had asked, cheeks flushed from too many glasses of wine. (Fiona only ever allowed herself a maximum of two glasses of wine at book club.) "It's not too late, you know. You're barely forty, right? You could have a bonus baby. An adorable little pink thing to dress up and parade around, like I do with Maddie." And Jane had giggled and sloshed white wine on Sylvia McCain's couch and Fiona had laughed insincerely and turned away to start another conversation, feeling a flare of annoyance (and not just because she was only thirty-eight). She didn't like it that Jane was suggesting she lacked something. She didn't like the way she felt when she talked to Jane, either, like she was always one step behind, like there was something she wanted to say but she couldn't figure out how to say it.

Jane had once been an investment banker, but then she'd married another investment banker and decided to Become a Mother. Fiona had briefly been a kindergarten teacher pre-motherhood, but going back to work made no sense after the twins were born and especially not after the family moved from Toronto to New York and she needed new credentials. Because she'd gone from teaching kindergarten to being a mother, she sometimes felt she'd never been anything *but* a mother. This didn't feel like a bad thing. She felt somehow more qualified than Jane, who now taught a Tabata class at a local gym, to "keep myself from going to shit completely," and drank too much almost every time Fiona saw her. Perhaps, if she had considered Jane a friend, she might have confided in her that she had *wanted* all boys. But she almost never told anyone that. She came from a family of all sisters, a mother, no father. And yet men made more sense to Fiona than women did.

Fiona had eventually risen from the couch, thanked the hostess, and gone home. *The nerve of Jane, to say something like that to me,* she had thought.

Now she pulled into the driveway and turned off the car's engine, seeing the crates stacked on the wraparound porch as she did. "Damn it," she said for the second time that day. It was produce delivery day. In the spring and summer, a farmer delivered his organic bounty to her home each week and she organized a co-op share with her neighbors. (In the winter it was every two weeks, and she set it up in her basement and didn't mind that people trooped through the house with wet boots every other Friday. In fact, she loved it, loved showing off her house, loved feeling that she was a hub in the neighborhood. The organic produce hub. Which seemed like a small thing, perhaps, to those without children—or to Ilsa, who had questioned her about it once. "Why wouldn't you just go to the farmers' market on Purchase Street on the weekends?"—but was absolutely not a small thing at all. She, by working directly with the farmer and orchestrating the weekly organic drop-off, was a part of something that was important.)

Except somehow, today, she had forgotten all about it. There were even a few neighbors standing on the porch, waiting. She felt her cheeks grow warm. *How* could she have forgotten? It was Friday. Every Friday, the produce came.

She got out of the car, leaving her groceries behind, and stepped onto the porch to help sort the vegetables. "I'm so sorry," she said to Michelle Turnbull and Alice O'Shea, who stood waiting. "I was just . . . I had an appointment that went late."

"It's fine, Fiona, we know how busy you are," Michelle said, and Alice smiled, but Fiona still felt flustered and exposed. When she finally went inside, too embarrassed to start unloading her piles of generic, big-box groceries—all the cereals and granola bars and bottles of juice she needed to keep the boys fed (not all fresh and organic all the time; she realized she just wanted people to believe that)—she felt as though her cadence had been thrown off. *Focus,* she told herself. But the Thing had seen its opening and was reminding her that it was coming. She shook her head. *No. Nothing is coming. Nothing bad is going to happen. I'm just tired.* She made an espresso in her single-serve brewer, then made it a double.

Tim came home from work early. He rubbed his eyes while he stood in the kitchen, reminding her of all three of the boys at once. Eliot was in the backyard because his "screen time" had ended, but the twins were both out, Beck at band practice and Cole at a friend's.

"The guests should start arriving around seven," Fiona said as she layered summer vegetables in a ceramic baking dish. Everything else was prepared, and Rita was outside, setting up plates, candles, cutlery, and napkins in baskets, ice buckets, and galvanized steel bins for microbrews, glasses, and a small minibar.

"Sure. Looking forward to it. Bit of a tiring day, but I'll just have a rest for a few minutes, then shower and dress." He walked into the kitchen. "Whatever you've been cooking smells delicious. Ah, your famous tian." He kissed her cheek as he passed, and she smiled, feeling herself relax slightly. She liked it when he called her dishes "famous." (She secretly considered a lot of the things she made "famous" and Tim had always seemed to understand this.)

She pulled two bottles of his favorite Riesling from the wine rack and put them in the fridge. When Tim was showered she'd open a bottle, or ask him if he wanted some scotch. She'd make their last day together before she went away a nice one, even if she *was* preoccupied with the party.

"Oh," Tim said, pausing on his way out to the screened-in porch, where he would often take off his shoes and rest at the end of the day. "We'll be one short. Michael had to fly to Copenhagen to put out some fires. This deal *is* going to happen but it's taking some massaging and one of us had to be there. He offered, because he knew we were having this do tonight. But he said Ilsa will still join us. They had already arranged for Sylvie to stay with the kids."

"Oh, well, she doesn't have to . . ." Fiona began, but what she wanted to say hung in the air between them. *I don't want her to.* She saw brief disappointment—in *her;* she hated that—on Tim's face. *I wish you had never told me,* she thought but didn't say. Because how could she fault her husband for always being so honest with her, for having a moral compass so strong he seemed constantly pointed in the direction of the truth?

"Michael said she's been looking forward to it. Something about wanting to meet that artist you said you'd invited?" Michael, Tim's business partner, was fifty. His divorce had not yet been final when Ilsa, then twenty-five, had flown in for a visit and Michael had become entranced with her during a dinner party. Fiona had been surprised when Ilsa had started to date him. But now Ilsa was thirty-three and they were seven years into a marriage, with two young children: a four-year-old girl, Ani, and a three-year-old boy, Xavier. Michael also had two older children, Alexa and Shane, from his first marriage, both of whom were now in college.

"The artist's name is Lincoln Porter," Fiona said. "His wife is coming, too." She had invited the Porters three years in a row, but they had always declined for various reasons.

Tim loosened his tie, took off his jacket. "What does he paint?"

"Impressionist landscape."

"Like Ilsa," Tim said, and Fiona felt bothered that he paid such close attention to Ilsa. But she didn't say anything because she knew, in a way her husband did not, that some things were better left unsaid. Like this: that once, her beautiful younger sister had tried to kiss her husband. It was after the very dinner party during which Ilsa had been introduced to Michael. Fiona had developed a migraine and had gone to bed, and Ilsa had volunteered to stay up and help clean. "I don't think she knows what she's doing," Tim had said the next morning over coffee, Fiona's limp hands in his. "I think there's a lot of pain there. Her marriage just ended. She's so young to already be divorced." Fiona had gritted her teeth. *So young.* Yes, indeed. Tim had asked her not to tell Ilsa she knew, and Fiona had complied out of loyalty to him only. "You should try to forgive her," he had said. "You're her big sister. Maybe you can help her." But Fiona had never been able to do either of those things.

"The Astors have a Lincoln Porter painting, above the fireplace in their great room," she said.

"Oh. Yes. The riverbed. Very nice. I'll mention to him that I've often admired it." He left the room and went to stretch across the chaise in the screened-in back porch.

Meanwhile, Fiona wiped the counters, then passed him to go check on things outside. She hadn't done all she had wanted to do in the garden that day. But it was only four-thirty—she had time. She picked up a small trowel from a bucket.

Later, when the phone rang, her hands were dirty and she wiped them on her pants, leaving streaks of dark on the khaki that she looked down at, surprised. *Why did I do that?*

"Hello?"

A pause. "I'd like to speak to—to Timothy. Timothy Sherman. Is he there?" The foreign lilt, the way the young woman asked if he was there, the upturn at the end of the question so different from the way she, Fiona, sounded when she talked.

"I'm sorry," Fiona said. "Could you repeat that, please?"

"Timothy Sherman. Is he there? Do I have the right number?"

Fiona swallowed hard. *Vienna.* It had to be. And somehow, she had known.

She stood outside the screened-in porch and listened, but could hardly fathom what it sounded like Tim was saying.

All she could think was, *Something happened.*

The phone rang again later. It was Ilsa. Tim was still upstairs. Fiona was standing in the kitchen, still in her gardening clothes with the dirty streaks. How long had she been standing there? Could she cancel the party? No. It was too late. She needed to get upstairs and get dressed.

"Hey," Ilsa said. She always sounded like she'd just gotten out of bed: throaty, luxuriant. "I can't *wait* to get out of the house. Do you need anything? Can I pick anything up?" The way Ilsa said "I can't wait to get out of the house" reminded Fiona of the way Ilsa had sounded as a teenager. Always longing to get away, to get out, to do something, anything at all. *You have it all, Ilsa. And yet somehow you always want more.*

"Hello? Fi?" Ilsa said.

"Sorry. No. I don't need anything. Just bring yourself. See you around seven." And she hung up the phone without saying goodbye.

Somehow she managed to shower and dress, although she couldn't remember doing it after it was already done and felt confused when she saw she had put her chin-length blond hair in a headband, applied concealer under her eyes, a small stroke of blush on each cheek, a little mascara, and that she was wearing a navy jersey dress and flat taupe sandals. Fiona on autopilot was as efficient as ever; she had even put on her good watch and diamond studs.

"Fiona," Tim said, from where he was sitting on the bed.

"Don't," Fiona said, and left the room, stopping just short of slamming the door. Eliot would hear.

When she came down the stairs she saw that Ilsa had arrived and was standing under a tree outside in the failing light of early evening. Fiona's sister now turned and walked toward the house, brushing grass or something from her dress as she did so. As though, Fiona thought, she had been sitting somewhere, maybe on a grassy hill, maybe at the park, waiting for an acceptable time to arrive. *Other sisters would say,* Come whenever you want. *But I guess I'm not that kind of sister.* She was carrying a bag in one hand and a little jacket in the other—it looked tiny, pointless, an accessory. She had on a teal silk dress with buttons up the middle and ruche up the sides. Her brown fringe fell into her eyes and the flyaways in her shoulder-length hair lit up in the dim glow of the electric candles in lanterns on the porch. Her left arm clattered with bangles as she reached up to ring the doorbell.

"Hello!" When she was inside, she kissed Fiona on both cheeks, and Fiona had to stand on her toes because she was in flats and Ilsa was in stilettos, high, strappy, and bronze. This annoyed Fiona, who thought about her floors, her grass. She didn't ask people to take off their shoes when they came over but always hoped they would be practical about their footwear. Ilsa never was.

"I'm sorry Michael couldn't make it," Fiona said.

Ilsa shrugged and stepped farther inside. "Is anyone here yet?"

"No. You're first," Fiona said, following her into the kitchen.

"Where do you want these?" Ilsa lifted two bottles of Veuve Clicquot out of the bag.

"You're far too generous. Thank you." Fiona took them and put them in the fridge, feeling irritated by them. It was *so* Ilsa. The two bottles of French champagne made everything else—the bottles of Riesling, the summer vegetable tian, now on porcelain appetizer spoons, the frenched lamb chops, ready to grill, the crostini—seem drab.

"Are you okay?" Ilsa asked.

"Fine. Why?"

"You look . . . tired or something."

"Gee, thanks."

"Oh, don't be so sensitive. You look perfect as usual. I just thought . . . But never mind. Can I have a drink? And where is that husband of yours? I have to chastise him for throwing my husband to those wolves in Copenhagen."

Fiona opened the fridge and stood still for a moment. *That husband of yours.* Jane, the outspoken woman from her book club whose comments had so distracted Fiona the evening before, had once met Ilsa and said, "Now, there's a woman I wouldn't trust around my husband." But she'd said it in an admiring way. Fiona, if she had known Jane at all, would have said something to Jane like, *You don't know the half of it.*

"He's upstairs. He got home late," Fiona lied, struggling to keep her tone even. Should she take another pill? *Bad idea. No.*

Ilsa wrinkled her nose at the Riesling. "Don't you have anything less sweet?" she asked.

"There's Pinot Grigio outside. Or I can open the champagne."

"No, no, that's for you and Tim. And besides, it's not cold."

The doorbell. Fiona took a deep breath. *You can do this. You can pretend nothing is wrong. You do it all the time.*

The artist was the last to arrive, with his wife. He was tall, with a dark suit jacket that seemed too formal and perfectly formal at the same time. His eyes were blue, his hair was white. Underneath the suit jacket was a white shirt, no tie. He was handsome in that overly masculine way Fiona didn't especially like (everything enlarged, hands, jaw, nose, brow).

Lincoln's wife stood beside him, gray-streaked blond and birdlike. Fiona couldn't remember her name. Anna? Elizabeth? Something traditional. She wanted to ask Tim because he never forgot anyone's name, but had managed to get through most of the evening speaking only to Tim when absolutely necessary. And this, Fiona decided, was not absolutely necessary. What did it matter what the wife's name was? For once in her life she was not going to be the perfect hostess, was not going to go around introducing people and matchmaking guests and worrying about every little thing. She nodded and waved to Lincoln and his nameless bird-wife and went to the bathroom, where she pulled the door closed and leaned against the wall, closing her eyes and attempting to compose herself. It was the second time that evening she had needed to do this.

When she emerged, Ilsa was leaning against the wall.

"I'm having trouble working up the nerve to introduce myself to him. Do you think you could do it for me?"

"Since when have you had trouble introducing yourself to anyone?"

"I'm feeling shy, I guess. He's an incredible artist." Ilsa shook her hair out of her eyes. "I once stood in front of one of his canvases and cried at the idea that no matter what I did, I would never be able to create anything so beautiful. He used to guest-lecture when I was in art school and I'd sit in the front row, starstruck."

"Well, I'd introduce you, but I can't remember his wife's name," Fiona said.

"I never said I wanted to meet his *wife*." Ilsa sidled past Fiona and the bathroom door clicked shut. Fiona stood for a moment staring at the closed door, thinking that she should have said something else, that there was something a little unhinged about Ilsa that night. But instead she walked away. She had to ask Rita to broil the crostini now and put out the salted tomato wedges. She had other things to worry about.

• • •

Later, Fiona saw Ilsa go back outside and walk to the back of the yard, where she leaned against the fence and talked to Jane. Jane immediately started to laugh and so did Ilsa, and then they were leaning against each other and talking as though they had known each other forever. Fiona felt something like jealousy. Why was it so easy for Ilsa to make friends? Why was it so impossible for Fiona? A moment later, Jane moved away from Ilsa, waving her empty wineglass, heading for the bar table. And, as Fiona watched, suddenly feeling like her backyard was not her backyard but instead a stage with multiple players, she saw Lincoln end the conversation he was having with Bill and Allison Du Pont beside the blue spruce. He walked toward Ilsa. He touched her wrist, lifted it, said something to her while she smiled up at him. Eventually he examined her other wrist. He was reading the tattoo that was there, Fiona realized. She was unable to look away as he gently moved the bangles aside.

Finally Fiona crossed the yard and approached, with the strange feeling that she was too late. "Lincoln, my apologies for being so rude and not greeting you and your wife." She emphasized the words "your wife" and directed them at Ilsa. Then she lowered her voice. "But I have to tell you something. I am mortified, completely mortified, but I cannot remember your wife's name. Please forgive me. And then remind me of her name and let's never speak of this."

Lincoln didn't move his gaze from Ilsa's face. And Ilsa didn't move hers from his, and Fiona wanted to slap them both back into reality. "Her name is Rebecca," he said. "I promise I won't tell her." Still, his eyes were on Ilsa's face. "I was just leaving, actually. Rebecca is already gone. Headache. It has been nice to meet you, Ilsa Bisette," he said. "And, Fiona, lovely party."

Then he walked away.

Fiona's voice was cold. "Just because you respect him as

an artist is no excuse to behave inappropriately," she said. "You're a married woman."

Ilsa laughed at her. "You're such a prude. Behave inappropriately? Come on. We were just talking. For two minutes, *maybe*."

"He was looking at you like he wanted to eat you."

"Was he really?"

"Ilsa," Fiona said, hoping her tone contained a warning.

"Relax, big sister. I won't ruin your party by allowing him to fling me on the buffet table and—"

"It's not a *buffet*," Fiona hissed.

"You're acting even more uptight than usual, you know."

"And *you're* acting like a teenage girl."

"Which is far better than acting like an old lady."

Fiona turned and walked away from her sister. She pressed through a small group of people and wished that all of them would leave her home immediately. Ilsa with her seductive grace, Lincoln with his contrived charisma, all of them, everyone, gone.

Tim, too, she realized. She didn't want him to be there, either.

So later, after the guests had finally departed—far too slowly—instead of sitting at the granite table with her husband, finishing the dregs of a bottle and dissecting the evening as she had envisioned doing earlier that afternoon, Fiona did something she never imagined she would do: she packed a bag for Tim (meticulously, of course) and told him to leave the house.

But she didn't feel any better after he was gone.

3
North American Black Bear (*Ursus americanus*)

In spring and summer North American black bears abandon their usually solitary behavior to socialize and procreate. While the male copulates with as many females as possible, the female only mates once every two years and gives birth every two to four years. In the years when the mother bears are ready to mate, they force their yearling cubs to stop traveling with them. This is in part to protect the cubs from the aggressiveness of the male bears during mating season.

lsa drove. She drove and she waited. Even as she moved fast, across pavement, along highway, she felt motionless and expectant. She would reach up and touch her bottom lip, which was slightly swollen from all the kissing, and she would think: *Shouldn't this at least hurt? I feel nothing.*

But then, about halfway to the cottage, just past Holland Marsh, where the farmers' market Fiona always insisted they stop at every summer for fresh produce was, Ilsa *did* feel something: she felt pissed off at Fiona for not being there. How could she have left Ilsa that message saying "I'm not coming, I've called the rental company, your name is now on the insurance for the car, don't forget your car seats" (as if she would forget the *car seats* for her own children!), and then turned off her phone? Ilsa had tried to call her sister several times afterward, growing angrier each time she pressed the call button. She hadn't been sure what she was going to say. Probably something like, *Come on, we've had fights worse than this, and you've never shirked a responsibility because of it,* in the hopes that using the word *responsibility* would bring Fiona back to her senses.

When Ilsa began to feel angry at her sister, she finally felt the pain she had expected to feel, a pain that now began to radiate into her heart, or the area where she assumed her heart was—her figurative heart, not the real one. Imagined pain, since there was really no such thing as a heart, not the way people talked about anyway. She looked in the rearview mirror at Ani and Xavier, both asleep, Xavier with his thumb in his mouth, hair in sweaty curls around his temples, Ani's eyes closed, the dark sweep of lashes visible even from the front seat, and she thought of Michael. Then she thought of Lincoln. Then she tried to just focus on the road, but she couldn't, so she pulled over and closed her eyes for a few minutes. She had never been good with long drives.

Ilsa had really only been pretending to be too nervous to talk to Lincoln the night before. In truth, she was waiting for him to come to her. The moment she had seen him, she had wanted him, specifically and in a way she knew was wrong, and so she decided that there was little point in talking to him if he wasn't a man who felt the same, if he wasn't a man who was willing to do such things. It had been a while, but Ilsa was still familiar with the nuances of seduction: mainly, that a man like Lincoln wouldn't want her to approach him. A man like Lincoln would want to hunt, and pounce.

So she waited and she watched him, strategically holding his gaze every time their eyes met. Finally, Jane went to get another glass of wine and he began to move across the yard, keeping her in his sights. When he reached her he immediately touched her, taking her right wrist in his long fingers and holding it up.

"You're a painter, too," he said. "Aren't you? I see paint on your wrists." Ilsa hadn't noticed it, but it was true. On the wrist that wasn't covered with bangles and ink (Ilsa had a French phrase tattooed on her left wrist) were streaks of dark purple paint, the color of bruises. "Maybe I'm just a house painter," Ilsa had said, and Lincoln had laughed.

"I can tell that you aren't. I know an artist when I see one."

"Really?"

"Really. What do you paint?"

"Nothing of value."

"Tell me your name. I'll find out if what you paint is of value."

"Ilsa Bisette." Her hair was back in her eyes. She brushed it away; the bracelets jangled. He had out his phone, and she tried not to let this annoy her. *He's checking to make sure I'm someone, and not no one.* He read his screen for a moment and then put his phone away and reached for her other wrist, his touch softer this time. He read the tattoo. "Gauguin's words," he said. Ilsa had been seventeen when she got the tattoo. Fiona had said, "You're going to regret that one day, when you're old and wrinkled and you have ink on your wrist," and Ilsa had said, "I seriously doubt it," and Fiona had said, "You seriously doubt you'll regret it, or you seriously doubt you'll ever be old and wrinkled?" Ilsa hadn't answered her. The tattoo read: *Je fermé les yeux afin de voir.* (I shut my eyes so that I might see.) Ilsa was considering another one, but wasn't sure which words to get.

Lincoln had leaned against the fence, and Ilsa had, too. He had looked up at the chaos of stars in the navy sky, then back down at her, and she had felt like one of the stars he had just been looking at, suspended in anticipation, light-years away from her life as it was—but, perhaps, seconds away from implosion. She had, for just a moment, had a grasping hold on the beginnings of a painting. *Star hanging in summer sky, about to fall.* "When are you leaving? My wife is already gone." Ilsa had cleared her throat. She had swallowed. She had tried not to feel disappointed. *What did you want him to say?* Something else. Something memorable. Something not quite so straightforward. And also, something that did not include the words "my wife."

Ilsa had not been planning to leave, but finally, when she found her voice again, she murmured, "Soon. Probably." "Do you live near here?" he had asked. She had nodded, unable to find a word, not even *Yes*, not even *Somewhat.*

"I'd like to walk you home," he had said. "I'd like that, too," she had finally managed, a proper sentence, because "I'd like to walk you home" sounded good to her. A little sweet, but a little suggestive. Still, when she spoke, her voice had sounded wrong, like it had been grated along something, smashed against the bricks. "I'll wait for you on the sidewalk," he had said. And then Fiona had rushed over, all blustering morality.

After, Ilsa had gone inside to the powder room, where she had stared at herself in the mirror and said, "You don't really want to do this." It was a line she was about to cross, and there would be no crossing to the other side of it again. She would become who she had never wanted to be. But she still crushed a mint between her molars, rinsed her mouth with water, and smoothed her hair and dress. She felt like a drug addict might feel. Sweaty, elated, ready for a fix. She said goodbye to Tim but ignored Fiona, whose face was white and angry and whose lips were pressed together like she was holding something in. *You're too boring to have feelings like this, to yearn for something more than your suburban lifestyle. It probably doesn't bother you that Tim doesn't kiss you properly anymore. Or maybe he does.* At this thought, Ilsa felt a twinge. *Maybe you're one of the lucky ones.*

As Ilsa had walked toward Lincoln, she thought of her days in art school. In particular, she remembered one afternoon when he had guest-lectured for her landscape drawing class.

As she had listened to him speak, she remembered thinking about who he might be as a person, behind the talk about art, beneath the layers of clothing. (Clothing: She even remembered what he had been wearing. A jacket and shirt, just like tonight. The shirt had been dark gray.) Now he turned, and in the streetlamp glow she thought, *Maybe I always knew he would come back into my life at some point, even just to . . .* but she didn't finish the thought because she wasn't sure what his purpose was. As he advanced, he looked to her like a lion so pleased that the best part of the kill had been saved for him: the heart, the loin. *Stop being so dramatic,* she had said to herself. "Hello," she had said to him. He had smiled, reached for her hand, pulled her to him until she was inches away (but neck craned, looking up because he was so tall, even with her in heels), and said, "Hello, gorgeous." (Again, she had experienced disappointment in his words. "Hello, gorgeous"? It was predictable. She didn't want predictable.) "Did you know," she had said, playing the coquette, "that once you were my teacher?"

Ilsa was driving again. She turned onto an off-ramp. She was getting close. The crunch of gravel beneath her tires relaxed her. No more pavement. Trees on either side. She opened her window. She felt some of the tension give way to anticipation. But she felt something else, too: an intensification of the ache in her chest. Because as she drove into the scenery, instead of taking it all in to store away for later, to process and distill onto a canvas the way she once could, she simply . . . didn't. She took another painful breath and then the feeling of nothing returned and she was back where she had started.

Ani was stirring in the backseat. "Mama?" she said.

"We're close," Ilsa said. "Really close." She made eye contact with her daughter in the rearview mirror and smiled. "Shh. Try not to wake your little brother just yet."

Before he left for Copenhagen, Michael had suggested leaving the kids with Sylvie for the entire weekend rather than taking them to Muskoka. "Maybe you just need a break," he had suggested, and she realized this was his way of acknowledging her distance from him. "Helen would be inconsolable," Ilsa had said, unable to look him in the eye. And this had been before the party, before she had officially betrayed him instead of just fantasizing about betraying him. Now she was glad she had insisted. At least when she looked at Ani and Xavier she could always count on feeling something. Her paintings of them were the only ones that were good anymore. But no one wanted to host an art exhibition featuring nothing but dozens of paintings of a toddler boy and little girl.

"How's it going?" Michael had asked her recently. "I feel like you haven't shown me any paintings for a long time." *Indeed. Almost a year. All I have is a canvas filled with dark purple strokes, a line for each day that has passed since I've painted, and now it's only purple, there is no white.* She had not said this to her husband, though. She had looked at him and felt angry with him. *How could you have not noticed until now?* And then she had lied and said she had an exhibition coming up.

But the date had come and gone and he hadn't mentioned it again. She felt relieved not to have to lie about it, but something had told her he knew and just chose not to say anything about it. There was a cruelty in this that he wasn't capable of understanding, but she felt it keenly.

Now Ilsa pulled the car into the marina parking lot. As usual, one of the indeterminate number of sons of Johnny, the owner of the marina and restaurant on the property—it was dilapidated-looking on the outside, with white and blue paint flaking from wooden boards and a sign that read FLIPPER'S SEAFOOD in uneven script; none of it (and especially the fact that fish don't even *have* flippers) betrayed the cult status of the lake-caught fish dishes—walked toward the car.

"How long are you staying?" he asked when she rolled down her window. She tried to remember his name. Was this one Benjamin or Conrad or Tom? They all looked nearly the same. Sun-bleached hair that probably went dark blond in winter, tanned skin, blue eyes. And there was another one, too, a younger one, and she had absolutely no recollection of his name but she thought it started with a *J*. She looked closely at the boy. Maybe this *was* the youngest one. There was something about the way he spoke, with a touch of pride in what he was doing that the other boys didn't have, not because they were disrespectful, but because they'd probably been doing it long enough not to want to do it anymore.

"Tuesday morning . . . I'm sorry, I don't remember your name."

"Jesse," he said.

"Right, Jesse." She always tried to be kind to these boys because they were motherless—or at least their mothers weren't present. Over the years, different women would pass through, vacuous blondes who all seemed the same to Ilsa. Inevitably, Johnny's girlfriends would become pregnant. And, just as inevitably, it seemed, they would leave Johnny and the baby to go back to wherever they had come from. "You'd have to be pretty unhappy to want to leave your baby," Helen had said once, and then had grown thoughtful and quiet before brightening up and saying, "I don't understand it. Johnny is a darling. One day we'll have to find him a *proper* woman. At least for a few seasons." A few seasons had been all any of Helen's relationships had ever lasted, and she never seemed to regret this.

"Can you take me out to the island soon?" Ilsa asked. Helen had long refused to get a motorized boat, so they had to depend on Johnny and his boys to ferry them to and from the island, for a fee. The boy named Jesse nodded. "Probably in about ten minutes. I'll carry your stuff down to the pier for you and then I have to go check in at the restaurant. If you go down to the store, Myra'll ring you up."

"Thanks." *Myra.* Perhaps, after all these years, Johnny had decided he needed another son. It struck Ilsa as a mean thought to have. But she still felt curious to see this Myra, the next in line. Would she be pregnant already? Ilsa opened the trunk for Jesse, then unbuckled Ani and lifted her out of her car seat and onto the gravel—"Check your sandal. Is it done up?"—before leaning back in and gently waking Xavier.

"Wake up, *mon chou*," she said into his hair. "Time for the boat ride, and then we'll be at Nanny's."

He opened his eyes and smiled. He was always happy when he woke up. Not like Ani, who took time to come back into the world. Xavier would often wake early with his father, but Ani would sleep in, shades drawn, like a teenager. On weekends she would come into Ilsa's room, and they'd sleep the morning away together. "Nanny's. And swimming?" His voice was hopeful.

"Yes, swimming. Of course swimming." She lifted him out of the car and kept him on her hip. "Nothing but swimming, if that's what you want."

"Cookies?" Ani asked.

Ilsa reached down and took her hand. "I'm sure there will be cookies. And strawberries. And blackberries." Ilsa kissed the top of Xavier's head, then put him down and reached for his hand, too. The three of them walked together toward the general-store area of the building.

Inside, as always, it smelled like fish. "What's that smell?" Ani said, nose wrinkled. "Freshly scaled and gutted fish," Ilsa replied. "*Gutted?*" Ani repeated. "It means . . . cleaned," Ilsa said. "It doesn't *smell* clean," Ani said.

The woman behind the counter had nearly black hair pulled into a high chignon, and was wearing a navy FLIPPER'S T-shirt over slim jeans. She had on reading glasses, which she

took off and put down on the counter. She was smiling at
Ani. She didn't look at all like one of Johnny's typical women.
For one thing, she wasn't blond. Also, she had pearls in her
ears, which struck Ilsa as out of place here. The woman now
looked at Ilsa, still smiling, and Ilsa saw something in the
woman's eyes that she recognized. A certain sadness. Ilsa
smiled back.

Johnny, also behind the counter, with a stack of receipts
and on the telephone, called this woman "babe" and asked
her to pass him a calculator.

A moment later, he hung up the phone. "Hey, Ilsa, how
you been?"

"Very well, thank you, Johnny, and you?"

"Not bad at all. So, the restaurant's a bit slammed with
breakfast customers right now. It might be ten-thirty before
Jesse can take you guys. That okay? I had to send him up to
help run some food. You and those cute kids of yours want
to go up and have a bite?" Ilsa found the idea of food unap-
pealing. "Are *you* hungry for breakfast?" she asked the kids.
Xavier didn't reply and Ani shook her head vigorously, perhaps assuming she'd be required to eat fish, and pointed out
a chocolate bar on the rack. Ilsa hesitated—it was processed,
full of garbage—but then picked up two bars and said, "We'll
take these and go for a little walk."

"I'll add them to your tab," said Johnny, looking back
down at his receipts.

The woman, Myra, cleared her throat. "I could take them
over," she said.

"Nah. Jess likes to do it. Needs to earn his keep." Johnny
didn't look up from his addition.

"It's fine. We don't mind waiting." Ilsa led Ani and Xavier
from the general store and out into the parking lot. They kept
to the side of the dirt road, as close to the trees as possible.

"Maybe we'll see a deer," Ilsa said. "Or a rabbit."

"Or a tiger!" Ani's mouth was already smeared with chocolate.

The only sound other than their footsteps on gravel was the electric hum of bugs and the occasional *caw-caw* of crows.

But soon Ilsa heard an engine up ahead and pulled them both sideways, off the road and onto a driveway, to wait for a pickup truck to pass. The driver waved at Ilsa and Ilsa waved back because that was what you did up north, to strangers and friends alike.

Now they stepped back out toward the road and Ilsa looked ahead. For a moment she didn't register what she saw.

A large shape. Fur. Moving out from the trees and onto the road.

A wolf? It was twenty feet ahead. No, too big to be a wolf.

Bear. She squeezed Ani and Xavier's hands and pulled them back. "Shit," she said aloud, then looked down at the children. "Shh."

"Tiger?" Ani whispered.

"Bear. Be still."

If only we hadn't decided to go for a walk, Ilsa was thinking. The bear had been crossing the road and now it stopped, as if sensing them there. *Of course it senses us. It probably smells us. Shit.* Ilsa wondered if they should run. But you weren't supposed to run away from bears, were you? *Big.* You were supposed to make yourself look big. She swept first Xavier and then Ani up into her arms. They jostled against each other and their legs dangled. Xavier giggled. "Shh," Ilsa said again.

Now the bear was looking at them, paused in the middle of the road, nose forward. She lifted her head—for suddenly Ilsa felt she was a she-bear. And what if she had a cub with her? Weren't bears supposed to be especially dangerous if protecting a cub? Ilsa squeezed her children until Ani whispered, "Ow," and tried to pull away. Ilsa squeezed harder.

Xavier dropped his chocolate bar. The bear blinked at the movement and sound.

The bear's and Ilsa's eyes were now locked. *Are you supposed to make eye contact with bears?* Ilsa wasn't sure but would have been unable to look away regardless, even if the bear had started to advance. She had the panicky thought that maybe she was getting what she deserved. And she found herself wishing for Fiona, a sudden, little-girl-like urge. "Did you know that whenever you were scared when you were young, you would call out for Fiona?" Helen had once told her. "I don't believe you," Ilsa had said. "It's true. It's how I knew you loved her," Helen had replied.

Fiona would know exactly what we should do right now.

The bear snorted, snorted, leaned toward them—and then shook her head from side to side and continued along her path across the road.

Ilsa stood still for another moment, listening to the crack of branches under the bear's paws. Then she put Ani and Xavier down and said, "Let's go back."

"Was it a tiger?" Ani asked.

"Bear. Mama bear," said Ilsa.

Xavier: "Mama's bear?"

"No, just . . . just a female bear. I *think*. I don't know why I think that, though." Ilsa tended to talk to the children as though they were adults. She didn't know how else to be with them. "I'm sorry about your chocolate bar, Xavier. We'll get you another one."

Eventually she felt her heart rate return to normal. The restaurant was in sight. The woman, Myra, was out near the dock, watching Jesse ready the boat for the short journey to the island.

"We saw a bear out on the road," she said to Myra.

"Oh, yes, there are a few around this year. Most of them have cubs, but there's one lonely she-bear who seems to wander up and down the road a lot. I hope she stays out of trouble. Some of the hunters up here . . ." Myra shook her head and didn't finish her sentence.

"How do you know it's a she-bear?" Ilsa asked.

Myra shrugged. "I just know. Something about her."

"I thought that, too." Ilsa looked into the woman's eyes again. They were intelligent, blue, pale. The sadness was still there.

Jesse motioned for them to get in the boat. Myra lifted a small life jacket, a life jacket for a child. It looked new. "Need this?"

"No, we have our own, thanks."

As the boat pulled away, Ilsa scanned the tree line, looking for signs of the she-bear. She saw a moving shadow and squinted: it was Myra, walking into the woods alone.

Liane was sitting on the dock when Ilsa, Ani, and Xavier arrived. She put down her book and stood to wave. Ilsa was surprised to see a kayak—*the* kayak—tethered to the dock. Soon the boat bumped against the other side of the dock and Jesse jumped out to secure it, almost immediately starting to unload the bags. Ilsa thanked him and gave him a tip, then hoisted each child onto the dock before stepping onto it herself. She hugged Liane. It felt like a long time had passed since she had seen her sister. Ilsa hadn't visited Toronto that year, and Liane had only been to Rye once, at Christmas. Ilsa looked at her sister and wondered what was different about her. She was wearing an old bathing suit of Ilsa's and it looked great, the black a perfect contrast to her pale and delicately freckled shoulders. "You look good," Ilsa said.

"Oh. I . . . forgot my suit," Liane said, and Ilsa waved a hand.

"You can have it."

Liane leaned down and kissed Ani's nose, which Ani wrinkled affectionately. "Hi, Peanut," she said, pinching one of her cheeks gently. That was when Ilsa saw it, glittering in the sun. A diamond ring. She leaned down to fiddle with a bag, then stood up and stretched her arms overhead. Liane was now kissing Xavier and tousling his curls. *Glint, glint, glint,* went the ring.

"What a glorious day," Ilsa said. "I'm so glad we finally made it, and didn't get eaten by a bear in the process." She started telling Liane about the bear sighting rather than asking her about the ring, which was what any normal sister would have done. That Ilsa wasn't immediately in rapture over her sister's apparently impending marriage to Adam, whom Ilsa disdained for a number of reasons, was no surprise. It's just that what she *had* felt when she'd spotted the engagement ring on her sister's finger was something akin to jealousy. *Of whom?* Adam, maybe. Or some nameless friend of Liane's who had received this news first, had perhaps even gotten a phone call asking for advice—"What should I say?" Liane would have asked, because the decision would have been too momentous for Liane not to look for external help. But then again, who did that? Ilsa had been proposed to enough times to know there wasn't generally enough time to make a phone call.

Even in jail, they offer you a phone call.

Ilsa finished the story about the bear, and Ani stood beside her and nodded, solemn. "I thought it was a tiger," she said.

Liane laughed. Then she turned to Ilsa, a serious expression on her face. *Here it comes, she's going to announce it.* But Liane didn't say anything about the ring. Instead, she said, "Fiona's *really* not coming? What the heck happened?" And Ilsa, to her own surprise, blushed and said, "We'll have to talk about it later," inclining her head toward Ani and Xavier to show that it wasn't appropriate conversation to have in front of them.

Liane raised an eyebrow. "O-kay," she said.

"I'm going to go put a suit on, say hi to Mom, and get a snack for the kids. I'll be right back."

Ilsa kicked off her shoes and walked up the pathway. She had her weekend bag, and one for both the kids. She also had two canvas bags of wine and food—food for Ani and Xavier, mostly: fruit, cereal, pasta. Otherwise, she had only Syrah, champagne, a baguette, and cheese. She realized she had packed the same way she did every year, assuming Fiona would have the food all organized, that they would stop on the way up and Fiona would shop for everyone the way she always did. Even as she had passed the farmers' market it hadn't occurred to Ilsa to stop to do anything other than have a little nap at the side of the road. She felt foolish for a moment, but she brushed the feeling away. They'd figure it out. *And won't you be surprised, Fiona, to learn that we all don't need you as much as you think we do?*

Funny, though. Ilsa had never realized she needed Fiona at all until that day, until the bear.

At the door, Ilsa ignored Liane's foot bucket—"Come on, it's fresh!" Liane shouted from the dock—and walked inside barefoot, tracking dirt and sand first on the tile in the mudroom and then on the pine floorboards in the living room and kitchen. After putting the food away, she took her weekend bag upstairs and dumped it on the bed in her room.

Ilsa's room was at the side of the cottage, facing the trees and the creek, with a gabled window and a bed built into the wall that was far too small for her but made her feel good to sleep in, like she was still a child and thus devoid of all responsibility. When they came up to the cottage, Ani slept in the small bed, Xavier slept in a large playpen, and she slept on an air mattress beside them. Michael had only been to the cottage a few times—he had his own family vacation property, on a small compound in Nantucket. Ilsa hated it there, mostly because of its perfection, and the distractions of televisions and telephones and screens of every description in every room. And also the way most of the people in his family seemed to avoid the water. The way they changed for dinner. The way when she dove off the boathouse his sister remarked at her bravery.

"I'd be *brave* if those waters were shark-infested," she had retorted once. But no one had laughed. "There *are* sharks around sometimes," one of the sisters-in-law murmered. "At least that's what I've heard." That had been the weekend Ilsa had overheard one of Michael's sisters say to a sister-in-law, "Do you think she's after his money?" And the sister-in-law had wearily replied, "Oh, probably. But she won't get any of it." Most of Michael's brothers were lawyers, and it was true that Ilsa had signed a prenuptial agreement. *I am* not *after his money,* she had wanted to say, wishing she had walked into the kitchen and caught those two by embarrassed surprise. *I married him . . .well, I married him because he's* staid. *And that was an enormous mistake. And I am the one paying for that, not him.* She didn't, though. She just asked Michael if they could go home a day early and he said, "Why, are you sick?" and she said she was, and they left.

Now she turned in a small circle around her room. There were canvases leaning against one wall. She realized they were two that she had brought up and painted the summer before. There were small splatters on the hardwood from when she had rested them there, still wet. Paint on the floor was not something Helen cared about, Ilsa knew, but she still stood and looked down at the splatters and felt guilty. She tipped a canvas back and looked at it, then let the canvas fall back against its mate. It wasn't great, but compared to what she had been painting lately—*nothing, goddamn it*—it was brilliant.

She pulled off her T-shirt, skirt, and underwear and looked at herself in the mirror on the bureau, trying to see what Lincoln might see. Breasts that were perhaps not as pert as they used to be, but weren't big enough to sag, with small nipples that Eric, her first husband—whom she had met at twenty-two, during a trip to Paris to see her father; he had followed her during a walk along the Seine, presented her with a bunch of flowers; she had been naïve enough to believe he didn't do this for all the girls—had once told her were the color of black cherries. Her stomach was flat, her skin smooth and lightly tanned already.

She raised her hands to her breasts and thought of the back of her dress, the night before. Back at home, clumsily unzipping it, she had realized that it was ruined. The delicate fabric had been pilled and mangled by the bricks on the wall of the half-finished house Lincoln had pressed her against when he had pulled her off the sidewalk during their walk home. She hadn't noticed at the time. She hadn't noticed anything, really, except the way it felt to be kissed.

Eventually they had come out from between the houses and had continued to walk, stopping every few feet. Ilsa had known the heels of her shoes were beyond repair, sticky with mud, stained with dirt. She hadn't realized about the dress yet. *How easy it is to ruin things.* A few houses before hers, he had kissed her one last time and asked her what the best way to contact her would be. She had given him her cell phone number. "It was delightful to meet you. I'll see you soon," he had said.

Now she looked away from herself in the mirror and opened a drawer, where she rummaged for her black bandeau, remembered Liane was wearing it, and settled on a burgundy tank suit.

She pulled suits for Ani and Xavier out of their bags, plus sunscreen, towels, and water wings for Xavier. And then she had that feeling she sometimes had, the one where she remembered for a moment what it had been like before children, when a bathing suit and towel for herself would have been enough, when she didn't have to worry about anyone else. And she felt a hollow sadness for even thinking about those days, and she focused on how much she loved her children.

She heard a floorboard creak. Helen stood in the doorway, her long, blond-streaked-with-gray hair messy. "Darling."

"Mom! Did I wake you?"

"I wasn't sleeping, I was meditating." Helen crossed the room and hugged and kissed Ilsa. "Good to see you," she said, studying her daughter's face the way she always did when it had been a long time between visits. Ilsa felt abruptly self-conscious, but Helen didn't say anything except, "You look beautiful," which was what she always said. "I'll get my suit on, too." Helen headed back toward her own room, removing her rumpled sundress as she went.

Ilsa turned away. Helen had never been the type of mother to hide her nudity, ever, and Ilsa couldn't remember when she had started looking away from her mother's body, and wondered when Ani would start looking away from hers.

Ilsa dove off the dock and swam down until she couldn't hold her breath any longer, and she still hadn't reached the bottom. When she came up, she felt cleaner, coldly vindicated. She paddled out farther, away from the dock, and she thought about her father, Claude, and the Catholic churches he had always taken her to during her trips to Paris to see him, starting when she was a girl. The summer before, Ilsa had traveled to Paris alone with Xavier, so Claude could meet his grandson for the first time. She remembered Claude had held the little boy aloft to show off to his group of friends, all of them already wine-soaked at midafternoon. (He had done it when Ani was born, too, held her up as though she were the baby lion in that movie and said, "Here she is, my little Anaïs!" He was the only one who called her that.) That afternoon, with Xavier, the friends had all cheered: artists, musicians, poets, all of whom found themselves but not each other fascinating.

Later that weekend, he had dragged Ilsa off to a church. "Why do you always want to confess?" she had asked. "Absolution," he had replied. "I think it really works." "In what way?" "If you do what the priest says, all is forgiven. So simple! And then you can just come back the next week." And he had laughed, removed his hat, and gone into the booth while Ilsa held Xavier and wondered if her son, almost two, who was staring up, up, up at the stained-glass windows, at the golden organ pipes, at Jesus on the cross, palms bleeding, face contorted but still pious, could understand any of this. He would not be this kind of man, this she knew already. But she—she was already who she was, and in that instant she had disliked Claude for it.

She had not returned to visit him since. She had thought about asking Helen again, as she had dozens of times throughout her life, exactly what had attracted her to Claude. But it wouldn't be straightforward, nothing like the way it probably was for people whose parents had divorced and, beforehand, had explained to their children where it had gone wrong. *We'll always love each other,* these people might say. *But we aren't* in *love anymore.* Whereas Helen had once said to Ilsa, "I was in love with him, but it was never sustainable. Isn't he a beautiful man, though? And you're beautiful, too, just like him. So I made a good choice, in the end." This had always struck Ilsa as surprisingly shallow. *You chose him so I would be good-looking? What about all the other shit that goes along with being the daughter of a man like that?*

Ilsa still shuddered when she recalled the one time Claude

had taken her to meet Madame La Boussière, the woman who paid his rent, and more. It had been like a scene in a play, one that you wished, when the curtain fell, you had never watched. The old woman languished on a couch, her blue eye shadow and foundation caked, her cigarette ash falling on the floor. She had squinted at Ilsa and said, "*Est-elle ta maitresse?*" (Is she your lover?) "*Non,*" Claude had said, patting the shoulder of the woman's loose kimono, taking the envelope from her ring-encrusted hand, telling her he'd be back the following week and would have more time to spend. "I don't ever want to have to see her again," Ilsa had said to him afterward, and he had said nothing in response.

"Watch out," Liane said from the dock. "The snapping turtle is around, and he's meaner than ever this year."

"Come on, get in. Maybe you can actually beat me to the floating dock for once."

Ani, Xavier, and Helen were in the shallow water close to shore, splashing and laughing. Liane stood, peeling off her Vampire Weekend concert T-shirt to reveal the bandeau. Ilsa noticed there was now a man on the dock next door, which appeared to be a lot closer than it used to be—she'd have to ask Helen if the Castersens had sold. He had a book in front of him, but he was watching Liane, who, instead of diving in, plugged her nose with one hand, held the bandeau in place with the other, and jumped awkwardly into the water. The man smiled and looked back down at his book.

Ilsa swam more slowly than usual and let Liane win.

Later, Ilsa put the children to bed and then she, Liane, and Helen sat at the bistro set in the screened-in porch for a late dinner. Helen had a pile of greens grown by someone named Iain and there was kamut mixed with canned mushrooms, and tempeh steaks that tasted freezer-burned. Ilsa tried not to think about what they would have had if Fiona had been there. Besides, there was also wine. It was making her feel pleasantly light-headed, and if she took a sip right after a bite of tempeh, it didn't taste so bad.

Later, Helen stood to clear the plates away and get dessert.

"So, tell me, now, why did Fiona get so mad at you that she refused to come here?" Liane asked when Helen was gone.

Ilsa swallowed. "She suspects me of being an extreme hussy."

"Sus*pects*?" Liane laughed, but then looked at Ilsa's face and stopped laughing. "What did you do?"

Ilsa hesitated. But she could tell Liane anything, couldn't she? And the fact that judgmental Fiona wasn't there made it easier to speak freely. "She had a party last night and it turns out her neighbor is Lincoln Porter, who is . . . well, a really great artist."

"*You're* a really great artist," Liane said.

"Ha. Thanks. But I haven't painted anything worth saving in ages, you know." Saying it aloud made Ilsa feel like she was falling into a pit.

"Come on, really? When's your next show?"

"No shows upcoming. I'm experiencing a dry spell. Which is maybe why . . ." Ilsa uncrossed her legs and put her elbows on the table. "I kissed Lincoln on the way home," she whispered, feeling pleasantly warm, like a teenager again, with a secret to share with her sister. "A lot."

"You *what*?"

Ilsa looked up, surprised at Liane's reaction. *Oh. Right. She just got engaged. She's probably feeling quite chaste.* "Sorry. Never mind."

"No. Come on. Ilsa!"

"What? Just forget it, okay?"

"Do you want Michael to find out?"

"Of course not."

"Then why would you leave Tim and Fiona's house with another man? Tim is Michael's best friend. And his business partner. What if he saw you? He would tell Michael, you know. He wouldn't keep it a secret just for your sake. And Fiona—well, she's mad. She didn't even come. This is not good, Ilsa."

"What's not good?" Helen was back, carrying a tray with a plate of grapes and three dishes of her soy ice cream.

Ilsa and Liane were silent. Then Liane said, "Ilsa made out with some guy," and Helen sat and reached across the table for Ilsa's arm and said, "Ilsa?" and Ilsa wanted to laugh at the ridiculousness of it all. *Why can't we just be normal people, a normal family? Why can't we have a mother who we can't talk about stuff like this with?*

Except Helen seemed oddly uncomfortable, too. Her eyes, rather than attempting to probe into Ilsa's and get her to tell all, were now downcast.

"Can we please forget I ever said anything? Please?" Ilsa pulled her arm away from Helen's and picked up Liane's left hand, flopping it back and forth while Liane kept it limp. "Don't we have other things to talk about? Like, why hasn't anyone mentioned this engagement ring? What a bunch of weirdos we all are. Let's talk about *that* instead." Ilsa actually felt grateful to Adam at that moment, for giving her something to distract everyone with.

Helen started rearranging the grapes on the plate. The awkward silence remained. "Yes, tell us about the ring," she said, and Liane gave them both a look that seemed oddly defiant.

"Adam and I got engaged," she said.

"Great news!" Ilsa practically shouted.

"I know you don't think so. You already told me you don't like him."

"I never did. I just said . . ."

"You said he was staid, and if I stayed with him, one day

there would be no way to leave. And that one day I would regret it."

Ilsa closed her eyes. *Staid.*

"Sorry," she said. "I didn't mean it." *I was talking about me.* She opened her eyes.

More silence. Then: "Let's rewind," Helen announced. It was something she had always said when they were little. Then she'd make funny noises with her lips, or walk backward around the room, and let the girls or herself have a "do-over." She didn't make any funny sounds or walk backward this time, though. She just lifted her empty glass and said, "A toast. To Liane, and to marriage, and to the possibility that maybe love *can* be, if you really work at it, everlasting. *Necessary.*"

The three of them clinked glasses, and then Helen looked down at hers, realized it was empty, and pretended to drink anyway.

4

White-Tailed Doe (*Odocoileus virginianus*)

A mother doe often leaves her fawn unattended for hours at a time, returning so the fawn can suckle and then leaving again. If a fawn needs her mother, she bleats to call out to her. Those does that do not have young, either because they are barren, failed to produce a fawn, lost a fawn to a predator, or are too old, are sometimes referred to as "dry does."

Sometimes Myra believed she had stayed because of the call of the loon, the howl of the coyote, and the doe with her fawn, standing in the dew-strung garden in front of the cottage. It was such a beautiful place—in the summer, at least.

The truth wasn't quite as simple. It was this: She stayed because she loved Johnny. She stayed because she never gave up hope. She tried to convince herself it didn't matter to her that he was never going to be able to love her back because he was the kind of man who was a little frozen on the inside, even if on the outside he seemed gregarious. She had once read a Leonard Cohen poem and thought of him: "I'm just another snowman standing in the rain and sleet, who loved you with his frozen love, his secondhand physique." Except, of course, he didn't love her, not even in a frozen way. *Really?*

an insistent inner voice would sometimes ask her. *Are you sure he's actually incapable of love, or are you simply justifying the fact that he doesn't love you? And regardless, is this the right person to be trying to have a baby with?* She tried to ignore the voice.

Perhaps if the four boys—the endless supply of sons had turned out to be a bit of a rural legend; Johnny also had nephews who worked at the marina, and they all looked alike—had ever shown any signs of needing her, she could have used that as a justification, too. But the reality was the boys, at seventeen, nineteen, twenty, and twenty-two, were past the point of needing a mother by the time she came along. The only moments she ever felt like a mother to them was when she picked up their dirty socks. She followed trails of socks through the house, muttering to herself, frustrated. She would put the socks in the washing machine and try not to feel resentful and imagine that at that moment she was probably feeling something that real mothers felt all the time: The Resentment of the Dirty Socks. She thought about what one of the inspirational books she had started buying when she went into town would tell her, that she was probably supposed to find a way to be grateful for all this, to stay in the moment and see the good. *But how can you be grateful for dirty socks and a man who doesn't really love you?*

There were days when she thought she would probably leave, too, just like all the other women had left before her. And still other days when she felt hopeful that things would change and she would get what she wanted out of this. (The love, the baby.) But, especially in the winter, there were also days she felt so barren she knew it was a permanent state. She didn't need a doctor's opinion. She was a dry doe, a term she heard one of the hunters in for an early breakfast use that morning.

The hunters had been arguing over the practice of shooting does that had fawns with them. From what Myra could understand, not knowing much about hunting aside from the fact that it made her feel nauseous, it was frowned upon to shoot a doe that had a fawn with her because that would also, ultimately, lead to the loss of the fawn. (Myra felt confused about this: So the life of a fawn mattered more to a hunter than the life of a doe or buck? Was this because fawns were babies and awakened some sort of empathic response in the hunters or because, if the fawn died an untimely death, this would be an animal the hunters would *not* one day get the chance to shoot at?)

Apparently some hunters were indiscriminate, not caring if they shot a doe that was accompanied by a fawn. But most hunters, Myra overheard these men say, took down stags and bucks exclusively whenever possible during hunting season. However, if they were absolutely positive of the absence of a fawn, they would also shoot "dry does" at will.

When she served the hunters their breakfasts she said to them, quietly, "I'm sorry, I overheard you talking and I'm curious. What's a dry doe?" They looked surprised, likely because Myra didn't talk to the customers much more than she had to—she wasn't unfriendly, just professional, or so she hoped people thought. (*I have an MBA,* she sometimes had the urge to say, when a breakfast was sent back or someone talked to her like she was somehow less than. But, she realized, half the people she served probably had no idea what an MBA was—and the other half would probably say, *Then what the heck are you doing in a place like this?*) The hunter with the red-and-black-checked jacket and the trucker hat said, "A dry doe is a doe with no baby." "Why doesn't she have a baby?" Myra asked. "She's either too old, or her baby died earlier in the year, or she failed at mating that season. So we shoot her if we see her and we're sure of it, since there's no danger of putting fawns at risk."

Myra had put the breakfasts down on the table, taking care to place the correct breakfast in front of the correct man and ask if he needed anything else *at the moment,* before going to the bathroom and closing and locking the door. There, she had allowed herself to cry for three minutes, staring at the wood paneling that was really wallpaper before returning to the dining room to continue serving breakfasts and brewing pots of coffee.

Now she was standing by the window of the cottage beside the marina, where she lived with Johnny and the boys, trying not to think dark thoughts. It was late June. The first official day of summer had just passed. But still, she had to force herself not to think about winter, and about how it would arrive, wanted or not, as always. "I don't know why you rage against it so much," Johnny had said to her once. "Winter will always come and there's not a thing you can do about it, especially up here." During the winter that had just passed, he had agreed with her that it wouldn't be a bad idea for the two of them, at some point, to go somewhere warm for even just a week. But it hadn't happened. When she'd brought it up in March, he'd suggested she go on her own. "You deserve it, My," he'd said. "You work hard. I know you hate the cold. Go somewhere. I'll buy your ticket. I'll pay for you to stay somewhere ritzy." But she didn't, even though she should have. She took too much solace in the way he called her "My," thinking maybe he finally meant it, that maybe he'd finally taken possession.

Also, she had been about to ovulate.

She didn't even bother tracking her cycle anymore, though, hadn't since around then, probably. She wasn't sure if she'd given up or not and didn't want to have to decide. Admitting she had given up would involve a period of mourning. Better to save that for winter, really.

She saw the boat approaching. It was Jesse, and he had the young woman with the red hair whom Myra had ferried over to the island alone the week before in the boat with him. Myra hadn't thought this woman was coming back until Tuesday and knew her car was blocked in by one of Johnny's trucks. She went outside and walked down to the dock.

"Hi," she said. "On your way back to the city already?" She noticed that the woman's pale face was blotchy and red in places.

"Yes. I'd like to get my car and leave," the woman said, in a tone that seemed to be trying to prove a point to someone who wasn't there.

Myra said, "I just need to move Johnny's truck. And I'll get the keys for you." Johnny wasn't there. He'd driven into town to run some errands. Myra thought about refunding part of the woman's parking pass, which would have been paid in advance as per Johnny's policy. This woman would have paid for more days than she had actually stayed. (Johnny charged five dollars per day for parking and insisted on no refunds. If she *did* refund money to this woman, he would probably be annoyed. "Summer is the only time we have to make any real money," he often told her. "And most of these cottagers have it to spend." As though she, Myra, didn't know about money or businesses or life. As though she, Myra, hadn't had a life and a job and a heck of a lot more knowledge of a great many things than he did before she arrived there and dashed her dreams against his dock.)

Now the woman was holding out money.

"What's that for?"

"For driving me back here early. I wanted to give it to him." But Jesse was already off the dock and walking toward the restaurant. "Just take it. Give it to him. He could probably use it."

Myra bit her lip, for some reason offended by this. What made this woman think Jesse *needed* that money? What if he didn't?

"Oh, no, it's okay, the ride back, it's on the house. Please, no thank you."

"I insist." The young woman pressed the fifty-dollar bill, one of the new ones, the plastic ones that made Myra feel like the rest of the world was passing her by and Johnny grumbled had the potential to melt, into her hand. "Just take it." Myra was going to protest again but instead she took the bill and put it in the pocket of her jeans to give to Jesse later.

"Thank you," she said. Then: "Let me help you with your bags." It was this, this *servitude,* that bothered Myra sometimes. She tried to channel gratitude, the feeling she had on good days, when she felt superior to the people still held in slavery to whatever electronic device they had in their pocket sending radioactive waves through their bodies as they asked her frantically if there was a cellular tower nearby. *Nope,* Myra would say. *But there's a pay phone.* And then she'd have the urge to add: *I used to work on Bay Street. But now I get to fall asleep to the sound of the loon's call and wake up to the sun shining on a lake as still as glass.* Something always stopped her from being so smug, though. Because she knew there were also nights when she fell asleep to the sound of ice cracking, loud as gunshots across the lake, and woke in a darkness so deep she might stay inside for days.

She hoisted the woman's bag out of the boat, then leaned down and adjusted the knot on the rope tethering the front of the boat to the dock.

Later, after the woman got in her car and waited for Myra to pull the truck out of her way so she could pull out, Myra sat and watched her taillights disappear and, unexpectedly, she felt envious.

But you could just go, too. If you really wanted to.

Myra had come to Flipper's for the first time during a girls' weekend at a nearby cottage with women she didn't see anymore. These women likely now thought she was crazy. She was probably now a cautionary tale. It all felt like a lifetime ago—and in some ways, she supposed, it had been. In other ways, it hadn't been at all. Half a life, really. *Stop feeling sorry for yourself.*

In reality, it had been three years.

Johnny had been tending the bar that night, mixing them margaritas, or cosmopolitans, or something predictable for a group of women of a certain age, which they were. He'd had a bartender's guide behind the bar and he'd been magnanimous, happy to serve them whatever they wanted even though they probably all seemed like a bunch of cackling hens to him. Now she knew it was because of the money he was making off of them, but she had thought at the time that perhaps he actually enjoyed his job, enjoyed serving people, and also, just maybe, that he enjoyed being around her, was interested even, in her. When she looked at him, the sleeves of his flannel shirt rolled up over arms that bore a tan that obviously reached the deepest layer of his dermis, the hair golden on top of his skin, she had very badly not wanted him to think *she* was a cackling hen. She had very badly, when she looked at him, wanted to go somewhere and kiss him. And this was not something that measured and shy Myra was prone to feel or be tempted to do.

"Who is he?" she'd asked her friend Wendy, the one whose family owned the cottage the group of women were staying at for the weekend.

"Johnny Hicks. Nice name, huh? Kind of appropriate, although he is rather delicious in a guy-from-the-sticks way. Very blue-collar. Rumor has it there's a different woman with him here every few summers. He gets most of them pregnant, they all have boys, and then they all leave."

Myra had leaned in, fascinated. "Are you serious? Come on. That can't really be true."

"For real. I don't even know how many sons he has, but

there are lots of them and they all look the same. So do the women: pretty and blond."

"How many women? How many sons?"

"I told you, no idea. But I think the first woman had two kids before she left."

"But *why* would they all leave?"

"Maybe because they're bored to tears."

Myra looked at Johnny and couldn't imagine being bored. She was staring at him so hard she barely heard Wendy say, "The winters here are pretty deadly. Depressing. Nothing to do but cross-country ski and listen to the ice crack. And let's face it, there's only so much sex you can have, even with a guy like that."

Myra proceeded to drink several more cocktails, and later, out on the deck, she kissed Johnny Hicks with her hands clasped up and around the back of his neck. She went back inside after and was convinced none of her friends had noticed—but of course they all had, and were talking behind her back with a cruelness borne of jealousy. (*Isn't she still technically married? What is she thinking?*) Later, she and Johnny snuck outside and kissed again and she ran her hands down his chest, over the softness of his shirt, and Wendy walked outside with two of the other women and they cleared their throats.

Eventually the women all left and Myra and Johnny went to his place. The boys were sleeping, so he said she needed to be quiet. She whispered things in his ear like, "What did you want to be when you grew up?" and he said things like, "What I am right now," and she thought that meant something great about him, like that he was, unlike anyone else she knew, exactly *who* he was. Really what it had meant was that Johnny took everything literally.

She had wanted Johnny with a hunger that had never truly been sated—and at least they still had that. Their bodies fit together in a way that she hadn't imagined possible but that *he* was clearly used to. He hadn't said to her, the way she had to him, *This is the best I've ever had,* or *All I can think about is making love to you.* Instead, in response, he had smiled and said something like, "Yep, it *is* pretty good, isn't it?" If there was one thing Johnny knew, it was his way around a woman's body. A woman's mind, though: that was another story. Especially a woman like Myra, it would turn out. "The others weren't like you," he had said to her once. She hadn't been sure if this was a compliment, but it did make her feel slightly comforted, and also superior and safe from being filed in the same folder as these other women. *Pretty, blond, unintelligent, gone.*

She had decided to take the fact that he considered her different from the others as a sign that perhaps he was interested in having her encourage him toward self-improvement. So she began: "Do you ever want to go back to school?" "Nope. I'm forty-four. That would be stupid." He had gotten up from the table, leaving his supper unfinished. And that was that. She had tried to ask again and he had snapped at her to drop it. Later, she would learn he barely had a grade ten education, but also that there were reasons for this.

She had never told Johnny what it was that she'd wanted. She had never admitted to him that when her former friend Wendy had said that women would come to live with Johnny and end up pregnant she had thought, with the misdirected clarity only a drunk person can have, that perhaps she had found her answer. That night, through the distortion of too many cosmopolitans or margaritas or whatever they were, she had seen a way to leave it all behind: the disappointment of the city, the starkness of the fertility clinics, the embarrassment, yes, *embarrassment* she had felt when the doctors had said there wasn't a problem with her, per se, and nor was there a problem with Colin, but that they couldn't really understand why she wasn't getting pregnant. In Johnny and the marina and the boys she had seen a way to avoid witnessing the inevitable dissolution of her marriage to Colin, too. (Oh, and technically, they *were* still married. Technically, they had been in the midst of a trial separation when she had, as he put it, run off to the woods. But it was such a tepid dissolution that neither of them had bothered to do anything about it. Three years, and she hadn't heard from him. She supposed she had always figured that as soon as she got pregnant, she'd get in touch about a divorce. And that in the meantime, if he ever met someone or decided he needed closure, he'd do the same. But nothing had happened in either direction. And she had not told Johnny about Colin at all, at first because she had been nervous about mentioning it and later because she had realized how pointless it was. It wouldn't matter to Johnny. He was never going to ask her to marry him anyway, so her being *technically* still married to someone else was of little consequence.)

Once, Myra had said to Johnny, "We should go to the city." It was fall, not yet winter, and the leaves on the trees in their yellows, reds, and golds made her think of fresh starts even though they weren't really, even though what the changing of the leaves really signified was a last-ditch attempt at being something before the ultimate descent into nothing.

"Like, for a weekend?"

"No. We should just go. We should sell this place and go. You're a natural restaurateur, and I could probably find you a backer. We could open up a restaurant and live in my house and . . ."

He looked at her strangely and then he said, "*We* should sell this place?"

"Well, I mean, *I meant* . . . I know it's yours, and—"

"And you have your house. If you want to go back to the city, you can. But I'm not going anywhere." And he'd shaken his head like she was crazy and walked toward the main house, his work boots undone, his laces dragging. She wondered as she always did how it was possible he never stumbled. ("Didn't your mother ever teach you how to lace up your boots?" she had once asked him. "My mother is dead," he had said, and she'd wanted to ask but knew he didn't want her to, so she didn't.) *I should really go,* she'd said to herself after that conversation. *He's right. I have my house. I should go.*

But although she had always believed this urge for going would eventually overtake her, she had believed it would happen in winter—probably this winter, when she finally accepted and mourned her barrenness and couldn't take it anymore. And so it came as a surprise to her that the way this red-haired woman left would make *her* think about leaving, even in summer. She had watched those taillights and thought, *I could do that, too. I could get in a car and just go. I don't have to feel jealous of this woman for being able to leave. No one and nothing is forcing me to stay here.* Would the boys be upset? Maybe Jesse would. Was that enough of a reason to stay?

Myra walked toward the store. Johnny was back and he stood in the doorway, apparently waiting for her, his smile slow and easy. "Walt Anderson brought his boat in to get the engine looked at and now he's heading back to the city and needs us to take it back out to his place on the southwest side of the island. But I've got Amos coming in to look at the stove any minute and the boys are all busy, except Jess. So can you go out there with him? You can drive our boat and he can drive Walt's, and then you can come back together."

"Sure," she said. "I'm just going to grab a water."

As she squeezed past him through the door he slapped her on the seat of her jeans. "You're looking fine today, you know," he said, and it felt like there were pop rocks, the kind they sold in the store in little packets, fizzing inside her chest, hopeful effervescence, her body and mind responding with desire. The call of Johnny's body to hers was a difficult thing to ignore. And maybe this time it would happen. Maybe, just maybe, when she was on the precipice of giving up, it would happen. She certainly wouldn't be the only thirty-seven-year-old in the world to get pregnant. So she winked at him. "Be sure to make some time for me later," she said, and he kissed her quickly and said, "You betcha, babe," and walked up the hill toward the restaurant while she stood in the doorframe where he had just been, now watching him, the water forgotten. *What if it happened? What if I did get pregnant? Would I stay if I had his baby? Would I really want to raise a baby here?*

Myra didn't know the answer to that. But one thing she did know: she'd never leave her baby here with him. She *would* be different from the other women in that way, too: if she left, she'd take her baby with her.

Maybe you don't love him as much as you think you do.

On the way back to the marina after returning Walt's boat, the water was rough and Jesse drove slowly. This pleased Myra. She was certain that if she had not been there he would have been far more reckless, because he was a teenage boy and that's what teenage boys did. (Jesse even had a battle scar to prove his recklessness, on his upper lip, from when one of the older boys—Myra couldn't remember who because it happened before her time—had gotten him with a fishing hook. It had been an accident, of course. The story was that Jesse had been walking around where he shouldn't have been. That was how things went in the Hicks household: Don't be stupid and you won't get hurt. And yet people did still get hurt.)

Now Jesse slowed the boat and directed it into the channel where the water was calmer but where he had to slow down even further.

"Your father wanted you back at the restaurant," Myra said quietly, wondering why she'd said that. She was tired. She didn't want to go back to the restaurant right away. Maybe he didn't, either.

He drove the boat in silence, looking over at her every once in a while. She eventually got the impression that he had something to say to her. This alarmed her slightly, mostly because she wasn't sure how to encourage him to say whatever it was he needed to say. As always, when faced with any sort of situation with the boys, it amazed her how little she knew. Was she supposed to talk to him, to try to draw him out, or to stay silent and wait for him to speak? She wished suddenly that she *was* his mother. Then she'd know exactly what to do.

She opened her mouth, then closed it, then sat and thought, selecting and tossing aside different conversation openers until they were out of the channel and he was starting to speed the boat up again.

"Jesse . . . wait. Slow down." He did. "Are you okay?" she finally asked. It was as good a start as any, she supposed.

He glanced at her sideways again. "Sure. Yeah. Well. Um. I'm good, actually. Because, I, uh . . ." He cut the engine. "Well, here's the thing: I got into school."

"Really? As in—"

"Yeah, as in university. University of Toronto. Into the forest biomaterials science program we talked about. Late admission, so, uh, well, yeah, I didn't think it was going to happen."

Neither had Myra. She'd known exactly when he should have heard back from the schools and had been torn about whether to mention it to him or not, to offer her support and empathy, to encourage him to try again the following year, or to apply to a community college, or to take some enrichment classes.

"This is amazing! I didn't—I didn't want to bother you about it, but I was hoping . . . and then . . . I didn't think . . ."

She realized she was talking exactly the way he did, in choppy half sentences.

"Yeah, well. I just thought I'd tell you. It's not like I can go or anything, but it's kind of nice to have gotten in."

Myra thought about what Johnny had said when she'd broached the topic once. "I don't have any money to send anyone to university," he'd told her, and she hadn't known what to say, but she'd known what she'd *wanted* to say, and several times since then she'd wished she'd said it. *I'll pay.* But if she'd said that, there was no telling what might have happened. Johnny might have gotten angry, or he might have been surprised to find out that she had money, that she had more than just her house in the city, which she currently rented out to two tenants, main floor and basement. "Have you told Johnny yet?"

A shadow of alarm crossed Jesse's face. "No. Because he'll just . . . well, I know what he'll say. And I don't have a full scholarship, so there really is no way to pay for it, and even if there was, well, where would I live? It's all just kind of a pipe dream, you know? But I wanted to tell you. Because I didn't believe you when you said I was smart enough to get in, but I guess you were right. I mean, sure, I was wait-listed and all, but I still got in, and I thought you'd be impressed, and I also wanted to say thanks because, well, it made me feel really good . . . even if I can't go." These words came out in a rush and she imagined it probably wasn't easy for him to say them.

Myra took a breath. She put her hand on his, on top of the steering wheel, and she spoke loudly and firmly to be sure he heard her, to be sure he understood her, to be sure he knew she meant it. "Yes, you *can* go. *I* have the money to pay for it and I *want* to pay for it and I won't take no for an answer." His mouth opened, but he didn't speak. "And I have a house in the city," Myra continued. "We'll live there." Then she swallowed and took her hand away. "I mean, because I wouldn't want you to live in my house alone, and also . . . I was planning on going back to the city anyway at the end of the summer. So it's perfect timing."

She thought about Johnny and the way he had kissed her earlier and the idea of making love to him later in his bed in the cottage beside the marina. *His* bed. *His* cottage. *His* marina. *His* life.

Funny. Instead of leaving behind a son, I'm taking one with me.

5

Great Blue Heron (*Ardea herodias*)

These large wading birds usually breed in colonies, in trees close to lakes or wetlands. Great blue herons are considered monogamous, not because they mate for life, but because they only have one mate per mating season.

ain had been the one to tell Helen that Liane was wearing her engagement ring. He was angry, she could tell. Or hurt. Or maybe both. "You didn't even tell me it was lost," he said. "You told me it was getting polished. Which, now that I think about it, is ridiculous. You would never do that."

"I knew I'd find it eventually."

"If we're going to be married, we can't hide things from each other."

"Sometimes things are better left unsaid."

"That's not a good philosophy."

"Maybe one of the reasons I never got married, then. I don't know the philosophies."

"It's not a marriage philosophy to tell people the truth. It's a general one. A life one."

And just like that, over the phone, while the girls were still there, they were in a fight. Or not a fight, but something. A tiff? Helen had grown tired of trying to classify these disagreements. *Why do we have to do this?* she wanted to say. *We never fought, not once, until you decided we needed to be tethered to one another by a piece of rock and a legal document.*

"Aren't you at least going to ask her why she's wearing it and saying she's engaged? I'm a bit concerned about her, to be honest."

"You hardly know her."

"She's your daughter. I want to know her."

Helen felt herself soften. This was part of why she loved Iain so much. He cared about Liane already, because he cared about Helen. And she appreciated it. But she still wasn't about to interfere.

"She'll explain it to me. I don't want to embarrass her. And also, she's had the kayak out. Did I tell you that? I think she's had some kind of breakthrough about Wesley's death and I don't want to get in the way."

"What if she *needs* to talk, though?"

"She'll come to me. You don't understand what it's like with daughters."

"I have a daughter."

"Okay, then you don't understand what it's like with *my* daughters. I never pry. It's just not my way. It always makes things worse. She'll tell me what's going on eventually."

"What if she doesn't, and she leaves, still wearing the ring? Then what will you do?"

"Liane wouldn't do that. She knows it's not hers. It's just a matter of time until she explains."

At that point, of course, her weekend with the girls was still chugging along, despite the fact that Fiona had not shown up, throwing the equilibrium off in a way that surprised Helen. Helen had told Iain she needed to get off the phone then. She had said, "I love you, I really do," and he had said, "I really love you, too," but he had sounded more exasperated than usual.

Then, two mornings ago, Helen had woken and gone

downstairs to make coffee. In the kitchen, she had discovered the butter dish open, finger-shaped gouges in it, and the ring in a juice glass filled with soapy water. *There's a chance I could have just dumped it down the drain,* Helen thought. *Then Iain would* really *have had something to be angry about.* But she hadn't dumped it. She'd taken it out of the glass and cleaned it with care, and when Ilsa came downstairs later that morning, Helen told her it belonged to a friend who had stayed at the cottage.

"Then why was Liane wearing it?" Ilsa had asked. "Is she not really engaged?"

"I don't know, I didn't get the chance to ask her. She left." *Without telling me anything.*

Ilsa had rubbed her head as though it hurt. "It's my fault she left. She got really mad at me yesterday because I went over and started talking to the neighbors and invited them for dinner today. We argued after you went to bed."

Helen wasn't blind. She had seen the man next door watching Liane, and Liane watching him. But, as usual, she hadn't said anything. "Ilsa—"

"I was just being *friendly,*" Ilsa had said, defending herself against the things Helen hadn't said yet. "They're our new neighbors. We should get to *know* them."

"They're just renters."

"Renters don't count?" Ilsa was now storming around the kitchen in a way she hadn't since her more tempestuous teen years. Morning light streamed in through the big kitchen window and Helen knew that it probably made her look old, especially first thing in the morning. *And* I'm *the one who's supposed to be getting married.*

"Why did Liane get so upset?"

"Because she thought I was interfering, trying to bring her and that neighbor man together, in an attempt to prove she doesn't really want to marry Adam."

"Were you?"

"No! I just thought it might be fun for her. The amount of lustful glances they were shooting each other from across the lake, Jesus! I thought it might help her to know that all marriages aren't sacrosanct, that maybe none of them are."

"Help her in what way?"

Upstairs, Xavier had called out, "Mama?" The day before, his nose had started to run and he had gone to bed with a slight fever.

Ilsa had stopped moving around so frantically, brought back to herself by the sound of her son's voice. "You know, we might just head home early, too," she said. She stood still, looking down at the butter dish. "I'm sorry. We had an off year, but there will be others. There always are."

"An off year," Helen had repeated.

"Maybe I'll come back later in the summer," Ilsa had offered.

"You're always welcome," Helen had said, surprised by how badly she wanted Ilsa to return, or not to go in the first place. But instead of trying to convince Ilsa to stay, she had walked down to the dock with her coffee to watch the sun finish its ascent. She felt lonely. Even though she had Iain, just a few cottages over, and a daughter and two grandchildren still in the cottage, she felt completely alone. What she wanted, she realized, was someone to talk to. A friend.

She thought about something Liane had said the day before. She had mentioned that she had been flipping through the cottage guest book that week. "And I saw an entry from Edie. What happened with you two, anyway?"

Helen had stopped what she had been doing—salting and peppering fish fillets she had thawed—and looked up at Liane, thoughtful. *Well, let's see. What happened? She ran off with Fiona's father, that's what happened. She turned out to be more envious of me than anyone else.* "I don't remember anymore," Helen had finally said. "Something silly. I think she lives in California. Or maybe New York City. I don't know. She got married." Helen had squeezed lemon on the fish and then rubbed the lemon over her hands before washing them.

"I went out in the kayak," Liane said next. "I don't know if you noticed."

"I did," Helen said carefully. "I'm proud of you." She covered the fish with a pot lid. She cleared her throat and waited. Maybe now Liane would explain about the ring. But she didn't. The conversation appeared to be over.

And then both girls had left and Helen was alone on the island with nothing to do but walk over to Iain's and admit to him that she had failed at her mission. She had spent the day and night with him, but now needed to go back to her place for more stuff. He was reading the paper, his reading glasses down his nose. She stepped in front of him, sandals in hand.

"I'm going for a walk," she said. "I need a few things from my place."

"Mmm-hmm," he replied, without looking up. He was upset with her still, she could tell. Perhaps she couldn't blame him. It probably hadn't felt very good to arrive at her cottage and discover her daughter wearing the ring, as though playing dress-up with some discarded trinket.

Helen put on her sandals, walked out the front door, and couldn't help but think the old Helen—or, perhaps more correctly, the *young* Helen—would keep walking away from this place and never return. And although she still felt like the same person (sometimes that didn't seem fair, mostly because of the crow's-feet), at sixty-four Helen was finally grown-up enough to know that walking away from a man like Iain, a strong, solid, intelligent, passionate, and, yes, *traditional* man like Iain, would be a mistake she'd regret, always.

• • •

Meeting Iain had happened for a lot of reasons and in a roundabout way. Mainly, the events that had set it into motion—or at least that had preceded it, had helped her identify her need—had happened because Helen had finally grown tired, one day, of eating dinner alone.

After an early morning spent doing yoga back in the rural village where she lived during the year, after her daily walk, after tending to her vast garden of herbs, the smells of which brought back so many different memories and made her feel a little sorry that every summer she would give the house to a house sitter (almost always an actor or painter or some other form of artist friend who needed somewhere to be) and spend most of the time on the island, after a visit to the library in town for a new crop of literary thrillers, after lunch with her friend Nina (wheat germ burgers at the Carrot Top Café), after a nap in the solarium, from which she woke, slightly disoriented, dreaming she was about to go on at Massey Hall, after realizing it was not in fact 1975 and feeling that perhaps she had slept too long (she had, and she'd never get to sleep that night), after watching the sun fade on the horizon from where she lay, after feeling hungry, moving to the kitchen, and beginning to prepare a meal—her idea had been kamut pasta, fresh tomatoes, basil, olive oil, a glass of wine, but instead she had put toast in the oven, sliced tomatoes, ground pepper, felt tired of cooking for one—after carrying it outside and turning on CBC radio to keep the silence at bay, after all this, she had had the following thought: *I am tired of eating alone. I don't want to become a woman who eats cereal over the sink, who ceases to care about her meals, or who constantly invites friends in for dinner, bustles around the kitchen, all the while thinking,* If you weren't here I'd go insane with loneliness. *I never used to be that woman, but I am getting lonely. My days I can fill fine. But at night, in the evening . . . well, I want someone to eat with. I want someone to cook for who isn't a friend. And, to be frank, postmeno-*

pausal or not, I wouldn't mind a good lay once in a while, and none
of the men in this town seem up for the task.

And so she stood and fetched her laptop, left her toasted
tomato sandwich, and drank her red wine instead—one glass,
then another—while she set up a profile on MatchedSilver
.com, a website that Nina had mentioned that day at lunch.
The name of the site had caused her to cringe, but she still
went on. *Gracefully Aging Flower Child Seeks Dinner Companion*,
she wrote, and immediately felt embarrassed. Still, she continued with a jumble of words that described her completely and
would likely put most men off.

She faltered for a moment—surely she would be recognized; or perhaps not; it was indeed no longer 1975—then
uploaded a picture a friend had taken of her at a party. In the
picture Helen was laughing while facing slightly away from
the camera. In the soft light of the photo, the white streaks
in her hair looked blond and her laugh lines were still visible
but softened.

She got a lot of messages. Some of them memorable because they were bizarre, some of them memorable because
they were pathetic, a few memorable because she was indeed
recognized (the "folksinging goddess of my not so illustrious
youth," as one man put it), but none of them memorable
because they were *memorable*. She began to grow frustrated.
This isn't going to work. If I'm going to meet someone, I'm going to
meet him in a different way than this. I always did before, didn't I?

Except in the life she had led before, it had been somewhat easier to meet men.

Helen had left her hometown of Mulmur, Ontario, at seventeen. When interviewers asked her why, she always said,
"Have you been to Mulmur?" and left it at that. But in truth,
it was a pretty little farm town she wished she could tell idyllic

stories about. Stories other than: "*My mother, Abigail, did all the things in her life because she had to, not because she wanted to, and sometimes I would see her looking out across our fields of potatoes with an expression of longing so fierce I wanted to take her hand and run away. But I knew if I suggested it her face would return to normal and she would smile and say, 'Why on earth would I ever want to do that?'*" Stories other than: "*My brother, Ellis, was 'not right in the head.' That was how the townspeople put it, but no one ever sought to figure out what the problem was, exactly. Then one night he came into my room, covered my mouth with his hand, and climbed on top of me, but I bit him and he screamed and my father came running.*"

Helen's father, Angus, didn't speak of what he had seen happening that night because he almost never spoke of anything. But he also didn't argue with Helen when she said two days later she was leaving, didn't have a response when Abigail cried and said, "But she was going to marry Beacan Wilson." (Later, though, when the cottage was put in her name, she recognized the small piece of property they had visited each summer, for quiet vacations during which Helen once swam the entire perimeter of the island and thought she might die from exhaustion, as an act of contrition. So she fought Ellis hard for it in court when he attempted to prove that their father was going senile and was not in his right mind when he bequeathed the property to her, then paid him what would have been his share to make sure he never came around, and gave him her share of the farm, too.)

It was 1968 when Helen escaped to Toronto and ended up flopping in an apartment with a group of Vietnam draft dodgers. At night she sang them the Irish folk songs she remembered her mother singing while cleaning, mending, or cooking, and one of the group told her she needed to learn how to play a guitar. "I already *do* know how," she said. "I just don't have one." So they pooled their money and bought her one.

Later, she moved into a Yorkville apartment with three

other girls, all of whom wanted to be folksingers, too. They started busking on street corners and trying to think of a name for the group they were going to form. Then Helen was approached by the owner of a bar. "What about my friends?" Helen asked. "Can they come sing, too?" But the man had said no, just her. The bar was called the Purple Onion. It was the same place where Buffy Sainte-Marie wrote "Universal Soldier." Helen went back to the apartment and packed her things into a bag before her friends could tell her to move out.

The record executive who discovered her was a king-maker, and also her first lover, and journalists would always ask about him, but she would refuse to say his name. "It was the first and last heartbreak for me," she would say, trying to sound cavalier. Closer to the truth would probably have been something like, *The first cut is the deepest,* but that line was al-ready taken. Soon, though, it became her trademark to sing songs that were anti-love, to preach, through her music, about how women didn't need men at all. She had been raised by a woman who thought the greatest thing Helen could aspire to was to marry Beacan Wilson. She had never once seen her father kiss her mother. Her brother had tried to rape her. "I'm not a huge fan of men," she would say in interviews. Of course, there were rumors that she was a lesbian, but Helen didn't care. (Abigail did, though. This was apparently the final straw. She stood up in church and publicly denounced her daughter. A childhood friend wrote Helen a letter to tell her about it.)

"Down with Love, Says Helen Sear," read her *Rolling Stone* cover line.

Success made her life a blur, until she turned twenty-five and walked into a party and met a man named Nate, the guitarist of one of the most successful rock bands of the era. He spilled his glass of red wine on her, then gave her his shirt to wear. She had wandered the party smelling like him until she believed at the end of the night that she knew him. (She never really did.) She went with him back to his hotel room.

Weeks later, when he went back out on tour, she discovered she was pregnant. She wrote him a letter. He didn't reply. She considered her options and decided that although she could exercise her choice not to keep the baby, she could also exercise her choice *to* keep the baby. She could purposefully raise him or her without a father—and maybe that would be even more controversial than anything she had done so far.

By this time she had been befriended by Edie, a trust-fund child (Helen had recently heard the term "trustafarian" and thought of her old friend, always with a twinge of bitterness) who wasn't musically talented but was intelligent and spontaneous and the perfect accomplice, with her long dark curls and aristocratic good looks in stark and appealing contrast to Helen's blond hair and wide-set blue eyes. "*We* can raise the baby together," Edie said. "Who needs a man?" That was how it had started.

Fiona was born, and she grew a little older, and then the seventies drew to a close and Helen passed thirty and tried not to notice. The songs she was writing were different, more offbeat and jazzy and not so popular with the North Americans, but the Europeans loved them, so she decided to go on an extended tour over there. On the night she met Claude, she had decided to procure a bike and ride it through the city, pretending to be a Parisian girl without a care. She wore a hat and sunglasses so no one would recognize her, but this made it difficult for her to see and she fell off the bike. Claude was standing on the street corner and he picked up the baguette and cheese that had fallen from her basket and said, "This won't do, will it?" and took her first to dinner and then to meet his delighted artist friends.

Her pregnancy was purposeful, although she didn't *quite* explain this to Claude. Still, he seemed pleased about it, in his vague way. He even tried to live with them back in Toronto, when Ilsa was a baby. But he couldn't. He missed Paris. He thought Toronto dismal in winter, repressed in summer. He loved Ilsa, though, and Helen promised never to keep her from him. It was when Claude was living with her that she and Edie began to drift apart, ever so slightly. A man sharing their space changed things.

The eighties weren't kind to Helen's career. She had been warned to expect it, but still, it stung. Her record sales were plummeting, both at home and abroad, and no one seemed to understand that she needed to evolve, that she couldn't just be the same girl, singing the same songs. She got restless and left the girls with Edie. She went to India for a month, because it seemed like the thing to do. She met Wes at an ashram when she was sitting on a cold floor trying to meditate. She had been unable to focus and had opened her eyes. He was watching her, his green eyes (the same as Liane's) bright. *I want you,* she had begun to say, over and over again in her head. *I want you, I want you.* And as they sat, wordlessly staring at each other, she had become positive that he was saying the same thing in his mind. Not in the base, physical sense, not *I want you* as in *I want to sleep with you* (although of course there had been that), but as in *I want all of you, inside, outside, all of it.*

She thought she had loved him most, when she did allow herself to think of him. And she wondered why that had done nothing to pull him back from the edge. "We can't choose who we love," she had said after he died. "I still would have wanted to love him, even if I had known there was no curing him."

It was this line, "We can't choose who we love," that Edie had thrown back at her when she had eventually confessed to Helen that she had seen Nate at a party—and had only approached him to confront him about Fiona, she had insisted—and ended up falling into a headlong affair with him that had somehow turned into a marriage at city hall. "Are you pregnant?" Helen had asked, incredulous. Edie was younger than her by a few years, but still. It seemed unlikely. "We might try," Edie had said softly, and Helen had thought, *This might be all my fault.* She had allowed Edie to live in her shadow, had many times treated her like a nanny—and then Edie, whether on purpose or not, had managed to attain the one thing Helen had never been able to. "I don't want to see you again," Helen had said. This banishing of Edie had been the worst heartbreak, though, because theirs had been her longest relationship, even if it wasn't sexual.

After all this, you're not going to find great love on a cheesy website, Helen had thought. *And maybe not ever again. That part of your life is over. Move on.* It was June and just about time to pack up and go to the cottage, so she deleted her profile before leaving town.

But then: On her first day at the cottage that year, the day before the girls arrived, Helen had gone for a walk. She had stopped when she had seen Iain in his garden and stood watching him, mostly because he was strange to behold. All those greens, in bushel baskets around him. He was wearing some sort of apron and carrying a basket but there was nothing unmasculine about him. He stood up and looked at her and she smiled and said, "Hi," and was about to make an excuse about why she had been standing there staring at him when he smiled back and said, in a voice that made her go weak at the knees (literally, they knocked together a little and she had to steady herself; she was *such* a sucker for a Scottish accent), "Would you like some greens? I have tons. Literally, I think." Greens. Honestly. Iain and his greens. But it was yet another of the little things she loved about him that added up to a larger sum: the way that he was so relentlessly himself. (Except, of course, when him being relentlessly himself meant him being relentless about the topic of marriage.)

He had walked toward her and they had started to talk. About the greens, at first: dandelion and chard, spinach and chicory, turnip leaves, rutabaga leaves, beet greens. "They're the secret to longevity," he had said. "Oh, good," she had replied. "I was getting tired of goji berries, turmeric, and the ground-up bones of wayward children." To her relief, he had laughed, but then they had stood in silence. She, searching for something else to keep the conversation going, had asked him if he had seen the two blue herons who were out on the lake most mornings. "Oh, yes," he said, "all the time. Aren't they a gorgeous pair?" Helen nodded and wondered what to say next, but then, thankfully, he had said, "Would you like to have dinner?" And she had said, "Yes, why don't you come over to my place and cook me some of your youth-preserving greens and I'll do the rest?" And he had said, "If you're sure, because I can cook," but she had shaken her head, wanting to have him come to her, although she wasn't sure why.

Iain came to dinner—to her relief, not bearing wildflowers or something equally trite, but instead two bottles of wine, one red, one white. "I wasn't sure which one you liked," he said. "What if I didn't drink at all?" she had replied. "Then I would have had to have them both myself," he said. "And besides, aren't you Helen Sear?" She had nodded, for some reason embarrassed to admit this. "I'm sorry," he said, sensing discomfort. "I didn't mean . . ." "That just because I used to be a folksinger I'm also a complete alcoholic? It's partially true."

She took the two bottles from him and stood looking at him and found she wanted to run her hands over his chest, to take off his glasses, to kiss him. Perhaps she would have done this, many years ago—in fact, this was exactly what the old *not*-old Helen would have done: put the bottles down and led him to her bedroom, taking her shirt off along the way, shrugging out of her skirt, no underwear, of course. However, it was one of the sad truths about aging that a person couldn't just do things like that, that a woman couldn't count on the fact that lifting one's shirt over one's head would render a man speechless—at least not in the right way. And that you needed to have at least a few glasses of wine, if not several, before the courage could be worked up to do any of it.

"Used to be?" he said. "You mean you aren't anymore?" "Well, it's been a while since I performed, but I suppose the label is stamped on me forever." That's how she sometimes felt, stamped by her songs, by the things she used to say.

Later, when the wine helped her lose inhibitions and she *did* lift her shirt over her head, he was sweet, said all the right things, made her feel good, maybe even great. And as time went on he also made her feel that none of the places she had gone to or the people she had been or the mistakes she had made in the past—many of these mistakes and much of this pain outlined in those songs she could never shake—mattered. She eventually came to feel that she could tell him everything.

This had not turned out to be true in all cases.

The night he proposed was also the night they'd had their first fight.

She had laughed before she had realized he was serious when he said, "Marry me." Her next response had been to say, "But *why?*" Also a mistake.

"Because I love you," he had said. "Because I want to wake up with you beside me every morning for the rest of my life."

"Every morning? What if you go on a trip? What if *I* go on a trip?"

"Come on, Helen, don't get all technical on me."

"We can still do those things even if we're not married.

Also, don't you want to know that every morning, when you wake up beside me, it's because I want to be beside you—not because I have to be, not because of some piece of paper?"

He had sighed and taken off his glasses and she had felt the first tingle of fear. *You could lose him if you don't do this.* "I suppose that's true. But . . . I want to be more to you than anyone else, than any of the others. Which I realize makes me sound incredibly insecure, and I'm not. It's not insecurity. I'm not trying to stake my claim, so don't suggest that, either. I just . . . I can't help it. I want you to be *my* wife. I want you to marry *me*. And I'm a Catholic boy at heart. It's how I raised my own kids. I'm not sure how comfortable I'd be living together if we didn't marry."

"Let me get this straight. You actually think that marrying me will somehow keep you out of hell?" Helen was having trouble keeping a straight face but when she looked at him she realized he didn't find any of this funny.

And so she had composed herself and said *yes,* because how could she not have? Iain was the kind of man who pulled out her chair, held the door for her, gave his seat to women on buses and subways. (Which, yes, she sometimes did think perhaps reflected a belief in him that women were the weaker sex, but still, it was endearing.) Iain always, always kept his word, when it came to her and when it came to others, his family, his friends, strangers even. He was her best friend, truly, he was the person she wanted to be with all the time, the person she thought of and smiled about when she wasn't with him. He made her feel like a better person, and this was no small feat. He was never threatened or frustrated when she became strident, never became annoyed with her when she jumped on a soapbox. "She's a lot of work, isn't she?" a friend had once said, and he had smiled and pulled Helen close and kissed her on the head and said, "An awful lot."

She also liked that he had his own life, too, and she knew he had been satisfied with it before she came along, that although he was a widower he had never been searching for a woman to fill a hole. He had been an agriculture museum curator before he retired. He sometimes seemed to come from another era, could make her feel as though the time and therefore her life was not in fact running through her fingers but was slowing down instead. He was humble. He was self-aware. He could be funny and goofy, but he could also be brilliant. And most of all, he loved her. "Worships you, more like," Nina had said. "I don't know how you do it, but you seem to have somehow landed yourself the last good one on the planet."

And the biggest fault she could find with him? That he wanted to marry her.

"I need to tell the girls first, before we set a date," she had said the night he proposed. "I can't just surprise them with wedding invitations in the mail. They don't even know about you."

"So when are you going to tell them?"

"Our annual cottage weekend."

"But that's months away."

"Six weeks, not months."

"Why can't you have them up sooner?"

"Because that's when we always do it."

"But maybe you could start a new tradition. A cottage weekend in May."

"The island is uninhabitable in May. All those bugs."

He had reached for her hand and she had felt relief at his touch.

"I'm sorry. This didn't exactly go the way I planned it," he said.

"You planned this?" This made her nervous. "It seemed so spontaneous."

"Well, it was. It *was* spontaneous, but I'd definitely been thinking about it. A lot. And planning it. And I was going to . . . well, I didn't think getting down on one knee with a ring would be appropriate, but the next step was going to be for me to give you a ring."

"You have a ring?"

"I have a ring."

"Oh, please, no." Helen had said that accidentally. "Oh, no. I'm sorry. That didn't sound right. It's just that I—"

"Don't like to wear jewelry unless it's costume. I know that. But I thought you might like this one. It's simple." He was pulling it out of his pocket. And it *was* a pretty ring. A square diamond—the words *princess cut* had popped into Helen's mind, although she had no idea how she knew this term—with an antique scroll setting. If she had ever wanted an engagement ring, this probably would have been the one. Although at that point even if she had despised it she would have pretended to adore it.

When she put it on, the mood lightened a bit. They shared a toast to their future.

But then time passed and she began to try to think of reasons not to marry him. That was why she had misplaced the ring. She had taken it off and placed it on the shelf and forgotten about it because she had read that line in the Martha Gellhorn book about how you should never marry a man who didn't like his mother. *He never speaks of his mother,* she realized. *And when he does, it's dismissive, disparaging.* She felt guilty about it later, knew he had his reasons—and very compelling ones, at that: his mother was an alcoholic who had hit him and his sisters regularly and eventually died of liver failure. But of course by then the ring was already destined to turn up on Liane's finger.

• • •

Helen returned to the cottage from her walk. He was at the table with a notepad. She could sense that his annoyance had not dissipated.

"Who do you think you might be inviting to the wedding?" Iain asked.

"Who are *you* inviting?"

"My kids. Some friends. Forty people, probably. You?"

"Why do you need to know?" She had intended to make amends when she returned, but now she was feeling defensive again.

"I'm just wondering how many we can expect. What to budget for this."

"I thought we agreed, something simple. And budget isn't an issue. I'll pay. Whatever you want."

"Of course I'm not letting you pay for our wedding." He seemed seriously affronted. "And it would help to know how many guests."

She boiled water in the kettle, measured matcha powder, whisked it into hot water, slid a mug toward him with a bit too much force. (Green liquid that looked like pond scum spattered across the table, some onto his hand.)

"Ouch," he said.

"I don't know who I'm inviting yet," she said. He said nothing, and she sat, watching him and feeling the anger begin to build.

"You're only hurting yourself with all this wedding business—and why?"

"I'm sorry, *what?*"

"*And why,* I said. So you can have an official piece of paper with both of our names on it?"

"It's more than a piece of paper to me. Why are you sabotaging this?"

"I'm not sabotaging anything. I want to be with you. I want to spend the rest of my life with you. But . . ." She searched for one of her reasons. "Well, here's the thing about committing to someone at our age: you actually mean it when you say you're going to spend the rest of your life with a person. The 'in sickness and in health' part has less of a far-off-in-the-distant-future ring to it. I just don't want to have to say it aloud and think about my own mortality."

"That's another one of your weak excuses. And we just won't say that part. Did you really think I was going to make you recite traditional vows?"

"Maybe I did, considering you want us to *be* traditional and get married."

"I can't change who I am, Helen."

"And I can?" Except she could see why he thought her more malleable, more changeable. She *was*. How many times had she reinvented herself over the years? But what most people didn't understand was that she had remained the same person inside. *"Marriage,* Iain. The very thing I always said I would never do for many reasons, but in part because . . . well, in part because I stood against it for so long!"

"Don't you think it's time to grow up? The era is over. Women know they have choices now. And you definitely proved you could do it, Helen. No one's going to fault you. Maybe no one will even notice."

She tried to ignore the fact that he had hinted that she didn't matter anymore. "You think getting married is what makes you grow up? *Please!* I grew up long before I decided I was *never* going to need a man to complete me."

He left his tea and went out to his garden.

"Your goddamn greens!" she shouted after him, and immediately wished she hadn't. Especially when he turned and shouted back at her.

"Fine, Helen, fine! If you don't want to marry me, then don't!"

And then, yet again, the ring was abandoned on a countertop. Many times after, she wished she had kept it. But she didn't. She left, went back to her cottage, and wandered from room to room. Eventually she opened the guest book and ripped out the page with Edie's entry on it, the one Liane had mentioned. She crumpled it up and threw it in the garbage. She tried to calm down. She didn't succeed. So she called Johnny and had him pick her up. She left without properly closing up the cottage and gave cash to have one of his sons do it. Who knew when she'd be back? She certainly wasn't going to spend the summer on the island now. Maybe it was a place that was now forever ruined. *And all because of a man,* she thought mutinously.

6

Red Fox (*Vulpes vulpes*)

*Although red foxes will dig their own dens, they seem
to prefer using dens that were made by other animals.
Depressions under buildings are also favored den sites.
While it is believed the red fox mates for life, pairs may
separate for a few months and rejoin during the breeding
season, or they might not rejoin at all.*

When the fox—which, it turned out, lived beneath the cottage—ate Rolf the guinea pig and the girls witnessed it, Gillian realized that she couldn't shield her girls from everything.

Afterward, when Isabel and Beatrice's sobs had slowed, when they were blanketed on the couch, huddled together watching a Disney movie—even though Isabel was thirteen and had told them she was far too old for Disney movies of any sort, which was probably true—Gillian thought perhaps she should go talk to Laurence. She hadn't had this thought in a while. She had been spending most of that summer so far trying to think of ways to *avoid* talking to him. But no. It was time. Something had to give. Somehow, the brutality of the fox had finally made her realize this.

She left the living room and walked into the kitchen. Her "husband"—she put mental quotation marks around the word now—was facing the window, a bottle of beer in his hand. His laptop at close hand on the counter meant that he was probably planning to go and write, and this filled her with irritation. Always, the *writing*. His other wife. His mistress. And, as she did every time she thought of his writing this way, as an act of infidelity, she felt welcome self-justification. She had done what she had done because he had never loved her properly to begin with. Did it matter that Daniel, in general, wasn't as passionate about life as Laurence, wasn't quite as handsome, certainly wasn't as intelligent? No, it did not. Because Laurence's intelligence was useless to her. Like a cocktail party anecdote. "This is Gillian and her husband. He's a novelist." Now the person's eyebrows would rise with interest. "His most recent book was short-listed for the Tamworth." Eyebrows up even farther, combined with a slight turn away from her and toward Laurence. "It's about what would happen if we knew exactly when the world was going to end—but not for a hundred years." Sometimes people simply turned their backs on Gillian at this point. *What about me?* she had often found herself thinking. *I'm a genetic researcher. One day I might save your daughter's life.* But no. That was not the sort of thing that mattered to anyone. Until they actually needed it.

"I think it's time we left the island," Gillian said. Laurence just nodded absently and continued to look out the window. She felt herself become angry. "We as in *I'd like to take the girls with me, back to the city. We as in not you. We as in us.* I think we should all talk, and then I think the girls and I should leave."

Now he was paying attention. "I don't want you to do that."

"I don't think they want to stay. And I especially don't think they'll want to stay once they know."

"Did you think about asking them what they want?"

"No. But I know them. And also, it's what *I* want."

He ignored this. Of course he ignored this. When had he

ever cared what she wanted? "Perhaps we should ask them together—after, as you suggest, we have the talk."

"Make them choose between us? Laurence, that's monstrous."

He clenched his jaw and looked away again, and this show of anger, however benign, surprised her. He hadn't displayed anger since it had all started. Mostly what he had done was spend time on the end of the dock reading, or upstairs in the tiny attic studio looking at the water (this was all she ever saw him doing) and writing (this was what he said he was doing). Oh, and of course he played with the girls, went for walks and canoe rides with Isabel, tickled Bea until she shrieked with laughter, read them their bedtime stories instead of Gillian because, according to Bea, "Daddy does the voices better and he snuggles longer than you do."

Meanwhile, Gillian, when the girls were otherwise occupied (with Laurence, or with television, or, in Isabel's case, with her computer or phone), wandered up and down the property line trying to get a cellular signal so she could return Daniel's numerous texts.

"This was not how this summer was supposed to go," Gillian said.

"And how was it *supposed* to go?" he asked through teeth still clenched.

She rolled her eyes. "*You* tell *me*! This was your idea, renting this place!"

Now he unclenched and spoke quietly, ever mindful of the girls in a way that to her felt self-righteous. Another reason to be angry with him instead of at herself. "I rented it before I knew . . . about . . ." He could never say it, though. "And it was *your* idea to visit with the girls on weekends. Listen, Gill, I'm not saying we make the girls choose between us, but yes, it's time to tell them, and we need to do it together, and we need to make them feel like they have at least some control over what's going to happen to them next—Isabel, anyway. Bea probably won't understand." He sighed and stepped back. She hadn't realized he'd been advancing. "After what happened with that damned fox, if you want to take them back to the city, you can, but they *are* coming back next weekend and the weekend after that. I can just come get them myself, if that's what you need."

"So you've thought about it. Me leaving." It sounded like an accusation, and she realized it was. *We agreed to this.*

"Yes. I've thought about it. I've thought about it a lot. I think about it all the time, in fact. What do you think, Gill, that I like living a lie from Friday to Monday, that I don't care at all?"

"You *act* like you don't care. Most of the time you act like this isn't even real. Like, for example, when you accepted that neighbor's, that *Ilsa's,* dinner invitation, as though it would even be possible or *probable* for us to go into the home of strangers and pretend that everything was normal!"

"I told you, I didn't know what to say, and didn't want to explain it all to a stranger, so I just . . . said yes." But his face had started to color. "Besides, it didn't happen, remember? She canceled, said something had come up and that she and her sister had to leave the island."

"*They* canceled. *You* would have gone through with it."

"When you come here, you walk around acting all wounded and pious. Do you actually think I don't know what you're doing, wandering around outside at all hours trying to get a cell phone signal so you can text *him* and tell him how bored you are? How horrible it is to be stuck on this island with your 'husband'?" She winced. He tipped his beer bottle back and emptied it of its contents, then opened the fridge and took out another one.

This was new. He had hardly been drinking at all, almost never joining her in a glass of wine before or during dinner.

She had thought perhaps this was because he hadn't wanted to share anything resembling festivity with her. But maybe he simply hadn't wanted to be even slightly the way he was now: out of control. She knew it wasn't for her that he hadn't wanted to be this way, but for the girls. Except now that the girls were off balance because of the incident with the fox and that stupid and pathetic guinea pig that had been all her idea, and she wasn't even quite certain the girls liked particularly, he was allowing himself to fall apart a little, too.

He swallowed more beer. "I don't want to upset the girls, either, but it's going to happen eventually."

I know that! she wanted to shout. *That's exactly what I was thinking!* But instead she opened the fridge, took out a bottle of white wine, and poured a glass.

He turned away from her and walked toward the sliding doors, presumably to go and sit on the end of the dock again, either a laptop or a book holding all his attention.

"This is your fault, too!" she shouted after him, not caring anymore what the girls heard or did not hear. But he didn't turn, or even flinch. He just kept walking away.

Laurence and Gill met when she was in the midst of her postgraduate degree in medical genetics at Oxford. Her roommate, Louise, had been dating an English major from Toronto and he had come to visit for a week with a friend. "He's a writer," Louise had said. "Apparently he wants nothing more than to visit the Reading Room in the British Museum Great Court. Will you take him?"

She still remembered that he had been wearing a blue button-down shirt and khaki pants the first time she met him—although, at the time, how could she have known that this would turn out to be his uniform, that the very things that had attracted her to him in the first place (his casual way of dressing, his constant five o'clock shadow, the way sometimes, when a story wasn't going well, she would notice that some of his nails had been bitten down) would eventually repulse her?

Back then, however, when he decided to stay in London, to be with her and write for a while, she would take those sore-looking fingers in her own, kiss them, and say, "It will work itself out; it always does. This block won't last for long," and he would smile and start to undress her and call her his muse.

This had happened a lot during their heady first days together. Whether he legitimately needed a muse or did not, he would end up undressing her frequently. They had been together only five months when she discovered she was pregnant. Her secret: There was a small part of her, a very quiet part, that had insinuated the following: *This wasn't supposed to be forever. You weren't going to marry a* writer.

When she told him about her pregnancy, he didn't react (later, this habit of his, too, would annoy her) but instead watched her face and waited to see what she would say next. "I want to keep the baby," she said, expecting her voice to sound more halting than it had. Instead, she had sounded very sure, and very grown-up—which had made her realize she officially *was* grown-up. This was an idea that did not immediately sit well with her, despite the fact that she had almost always been called "mature for your age." "I just don't think I can—" she continued, but he put his hand on her forearm and said, "You don't have to explain."

It was different after that. She no longer felt like his muse. Her stomach distended and she hated it. He said she was gorgeous. An earth mother. Later, *arabesque.* She began to have strange dreams about leading a different life, about being in the pages of one of those Choose Your Own Adventure novels that had made her feel so uncomfortable as a child (Was it really okay to choose your own book ending? Perhaps this was why she had never been able to identify with Laurence's need to write books) and simply deciding to go down another path that did not include Laurence. Then she'd wake up and realize she didn't have a choice.

Isabel arrived. Laurence was a perfect father, but Gillian suffered from what she realized now was postpartum depression. It took her months to connect with her daughter. She said that nursing hurt, but it didn't. It was just that the close contact made her uncomfortable in the same way getting massages or facials at spas did. When she had tried to explain this to Laurence, he was incredulous. "But this is your *child*," he had said. "You should be on my side!" she had shouted, and he had put his hand on her arm. "Please. Don't shout. There aren't sides here. We're all on the same team now. Me, you, and Iz." His private little name for her.

She had eventually come out of the depression, but the feeling of being the "other" in the family had never dissipated, not even years later, when she decided they should have Beatrice in an attempt to grow their family unit to a size that would be big enough to include her, too. This had failed, of course. A child can't save a marriage. Gillian should have known this. And poor Beatrice. She was a colicky baby and still cried more often than not, as though she knew the weight of the future of her parents' marriage had always rested on shoulders too small to bear the load.

Daniel was a scientist. They met on an advisory panel. She had not immediately liked him. But when he asked her, later, if she had, she said, "Of course I did. I couldn't stop watching you."

Jasmine, the divorce lawyer, had explained to Gill that it would take nearly a year for the divorce to be finalized. She was okay with the wait, but it made Daniel, who had already separated from his wife when they began their affair in earnest, edgy. It was as though he expected her to change her mind.

It was difficult for her to explain to Daniel why she wanted him—and she didn't want to tell him that the very reasons she wanted him were so opposite from the reasons she had wanted Laurence (or that maybe it was *because* he was the opposite of Laurence that she wanted him at all). So she just told him that it was difficult but that she was working on it, trying her best, that she loved him, of course she did, for reasons that she found challenging to explain simply because she was so logically minded. This placated him. He liked it when she mentioned logic, especially in relation to her own mind. (There: a reason. Because he appreciated logic and especially hers. And also, secretly, because his achievements were never going to outshine her own.)

She pushed Daniel from her mind and peeked in at the girls. Beatrice was still watching the movie. Isabel was tapping away at her iPhone, holding it up, searching for a signal the way her errant mother so often did. Gill forced herself to smile. Then she returned to the kitchen to make a salad and take out the fish she intended to parcel in foil and grill for dinner. Later: "Go get your father for dinner," she instructed Isabel. And Isabel did, and Laurence, her "husband," entered the cottage, did not drink any more beer, declined her offer of wine during the meal, chatted and laughed with the girls, and also offered to hold a special memorial service for Rolf the next day. The talk didn't happen. She avoided looking at Laurence and could tell he was avoiding looking at her, too.

Later, everyone went to bed, Gill in the master bedroom, Laurence on a futon in his upper-level study. As she climbed between the sheets, she had a sudden sense that all was as it should be, but this feeling didn't last for long. It never had.

• • •

The next morning, Gill woke early, before Laurence—although it didn't especially matter, now that they weren't in the same bed—and went for her daily run. The reality of what they had been doing now felt to Gill like the act of peeling a Band-Aid away slowly. *And the dirty line around the Band-Aid is still going to be there when the Band-Aid is peeled away, and scrubbing that off is going to leave the skin raw and itchy.* She tried to run away from this thought, but the pounding of her feet seemed to insist on the metaphor. *I've been married to a writer for too long.*

Gill hadn't brought her phone with her as she usually did when she ran. She hadn't wanted to talk to Daniel, or anyone, that morning. The next time she spoke with Daniel, she had decided during her sleepless night, she would have something definitive to say. *No more pretending. We told the girls. I'll introduce you soon, but not yet.*

As she ran she thought about how, before the argument they had had in the kitchen after what had happened with Rolf, their only other argument had been about Laurence wanting to try counseling. Back in the city, back before all was revealed, he had said to her, "If we go, I'll feel like at least then we'll know we tried everything."

"But do you see the way you're talking? *Then we'll know we tried everything.* Past tense, as though our marriage is a dead thing. Because you know it isn't going to work, and then we'll have gone through the agony and embarrassment of sitting in front of someone we don't know, airing our dirty laundry, secretly waiting for him or her to tell us we're right and the other person is wrong. And besides, we *did* try everything: we tried having Bea. That was giving it our all, *that* was trying. If a child wasn't going to bring us together . . ." There it was: the logic. Laurence didn't like it as much as Daniel did, though.

But actually, there was one other argument, wasn't there? It had happened after she had told him about Daniel, referring to it as an "emotional" affair only, feeling slightly sick about the lie but also not wanting to take any chances. She remembered feeling angry at his lack of reaction. She remembered how she started to argue with him. "*You've* had countless emotional affairs, you know," she had said.

"What are you talking about?"

"Your characters. The perfect women you create because you aren't *with* the perfect woman."

"Gill. You've got to be kidding. You can't accuse someone of having an affair with a fictional character."

She remembered that she had lost all hold on her precious logic in that moment. "Oh, yeah!? Well, that's exactly what I'm doing!" she had shouted, before storming from the room.

For years she had pored over his manuscript drafts, or the typed, discarded pages she would find in odd places, but it was never, ever her, not even a single characteristic, and it never had been. Even that summer she hadn't been able to quit the habit of snooping through his work, and one afternoon when he was swimming with the girls she'd found herself reading a short story about a red-haired woman. This one seemed more vivid than all the others, and awakened a jealousy in her she thought had gone dormant. She felt so vengeful, there in the attic of the old cottage, that she had very nearly deleted the story from his hard drive. But she hadn't.

Gill slowed her pace when she realized she was gasping. She turned and began to jog slowly back toward the cottage.

Down the driveway, and the jogging stopped. Laurence, Beatrice, and Isabel were standing beside the water. Gill realized they were having the memorial service for Rolf and felt stung that Laurence hadn't thought to wait.

Laurence was holding a piece of paper, which he passed

to Isabel, who started to read in her clear young voice. Gill realized it was a poem. Emily Dickinson.

> *After great pain a formal feeling comes—*
> *The Nerves sit ceremonious, like Tombs—*
> *The stiff Heart questions was it He, that bore,*
> *And Yesterday, or Centuries before?*
> *The Feet, mechanical, go round—*
> *Of Ground, or Air, or Ought,*
> *A Wooden way*
> *Regardless grown,*
> *A Quartz contentment, like a stone—*
> *This is the Hour of Lead—*
> *Remembered, if outlived,*
> *As Freezing persons recollect the Snow—*
> *First Chill—then Stupor—then the letting go—*

Gill looked down at the wedding ring she still wore on her left hand. It felt very heavy. She had lost weight that summer from the stress, and the ring slid off easily and landed in her other palm. She looked forward, at Isabel. Should she give the ring to her? Would she even want it? She closed her palm around the ring and walked toward her "husband" and daughters. "We should go inside and have a talk," she said when she was close enough for them to hear her.

She hated that this would be a moment Isabel was likely to always remember, that Beatrice would have a foggy awareness of. She squeezed the ring more tightly until she was sure it would leave a mark.

7
Eastern Gray Squirrel (*Sciurus carolinensis*)

The eastern gray squirrel has two breeding seasons each year, the first in winter and the second in summer. Each of the mating periods lasts for about three weeks. Generally, only females over two years of age will breed in both seasons. Courtship behavior begins when a receptive female calls continuously from a treetop with ducklike sounds. Several males soon gather and often fight to determine the dominant animal. As they congregate, the female becomes agitated and begins to race through the trees, followed closely by all the males. When she is ready she will stop and allow the dominant male to mate with her.

Liane almost didn't see the short story that changed her life. She had considered canceling her subscription to the *Malahat Review* but had changed her mind about it at the last minute. Still, when the fall issue had arrived in the mail, she had ignored it in favor of the other things she had been reading lately, articles in magazines she had never thought she would buy but now did in an attempt to make her life more fun. Her new life, the one she now led alone.

Liane had previously lived in a condo with Adam in High Park. They would regularly take their dog, Atticus, to the off-leash park, where the Labradoodle (Adam had insisted it was the perfect choice for them, because these types of dogs did not shed or produce allergens; when he had first said the name of the breed she had thought it was a joke, but she hadn't known the half of it—at the park, she met owners of schnoodles, whoodles, Jack-a-Bees, and Peke-a-Poos) would happily chase squirrels or other dogs, but mostly the squirrels.

The proximity to the off-leash park was mostly why Adam had gained sole custody of the dog when Liane left, or at least that was how she had allowed it to be justified. The truth, though, was that Liane had liked Atticus but hadn't ever really loved him. Perhaps the fact that she'd let him go so easily made this obvious, but she hoped Adam didn't know. It felt like yet another failure, piled on top of her failure to stay with him.

Either way, now she lived in a Queen Street West apartment, above a store that sold wool. When she had gone to see the apartment, she had stood on the street and looked up at the window box filled with red geraniums and felt certain that this was the place where she was going to start her brand-new, happier life. The wool store, the flowers, her standing on the sidewalk. She had closed her eyes for a moment and breathed through her nose. *Yes. This is the place.*

She had considered calling her mother or one of her sisters, just to check. But she hadn't. It was perhaps the first decision she had ever made in her life without checking it with someone else. Her life had always been defined by her roles: daughter, little sister, girlfriend, student. Now she wasn't a girlfriend or a student. And while she was still a sister and a daughter, she was pulling back. Not forever, just for now. *You need to be Liane. You need to find out who that is.*

But, just over two months later, the Indian summer the city was experiencing in late September had turned the geraniums brown and sorry-looking. And Liane was feeling lonely and suspected that *she* was probably a bit sorry-looking as well.

It was morning, and she was on her way to work. She was early because she'd recently read an article, in one of those magazines she had never needed before because there had always been so many females in her life who gave advice, about not being late. One of the suggestions had been to add a half hour of time to any estimate. So Liane had started doing this, which meant that now, instead of being late, she was often early. For some reason, being early for things made her feel even lonelier. There was something about the rush from place to place, she realized, that had made her feel vital, necessary, part of something, not alone. So now she was dawdling at her front door instead of leaving.

She looked over at the window and decided she was going to water the sad brown geraniums one last time. Perhaps when she returned home from work later that day a miracle would have occurred: they would be restored to their former crimson glory and she would be as happy as she thought she was going to be when she signed the lease for the apartment.

After she opened the window and watered the flowers, she closed it again, latched it, picked up her bag containing her laptop, novel, and lunch, considered bringing the *Malahat Review* with her but didn't, and left the apartment, walking down the stairs with their weathered black treads and out onto the sidewalk. As usual, she stopped at the coffee shop at the corner to have her porcelain travel mug filled with light roast. A squeeze of agave syrup, several dashes of cinnamon because yet another article had touted cinnamon as the cure for all ailments.

She looked down at her watch and found she was still twenty minutes ahead of schedule. But she could see a streetcar pulling closer and so, out of habit, she rushed toward it, feeling a sudden and unexplainable urgency rise within her: *I must catch this particular streetcar now.*

She was out of breath when she boarded, fumbling for her

transit pass, juggling her coffee and her bag. Her novel fell out at her feet, a beat-up copy of *Cat's Cradle* she'd purchased at a secondhand shop nearby and thought that for $1.75 why not? The streetcar was crowded and she clung to a pole and wondered, *Why did I do this? I'm not even late.* She thought about reading the now even more battered Vonnegut novel, but hated to read standing up. So she looked at her own reflection in the window as the streetcar passed through a tunnel of tall buildings, and soon she was nearly at the subway.

She was pushing through the crowded streetcar to get to the door when she saw a man standing a few poles over, reading. And she was sure of it, immediately. It was him. His hair was the same color, his nose the same shape, his lips curved in the same way.

She was filled with elation. There was *purpose* to the watering of the dead geraniums, the pointless rush for the streetcar.

She had gained confidence in the weeks since she had started standing in front of classrooms full of students on a daily basis and acting like she was in charge. She had even found she liked it, much more than she thought she would, and even without Adam standing on the sidelines, prodding her in the direction he wanted her to go in. So she bravely walked toward the man on the streetcar, determined to introduce herself. He turned his head and looked up from his book. She read the title. *How Do We Fix This Mess?* It was about the global financial meltdown. *He would never read that.* She didn't know him well, or at all, but she knew that much.

She felt foolish. *It was because of the dream, probably.* Her stop arrived and she exited the streetcar, thinking about it as she walked down the steps, out onto the street, and down into the subway. It had been one of those dreams you wake up from but then want to fall back into again. Only, when you close your eyes and try to redream it, it isn't quite the same. The dream was very simple—unlike her others, which made her feel confused when she woke up. She had been on a streetcar, just like the one she had been riding moments before, but this one was practically empty. And then she saw him, standing even though there were seats all around him, reading a book. He had looked up and seen her and she had taken three steps and stood before him. He had put his book down on a seat and opened his arms and said, "Come here," and she had done just that, stood right up against him, her chest perfectly aligned with his chest, her heart perfectly aligned with his heart, their two hearts beating against one another while the streetcar moved through the city for miles and miles and miles. When she had woken, she had closed her eyes, but the feeling had already disappeared. What had the feeling been? *Absolute calm. Perfect rightness.* And a little bit of sadness, too, but maybe that had just come from the waking up and realizing it wasn't real.

So here you are, pining after a man you never even really met. Tears blurred her vision. She looked down at the floor. *What is wrong with me?* Because of the tears and the way she was squinting, for a moment the floor of the subway platform bubbled and wavered below her. The floor appeared so insubstantial that she had the thought that if she stepped onto the blurry, wavy spot, she would disappear. She would have finally found her door in a tree, her portal to another world. What would she feel, she wondered, if she *did* find herself standing in another world, one that existed below the subway platform, one that only a select few people knew about?

Relief, she realized. *Relief that this is not all there is.* And in that moment Liane understood why people needed religion so much: mysticism, the concept of another realm just beyond the fingertips of humanity, was very soothing. Of course, Liane was an academic and a realist (she tried to believe in magical worlds the way her father had told her to, but could never truly), and she wasn't religious. It was just nice to finally understand it. She blinked away the tears and the subway floor became solid again.

"Liane, why aren't *you* married? You're intelligent, attractive . . . ?" It was Grace Arnold, who taught Marriage, Reproduction, and Kinship 302, and she was speaking in the leading tone Liane recognized to mean she was making a point. But Liane hadn't been paying attention to the conversation between Grace and Tansy, the professor whom she assisted (who knew Liane was recently *dis*engaged and shot her a sympathetic glance). She had instead been eating an apple for breakfast and reading a copy of *The Walrus* she'd picked up from a table (secretly and guiltily wishing it was *Women's Health*) because she had been early for work, of course, but not early enough to actually accomplish anything.

Now a piece of apple caught in her throat and she started to choke.

"I'm sorry, *what's* stopping you from marrying?" Grace prompted.

Liane wondered if she would die, right there in the anthropology faculty lounge. Someone would shout, *Is there a doctor in the house?* and all her colleagues would say, *Yes!* But no one would be able to save her, and they'd all be forced to admit that they weren't *really* doctors, but, rather, academics. The timeless argument would ensue. Rigor mortis would set in.

"Perhaps it's that the biological urge is weakening, generation by generation?" Grace continued.

Another cough. Liane swallowed the now vile-textured chunk, cleared her throat, and said, possibly because she was light-headed from the choking, "Actually, I used to be engaged, but . . ." *But what? Why would you say that?* "It didn't work out."

After Liane spoke, a few of the others in the lounge looked

up before returning to books or reports or research or lecture notes or other conversations. *That's right. I used to be engaged to the dean's son. It's how I got this job. And I still have it. Because in this particular day and age, you can't fire or not hire someone for breaking an engagement.*

"How long?" Grace asked.

"How long what?"

"How long were you engaged?"

"Oh. I . . . don't really know." *About a minute? Never officially? I stole a ring I found in my mother's cottage and pretended it was mine?*

"And would you do it again?"

Liane thought about this. "No," she said, and knew she was being honest. *No, I would never wear a fake engagement ring and pretend everything was fine and alienate myself from my sister, never again.*

Grace nodded, then turned back to Tansy.

Liane sat for a moment, unsure of what to do, then looked back down at her magazine and pretended to read as she listened to Grace continue to argue about whether, in a few thousand years (presuming the world made it that far; Liane *thought* this, but didn't say it, the current trend in the lounge being optimism), the concept of marriage would be seen as an ancient ritual, or would still be one of the vital constructs of society, however unattainable and unrealistic it had become for almost everyone. Tansy was arguing, slightly less vociferously, *for* marriage.

"We've evolved," she was saying. "We may not be monogamous by nature, but people need companionship, especially as they grow older. It just makes sense."

"Does it? More and more people are choosing *not* to marry, though," Grace declared. "We all know this. We have an example of this right here in our own faculty lounge." *Who, me?* Liane turned her head from side to side. Everyone was looking at her. She realized that she had made it sound like she was against marriage, and she hadn't intended to convey this.

"So it might be evolution. Yes?"

This was a habit of Grace's. *Yes?* she would say, and people would nod (or at least Liane would, because she had a habit of nodding when people said, *Yes?*) and then realize they had unwittingly supported her point. "We might be evolving *away* from monogamy rather than toward it. Simply wanting a companion when you're old is not a sign of an evolution, Tansy. Plus, the instances of *re*marriage are going down. Yes?" Now Liane did find herself nodding without wanting to, even though she, technically, was not part of the conversation but rather an unwilling illustration. "Some people are trying it out once, realizing it's not for them, and moving on with definitive absolution. Look at your mother, Liane!" Now Grace clapped her hands, and Liane blushed. "Wasn't she a pioneer of all of it?"

"Um. All of what?"

"You know, the beginning of the shift away from the idea that women needed men. The whole a-woman-needs-a-man-like-a-fish-needs-a-bicycle movement?"

"There was an a-woman-needs-a-man-like-a-fish-needs-a-bicycle movement?"

"But you're only talking about it in terms of women and men," Tansy butted in, seeing her opening. "What about gay marriage? Why has it been such a hard-won fight, then, if no one cares about marriage anymore? Why is it that gay men and lesbians are fighting to be recognized as married couples?"

"For the financial benefits," Grace said dismissively. "And probably because they want to be able to have a party and get gifts and money, just like all the straight people have been doing for years." Now Grace glanced at Liane, and Liane felt like she'd been caught at something. "How old are you, Liane? Thirty-five?"

"I'm thirty." Liane liked her job but suddenly wished she worked at a regular office, where the staff gathered in the lunchroom to talk about *So You Think You Can Dance,* or some other show she had never watched but had seen listed in the online grid she searched regularly for documentaries. Liane didn't know from experience, never really having worked anywhere but at a university, but she imagined people at places of work not solely focused on intellectual development understood, among other things, that you *never* overestimated a person's age, that you *always* erred on the side of extreme caution when guessing at it. Perhaps these imaginary coworkers wouldn't be book-smart, but they'd have a different kind of intelligence. They'd notice if you wore new cowboy boots, for example. Or seemed to be making an effort to eat more salads after reading that carbohydrates were the prime culprit of abdominal fat—because although you were admittedly not ancient (not compared to most of the other professors, but definitely compared to the students), you had still started to notice a few changes, a metabolic slowdown that left you wondering whether, on top of being alone for the rest of your life, you were also going to end up with one of those stomachs that could only be described as a "front bum."

Indeed, this was not the kind of discussion that could be had in the anthropology faculty lounge.

"Sorry," Grace, who wore masculine button-up shirts every day (possibly for the very purpose of concealing a front bum, Liane thought, and then felt guilty about it) and likely cared nothing about what age people thought she was (if Liane were to guess aloud, she'd say forty-five, but in reality Grace seemed at least fifty), said. "I always forget how young you are. Our faculty wunderkind, teaching and about to be published already." She said it warmly; some of the other professors weren't as kind, were in fact *un*kind, in subtle, insidious ways. But Grace did not appear to be prone to envy. Liane always, when meeting a person for the first time, gauged the level of envy he or she was capable of.

"No worries," Liane said, being sure to smile and make eye contact. She had learned a lot about human interaction in the faculty lounge. Then she looked down again, hoping that Grace would somehow forget about the line of questioning— why did she need to know how old Liane was, anyway?—and turned a page of the magazine, pretending she was very engaged in the article she could no longer remember the topic of. She read the first few sentences of a paragraph in the middle of the page: "*In principle, the advent of a highly capable artificial intelligence that can take over the cognitive burden of running the world sounds quite nice. As British mathematician I. J. Good wrote in an influential paper in 1965, 'The first ultra-intelligent machine [is] the last invention that man need make.'*"

The sentence made Liane feel dread, both because of its content—she was understandably threatened by the idea of artificial intelligence—and because she had somehow made it nearly halfway through an article without absorbing its topic. She had thought she was reading an article on polar bears interbreeding with grizzlies. *That was last week. You read that article last week.* This made her think about another article she had recently read, about the importance of flossing your teeth. Apparently not flossing your teeth could increase your risk of dementia, even lead to early-onset Alzheimer's. *Oh, great. Maybe that's what I have.*

She flipped backward, away from the image of robots running the world and the idea that she was becoming demented, but couldn't settle on anything. Then she realized Grace was saying something else to her. "Pardon me?"

"I've been thinking of holding a panel discussion on marriage for my postgraduate class, and I was wondering if you might be willing to be on the panel. The students will likely be able to relate to you. And they might find your situation interesting. Engaged once, and now certain that marriage is not for you." Grace paused. "We won't, of course, get into any private details. Just a brief overview of your situation, followed by a discussion that will be largely academic, not personal. Yes?"

"Well, I mean, it's not exactly what I said, that marriage isn't for me. I just said . . . you know, that I wouldn't . . ." She wished for a moment that the apple chunk had done its job. She stood. "I have a tutorial, which I am about to be late for." Her voice was strange, too bright. She gathered her belongings before crossing the room to check her mailbox.

Tansy and Grace moved on after a brief, awkward moment to the subject of procreation, and what would change about the practice ("practice," that's what they called it, as though it, *sex,* especially for procreation, was not something they themselves engaged in) without the tenet of marriage to sanctify it. Would it be like *The Handmaid's Tale,* but without the strange sex scenes? *Yes? No? Maybe?* Liane stood with her head bent toward her mailbox and continued to listen, counting to ten in her head. Then she would leave. After she got to ten.

"Will men be unnecessary, will sex be for pleasure only, is sex *already* for pleasure only, for almost everyone except Catholics and Mormons, and those unlucky people currently in the throes of 'trying' to have a baby?" (Grace was truly on a roll.)

What if Liane had not stood to leave? What if she had stayed in her seat, and Grace had asked her, *Do you want to have children, Liane? You don't need a husband to do that anymore. So? Yes?*

Maybe. But it would have to be with the right person. And I don't think he exists, except in my imagination, Liane would have answered, without being able to stop herself. And then everyone would have known absolutely everything there was to know about her.

Time's up.

Outside, Liane turned down St. George and began to walk toward the King's College building, one of her favorites on campus. She slowed. She had been exaggerating about being late for her tutorial and now, yet again, she was going to be early. She looked across the field in front of the building, with its soaring central tower, and thought of what she knew about the field: that below it was a buried pond. During the cholera epidemic in the 1800s, this pond had been found to be teeming with cholera and had been subsequently buried. Liane had always wondered how it was even possible to bury an entire pond, and felt strange when she walked over this area of the campus, especially during damp weather when the ground yielding beneath her feet made her imagine sinking down into the ancient and still-infested waters. She usually skirted the buried pond, even though it took her longer to get to class.

Now she saw a young man crossing the field and slowed further. There was a woman jogging after him across the field, calling out something. Both of them looked familiar. "Jesse!" The woman called, and the boy stopped walking and turned. She was holding a textbook, which she handed to him. "You forgot it, and I knew you needed it," Liane heard the woman say. The boy was Jesse, Johnny-at-the-marina's son. And the woman was the one who had been at the marina in the summer. She handed Jesse the textbook. It was so out of context that Liane had stopped walking altogether and was simply watching them both. "I was coming this way anyway, and I knew where your class was, so . . . I'm glad I caught you," the woman said. "Your phone was off." The boy smiled. "Thanks," he said. "I usually turn it off during lectures. Sorry. I'll see you later." "See you later." The woman turned and started walking away. She didn't see Liane.

Liane had just assumed she wasn't his mother, that the mother of this boy had been one of those blond women who had lived with Johnny for a time, but now realized she had been wrong. She thought about catching up with the boy and saying hello, welcoming him to campus, telling him she taught there, but she didn't really know him. Instead, she continued walking along the perimeter of the field, keeping to the edge of the buried pond.

Inside the classroom, she shuffled her notes. She would be discussing Norwegians, and how they believed envy to be the enemy of happiness. The Norwegian term *skadefryd* (otherwise known as *schadenfreude*) related to modern superstitions about the potential to do damage with thoughts, mainly because the word, literally translated, meant "to harm joy."

She felt the nervous flutters in her stomach, but they weren't anywhere near as debilitating as they had been during her first few classes, when her cheeks had been embarrassingly blotchy and she'd heard a few titters spread around the room as she cleared her throat repeatedly. She had retreated to her office and signed up for an online course in public speaking, practiced in front of her mirror at home at night, thinking this was one of the good things about living alone. The lecturing got better. (Later, also while online, she had checked out her rating on a site called RateMyProfessor.com and noticed, with guilty pleasure, that in addition to good reviews from her students, she had also gotten a chili pepper in the "hotness" column.)

Now Liane stood before the students gathered for her class and started to speak. The students bent their heads, taking notes by clicking keyboards on mini-laptops or tapping iPad screens. When Liane remembered her own years in university, the sounds of pens scratching, papers rustling, the interaction involved with borrowing someone's notes, making a copy, returning them reverently, she always felt nostalgic.

Eventually it was eleven o'clock. As usual, a small group of students waited to ask Liane questions about the lecture, and she patiently answered them. You couldn't know whether you were going to be a good teacher until you actually became one, and Liane was. This made her feel proud of herself. She had a calling, a vocation. It hadn't all been for nothing. When the students were gone, she left the room. She opened the heavy doors to go outside and felt the wind on her face and realized there was a hint of coolness there. Perhaps summer was finally retreating. This made her feel wistful for the kind of summer she had thought she was going to have but hadn't. A small knot of students brushed past her, talking, laughing ("What do you want to do now?" "I don't know. Coffee?" "Frisbee!"), and Liane felt the jealous knot form. She looked away from them.

Later, when Liane got home, she made tea and decided sadness and loneliness had won over hope: she threw the geraniums into the trash. Then she decided to take a bath in the claw-foot tub. And she picked up the *Malahat Review*.

The magazine was in her hands, getting slightly wet, and the neroli-oil-scented water was nearly up to her chin. She flicked through the pages until a title caught her attention: "The Snapping Turtle." By Laurence Gibbons.

It was a short story about a man who was an intelligence investigative specialist for the Ministry of Natural Resources. He was spending a summer month at a cottage so he could keep an eye on a group of men believed to be illegally harvesting turtles from the wild, but ended up spending the time he was supposed to be spending performing reconnaissance on the men watching a redheaded woman swim in the lake each morning and read on the end of the dock each afternoon. He started leaving books for her on the end of the dock, secured by rocks.

The story ended with the man wracked by guilt—he had failed to find out if the men were indeed poaching turtles illegally, and also, one day, the woman simply never returned to the dock and he was left with a sense of longing, both for the woman with the red hair (Red hair! Liane dropped the magazine into the tub when she read this, then picked it up and continued to read the story from the soggy pages) and the life he had always hoped to lead, one he felt slip away from him that summer. "Life is full of what-ifs. And should-haves. And did-nots," she read. "And he was afraid of what it meant that these what-ifs seemed to be growing further and further apart in his life. Eventually they would run out completely, like the turtles whose numbers were dwindling because people like him were supposed to be doing something about it but weren't. Eventually they would disappear forever, and all he would have would be his regrets and the memory of the color of her hair."

She wrapped herself in a towel, spent a few minutes attempting to dry the magazine with her hair dryer, and left the bathroom, turning on her laptop and sitting down damply on the couch, waiting impatiently for the laptop to boot up. Her hand shook as she typed the name into Google.

She read his bio, but it was only the final sentence that registered, and that she repeated, over and over. "Laurence Gibbons lives in Toronto with his wife and two daughters."

But still.

At one point, she put the magazine—one of the pages had been scorched by the hair dryer and she'd given up trying to dry it, so it was still damp and resembled in some places papier-mâché—into the trash with the dead flowers.

Later still, she picked it out and shoved it to the back of a drawer. It was starting to disintegrate.

Finally, hours later, she made a decision. She took the magazine out of the drawer. She called Helen. "How *are* you?" Helen asked in the way that she always asked it, even though Liane hadn't called her back in weeks, even though she had hardly explained any of what was happening in her life to her mother. There was no accusation about any of that in Helen's tone. There was just the expectation that Liane would tell Helen how she really was. Helen never expected people, especially not her daughters, to just say *Fine* or *Good* or *Okay* when she asked how they were.

"I'm . . ." Liane couldn't explain how she was to any degree of satisfaction, so she avoided it. "I'm wondering if you have Iain's phone number," she said, as casually as possible. "You know, that man who now owns the old Bachman place? The guy with the greens." "Oh, I know who he is," Helen replied, her tone different now, less inviting. "May I ask why you need it?" "It's . . . I have a question about greens." "A question about greens," Helen repeated, but Liane didn't elaborate. "Well, I do have his number. This is his cell, so wherever he is, you should be able to reach him." Liane wrote down the number. "Thanks, Helen. I'm sorry I can't talk. This is kind of important. But I'll call you back, okay?" "Please do. I miss you. I worry about you. And . . . could you please tell Iain I said hello?"

"Sure."

"Actually, no. Don't. Don't, okay?"

"Oh-*kay*. 'Bye."

Iain picked up right away. She felt embarrassed and shy and also realized she had no plan. What exactly was she going to ask him? How was she going to explain this? "Hello, Iain, it's Liane here," she said, realizing if she didn't say something he was going to hang up. "Liane, Helen's daughter, we met this summer?"

"Of course I remember you," he said, his tone warm. "How *are* you?"

"Good. Fine. Yeah. So, thank you. It's just . . . that you seemed to have a pretty good handle on island goings-on and I was . . ." She trailed off. *What? I have a crush on a married man and am wondering if you think there's any chance he has marriage problems?*

"Hello?"

"Hi. Sorry. Hi. Okay. So you know that couple who rented out the Castersens' place this summer? That man you said was a writer?" She thought quickly, and found a place to start. "I wanted to buy his book, the one you were talking about, about the end of the world . . . and I was wondering if you could just confirm his name for me."

"Laurence Gibbons."

"Laurence Gibbons. And is he . . . are they still renting the cottage, or . . . I guess they've gone back to the city by now, right . . . ?"

"Actually, no. It appears Laurence has moved into the cottage. I have no idea when he plans to leave, but I keep telling him the lake will freeze eventually and he'll have to take a snowmobile out to the mainland if he wants to leave."

"He's still there?"

"Oh, yes. And all by himself, for the most part. We've taken to having coffee from time to time, and it turns out we're both bachelors. His girls are still coming up some weekends, and he goes back to the city, but the wife—well, apparently she's no longer his wife."

Liane's mouth had gone completely dry. "Oh," she finally managed. "And he's still there?"

"Yes. Still here."

"On the island."

"That's right."

"I have to go," she said. "Thank you for this information. I'm . . . I'm really looking forward to buying his book."

He cleared his throat. "Could you . . . tell your mother I said hello?"

"Definitely. She says hi, too," Liane said, figuring it would probably be okay to tell him that now that he had asked her to extend a greeting to Helen. Strange behavior on both of their parts, but Liane didn't have time to think about it.

She hung up. She looked around her lonely apartment and back down at the burnt and waterlogged magazine in her hand.

And she made another decision without consulting anyone.

part two

Love never dies a natural death. It dies because we don't know how to replenish its source. It dies of blindness and errors and betrayals. It dies of illness and wounds; it dies of weariness, of witherings, of tarnishings.

—ANAÏS NIN, *DELTA OF VENUS*

8
Barn Owl (*Tyto alba*)

The barn owl does not have a specific breeding season; it mainly depends on food supply. To attract the female, the male barn owl uses a special call. He also hovers in front of the female to show off his chest and belly. This is called the moth flight. During courtship, the male and female hoot and chase each other while in flight. Though some owls are monogamous, the barn owl may have different partners to produce several broods.

Him: "Fiona. This can't go on forever. You won't speak to me, except when the boys are around. And you think this pretending is fooling them but it isn't. No one in this house is happy. We have to talk about this."

Her: "You lied to me. You've been lying to me our entire lives."

Him: "I told you . . . I told you I had my reasons. I told you I was *sorry*."

Her: "And having your reasons and being sorry doesn't change anything. Yet somehow you expect me to be fine with it, to forgive you and allow you to—let this *situation* become a normal part of our lives."

Him: "Please stop referring to this as a 'situation.' Please stop refusing to say her name. She's a person."

Her: "I still don't understand why you won't fly over there and insist on a paternity test. Then maybe we could finally put all this behind us."

Him: "You're being incredibly cruel."

Her (beginning to retreat): "Oh, yes. That's right, why would you need a paternity test? *You've* always known. You just decided not to tell *me*. Please, just go away. I can't talk to you. I don't *want* to talk to you."

Him: "You can't shut me out forever."

Her: *Slams door.*

Fiona had lost count of how many times Tim had said, "You can't shut me out forever," to her in the preceding five months. And she was beginning to believe he was very wrong—she probably could shut him out forever. Some things just became habit. But then, the day before, he had told her he was no longer going to stand for it. *He* had said that to *her*. It made her realize it was what she should have said in the first place, if it was how she really felt. She should have said, *You have made my life into something I never wanted it to be. You have brought into my life the very thing I have always avoided. Everything was supposed to be perfect, and now it's not, and I can't forgive you.*

She was in her office, sitting at her desk, staring at the list on her blotter. *Read book for book club* was the first item.

The book club meeting was tonight, at Angela Tanner's house. Seven years in the club and she had never failed to read the book. But she had only been able to manage a few chapters of this one. The protagonist was vapid, and although the book was set in Morocco, Fiona got the feeling the author had never been there. This bothered her inordinately. The idea of spending the rest of the afternoon reading the book was unfathomable. So she crossed the item off her list, tapped at her iPad, and called up the title of the book on Amazon, then read the synopsis and a few reviews. Most of them were favorable. "People are sheep," she said aloud. She had been talking to herself aloud a lot lately. She hated to admit she had no one else to talk to.

There was a time when book club meetings had been one of her favorite social events. She had loved when it was her turn to host, had made it a point to outdo herself every time. The previous year, her hostessing duties had landed in the winter months and she built a fire, mulled wine and cider, braised rabbit and tucked it into phyllo cups, roasted grapes and served them with pillows of carefully selected cheese and chewy bread from the most well-known chef in town.

"It still just tastes like bread to me," Tim had joked with her later, after everyone was gone and he had emerged from hiding in his study. She remembered that even though she valued her association with these women she had been relieved to see his familiar face at the end of the night. She could finally relax, sitting with him, discussing the night over the remains of the wine and the bread with his favorite sweet churned butter.

Fiona steeled herself against the good memories of Tim and decided to call Angela, the book club meeting hostess that evening. "I just wanted to ask if I could bring anything," she said. "Dessert?"

"Oh, no. I've got it all under control."

"Perfect, then." Fiona paused and wondered what it would be like to say to Angela, *Could you meet me for a coffee? I need someone to talk to.* Instead, there were a few beats of silence. In the yard she heard the owl, hooting softly the way it did. ("Aren't owls nocturnal?" Eliot had once asked, after he learned the word in school. "Not ours, apparently," Fiona had said.) "See you tonight, Angela," she said, and hung up the phone.

Our owl.

Our house.

Our life.

All ruined.

• • •

That night, Fiona sat on Angela's couch in her walk-out basement with its salmon-colored walls and fawn-colored rug and
plush, Moroccan-style cushions everywhere, some of them
covered in tiny little mirrors, gilt mirrors on the walls, vast
geometric paintings. *Won't Tim laugh when I tell him it appears
she actually redecorated in the theme of the book,* she thought, and
then experienced that familiar drop in her spirits. She imagined what she was experiencing was similar to bereavement,
the way a person who has lost someone picks up the phone to
call them, then realizes they're gone and experiences the loss
afresh. Perhaps she and Tim hadn't been as close as they once
were—all the traveling, the long absences had taken their
toll—but he had still been her confidant, the person she told
those petty details to, the ones that didn't matter especially
but that you had to tell *someone.*

The food was set out on a low table before the women,
dates and almonds and figs and goat cheese rolled in something and doused in oil, tiny hollowed-out pumpkins filled
with spiced and roasted seeds, spiced meats threaded onto
skewers with mint yogurt dipping sauce. Later, Angela was
bringing out tagines, she had said. Lamb and apricot and
spicy vegetarian. "She doesn't make any of the food herself,
you know," whispered Nancy Wells, on Fiona's left. "The
nanny does it, and Angie takes the credit."

"Isn't that what you pay people for? To do things and let
you take the credit?" Fiona said, surprised by the harsh sound
of her voice. She decided to ignore Nancy and the food and
focus on her wine. But eventually her glass was empty, so she
looked around.

Who are these women? She felt isolated from all of them,
even though she was literally rubbing elbows with both Nancy
and Johanna Edwards. *I don't even think I like most of them.* She

refilled her wineglass, thinking she'd have more than her normally self-allotted two glasses. Perhaps she'd have *three* glasses. Or had she already had three? Well, maybe she'd have four. And what was more—

"What's more," she said aloud, realizing it was a complete non sequitur. She sounded crazy. What's more *what*? "What's more, I hated this book." *That's what.*

Jane raised an eyebrow. "Really? *Hated* it?" There was a hint of admiration in her voice.

"Yes. Hated it."

"That's not a very constructive criticism," said Nancy, moving her elbow away from Fiona's.

"No. I suppose not," Fiona said. "I shouldn't say I hated *all* of it. I just hated the few chapters of it I actually managed to read."

There was silence. No one had admitted to not reading the book before.

"*I* liked the way she accepted herself," said Carole Huntziger. "I liked the way she didn't try to be someone she wasn't. You just knew that if she'd lived in our age, she wouldn't be running out and getting . . . *you* know, Botox or something like that. Those fillers, the ones that are supposed to plump you up but really make you look like a clown."

"What's so wrong about getting Botox?" Fiona asked. *And don't pretend you don't know what those fillers are called. Everyone knows you had your lips done last year and pretended it was some special lipstick you bought.*

"First off, it's *poison*. It paralyzes the muscles in your face so you can't smile," said Nancy. Her husband was a doctor and that made her the group's resident medical expert. "There are potentially *devastating* side effects. Did you hear about the doctor couple who injected each other and ended up *paralyzed*?"

"Well, sure, okay, fine, it's a toxin." Fiona realized she was slurring, that what she had actually said was "toxshin." Three glasses, four? How many had she had? "But . . . but is it so wrong to want to feel *good* about yourself?"

"You need bovine toxin injected in your face to feel good about yourself?"

"I'm not talking about *me*. I'm just saying." (Which sounded like, "I'm jusht shaying." *Uh-oh. I should have eaten at least one of those stupid dates.*) "Why are we judging people who do these things? Not everyone who has these treatments looks terrible. Do they?"

Nancy leaned forward with interest. In addition to being the medical expert, she was also the most notorious gossip. "Why are you so focused on this? Have you recently had something done?" But she sounded dubious, like probably Fiona would look better than she did, especially lately, if cosmetic intervention were at play.

"I guess all I'm trying to say is, are all the people who do things like this really unworthy? Not as good as the ones in this crappy book because they don't walk around saying things like 'I've grown accustomed to my own face' and, 'I've learned to love myself, which is the greatest love of all'?"

"I don't think she said, 'I've grown accustomed to my own face,'" said Carole.

"Or that last part. Which I think is a Whitney Houston song," ventured Jane in a tone within which Fiona detected kindness, not mocking, and felt grateful for. "But I think you're right. It got to be a bit much. I didn't finish it, either . . ."

Fiona looked at Jane. She was smiling at her, shaking her head a little as if to say, *You and me, we're actually the only normal ones here.*

Fiona realized she wanted to leave. Immediately. She suddenly wanted to be anywhere but there, with the neighborhood wives whom she had once felt so firmly and smugly in a group with, regardless of whether she actually liked them. She remembered a time when the very existence of these women in her life, the fact that she was friends with them, had made her feel as though she had won some sort of contest. And also as though she had succeeded in being nothing like her mother, who had never understood the importance of sorority in a broad sense, versus a pour-your-heart-out, leave-yourself-bare, get-yourself-hurt sense.

Except now Fiona *wished* to pour her heart out. But even though she was clearly upset, not one of the women asked her if she was all right, not one of them leaned forward, rubbed her back, poured her more wine even though she clearly didn't need it, and said, *Is everything okay, Fiona? Do you need to talk?*

Instead, after a brief silence, the conversation about the book began to rise around her again.

Fiona stood. "I'm going to take myself home," she said. "I think that cheese was off. My stomach is upset." They ignored her. She heard someone whisper, "She didn't eat a thing."

On the way out, she looked at herself in the mirror and attempted to smooth the furrows in her brow. She couldn't. She looked angry, permanently. *But I'm not angry. I'm sad. I'm scared. I'm lonely.*

She heard a sound behind her, and saw Jane's face and torso now beside her in the mirror. Fiona noticed Jane's brow was perfectly smooth. "Hey," Jane said. "Maybe you shouldn't drive . . ."

"I'm only a few streets away," Fiona said, but she let Jane take her elbow, knowing she was right.

When they were outside, Fiona gave Jane her keys.

"I'm embarrassed," she said.

"Don't be. You were fantastic. And I agree with you completely, by the way. It's about time someone stood up to those old biddies."

Fiona found herself laughing. "Old biddies? But we're all basically the same age."

"That may be, but there are some nights I sit at those book club meetings and feel like the youngest person in the room, by decades. Don't you ever?"

Fiona was silent. And then she said, "No. Never. Most of the time I feel like the oldest. Also, once you said I seemed like I was in my early forties. But I'm only thirty-eight."

"You don't *look* like the oldest. I'm sorry I said that. It's just that you're so accomplished—wise or something. Honestly. You look fantastic. But you know, *I* get Botox all the time, and no one ever, ever notices. My dermatologist is a wizard."

Fiona turned to her. "Really? But your face . . . moves."

"That's because he's so good. It's undetectable. Baby doses. That's the secret. Do you want me to get you an appointment?"

"Do you think he could fix these?" Fiona frowned at Jane and ran a finger along the ridge between her brows. She realized she had never done this, never sat in a car—or anywhere—with a woman who wasn't her sister, and discussed something as frivolous as wrinkles. *Girl talk, that's what it's called. And you've never even had it with your sisters, if you're being honest with yourself.*

"In his sleep." Jane rifled through her purse, pulled out her phone, and started texting. "I bet he could squeeze you in tomorrow."

Fiona felt pleased. Tomorrow. Tomorrow she could actually take action about something that was bothering her. "Thanks," she said to Jane. "Let me know if he replies."

"He's usually pretty quick."

"Let's go." Jane turned on the ignition and pulled out of the parking spot, squealing the tires slightly. She looked at Fiona sideways. "I did that on purpose," she said. "We're making an escape. I thought maybe you'd smile. While you still can. Ha, get it?" Jane drove until they were close to Fiona's, and then pulled over.

"Fiona . . . is everything okay with you?"

Fiona didn't say anything. Then: "I don't think so. No. Not really."

"Do you want to go home, or do you want to go somewhere and talk? We could leave your car here and walk down to one of the bars by the water. It's not *too* cold."

"That's just what I need," Fiona surprised herself by saying.

"Margaritas? Really?"

"Trust me, you need one. Wine is too mature. We're supposed to be having fun."

When it arrived, Fiona sipped the sweet-sour drink and looked out through the window of the bar at the water and the moonlight shining on it. She thought of the swans she had seen, all those months before.

Jane was sliding a finger along the side of her glass and putting the salt directly on her tongue. When she had ordered, she had asked for an extra-salty rim. She had smiled at the waiter in the same way Ilsa would have: sexily, conspiratorially.

"Are you and my sister friends now? I saw you talking at my party. At the start of the summer."

"Oh, right, yeah. I liked talking to her. She's really . . . just something, isn't she? But I haven't seen her since, no. Although I thought maybe we could ask her to be in the book club. Liven things up a little?"

Fiona shook her head. "Ilsa would never be in a book club," she said. "No offense."

"There was a time I would never have been in a book club, either. But here I am. Unless we're kicked out for admitting to not reading the book and then making a dramatic escape."

Fiona felt the salt stinging her lips, which she hadn't realized until now were so chapped. She looked across the table at Jane and thought: *The old Fiona would never have even considered confiding in Jane, a woman I hardly know. But here I am, just waiting for her to ask what's wrong again, so I can tell her everything.*

In the end, she didn't even wait for Jane to ask.

"I think my marriage is ending. I think it ended back at the end of June, when a phone call came in . . . and I . . . I haven't done anything about it except . . ." Fiona closed her eyes and swallowed more tequila.

Then she told Jane how she had waited inside the kitchen that afternoon while Tim talked on the telephone to the foreign-sounding young woman. When the talking had stopped, she had assumed the call was over. "But he didn't come inside, and finally I went out on the porch, and he was just sitting there, looking down at the phone. I asked him who the call was from and he told me to sit down, so I did."

Fiona remembered his explanation had been halting and hushed. "That," he said, not looking up from the receiver, "was a young woman named Samira. A young woman named Samira from Vienna who believes I am her father."

"But you're not, of course."

No hesitation. "I am."

"What? How can you . . . what did you . . . I don't understand."

Now he looked up. She didn't recognize what was in his eyes. Guilt, shame, fear. She had never seen any of these emotions in Tim before. "Her mother was a woman I met just after college, when I was traveling in Europe. In Vienna. Before I even met you. I spent a few months there and we . . . This was a long time ago . . . I never imagined—"

"Never imagined what? Do you really think this is true, that this woman calling you is actually your daughter? Don't you know that scams like this happen all the time? You can't just take something like this at face value!"

Tim had looked at her for a moment that stretched taut. "I knew," he said. "I knew about her. Marta contacted me after . . . when she knew she was pregnant. I was already gone, had run out of money, so I had to go home. She sent me a letter, she told me she thought I should know she was pregnant, she was certain it was mine, she was keeping it, she was moving back in with her parents, and she didn't want anything from me." Silence. Fiona supposed he expected her to form a response, but she felt numb. He started talking again: "I was twenty-one. I didn't know what to do about it. So I didn't do anything. But then . . . months later, I *did* try to get in touch with her, but I couldn't. And the years passed, and I met you, and . . ." He sighed. "Part of me always thought this call would come. I never stopped wondering . . . I never knew what to do . . . I hated that you didn't know. I vowed that I would never keep anything else from you."

"My honest-to-a-fault husband," Fiona now said to Jane. "It was always all about his guilt."

Jane's finger, salt-covered, was still poised before her mouth. "Even all these months later," Fiona continued, "I sometimes question whether this conversation actually happened, whether it's even possible that Tim could have harbored a secret like this for all of these years. My entire life, all I wanted was to avoid drama like this. It gets so tiresome. It was my childhood. And yet, I walked right into it by marrying him."

Jane wiped her finger off on her cocktail napkin and took a sip of water instead of margarita. "What did you do, after he told you?" she asked.

"I didn't do anything." Fiona realized how it sounded when she said it aloud. Ludicrous. "Actually, that's not true. I took a shower. I got dressed. I hosted a cocktail party. You were there. And I've barely spoken to him since. But a few days ago he told me we no longer seem to have a marriage, and that maybe we just need to end it, put it officially out of its misery."

Jane's dermatologist had texted back when they were two more margaritas in. Which was how she ended up in a chair at Dr. Solway's office the next afternoon, squeezing a rubberized set of red lips emblazoned with the name of a collagen-dispensing company while the doctor injected the much-maligned (at least in certain book club circles) bovine toxin into the "number elevens" between her brows.

When the doctor jabbed a second needle into her forehead, she flinched.

He patted her hand. "You'll be okay," he said. "It'll all be over in a minute."

"No, it won't."

"Really, it will."

Another jab, and she closed her eyes. How was it possible that so much time had passed since that afternoon when everything in her life had changed? And yet, just like she had told Jane the night before, she had done nothing about it at all except feel herself fill with hatred and bitterness and loss. And now, with the needle to her forehead, steadily emptying its toxic contents, she realized she was now *literally* being filled with poison. *How fitting.*

Later, in their bedroom, after the late June party was over, Tim had pleaded with her.

"It was a mistake, but it doesn't mean that our entire lives have been . . ." He sat down on the bed beside her. "A lie."

"Get off my bed," she had said.

"Do you know why I didn't tell you I had a daughter somewhere out there?"

"This should be good."

"Because I knew you wouldn't have married me."

"Are you trying to blame me for this?"

"I'm not saying I was right. I was wrong, and you have every right to be angry with me. Trust me, I *thought* about telling you, so many times. I wanted to share my secret with you, but I was too afraid you'd see it as a deal-breaker and I'd lose you, all because of something that . . . something that, to be honest, never even felt real. Until now. A stupid mistake that I made when I still felt like I was a kid. A mistake I've never really known how to fix." He put his head in his hands.

"You underestimate me!" Fiona had shouted. But it *was* true. She still had clear sight of who her younger self had been, and she was not much different now. She knew she would have judged him harshly and would most certainly not have still married him if she had known he had an illegitimate child from a mistake made in his early twenties that he had never done anything about.

"I was scared," he continued. "I remember you said something to me back then, something about a friend of yours who had married a man who then found out he had a child with an ex-girlfriend." Fiona remembered. Laurie Jackson. Oh, how she had pitied Laurie Jackson. "I knew how perfect you wanted your life to be, how different from your own upbringing. And I . . . I got scared. And then it was too late."

Fiona had pushed herself away, up off the bed, and gone to stand in a corner of the room.

"Get out," she had said. Tim had flinched as though she had slapped him. But he had still apologized to her again, his hands held out in supplication.

"Get out," she had said again. "Go."

"Aren't you going to your mother's cottage tomorrow? Perhaps a few days of distance, and then we can—"

"I'm not going anywhere *now*. *You* have to leave."

He had. Fiona had no way of knowing where he went because they never discussed it afterward. He had returned the
following afternoon. She had thought about throwing him
out again, but she was beginning to worry about the boys, who
had asked her several times why she had canceled her trip and
had been unsatisfied with her vague explanations. "You always
go," Eliot had said, a perplexed expression on his face.

"Well, I'm not this year," she had snapped.

In the weeks that had followed, Tim did not grovel, because Tim was not a groveler. But he did try to talk to her.
Finally, she relented.

They sat at the dining room table, she at one end, he at
the other.

"I don't know what to do," he began. "You're my best
friend, Fiona, you really are . . . and this huge thing is happening to me, and I can't talk to you about it. But I wish I could,
because . . . well, because you'd know exactly what to do."

"No, Michael is your best friend," she had said.

He had shaken his head and she had been powerless not
to think, *You're mine, too*. But she wouldn't relent. She *couldn't*
relent. She had her reasons, her own secret, and especially
now, even though she knew how hypocritical it was, she had to
hold fast to her ideals. *But why? Why?* There was a weak inter-
nal voice she had to struggle to silence. *Because this is a betrayal
of* me. *Whereas my secret has absolutely nothing to do with him.*

"I can't help you with this," she had said, and left him sitting alone yet again.

A few days later, he had approached her once more.
Something about him had changed. He was no longer seeking forgiveness. "I think you should know that I'm seriously
considering offering to go visit, or asking her if she wants to
come here. I think it would be cruel at this point not to—"

"You can't do this to us, Tim. She cannot come here. What
will the boys say? What will they think?"

"I don't know what they're going to think, but I can't keep this secret anymore, whether or not you want to deal with it. I don't want to shut her out. None of this is her fault. And now that Marta has died"—here Fiona had breathed in sharply; this she had not known, and how could she have, since she had been refusing to allow Tim to talk to her?—"she's alone, and she's twenty-two, and she just . . . she wants to meet me. And I don't want to say no."

"What you need is a paternity test."

"You're being incredibly callous. Her mother just died. This is my responsibility! I can't hide."

"How convenient that you're not going to hide from this mistake now that you can't."

He came closer, stood before her. "What am I supposed to do? Never invite her here, never go there to visit, never suggest we should meet in person? Destroy her self-esteem completely by rejecting her?"

Fiona closed her eyes. "Please stop."

"Whether you like it or not, I am her father," he said. "I can't reject her. I could never live with myself if I did. If you can't understand that—"

Her eyes flew open. "Then what? If I can't understand that, then *what*?"

He appeared startled by her anger. "I don't know," he said.

The doctor had finished his injections. He handed Fiona some tiny gel ice packs and said, "We'll deal with those sun spots the next time you're in. I have some fantastic new laser treatments with barely any downtime. And you really do look great for your age, by the way. It was just those furrows, and they'll soon be gone."

"I don't feel anything," Fiona said, standing.

"It can take up to a week for the effects to show," said the doctor. "Give it a little time, then call the front desk if you think you need more."

Fiona used the restroom before she left. She stared hard at her face but still saw her same pale, haggard-looking self. She felt disappointed. She had vowed that today something would change. She hadn't counted on having to wait up to a week for the full effect of her resolution.

"The truth?"

Jane had texted to see how the appointment went and Fiona had suggested meeting for coffee because the idea of going home held no appeal.

"The truth. Come on. You have to tell someone the truth about yourself, and since you won't go to my therapist—"

"It would be too weird to share a dermatologist *and* a therapist."

"Oh, who cares? But either way, you have to talk. There's got to be more to this. I hope you don't take this the wrong way, but you're being a little irrational, and it has to be coming from somewhere. Husbands have secrets. At least he didn't cheat on you." Something about the way Jane said this made Fiona think that perhaps Jane's husband, a lawyer with a receding hairline, a Maserati, and an entitled attitude, had.

"Okay. Fine. The truth. There's something about me no one knows. No one in the world except my mother." Fiona's heart started to pound, fast, but it wasn't an unpleasant sensation. She felt like she was driving a race car around a corner. If she slammed on the brakes now, she would spin out. "Tim, and Ilsa and Liane, too—everyone has always believed that Helen just didn't know who my father was. But my mother *did* know. When I was in my late teens, and graduating from high school, she had this falling-out with her best girlfriend. Aunt Edie." Fiona paused. It still stung. It probably always would.

"I overheard them arguing. They kept saying the name *Nate*, and then *my* name, always in lowered voices. And I figured it out. This man was my father, and Edie was somehow about to marry him, and Helen was livid. I was angry, too, when I realized Helen had kept his identity a secret from me my whole life." Fiona could still hear her own voice, shouting at Helen: "Why did you lie about this? What is the matter with you?"

"Because I didn't think we needed him," Helen had said. "Because I wanted to protect you from ever feeling rejected, the way I did. The way I *do*."

"Who is he?" Fiona had asked.

And Helen had said the name of a guitarist in a band that had grown popular in the seventies and had never lost momentum. Fiona had been rendered momentarily speechless. "Holy," Jane breathed when Fiona said his name to her.

"After Helen told me, I said I was going to contact him," Fiona said to Jane. "Helen told me not to do it. She said he was selfish and always had been and that I needed to be prepared for the fact that he might not acknowledge me. She said . . . she was afraid I would get hurt. But Edie was like a mother to me, too, sometimes more than Helen. I couldn't imagine she would marry a man who wouldn't want me. I even envisioned . . . well, I even envisioned this whole other life, with him, and Edie, and . . ." Fiona started to blink quickly. *No. I won't go there.*

"But it didn't turn out that way. And your mother knew what would happen, and that's why she kept it a secret."

"Is *that* how you see it? I never did. I think it was Helen's own pride. *She* was used to blowing men off, not the other way around." Still, Jane's words had given Fiona pause. Wouldn't Fiona want to protect her children from the same kind of pain? *I would never put my children in that position in the first place, though.* "Anyway, I was sure he'd want to know me. First I sent a handwritten letter, and then another, and then, finally, I delivered a written entreaty to his assistant." Fiona had memorized the reply, but not on purpose. "The assistant wrote back: *Please, stop contacting him. This comes directly from the man himself.* So I contacted Edie. She asked me to have coffee. She told me that I should just let it all go, not try to force myself on him, understand who he was. I asked her to talk to him for me and she—she said no. She said he was a very particular kind of man, and that I shouldn't think he was a bad person; I should just try to understand that I needed to let it go. She suggested she and I remain close, in secret. I never saw her again after that. She sent a few letters. I ignored them."

"I'm sorry," Jane said. "That must have been awful. And this happening with Tim has brought all those old wounds to the surface, right? Plus, Tim is acting exactly the way you probably wished your own father would have acted."

"It's just so *fucking* dramatic." Even Fiona was surprised by her own harsh wording. "Do you see? Do you see why I can't stand this? Why I never wanted my life to even remotely resemble the soap opera of my youth?"

"Was your mother in love with him?"

"No, I don't think so. Helen had so many 'loves of her life.' She went through men like they were handkerchiefs. She once referred to all our fathers as 'the sperm donors.' As though she had no clue that they were actual people who were going to have an effect on us no matter what sort of brave new world she thought she was trying to create." She shook her head. "I just wish she would have been more responsible."

"You sound like you're talking about a daughter, not a mother."

"That's what it felt like, growing up. I hated it."

"So, what are you going to do? About Tim? You don't really want it to be over, do you? Spouses do lie to each other, sometimes even keep secrets from each other." Jane gave Fiona a meaningful look. "It doesn't have to be the end of the world."

"My secret's different."

"How?"

"It's not a betrayal. It's about me, my past, nothing that could come back to haunt him."

"Except now it is, because it's informing your behavior—but he has no way of knowing why you're reacting this way. Fiona, the man made a mistake."

"I never wanted to be married to a man who made mistakes." Fiona looked down at the table, at her still-full coffee cup, the leaf pattern the barista had made for her melting into the foam. "And anyway, I don't think we can turn back from this path we're on. He said what he said, about us being over. He also said we should see a mediator and figure out how to be apart, since clearly we can't be together."

Later, Fiona drove toward home and saw a sign at a market advertising Thanksgiving turkeys. IT'S NOT TOO LATE, the sign read. She slowed. Thanksgiving. She had actually forgotten. Nothing like this had ever happened to Fiona before. She normally ordered an organic, grain-fed turkey from a local farm months in advance and planned a complicated dinner with all the trimmings.

The sign had said IT'S NOT TOO LATE, though. She could still get a turkey. She gripped the steering wheel and pressed her foot on the gas. She would have Thanksgiving, if not for her, if not for Tim, then for the boys. Their lives had been in disarray for months, and Fiona knew no amount of pretending could conceal this. The summer had been especially hard. Normally Fiona loved packing up and heading to Tim's family's summerhouse in Maine, where they stayed for the month of August, Tim working from there and flying back and forth to meetings. She always greeted the change in routine with great anticipation, happily packing for herself and for Tim, and for the boys; eagerly planning meals and guests and activities and maintenance projects, day trips, small projects.

Almost none of that had happened this year. She had hardly socialized, had approached every task with a sense of dread, even shopping and cooking. Was it because of this that the boys had seemed so distant, so wrapped up in their own lives, or was this just a normal teenage phase? For the first time, neither of the twins worked at Stott's Marina. Instead, they had taken jobs as busboys at a nearby restaurant. "You're *fourteen*," she'd protested. "You can't work at a *bar*." But it wasn't a bar, they told her. It was a restaurant. And they were going to make more money than they did at the marina because they were going to be included in something called a "tip-out" every night. She had still said, "No, no, you'll work at Stott's like always," but then Beck had told her that Tim had already given them his permission. Which had started yet another fight she and her husband never finished.

The twins working at the restaurant had, as far as Fiona was concerned, effectively finished off the ruination of a summer that was already ruined to begin with. It had thrown Eliot off because his brothers weren't home at night and slept most of the days away, and it had thrown Fiona off because she was used to a different routine. Plus, she worried about them when they came in late. She couldn't sleep. She bought over-the-counter sleeping pills, but they didn't work.

At a stoplight, she caught a glimpse of herself in the rearview mirror. The furrows were still there and she was pretty sure she saw the beginnings of a bruise. She moaned, and was surprised by how desperate it sounded. Had it come from her, or was there an animal trapped in the car?

"This is not a marriage." *He* had said that to *her*.

At home, she poured a glass of Pinot Grigio, even though the doctor had suggested that it might be wise to avoid alcohol for twenty-four hours because of the blood-thinning effects.

She plunked in an ice cube, thinking briefly of the way Tim, the vinophile, always disapproved of this. She added another cube and held the glass against her forehead. Then she went upstairs and took one of her pills, which had been happening so frequently lately she had had to visit her doctor to ask for a prescription refill. "We've been traveling a lot," she had explained. "And you know me, my fear of flying . . ." In truth, Fiona wasn't afraid of planes at all. It was life that terrified her, especially now.

She returned to the kitchen and sat at the table alone. She could hear the boys upstairs, but hadn't called out to them to tell them she was home. Instead, she sipped her wine and sat, looking past the kitchen, through the living room, and out the windows at the front of the house. There was something wrong about the windows, she thought, standing to top up her half-empty glass and trying to ignore how woozy she was feeling. It was probably the Botox. *The windows. They're too empty. That's the problem.*

Right. I need to decorate. Thanksgiving, Thanksgiving.

When the boys were younger, they used to make construction-paper cutouts to mark each season and paste them all over the main-floor windows of the house. It was a throwback to her days as a kindergarten teacher, and she did it even though she knew she could have purchased expensive decorations for every occasion.

In the winter, enormous snowflakes festooned the thick wavy-glassed windows in their heavy panes. In spring, flowers and butterflies and ladybugs. In summer, it was big orange suns and multicolored beach balls. Autumn was leaves, of course, orange and yellow and sometimes brown.

She sipped more wine and thought that perhaps the boys would like to work with her on a craft project. *It's been so long since we did something like this together.*

She stood and went to the basement to gather supplies.

Scissors, paper, glue—everything she needed was still in the long-neglected craft cabinet.

"Beck, Cole, Eliot!" she called. They were supposed to have been doing something upstairs; she had given them instructions at some point, hadn't she? *Yes. Right, making beds.* They were supposed to have made their beds, and then, once they'd made their beds she had said she would allow them some extra "screen time." Which meant video games, a poison she had been unable to keep from her house. She would perform the bed inspection later. (What this really consisted of was her remaking each bed in the proper way. At least they were trying, and that was the point to Fiona, that she would raise young men who would *at least try,* who would live in apartments where the sheets and duvets had been pulled up over the pillows, and the socks and underwear had been picked up off the floor and put away clean in drawers, perhaps not folded perfectly, but away. They would be more likely to find nice girls to marry if they did this. She wasn't sure why she believed this, but she did.)

Now she put down three pairs of scissors on the table.

"Time to help me make leaves for the windows!" she called. "Leaves! Autumn leaves! For the window!" She felt like a vendor at a baseball game. She sipped more of her wine. No answer from the boys. Fiona laid sheets of orange, red, yellow, and brown paper on the table, smoothed them with her hand, tried again. "Okay! It's officially leaf-making time!" she called.

"We're playing," shouted Beckett.

"If you have something to say to me you can come downstairs and speak to me, not shout it down the stairs!" Fiona realized that she was breaking her own rule with her booming voice. *But tough. I'm the mom. I get to take some liberties. This is not a democracy.*

"Um, Mom? We don't want to make leaves!" Eliot seconded.

"I have band practice soon anyway!" shouted Beck.

She opened the fridge and pulled out a bottle of organic milk, one of dozens in returnable jugs that were delivered to her door weekly, then left on the porch to be returned and refilled. She liked lining them up on the porch. She had been pleased when a neighbor once said, "Your boys drink so much milk!" And it was a rainy day with a prewinter chill in the air. She had heard it was already snowing heavily farther upstate. *The perfect day for a warm drink.* She poured milk into a stainless steel, copper-bottomed saucepan and turned on the burner of her gas stove. Medium low, or the milk would form a skin. When it was hot enough, she opened her mouth to shout, then thought better of it, turned the milk way down, got the cocoa powder and organic cane sugar out of the cupboard, plus the cinnamon, which the boys had always enjoyed a pinch of in their hot chocolate, lined it all up on the counter, and climbed the stairs.

The boys were in the upstairs rec room, slumped in beanbag chairs, indeed playing video games. In addition to the cacophony of noise emanating from the screen, some sort of car-race game that seemed to rely on crashing, the boys were making *rrrr*-ing and *vrrrrom*-ing and *eee-eeeeeeee-smaaaaaaaaaaaaaaash*-ing noises with their mouths.

"Boys, it's time for us to make our decorations for the window," Fiona said over the din. "You said you'd help me. I'm making hot chocolate."

"Mom, seriously, hello? We haven't done that for years. We didn't say we'd help you. You never even mentioned this," Beckett said, without looking up. Eliot had paused his game—her youngest was still eager to please her, sometimes. Now he unpaused.

"I don't feel like it, either," Eliot said, watching his older brother carefully, then saying, "Oh, man!" When his car crashed because he wasn't watching the screen.

Fiona sighed. "Well, fellows, I can't do this project by myself and then hang it on the window and pretend I made the autumn decorations with the three of *you.* That would be . . ." *Lying. That would be lying. Pretending we still do things together as a family. And it would also be stupid. And pointless.*

She took a breath. "Okay," she said. "Okay. You feel like playing games right now. I hear you." This was exactly the kind of conversation it said to have in *How to Talk So Your Kids Will Listen and Listen So Your Kids Will Talk.* The fact that she was nailing it made Fiona feel good again. "I hear you, and I understand. Playing video games is fun, and it's a wet day outside and so it just makes sense that you would want to relax together. So, that's fine, continue your game, and maybe later, when you're feeling hungry or thirsty, you can come downstairs, and I'll make that hot chocolate and a snack—and we'll make a few leaves, too. And then you can go back to playing your game again. Deal?"

Eliot smiled and nodded. "Deal!" His car crashed again.

"I'm not going to help you make the flowers at all," Beck called after her, and there was a warning tone in his voice. "I told you. I have band practice. And you're being weird!"

"We're not making flowers!" she shouted. "We. Are. Making. *Leaves!*" Then she stopped and swallowed hard. "I hear you and I understand," she called over her shoulder as she headed for the stairs, but not before she heard Eliot say, "What's with *her*? Is she drunk or something?"

"Not Mom," said Cole. "Maybe it's menopause."

She walked carefully down the stairs and, when she got to the kitchen, took her glass, which was nearly empty, and dumped it down the sink. She dumped the milk down the sink, too.

What she needed, she realized, was to go somewhere. Alone. *This weekend?* She sat, biting her lip. She thought about making her chestnut soup, her dinner rolls in the shape of turkey tails, her squash stuffed with wild rice, her cranberry-orange relish, the four kinds of pie, one for each of them—for Tim, pecan; for Eliot, pumpkin; for Beck, raspberry; and for Cole, cherry. Her eyes filled with tears.

She took out her phone and typed *life-changing weekend* into the browser, then added the word *spa*, and then, thinking about the wine and pills, *detox*, and then, thinking about how tense her shoulders felt, *massage*, and *upstate new york* because she knew she didn't have the energy to go too far. She clicked on the fourth link from the top of the search results. "Top Ten Detox Spas in New York." She went to the Web page of Crystal Springs Body Mind Spirit Retreat and Spa. Apparently the resort sat on a large deposit of healing quartz crystal, which was purported to clear the mind and restore the spirit. Fiona hesitated. *Too new-agey?* She clicked on the link anyway. She read about the forested trails, wildlife and meditation gardens, the well-appointed spa. "We offer everything from two-night packages to 21-night life-transforming retreats." Fiona closed her eyes. Twenty-one days. And a life transformation, too. Now, *that* would be nice.

But she couldn't go away for that long. A week, though. Maybe she could actually manage a week, if she left first thing the next morning. She went to the booking page. There was a room available. Fiona had never done anything this impulsive before.

After, she put away the craft supplies and went upstairs to take a nap. She didn't wake up in time to make dinner. When she went downstairs, disoriented, Tim and the boys were eating pizza at the kitchen table, straight from the box.

9

Eastern Cottontail (*Sylvilagus floridanus*)

During mating season, male Eastern cottontails often fight with each other. The male and female also perform a kind of mating dance: the male chases the female until she stops, faces him, and boxes at him with her front paws. At some point, one of them leaps straight up in the air and the other follows suit. Eastern cottontails are polygamous.

lsa closed her book and ran her right arm over the empty space on the opposite side of the bed. Michael was still in his office but it was getting late. She stood and went into Ani's room to check on her, where she stood and watched her sleep, then kissed and stroked her daughter's cheek. She eventually took her hand away and shut the door softly on her way out, then went into Xavier's room and stood over the crib he still slept in because he had never once tried to climb out of it, wishing she could lean in and kiss his face but knowing she wouldn't be able to reach, and if she lifted him up, she'd risk waking him.

Back in her room, she pulled on a black silk chemise. She looked at her reflection in the mirror and pinched her cheeks, hoping for color. *You have to keep trying,* she told herself. In the kitchen, she got a bottle of red wine and one glass. *No. You have to get two glasses. You have to have a glass of wine with him or he'll wonder why you aren't.* Then she walked back up the stairs. Michael's office door was closed. She tapped with one fingernail.

"Come in." She pushed open the door.

"Hi, there," she said. He didn't look up from his computer screen.

"Hi."

"You okay?"

Now he looked up. "I'm still dealing with the fallout from the Copenhagen disaster. Now that it's in the news, we have shareholders to answer to, and it's not pretty. More cutbacks. I'm just trying to . . ." He shook his head. "Never mind, it won't interest you."

"Tell me," she said.

"It's nothing. Complicated." *There. He dismisses me. I'm not a partner. I'm not even a friend. I'm just here.*

"I thought you might need a break." She held up the bottle and tried to stop herself from building a case against him. *You need him, really need him.* "I have wine. And . . ." She trailed off, hoping he would notice the lingerie.

"I'm sorry," he said. "I have another few hours here at least. Have a glass without me. I really can't stop."

She felt cold. She wished for a robe. She wished not to be holding two glasses and a bottle. And she also wished not to feel as relieved as she did. *You need him to do this. You need him to make love to you.* "Are you sure?"

"Positive. Sorry." He was already typing.

She closed the door behind her, went downstairs, slid the wine back in the rack, poured herself a glass of orange juice, and turned on the television, even though she hated television. She stopped on a show about lottery winners. All of them had destroyed themselves one by one. She sat, depressively mesmerized, as each winner said he or she wished the money had never materialized. She suddenly felt the same way about her own life. She had won the lottery and squandered it without shame.

She changed the channel and ended up on one of those commercials with the sad music and the crying children, their huge dark eyes pleading with the screen, the flies crawling on their foreheads. When the camera zoomed in on a toddler too weak to brush away the flies that were crawling on her eyes (*on her actual eyeballs*), Ilsa did what the earnest celebrity was telling her to do and made the call. "Two, please," she said. "I'll take two." But saying this did nothing to assuage her guilt or tamp down her fear of what was about to happen to her. What *was* happening to her. In fact, it made it worse. She had said, "I'll take two," like they were puppies in the window for the taking, pieces of candy, pairs of shoes. "Actually, three," she amended, but this didn't help, either, despite how pleased the phone attendant was with her.

"You're a wonderful person," the attendant said.

"I'm not. Really. I'm not."

After returning home from the cottage early, Ilsa had tried to resist Lincoln. As frustrated as her conversation at the cottage with Liane had made her, it had also forced her to think about what she was doing. And perhaps she had also thought that the rift between her and Liane, something so foreign to her, so sad, so lonely, would somehow heal if she stopped what she was doing, if she heeded her younger sister's cautionary words. Thus she was able to ignore the first two texts he sent her, saying things to herself like, *No. I'm not going to do this. Yes, I'm bored in my marriage. Worse than bored: suffocated. Yes, most of the time I feel like Michael doesn't see me. And yes, part of the time I feel like I don't even want him to, would* rather *fly under his radar. But what I need to do is* make *him see me. I need to try to be a better wife. A better person. A better everything. I can't just throw this all away. I made a commitment. And there are the children to think about.*

One afternoon, though, she took the train into the city to meet a friend. On the subway, a man sat across from her, a construction worker, dirty boots, paint-spattered hands, a cooler at his feet. He was handsome, young. He watched her appraisingly. Every time she looked up from her book their eyes met and her cheeks felt hot and *she* felt hot and she thought to herself, *What if I wrote him a note on one of the pages of my book and handed it to him. A note that said,* Do you want to fuck me? Get off the train at the next stop. The depravity of the thought surprised and slightly disgusted her, but she was also captivated by the fantasy. She held the man's gaze for a long time as her stop approached. The train slowed and she got off and didn't look back.

A week later, at a gallery opening Ilsa forced herself to go to so she could somehow begin to feel part of the art world again, Lincoln was there, and this made her believe it was fate. She had walked slowly around the room, looking at the paintings, coming closer and closer to him. Finally, he had come to stand beside her in front of a canvas. "Are you ignoring me, Ilsa?" he had asked. She had kept her eyes on the artwork. "No," she had replied. "Just delaying the inevitable." They had shared a taxi from the city to Rye, but, to her surprise, he had not touched her in the taxi, during a ride that took nearly forty minutes. Then: "Stop the taxi at the end of Elm," he had instructed. This was a few blocks away from her house.

Outside of the taxi, he had taken her hand, and they had walked. Soon they were back where he had kissed her the first time. It was so dark she couldn't see.

This is wrong. He had lifted her skirt, pulled down her panties, moved closer: *How did this happen so fast?* She had felt as though she were moving through water, like a person in a dream who wanted to stop something but couldn't because the air somehow weighed a thousand pounds. "No, we can't do this. Not here, not now," she had finally said.

"But we will," he had said. And then he had walked away and left her there, alone in the dark.

She had become instantly disoriented. She couldn't see. *How dare he? How dare he? Asshole. Cad. Lincoln fucking Porter.*

Eventually she had straightened her skirt and ventured out from between the houses. A rustling in the dry brush made her stop. Panic made her chest feel constricted. But it was just a rabbit. It jumped out of the darkness and she tried not to scream, tried to see the humor as it hopped away, its tail bright white in the pitch-black.

He was standing in the shadows, waiting. "It was just a rabbit," he said. "Were you scared?"

She had brushed past him and walked quickly, her heels sinking into the grass until she reached the sidewalk again.

"Ilsa! Wait!"

"No! This was a mistake. I didn't know you were so— Clearly, I thought you were someone else."

He had caught up to her in two strides.

"I'm sorry. I was just playing a game with you."

"I don't play games."

"Are you sure?"

He had grabbed her arm and pulled her to him, kissing her roughly. She had kissed him back for a moment but then pulled away and looked up at him and, to her shock, had sobbed aloud, a harsh, choking sound. His expression had changed immediately.

"Ilsa—"

"You're scaring me," she had said. "Please, just let me go. I need to get home."

He hadn't let go of her but his hold on her had softened. "I'm so sorry. I didn't mean to scare you, gorgeous Ilsa. Beautiful girl." And he had stroked her hair, pushing her bangs up and away from her eyes, then kissed her once, very gently. "I thought . . . forgive me, I thought this was what you wanted. You gave me the impression that you wanted to be . . ." He shook his head. "I'll walk you home."

Swiftly, Ilsa became indignant. "I gave you the impression that *what*? That I had just read one of those soft-core S&M novels all the housewives in this neighborhood are getting horny about and decided I wanted someone to play rough with me, too?"

He smiled and shook his head. "Not you. You don't read those books, do you?"

"Of course not!"

They had continued to walk. She had known with doomed certainty that Lincoln clearly wasn't in the same situation or place as her, wasn't struggling with the morality of this, wasn't finding this difficult to do at all, was in fact trying to play *games* with her. She didn't know him well and yet she felt she did, felt she could see the way he moved through life like a man at a buffet, choosing among the items that were presented to him, sometimes when he wasn't even hungry. And there she was. The girl on the half shell. It would be a shame to waste her when she was clearly so ready.

She had allowed another gentle kiss a few houses from hers, and then he had walked away and she had quietly unlocked the door and gone inside and held in another sob and thought, *That's it. I'll never see him again, at least not intentionally.*

Liane had called her, later in the summer, and Ilsa had said, "I'm sorry," even before Liane could say hello. "I don't know why I didn't phone you," Ilsa had continued. "Nothing like this has happened to us before, and I felt terrible and stupid and I never picked up the phone because I didn't know what I would say."

"No, I'm sorry. I shouldn't have left the cottage like that, and I should have called, too—but here's the thing. I sort of needed to be on my own. I needed to make some decisions without asking for help. I've never done that before, so . . ." Liane cleared her throat. "I left Adam," she said, and Ilsa felt guilty for feeling so relieved, and also happy that she had been right about him being wrong for Liane.

"Oh, Li. Are you doing okay?"

"I think so. It was a fairly clean break. Very ordered. Very Adam. I'm staying with a friend for now, but I've lined up my own place, and I'm really—*yes*, I am happy about this. I made the right decision." Ilsa thought that Liane sounded partly like she was trying to convince herself and partly like she was genuinely happy. She decided being partly happy was half the battle and that she didn't need to worry about her. Then Liane had said, "How are things with Michael?" and Ilsa had said, "Fine. A lot better." And Ilsa had decided that she would make this statement be true. *I can and I will forget all about Lincoln. And about the desperate housewife cliché I'm becoming. About how I'm like my father in my appetites, how I fantasize about having sex with random people on subways.*

So she gave her husband massages when he came in late from work. She left notes for him, asked him to dinner. (He couldn't, both times she asked.) One night, she cooked his favorite, coq au vin, which he picked at before saying he needed to go upstairs and sort something out, that she shouldn't wait up for him, that he was sorry, he just wasn't hungry. She had been wearing a new matching lace bra-and-panties set under her dress. Of course, he had no way of knowing this, but she still felt resentful. Another strike. *If he really loved me, the way I need to be loved, he would have known.*

After he had gone upstairs, she had dumped the food in the garbage, even though she had known it was petty and wasteful to do so, even though there was a famine in the Horn of Africa and so many people didn't have anything to eat. And then she had gone to her handbag and taken out her cell phone. She had stared down at it.

But she had been unable to bring herself to send Lincoln a text message. In truth, she despised text messages. Liane had once said it was probably because she was an artist and excessively tactile. Even Michael, at first, had understood this, had sometimes sent her handwritten letters from New York instead of emails, when she was still living in Toronto. It was the care he took in his pursuit of her—Michael got what he wanted, or at least back then he did—that had caused her, however temporarily, to actually fall in love with him instead of just wanting to fall in love with him, instead of just wishing she wasn't in love with someone else. Sometimes these letters came with plane tickets enclosed, or letters attached to presents that were both beautiful and thoughtful. (Her favorite, an armful of white-gold and aquamarine bangle bracelets; another time, a weighty art book she had casually mentioned wanting to read, with a beautiful, hand-painted bookmark inside.) If he had not done these things, she probably never would have been able to convince herself that marrying him was a good idea.

This had been a different Michael, though. A happy, confident Michael. It was incredible to Ilsa how much of her husband's being was tied to his company. She had at first kept telling herself it was normal: Wasn't *she* tied to her art, wasn't it destroying *her* slowly inside that she couldn't paint? But somehow she saw what Michael was going through as different. While he fought desperately to improve his company, he allowed their relationship to starve and himself to decline from the stress. She didn't respect this. Once she had said to him, "Is this really worth it? We could live on less." And he had looked at her over the rim of his glasses, laughed bitterly, and said, "Perhaps *we* could, but my ex-wife couldn't, and my children couldn't." She felt sorry for him then. But this didn't temper her resentment.

Two days after she dumped out the coq au vin, when she arrived at her studio, shoulders already beginning to slump dejectedly in preparation for another fruitless morning, there had been a postcard leaning against the door. On the front was an image of Gauguin's *Nevermore (O Tahiti)*, and on the back, Lincoln had written: *Ilsa Bissette, I'm longing to kiss you again. Where have you gone?—L.*

Bold of him, she thought. How did he know her husband didn't accompany her to her studio, that her neighbors weren't nosy, that this wasn't an invitation to be found out?

She had picked up the postcard and brought it inside, then stood looking alternately at it and at the morning sunlight streaming through the window and the dust motes dancing in the air. Then she had sat down and started a painting that was not terrible, that was not heavy with dark purple—like the color Lincoln had seen on her wrist the day they had met, part of a palette of dark, depressing colors she had been working with, even though she hated them—but was instead light and alluring.

Her elation had not lasted. She didn't know how to respond to his postcard. She still couldn't bring herself to send a text message, wasn't sure if she should call, and couldn't very well walk over to his house. Yet for a week the postcard lit the edges of her life with the something that had been missing.

Until Michael casually asked her if she had any shows coming up, any paintings to sell, and she felt the light go out. "No," she had answered, wishing she could offer an explanation.

"I'm wondering if it makes sense for you to have the studio anymore," he had said, and she had hated him in that moment even as she knew it was true. "Perhaps we could just set up the spare bedroom as a home studio? Or maybe the basement?" The basement. The *basement*. Didn't he know she needed light? And yet, she knew he had a point. Did it make sense to pay a monthly rental on a room where she went to do absolutely nothing? No, it didn't. But she needed the space, desperately, had needed it always and even more so after having children, whom she loved but also felt crowded by at times. It was hard, when she was at home, not to think of them and what they were doing or what they would be doing when they returned, or what she had said to them last. She needed a place to go that was only hers, so that she could otherwise be what they needed her to be. She felt angry at Michael for suggesting that this be taken away, and angry with herself for not being able to produce enough to sustain it. "*You're* the one who said once we could try to live on less," he said later, in response to her sulking. When she left for her studio, she had slammed the door, hard. Ani and Xavier were at the park with Sylvie, or she wouldn't have done it.

At her studio, she cut out a small, postcard-sized piece of stiff paper, and she did something daring, something she used to do when she and Michael were dating—and not just Michael, but also Eric, her first husband. It seemed even more daring now. So much was at risk.

This painting was the curve of her waist, the rise of her hips, and the top of her thigh. She stopped there. She let the painting dry for a day, then wrote on the back of the make-shift postcard: *Next time, knock. I'm at my studio most days, at least until three.*

She thought about traveling into the city, all the way to his studio, but knew that would be a mistake. He wasn't like her, virtually unknown. She couldn't just walk in and prop a suggestive postcard against his door. He probably had an assistant who would intervene, toss this piece of perceived fan mail in the trash. So she looked up the name and address of his studio on the Internet and put the painting in an envelope and mailed it before she could change her mind. She felt sick with anticipation.

Four days later, midmorning, there was a knock on the door of her studio. Ilsa froze before the canvas she had just begun to dab at without purpose. She stood, threw a drop cloth over it, wiped her clammy hands on one of the paint-spattered hand towels on a hook by the sink, took a sip of water. Another knock.

"Coming!"

She opened the door.

He smiled. "Hello there." She was about to return his greeting and invite him in but he was already pushing open the door. He closed the door, put one hand on the small of her back, one on the back of her head, and kissed her, tongue plunging in, no time for pleasantries. She moaned softly and accepted that she wasn't in the *mood* for pleasantries. *He knows this about you, even if you don't want to admit this about yourself. Maybe you really do just want someone to play rough with you.*

Kiss me, kiss me, kiss me. And he did, endlessly, until she needed air, pulled her head away. "Good morning," she said, meaning it to sound coy or cute, but it didn't work. He left her standing alone and began to stalk her studio, his height and bulk making the room, with its high ceilings and exposed brick, seem somehow smaller to her, like when you return to a place you spent time in as a child and realize it wasn't as grand as you thought it was. He reminded her of a lion again, this time caged. He looked like he might roar without warning and begin to rip canvases apart, knock paint pots to the floor, trash the place, and leave simply because he had to, because the energy inside him was too much to contain. *This genius, this man, is in my studio, touching my things, in my space.* It made her feel special. But also, powerless and inadequate.

Many of her canvases were shrouded, mostly because she just didn't want to look at them anymore. He lifted shrouds indiscriminately and she was reminded of the way he had so carelessly lifted her skirt that night in the alley. He looked underneath, let the sheets drop, moved to the next. "Show me more," he said, and she obeyed wordlessly, standing by as he flipped through her paintings.

"You lack passion," he finally said, and it was like a slap. *I didn't ask you to come here and critique my work,* she wanted to say. "You don't lack talent, though. There's something here. Raw, but here. A soul." And now the sting was gone and she was glowing, humming inside. Lincoln Porter had not told her that she was talented but he had told her that she *did not lack talent,* and he had made reference to her soul.

"More," he said, "are there more?"

She bit her lip. "A few." She opened a cabinet. He flipped through them quickly.

"Nothing else?" She pulled out some much older canvases, canvases from years and years before, and realized too late what was at the bottom of the stack: the paintings she used to do for Michael. "We should store these at your studio," he had said to her once, and she had imagined he was afraid one of his children might find them. "What do we have to be ashamed of?" she had asked, and he had just shaken his head. She remembered he hadn't been comfortable posing but he had let her take some pictures and she had found it so arousing. She had loved painting him. She had never done it for anyone else. Now she thought, suddenly, that she would not like to paint Lincoln, as much as she was infatuated with him, would not like to have to linger over his aging body, would much rather focus on his mind, close her eyes and let him kiss her and touch her, listen to him speak.

He didn't come here to talk, though.

He was still going through the stack. "Hey, what are these? They're in a different style."

"Oh." She blinked. She had almost forgotten she still had those, the ones Eric had painted of her, when they lived in Paris. Two years. A blur. Sex, art, heartbreak. She reached for the paintings in his hand. "No, not those," she said. She hardly thought of Eric anymore, but she did now, looked down at the painting and remembered this one, how he had painted her lying naked on his bed, and himself, too, what could be seen of him in the mirror. The short-lived marriage had ended because she had caught Eric, a rising abstract painter, making love to his mentor's daughter. He had seemed surprised at her anger. "You're free to have a lover, too, you know," he had said. "I thought you knew that . . ."

"I don't want that!" she had screamed, and then she had screamed other things, too. ("She is seventeen fucking years old!" for example. He was shocked, laughed at her, said, "You might have a French father but you're American, aren't you?" "Canadian," she had sniffled at him. "I'm from Canada.") She left him, flew back to Toronto, borrowed money from Helen she would never be asked to pay back, and moved into the Annex, which was where she had been living when she first met Michael, in an apartment with polished wood floors like her studio, and a bed with a wrought-iron frame, and a big window with a view of Casa Loma. She attended art school during the day and worked as a coat-check girl at a jazz bar on weekends. She remembered how Michael had asked her to quit that job, said he would send her money if she needed it, and how she had said, "I don't want to be treated like I'm your mistress." He had proposed on his next visit.

Lincoln was now holding up one of the paintings she had done of herself.

"This is like that one you sent me. And *that* was good. *These* are good. And not just because of your body, your tits. *These* are *good. These* are what you should be doing. Paintings like this." He held up one of her husband. "And this." He took the painting she was holding away from her.

She swallowed hard. "Nudes?"

"Not nudes. These are more than nudes. And I'm sure you're capable of an even higher intensity of eroticism, aren't you?" Now he had put down both paintings and was pulling her to him. "*Aren't* you?" She was wearing one of Michael's old dress shirts and he opened it roughly, popping all the buttons. Then he unhooked her bra and let it drop to the floor. "Beautiful," he said. "*Better* than in the painting. But not by much."

Now she was unbuttoning his shirt and running her hands along his chest. And he was unbuttoning and unzipping her slim black pants, sliding them down her legs. Soon she was standing before him in nothing but her black lace thong. Their mouths had not parted. He pressed her against a wall and she undid the button and zipper of his trousers. They were both breathing hard and the sound of this, and their sighs, filled the room. They knocked over a stool. She pulled off his pants. He slid off her underwear and plunged a finger inside her and she moaned and arched against him. Two fingers, three, "Ahhh. *Yes.*" He put his hands on her hips and she lifted herself up and wrapped her legs around him as he entered her. She moved her hips, he moved his. He bit her neck and she clawed at his back. She felt her backside slapping lightly against the wall, wondered what her neighbor might think, if he was there painting. This just added to her arousal. Faster now, her moans and his becoming as rhythmic as the sound of her body against the plaster. She pulled him deeper inside her with each thrust. She heard herself say, "*Fuck me, fuck me,*" and heard him say, "*Yes. Yes.*" He shuddered and came and so did she.

And then it was over. He put her down, and she stood before him, naked and panting, her legs wobbly.

She found the old dress shirt and wrapped it around herself, and when she turned around, he was buttoning his shirt. She wondered what they should do. She had stools they could sit on, she could make tea. She opened her mouth to make the offer, but he silenced her with a fast kiss.

And then he left.

When Ilsa had told her mother she was marrying Michael, Helen had asked her why she was getting married again.

"Because I love him."

"Well, yes, but . . ." Things were left unsaid that Ilsa had been incapable of understanding at the time, but did understand now. What her mother *had* said, quietly, was, "Is it because . . . I'm sorry, but I have to say this: Is it because he's like a father to you, like a father you never had? I mean, we both know you *have* a father, but Claude is more like . . ."

"Like a boorish uncle, thank you, I know that," Ilsa had snapped, and they had proceeded to fight, which was rare. "Did it ever occur to you that I don't *want* to be like you?" Ilsa had eventually shouted, and Helen had flinched and said, "No, it didn't occur to me, because sometimes I think, of all three of you, you are the *most* like me, which is why I felt I could be so honest with you. I regret that now."

Ilsa had said nothing to this, but she remembered feeling wretched. She had, especially when she was younger, wanted to be just like Helen. But as she grew older she had realized that Helen was only pretending to have no true need for men. Her strength was somewhat of a façade; she ached and felt lonely like everyone else. Perhaps in response to this realization Ilsa had developed a yearning for men that was even stronger than her mother's unacknowledged one.

Helen had spoken again: "Are you doing this to prove it, to prove you aren't like me?"

"You make it sound like I'm doing something wrong. I'm marrying a man whom I love and who loves me. A good man. A dependable man!"

Helen had nodded. "Yes, he is those things. And he certainly has made his intentions with you quite clear. But, Ilsa, you might need more than good, you might need more than dependable. You might not think that now, but there might come a day . . . and he's not the type to . . . be flexible in his arrangements."

"Do you think that's what I want? Because I could have had that with Eric, and I didn't want it! To live that way— why bother making the promise in the first place, then? If I wanted to live like that, I wouldn't get married at all. But I am. I'm making this choice. I need you to support it."

"I just want you to be happy. Forever. I'm sorry I didn't have the correct reaction to your announcement and I *do* support you."

"I will be happy," Ilsa had said, defiant. "And by the way, even though you never got married, you didn't always seem to be so happy. What about when—" She had been about to say, *What about when Wes killed himself?* but she stopped because even in her anger, she knew that would be a cruel thing to bring up.

But Helen had known what Ilsa had been about to say. "Even if I had known the outcome, I wouldn't have changed anything," she said, her mouth smiling but her eyes sad. "I think love is a good thing, in any form. Even when it hurts. The pain often leaves behind a beautiful memory." She had seemed to realize something as she spoke. She had reached out and put both her hands on Ilsa's shoulders, squeezed, and then let go. *Go forth and get yourself hurt,* was what the squeeze had seemed to say. *There's nothing I can do.*

They never spoke of the discussion again. At the wedding, Helen had smiled, smiled, smiled. So had Ilsa, so had everyone. Especially Michael. He hadn't wanted the big wedding at first, had insisted it be small. "This is my second, after all," he had said to her. "And yours, too. Let's be reasonable." "But last time . . . last time, I eloped," Ilsa had said. "This time, I *want* it to be extravagant." In fact, she had needed it to be extravagant. And he had never said no to her, not in those days, so she had her lavish wedding. And it was a perfect day.

One day, though. That's all a wedding is. Ilsa knew that now. One day, and perhaps a few golden weeks away, during which time your new husband might schedule conference calls and suggest you go shopping to keep yourself busy, and you might realize you've already painted yourself into a corner.

Lincoln didn't call, or text, or visit her studio, or leave any notes. Three weeks passed. Ilsa couldn't eat. She couldn't stop thinking about him. The only time she was happy was when she was with Ani and Xavier, and even then it was tinged by guilt. She could hardly stand to be around Michael. When she sat beside him in the car, she would think, *I could tell him, right now, what I've done. And it would probably all be over.* The fact that there was something between them that could end everything began to wear on Ilsa. She became silent—and Michael was *already* silent, lost in his own concerns. So when they were together, they barely spoke.

One day, Ilsa heard a song on the radio, and the lyric "the opposite of love is indifference" made her cry, instant tears that felt sharp. She had never been the type to cry over songs, and hadn't she known that line all through her life? It was nothing unique or new. The problem was she now felt it, acutely. Indifferent to the man upstairs, the man in her bed. Ani was coloring at the table and she looked up. "Mommy?"

"I'm sorry. I'm so sorry, darling."

• • •

Weeks passed. Ilsa tried to forget, tried not to feel used and humiliated. Then, one morning, there was a knock at Ilsa's studio door. She sat in front of the canvas and thought, *No, I just won't answer.*

But when the knocking stopped she felt sick. Was he gone? She stood.

Knock, knock. She nearly fell to her knees with relief. She opened the door and she didn't say, *Why haven't you called?* She simply said, "Hello," and pretended to be happy to see him, pretended it was normal that he would just be surfacing now, pretended she had other lovers, that she hadn't been pining for him, no, not at all.

He didn't look at her paintings this time. And this time he also didn't press her against the wall. He asked her if she had a blanket and she laid one out on the floor. She said to him, "We should really use a condom, last time we . . . it was all so rushed, but we really should," and she fumbled with it and he didn't help her. Afterward, her spine hurt. "I'll call you," he said, before he left, and she despised the way she clung to the hope that he would.

The night Ilsa went into her husband's office with a chemise on and carrying a bottle of wine, she had known she was pregnant for about a week. And she knew it was Lincoln's because she was unable to remember the last time she and her husband had had sex.

I'll try again tomorrow, she decided after the rebuff. Then she repeated it inwardly like a mantra: *Tomorrow. Tomorrow.*

She was terrified, she was sick, both literally and figuratively, but she also knew that she didn't have any options. She wasn't going to get an abortion. She had considered it, yes, but had known it would be a secret too terrible to keep. And it wasn't the baby's fault. *Baby. It's not your fault, baby.*

Days passed, and she didn't try again with Michael. *What are you going to do?*

She nearly lost track of the passage of time, until Fiona called and said, "I'm not doing Thanksgiving dinner," her voice sounding strange, as though she had just woken up, and Ilsa had realized that time was passing alarmingly fast. *How far along does that make me?* She hadn't been feeling well that day. A stitch or a cramp had been bothering her. Probably the uterus starting to stretch. *I can't ignore this much longer.*

"I'm . . . traveling. Going away a few days. So I can't."

"You're traveling? Alone?" Ilsa had said. "Where?"

"It's—nothing. Nothing. Just something I couldn't avoid."

"Fiona, are you all right?" Ilsa and Fiona had never discussed what had happened that night at the party. Like everything else, it seemed, Fiona had swept it away, pretended it wasn't an elephant in the room, but every time Ilsa had seen her, she had sensed some sort of distress. She could hear it in her voice now, over the phone line.

"I'm fine. Just busy. What else is new, right?"

"Right." Ilsa held the phone tight to her ear. She wished she could confide in Fiona. Fiona always knew exactly what to do about everything. "Will Tim and the boys be on their own? Should I have them over, cook them something?" Ilsa had never offered to do this for Fiona before and was sure her sister would decline, explain that she had precooked a seven-course meal that she would have the housekeeper serve in her absence.

"Could you? It's why I'm calling."

"Oh. Well, of course. Will you ask Tim for me? Find out what time works best?"

"Why don't you just call him yourself? He's at the office."

So Ilsa had called, feeling nervous as she punched in

Tim's extension, even after all this time. She had never actually called him directly before, so she had had to use the company directory, and felt odd about calling the office and not speaking with Michael. When Tim picked up he sounded distracted. "That would be good," he said. "We were probably just going to order pizza again." *Again.* Strange. Ilsa wondered for a moment if perhaps Tim and Fiona were having problems, and tried to catalogue how this made her feel. Nothing. It didn't make her feel anything. She felt relieved by this, but still concerned for her sister and for Tim. *But no, not possible. Those two are the most solid couple in the world.*

"Five o'clock, then."

She had hung up and wondered what she would make. She'd never cooked a Thanksgiving dinner before and it seemed a bit late to get a turkey.

Her phone rang, and she looked down at it. *Lincoln.*

"Where have you been?" she asked before she could stop herself, and hated the sound of the words when she said them.

"At a retreat in the Himalayas. No phones. No wireless. Poor Ilsa. Don't you like waiting for release?"

She was silent. Her eyes stung. "Hello?" he said. "Are you still there? I have a few hours free. I can be there in ten minutes."

"I'm busy," she said. "I'm planning *Thanksgiving.*" She placed emphasis on the word as though it gave her credence in some way. *I am a woman who plans Thanksgiving dinners for people, for my family.* She understood, finally, what it might feel like to be Fiona, to be able to hide behind pressing responsibility.

"How about a drink, then? Tonight? Come on. Surely you can get away from your turkey for a few hours?"

She hated that she felt such elation. She didn't answer him.

"Ilsa," he said, and his deep voice turned her name into something like a purr. "I can't stop thinking of you. Your heat, the way you feel on my fingers, the way you respond to me, the way you're not afraid to *want*."

She held her breath.

"*Ilsa.*"

"Yes?"

"Have a drink with me at least? I must see you."

"Yes," she said.

They went to a dark, wood-paneled pub. It seemed like a mistake, to be out in public together in such a small town.

"You have a Mona Lisa smile," he said to her. And she thought, *That's one of the most trite things I have ever heard a man say.* It was a line he probably used on other women, too. She pushed the thought away and showed her teeth the next time she smiled.

He was attentive, different than she had ever seen him. Sweet, even. *This is when he falls in love with me,* she thought, and started to relax and allow room for relief. He was going to fall in love with her. Maybe it would be easy. *But even if he falls in love with you, what will you do?* Ilsa didn't know, but still clung to the comfort of her thoughts.

As if to confirm what she was feeling, he said, "Your eyes are amazing, what color are they, I can never remember." To which she replied, with insouciance that felt too studied, "Gray? Blue? They're always changing." He smiled like she had said something brilliant; his foot was out of his shoe and nestled against her calf. They talked about nothing, about everything, about childhood and family and her, a lot about her. How her art was going, what she had been doing. He said he had missed her.

Later, he excused himself to go to the restroom and it

was twenty minutes before he returned to their table. She watched him, pausing at a table, not just nodding and smiling at the people who had noticed him, but stopping and talking, having a conversation that seemed to her to be unnecessarily long. She felt irritated and hot. The half glass of wine she had allowed herself had upset her stomach. She waited and tried to maintain a sexy, alluring pose, crossed her legs, uncrossed them, sat this way and that, grew tired of it, slumped a little, then sat up and crossed her legs again at just the right moment; rare, lucky timing.

She wondered who the people, who now were watching him and talking to each other as he walked away, thought she was—for she was clearly not his blond-gray, birdlike wife, the one who so often appeared alongside him in the society pages, who had been with him that night at the party.

Whoever they thought Ilsa was, at that moment she knew with clarity that if they suspected she was his lover, they would judge *her*, not him. She felt resentful of this.

His mood had changed. "Have you had enough yet?"

"What do you mean?"

"Shall we go to your studio?"

She shook her head.

"Why not?"

"I just . . . I don't want to. Tonight I just want to sit here and talk."

"We've been talking." He sounded tired. She sat looking at him. "Fine. What do you want to talk about?"

She thought for a moment. "Do you think we were meant to meet? Do you ever think it was . . . destined?" She realized how stupid she sounded, how girlish, and wished she could rewind the words back into her mouth, the way her mother would have tried to do.

His expression was disinterested. "I don't know, maybe," he said vaguely. "I try not to think too much about fate." His eyes were roaming the room, but returned to her, intense once again. "You have secrets, don't you? Tell me some of them. If we're going to sit here and talk, you might as well make it interesting for me." He leaned in.

She felt like she was in shock. She shook her head slightly. She felt the anger she had been trying to suppress surface and begin to simmer. She thought about saying it, saying, *I'm pregnant, and I know it's yours because my husband and I never have sex.* She imagined that his expression probably wouldn't change very much. Then she thought of how she had felt that night at Fiona's party, when he had watched her, his unwavering gaze like a dim spotlight. Wherever she moved around the yard that night, the beam had swung along with her.

"I do have a secret," she said. "You were right that night, about me being a bored housewife."

"I don't know that I ever said that—"

"I never should have married my husband. It was a mistake."

"Everyone thinks that. It's because marriage is a mistake. But it's a necessary evil. Don't fight it, my dear. You are where you are."

She ignored him. "I only married him because—because I came back from France heartbroken, because my first husband betrayed me and made me feel like it was what I wanted, and then . . . I came to visit my sister Fiona, to see her kids, and I met Tim, and I thought I was in love with him. Or maybe I was in love with him. Who knows? Being in love doesn't mean anything anyway. It's fleeting, all hormones."

"So young to be so jaded."

"I zeroed in on him and decided I wanted him. Because he was so good and so safe, and because Fiona—well, she seemed so content, so untouchable. I wanted to be untouchable, too."

"Now, this is interesting," Lincoln said, and Ilsa wanted to reach across the table and slap him, watch as her wedding ring left a welt on his cheek. "What happened? Tim couldn't resist you, right? Who could? Especially years ago. I bet you were even more tantalizing when you were young."

She gripped the table to keep her hand down. "Of course he resisted. Because he's Tim. He is good. He's probably the best man on earth. He said such lovely things to me, too, and of course they made me love him even more, at least for a time. Then I met Michael, and I thought I had my solution. Not Tim, but similar. Similar enough. I finally stopped dreaming about Tim, stopped wanting to stay in bed all day just to have the feeling of being with him, even if it wasn't real. In Michael I thought maybe I'd found a substitute, that I could have the safe, perfect life my sister had, and be safe and perfect, too, and freed from . . . from who I really am. *And* from people like you." She reached across the table now and picked up Lincoln's hand, which was limp. She dropped it back on the table, where it landed with a soft thump, like he was a corpse already and not just an aging man. "I need to go home," she said.

He lowered his eyebrows. His hand was still in a dead-looking pile on the table. "Very well. I trust you can hail yourself a taxi."

And that was that.

"How was the gallery opening?" Michael had asked Ilsa when she got home. He was on his way up the stairs, but he turned.

"Fine." She looked up at him, forced herself to meet his gaze. "Fiona isn't doing Thanksgiving this year, so I told Tim to bring himself and the boys here for dinner."

"Okay," he said, not commenting on how odd it was that Fiona wasn't hosting this year. He continued up the stairs, then stopped again. "Hey. I have to ask you something." He walked down the stairs and picked up four envelopes from the side table. "Is this some kind of mistake? Did you adopt four children? There've been a lot of charges on the credit card. "

"I . . . it *must* be a mistake. I'll call them tomorrow."

"There are a few other things for you," he said, and she stood and studied his face, holding the letters he had handed her.

"Do you want to stay up and . . . have a glass of wine with me?" she asked.

"I really shouldn't. I have a seven a.m. meeting tomorrow." He turned and started walking up the stairs, his footsteps creaking in all the same places as usual.

"Michael?" she called. *I'm no longer following your unwavering path through our existence. I've gone off the rails and am potentially heading toward some sort of impact and you haven't even noticed.*

The creaking stopped. "Yes?"

She walked to the bottom of the stairs and held out the envelopes. "I lied. I'm sorry."

"About what?"

"It wasn't a mistake. I was up late one night and I couldn't sleep and got stuck on an infomercial and there were all those children with the flies crawling all over their heads, and there was one, she was Ani's age, and she had flies crawling across her *eyeballs* . . ." Ilsa took a deep breath, gulped in air. It felt like confession, this. She now understood what her father had been talking about, why he went into those confessional booths, performed such sacrilege. "So I adopted three at once, and then called back the next night to adopt one more," she finished. *As my penance,* she did not add.

He peered down at her, his eyes barely visible behind his glasses, which were reflecting the light from the lamp at the bottom of the stairs. *My silver fox,* she used to call him. Now he spoke in a paternal tone. "But, Ilsa, it's a bit unreasonable, don't you think? Two hundred dollars a month . . ."

"It's not as though we can't afford it," she said.

"What do you know about what we can afford?"

"I'll sell paintings."

"And this is how you want to spend the money from your paintings?"

"It's my money." She felt like a sullen child. "I'll spend it in any way I want."

"Your choice," he said, and turned, continued creaking up the stairs.

"Michael, please. Just wait."

He turned. She took off her shoes and met him in the middle of the staircase. She kissed him and he kissed her back, but she sensed hesitation. *When did this happen to us?*

"I'm sorry," she said. "I miss you. I miss *us*." But this wasn't true and she knew it. What she really missed was herself. Still, she kissed him again.

"Let's go to bed," she said.

The next morning, he rolled over in bed and slung a leg across her body.

She got out of the bed and went to the bathroom, turned the shower on, hot.

She had been in the shower five minutes when she heard the bathroom door open. She thought for a moment that it was Ani, up early and needing to pee, but when she realized it was Michael, she felt irrationally annoyed.

He pulled aside the curtain. "Morning." He squeezed into the small shower. She had conditioner on her hair and was exfoliating her legs and she smiled back but with gritted teeth as she moved out of the stream of water and stood in the cool air while he began to wash his hair.

"Got to make that early meeting," he said. "That was fun last night." And a wink.

She rinsed her hair and her legs. "I'm done. Enjoy."

"You okay?"

"Just tired."

She got out of the shower and wrapped a towel around her head and one around her body, then looked at herself through the steam forming on the mirror. She blinked a few times, reached for her eye cream on a shelf, and patted away the stinging.

10

Eastern Coyote (*Canis latrans*)

In general, mated pairs of coyotes are monogamous and packs consist of close family members. This need for a dedicated mate exists in part because of the high demands the pups place on their parents; most are born in large litters and require an extended period of training and care to learn to hunt and survive. Sometimes, however, coyotes practice polygyny, and two females raise pups with one male in one den—but this is rare.

t seemed later than it was—because the glass of wine Helen had ordered to her room had made her drowsy and she had tried to write and then eventually given up, made tea, felt officially ancient, and crawled into bed—when the phone rang.

"Hello," said an unfamiliar voice. "My name is Iris McKellah and I'm calling about Fiona Sherman. She has you listed here as her emergency contact."

Helen felt a shock of fear, instant, numbing. Her sleepiness evaporated instantly. She thought, *I've waited so long for a call like this about one of my children that I forgot I was waiting.* "What happened? Is she . . . hurt?" Unthinkable, the other option. No, she couldn't be. Not Fiona. Never Fiona. She was the strong one.

"Well, not exactly. I mean, she's hurt*ing*, yes. But she's not hurt, not physically."

"I'm confused," said Helen.

"I run the Crystal Springs Body Mind Spirit Retreat and Spa here in Neversink, New York, where Fiona is currently a guest. She checked herself in yesterday afternoon."

"Checked herself in? Is it . . . a rehab center?" Then Helen laughed. Of course not. Fiona wasn't in rehab. "Good lord," she said to herself, before realizing you couldn't talk to yourself when you were actually on the phone with another person.

"Oh, no, not a rehab center. A place where women seek positive change, so perhaps you *could* call it a life rehab. I own it, and am also the chief chakra and aura therapist." Helen could picture Iris. She was likely wearing several multicolored scarves and earrings made of feathers or some repurposed, recycled material. (Probably very similar to the ones Helen herself usually wore.)

"Are you sure you have the right Fiona Sherman?"

"I can't imagine how there could have been a mix-up."

"And what's wrong with her? Is she sick?"

"I did a reading this morning—Angel Cards—and was told she needed external help. A friend, I assumed, although one of the cards also suggested sisters. She doesn't seem open to making any friends here, though, and especially not *sister* friends, so I thought . . . well, you *are* a friend of hers, aren't you? She put you down as the person to call in case of an emergency."

"Well," said Helen, and then wasn't sure how to continue. *Well, I'm not exactly her friend. And I don't think she likes me most of the time. I always* wanted *to be her friend, though. That was my goal, when I became a mother to her—my first baby, so beautiful, so stoic, so different from me—to be a friend instead of just a typical mother. I failed at that, with Fiona at least, but I really did try.* "I'm her mother," she said.

"I see. Do you think it might be possible for you to come out here for a few nights? I won't charge you, of course. Fiona has a large room. You can stay in there. It seems the only answer. Are you able to?"

Helen looked around her hotel room, at the papers and the clothes and the wineglass and the tea mug. She had checked into the Chelsea, but it was just a stop among many. Over the summer, she'd also visited San Diego, Paris, Toronto, and an old friend in Munich. Then fall had arrived and she had decided she would hole up and finally write her memoirs because Edie had done it, written all those things about her in her memoir that only sold because Edie was Nate's wife and Helen's friend. Maybe she'd stay for a week. That would be enough to get a good start. And, she decided, she'd write it all by hand, the way she used to write her songs.

Except that memoirs weren't songs. And it was just easier to write on a computer. Not having brought one, Helen felt stymied rather than inspired. "Yes, I'll come."

"And are you far from here?"

"I'm in New York City at the moment."

"It's only about a two-hour drive." Iris said it as though it were as simple as driving around the corner to pick up eggs. And maybe it *could* be that simple. *Your daughter needs you, so you go.*

It was just that Helen couldn't come to terms with the fact that Fiona needed anyone. It was making *her* feel helpless. "How do I get there?" she asked.

"There are directions on our website."

"I don't have a computer with me here," she said, feeling embarrassed.

Iris recited directions, and Helen wrote them down. "See you soon," she said, and hung up.

All summer, Helen had felt like something was missing. She had been afraid that that something was Iain, whom she had been trying hard to convince herself she didn't miss. But she now realized what the hole was: it was the girls she missed. All of them together, warts and all. She'd seen them, yes, had visited them all, but they had not all been together at once. She thought about the last time she had seen Fiona, during an early fall visit to Rye. She hadn't seemed like herself, but Helen had thought perhaps it was early menopause. She'd had it early, too. It was the likely explanation, Helen reassured herself now, and this Iris just didn't realize.

But still, it was an opportunity. She needed to seize it.

"Ilsa?"

"Hi, Mom." There was a clatter in the background.

"You sound busy. Should I call you back?"

"I'm cooking. Thanksgiving dinner." There was another clatter, and a sigh. "Although it's not going that well."

"What are you making?"

"I was trying to re-create Fiona's menu. Huge mistake. Do you have any idea how high-maintenance chestnuts are?"

"I'm calling because I think I need you. Correction: Fiona needs you." She explained about Iris's call. "I don't know if there's really anything wrong with her, but I thought we might as well go and check it out. It seems like a good chance for all of us to be together, since our early summer weekend was such a bust this year. I'm calling Liane next. If I can pry her away from her brand-new knight in shining armor—who is an absolute *doll*, by the way—I can use my points to fly her down. And I called Iris back to see if we could get our own room and she said of course. She loves the idea of all of us coming. Although I suppose if you're doing Thanksgiving dinner, you can't . . ."

There was a sound like a spoon and pot banging into the sink. "I'm officially not cooking any longer," Ilsa said decisively. "Tim and Michael can handle it. Or they can take the kids to the football game at the high school and eat hot dogs. At this point I really don't care. I'm just not a traditional feast type of girl, it turns out. So how do I get there? Should we meet somewhere first?"

"I think you're about an hour and a half away and I'm two."

"Let's just both start driving and see who gets there first."

"Road trip!" Helen said, but Ilsa didn't laugh.

It was dark when Helen turned her car down the spa's driveway. She had been in the car for an extra hour, having turned off the GPS Iain had once given her because she was always getting lost. It felt a little pathetic to be actively defying someone she hadn't seen or spoken to in months, not since that afternoon at the cottage when she had shouted at him about his greens and he had said, "You should go," and she had.

I didn't want the GPS. I told him I didn't need to be told where to go all the time, that I'm excellent with directions. And then he had said, "I just always want you to be able to find your way back to me."

She felt a plummeting sadness. Just then, she hit a patch of black ice and started to skid and thought, *What if I die out here, what if this is it?* but she felt nothing at all in response to this thought.

She turned on the GPS.

Soon, at the insistence of the disembodied voice, she turned into the parking lot of the spa, stopped the car, and cut the engine. The building was constructed of stained wood planks with churchlike windows, and there was an ivy-covered stone tower with a peaked roof in the center. She could see there was a lake. She looked around the lot and saw Ilsa's car. The windows were fogged up. She must have been sitting inside, waiting.

Helen got out of the car and walked toward Ilsa's car, carrying her small bag. Ilsa wiped the fog off her window, peered out at her mother, and then reached into the backseat for her valise and got out of her car. Helen embraced her and told her she looked beautiful instead of tired. *This spa weekend will do* her *good, too.*

"We can surprise Fiona, and then maybe you can take a bath and go to bed," Helen said.

"Surprise her," Ilsa repeated. "Do you really think she's going to be excited to see us?"

"She takes on so much. Maybe she's just stressed out. Maybe we can *convince* her to be happy we're here."

"Helen. This is Fiona we're talking about."

Helen grimaced slightly. "Maybe we need to wait until Liane gets here?" Liane had always been their buffer. And she was taking an early morning flight. She'd be there, in a taxi, in time for a late breakfast.

"We can go to her room, all three of us, in the morning," Ilsa said.

"That's a better idea, isn't it?"

They walked across the lot, pushed open the heavy door, and entered a lobby with stone walls and high ceilings. It was empty, but there was a bell and a sign that read PLEASE RING. Ilsa sat down in a chair. Helen didn't want to seem impatient; she could already tell this was no place for impatience—there was a sign beside the bell that read ANGELS GIVE US FAITH TO WAIT FOR MYSTERIES TO BE REVEALED—so she stood and waited. Finally, though, she leaned forward and tapped the bell gently. Then she went back to the pamphlet she was reading, which said that the center rested on a mineral deposit with healing properties. There was a labyrinth for meditation, a sea salt pool, a green-tea hot tub, infrared saunas, a spa, yoga, guided meditation, vision-boarding, and, of course, the chakra readings and color therapy sessions.

A moment later, a woman with shoulder-length dark hair—she was likely the same age as Helen, but her skin was smooth and her eyes were clear and Helen felt momentarily envious, having just that morning looked in the mirror and compared her own skin to an old piece of flannel—rounded the corner. She was wearing a white blouse, several colored scarves, dangly earrings (exactly as Helen had suspected), and black yoga pants. Her feet were bare.

"You must be Helen. I'm Iris. Thank you so much for coming. And is this one of the sisters?"

"Yes, I'm Ilsa." Ilsa stood. She extended her hand, but Iris hugged her instead, then turned and hugged Helen. She smelled of patchouli.

"And your other daughter is coming first thing in the morning?"

Helen nodded.

"This is so wonderful. I really feel we're gathering the forces Fiona needs to survive this."

"That's the thing: survive what?" Helen said.

"What she's going through," Iris said.

"But *what* exactly is she going through?"

"Let's just go upstairs," Iris said. "I'll take you to Fiona's room first, and you can get settled in your own space later."

"Um, well—" Ilsa began. Helen opened her mouth to speak, too, but what was she going to say? *Actually, we thought we might hide in our room until Liane, our buffer, gets here. Fiona doesn't like either of us much.*

Iris stood, her head tilted slightly, waiting for one of them to voice whatever it was they wanted to say. But neither of them continued.

"Has it ever seemed to either of you that Fiona has a drinking problem?" Iris said.

"*Never.*"

"I'm not even going to answer that," Ilsa said.

"What about prescription abuse?"

"Are you joking?" Helen said.

"Of course not." Iris shook her head. "This is not a laughing matter, not at all." She said it like it was all one word: "a*tall.*" Helen felt chastened. "Fiona is in a very dark place. I'm just trying to figure out where it might all be coming from. She has one of the saddest, most despairing auras I've ever seen. Her chakras . . . they're in wild disarray."

As though that explained everything, Iris turned and started walking again, up a staircase and down a hallway painted pale yellow and lined with wall sconces and doorways, before tapping on a doorway with the number 212 on the outside. No answer. She tapped again. "Fiona? It's Iris." Still no answer. Iris frowned, and Helen began to feel sick, scared. Before she could stop herself, she reached up and banged the door with her fist. Iris looked startled.

"Fiona!" Helen shouted.

"Mom," Ilsa said. "She might just be sleeping. Maybe she took a sleeping pill."

"I have the master key," Iris whispered. "I'll let us in and we can see if she's okay."

It was only when Helen was standing beside the bed her daughter was sleeping in, when she had touched her chest softly to make sure she was breathing, the way she had when each of the girls were babies because she had a friend who lost a child to crib death and the memory of her haunted eyes had never left Helen, that her own breathing returned to normal. The light from the hall and the noise of the three of them entering the room didn't cause Fiona to stir. And there was indeed a bottle of Tylenol PMs on the end table beside Fiona. Only a few were missing—Iris had checked the bottle like she was a forensics expert, and Helen had found herself waiting, holding her breath. But no. She hadn't done anything drastic. *Of course not. Not Fiona.*

"We shouldn't wake her," Iris said. "You'll have to see her in the morning."

"I agree," Helen whispered, feeling relieved. They filed out of the room.

"I still can't believe that crazy woman called my emergency contact," Fiona said the next morning at breakfast. She was rubbing her head like she had a hangover. She saw Helen watching.

"Caffeine withdrawal headache," she explained.

"You have to admit, it's pretty funny," Liane said, pouring more of the chai tea from the carafe on the table into her cup. She dumped in almond milk and looked up. "Seriously, no coffee here? None at all?"

"None," Fiona said. "I made the mistake of asking and got a lecture on the evils of caffeine at such high levels. I'm definitely the black sheep around here."

"Think of *that*," Ilsa said.

"No booze, either. Apparently a lot of people come here to detox."

"I see." Helen tried to arrange her expression in a manner that wouldn't betray her disappointment that, in addition to no coffee with breakfast, she was also not going to be able to have wine with dinner.

Meanwhile, Fiona's mood was oddly buoyant. She had been happy to see Liane, at least, and seemed to be tolerating the fact that Helen and Ilsa were there. But Helen was unsettled. Fiona seemed fine—so what was this dark problem Iris was talking about?

Helen cleared her throat. This wasn't easy for her, but she had to ask. "Fiona, why did you put me down and not Tim as the person to call in case of emergency?"

"He's out of town," Fiona said without missing a beat.

"No, he's not," Ilsa said. "*You* asked me to cook dinner for him tomorrow. He most certainly is in town."

"That's right: I asked you to cook for him and the boys," Fiona said, her voice now irritated. "What happened to that, by the way? I guess they'll be having pizza?"

"Hot dogs, actually. And you heard Helen. That woman said it was an emergency, and I'm a good sister, so I came. Besides, after about an hour of trying to emulate you in the kitchen, I needed a spa weekend, too."

"Spa weekend," Fiona repeated. "Is that it, Helen? You think this is fun?"

"I didn't call it a spa weekend, Ilsa did. And besides, whatever it is, we're here because we're worried about you and we love you. So if something is going on with you, I think you should tell us."

"Are you sure you're not just here for the color therapy and meditation labyrinth?"

Helen frowned. Why had Fiona always made it so difficult to love her? And why did she always have to be right?

Iris had entered the dining room and was walking from table to table, talking to the guests. Her feet were bare again. She arrived at their table. "Ladies! Good morning. What's on the agenda for today?"

Fiona didn't say anything.

"I really need a pedicure," Liane ventured. "And, um, do you have family counseling?" But no one laughed and Iris smiled sympathetically.

"Check in at the front desk after breakfast and see if they can book you in for one. There's also yoga right after breakfast, vision-boarding before lunch, and mindfulness meditation at two. And tonight . . ." Iris smiled and clapped her hands together lightly. "This is exactly what you need. There's a new moon, so we're doing our traditional fire ceremony by the lake. All guests attend. You'll be there, ladies." She put a hand on each of her shoulders, and walked away from the table.

"For someone so new-agey, she's surprisingly bossy," Ilsa said.

That night, they stood by the fire, side by side in jackets and scarves and hats: Helen's hand-knit and wool, a long scarf draped many times around her neck; Liane in layers of sweaters, one with a hood, and her jean jacket; Fiona's a navy beret-style cap, no scarf but a high-buttoned neck on her pewter-gray coat; Ilsa in a bell-shaped red coat. She had forgotten a hat, so Iris had lent her a multicolored woolen one that looked out of place, but still, she was striking.

Iris was holding a copper bucket. It was filled with pink and amber stones. "I add a little bit of a twist to the traditional fire ceremony by incorporating these rocks into it," she said, smiling at each of the women gathered before her, her head turning so she could make eye contact with each of them. There were about two dozen. "Since there are so many rocks and crystals around here and they have healing properties, I like to make use of them. What I need you all to do right now is go into the bucket and choose the rock that seems right to you. Don't overthink it, whatever feels right, whatever your fingers land on. Then just hold it, or put it in your pocket. You'll keep it with you until the end of the ceremony."

They each did so. Fiona went last, Helen noticed, but at least she took one.

Now Iris picked up some small strips of paper, and handed one to each woman, along with a pen. "Write on this paper your deepest, most fervent wish for yourself and your life. Long-term, short-term, whatever it is that's most important to you. We'll use the power of the new moon to help you manifest your goals, your desires." Helen heard someone snort softly. She was sure it was Fiona. She didn't want to look at her. Iris also handed out small pieces of cardboard so they'd all have something to write on.

Helen looked down at her blank scrap of paper. *Whatever it is that's most important to you.*

My girls, she thought. *My girls are most important to me.* She had believed, when she became a mother, that she would not be one of those women who was defined by motherhood. Maybe that was why Fiona resented her so much, because Helen had fought against the maternal pull a little, when she was pregnant with Fiona and when Fiona was an infant. In some ways, she had been trying to make a point, not trying to *become* a mother.

She wrote: *I want my girls to be happy. That's all I want for my life.* Writing this made her feel a little sad. Her own mother had been a martyr and it had done nothing but drive Helen away. It wasn't easy to exist when there was a person in the world so uncomfortably invested in your happiness. If you didn't attain it, you felt like a failure. Helen sometimes marveled at how, even though Fiona had never met Abigail, she was in so many ways the same type of mother.

Helen looked around the circle. Everyone else seemed to be either thinking or writing. Except Ilsa, who was just staring into the fire. Helen underlined what she had written. She worried about her girls now more than ever, she realized.

"Is everyone ready?" Iris said. She was now holding a bunch of sage and a lighter. Helen breathed in the evocative smell of wood smoke. She looked out across the lake, then up at the sky. The air was cold. Winter was coming.

"I just want you all to know I saw coyote tracks out here this afternoon when I was preparing for the ceremony," Iris said as she lit the sage and waved it around. It smelled to Helen a little like a turkey cooking. "I found that interesting. He must have been around today. So we welcome his spirit energy, and his ability to help us adjust to the way things are, rather than fighting against them or fruitlessly wishing for them to be different."

Now Iris asked the women to form a closer circle around the fire. "Come on, get close, don't be afraid to touch one another. The touch of another human being is a blessing. It should be *celebrated*." Fiona was standing beside Helen, and Ilsa was on her other side, and Liane was on the other side of Ilsa. Iris was speaking again. "The traditional fire ceremony is a Native American tradition that can be about many things: letting go of the past, inviting in the future, or simply being grateful to the divinities. I like to do it during the new moon and focus on intentions: inviting goodness, saying goodbye to what we don't need, focusing on what we need to do to move forward. Generally, something is brought to burn in the fire, and that's what we're going to do with those pieces of paper you just wrote on. But before we can welcome these things into our lives, we need to get rid of what we no longer need." She put the sage out in a bucket of water and held up a small rock. "I want you to take your rock or stone in your hand."

Helen did. She felt her daughters around her, reaching their hands into their pockets.

"Now I want you to think of something that's been dragging you down. An emotion, a feeling, a thought pattern, anything. Something that you need to let go of. It can be helpful to boil it down to one word. Say that word in your mind as you hold your rock. When you're ready, walk to the edge of the lake, and throw your rock in."

Helen was surprised when Fiona walked to the edge of the lake first and flung her rock, then returned to stand by the fire, her piece of paper in her hand tightly folded. She was already starting to hold it out to the fire. "Wait," Iris whispered to her.

Helen looked down at her stone, a small pink quartz. *Regret,* she thought. About Iain, about the mistakes she had made, about everything. *And I need to stop trying to write my stupid memoirs. It's all been said, and I don't need to go back and nitpick.* She walked to the edge of the lake and threw her rock as far as she could, then turned away, picturing it sinking to the bottom. She saw Liane then, about ten feet down, standing by the water. She realized her daughter's shoulders were shaking and she quickly approached. "Liane?"

Her daughter looked up and wiped a tear from beneath her eye. "I was so skeptical when she was talking, and then I took this rock, and the word *grief* came into my mind, and I thought about my dad and . . . and now I'm just standing here, afraid to let it go. But I want to, because everything in my life is so great right now . . . but I still feel so sad sometimes. And I think it might be because I'm holding on to him."

Helen reached out her hand. "Can I hold it for a minute?" she asked, and Liane nodded. Helen took the rock and squeezed it.

"It wasn't us, you know," she said. "It wasn't our fault."

"I know," Liane whispered.

"He was depressed, and it is a sickness, but you don't have it. And you're not going to get it. Okay?"

Liane nodded again, but the tears still fell.

"And just because you let go of this, of the sadness and regret about what you may or may not have been able to do to help him, does not mean that you are letting go of *him.* He will always be inside you. The good parts of him. And there were many. He was the most incredible person. He loved you so much." Helen opened her palm and looked down at the stone. It was dull and flat, but there were little flecks of brightness. "I'm going to keep a little bit of this grief for you, okay? I'm going to hold it for you, and whenever you want to talk about it, I'm here." She squeezed the rock in her palm again, then looked up and pressed the rock back into Liane's hands. *Oh, Wes. How I wish things could have been different.*

As Helen walked away, she heard a small splash. She also saw Ilsa, up ahead—but Ilsa didn't throw her rock. She put her rock in her pocket and walked quickly back to join the circle before Helen could catch up.

Back at the fire, Iris said, "Please give your pieces of paper to me." Then she cleared her throat and held the small pages before her. "Now it's time for us to trust each other. This is not a traditional element of the ceremony, but in the spirit of sisterhood that I like to foster here, I think it's important. I'm going to pass these pieces of paper around. You'll each get someone else's. I want you to read it, and I want you to focus on wanting what this person wants, this person you may not even know, just as much as you would want it for yourself."

Iris handed Helen a piece of paper. It was folded in two. Helen opened it.

I wish none of this had happened. I wish Tim and I could go back to the way things were, that Samira didn't exist, that my life could return to the way it was. I wish to be happy again. She looked at Fiona. Her daughter's eyes were wide with something that looked like fear. *I asked that for you,* she said silently to her daughter. *Happiness, yours. That's all I want. All this other stuff . . . you can talk to me.* She said this internally and willed her daughter to hear her, but knew she didn't. *If you want her to know these things, you have to tell her.* Fiona looked away, back down at the fire, and Helen struggled to focus on what she had been tasked with: desiring all this for her daughter, even though she didn't quite understand it. It wasn't hard, when she cleared her mind. Iris had asked them to want something for another person just as much as they would want it for themselves. But Helen knew she could never want anything for herself as much as she would want it for one of the girls.

"Now put the papers in the fire," Iris said. Helen and Fiona stepped toward the fire at the same moment. When Fiona put her page in the fire, Helen saw the word *girls* just before it burned. Then Fiona turned and strode away from the fire and toward the labyrinth. Helen did not hesitate. She followed.

After the weekend, Helen decided to go back to New York and ask Edie to lunch. She thought Edie would say no, but she accepted.

Helen couldn't sleep the night before.

"Let's order the antipasti for two," Edie said, and just then, and only for then, the years were not between them, the passage of time and all that had happened was not sitting as an uninvited guest at the table. But then Helen looked up from the menu and saw again how Edie had changed, how sleek she was, how unfamiliar. The years had passed, and everything that had happened had indeed happened.

Helen sipped white wine. (This was something that had changed about *her*: in the past, Helen would drink only red wine, believing white wine to be for women of a certain age only. Now she was of that certain age, and knew that a glass of red with lunch would give her a headache and a hangover by three o'clock in the afternoon.) "Exactly what I wanted," she said to Edie, even though she had been considering the Salmone Dijon. She was ravenous after her weekend of spa food.

"And a mixed salad," Edie said to the waiter.

"And plenty of that fantastic bread," Helen added.

The restaurant, Volare, on West Fourth, was where Helen and Edie used to go together once every few weeks when they were younger. (Much younger. All those years, they really had passed.) It was "their" place, or it had been. They had never taken men to the hideaway of a restaurant, even though it would have made sense, with all the candles and the romance. "I enjoy your company over a romantic dinner more than anyone's," Edie had once said to Helen. "If only you were a man." And they had laughed. "Thank God I'm not," Helen had replied.

"We should get prosecco with our lunch," Edie said in a conspiratorial whisper Helen recognized, but that seemed out of place. Her hair was in a chic twist and she was wearing a pantsuit with a scarf tied at her neck. Diamonds at her ears. An expensive-looking watch. It made Helen, in her long skirt, bangles, and woven top, feel dowdy and underdressed. It made her understand why Nate had wanted to be with Edie. This was the kind of woman you could mate for life with. She had an aura of mystery. Maybe he still didn't know her, even now, because Helen certainly hadn't ever.

"Are you all right?" Edie asked. There was a lilt to her voice. As though she had taken on Nate's accent. Helen hadn't asked about him yet. But she would. She would do what she had come to do. She thought of Fiona, in the labyrinth, and the tears on her cheeks and the anguish in her voice. *What a fool I was to think that these men would have no effect on our lives, just because I pretended we didn't need them,* Helen thought. "I'm great," she said aloud, forcing a bright tone. "I just had a spa weekend with the girls, all three of them."

"Good. How nice for you." A beat of silence. "You know," Edie said, "we did what we said we'd never do. We let a man come between us."

"It was a bit more than a man," Helen said. "And it wasn't me, it was *you.*"

"Well, I'm sorry. Like I said all those years ago, we can't control who we love. You of all people should know that."

You of all people. What was that supposed to mean? Helen sat silent. Then she said, "How is Nate, anyway? *Still* touring? *Still* trying to pretend he's twenty?"

"Still doing what he loves to do," Edie corrected her, and Helen felt reproached.

"We've been married twenty years this spring, you know. Marriage isn't easy. But it works for us. And we're happy. And he's well. He sends his regards." All this came out in a rush, as if rehearsed, except it seemed she'd lost her nerve somewhat when she started speaking. *Nerve.* That was what Edie had. People would say that about her, "That girl has a lot of nerve." Helen had once loved her for it.

"Oh, come on. You didn't tell him you were meeting me."

"You underestimate me, *and* him. It was all so long ago, Helen. Water under the bridge."

The waiter had returned and Helen felt a sense of relief at the sound of the cork being released from the bottle.

"So. How *are* the girls?" Edie asked. "Your wonderful, wonderful girls. I've missed them."

"Ilsa has exhibitions in the city from time to time," Helen said. "She's a very talented artist. And Liane is in Toronto. She's teaching at the University of Toronto now. And she's in love with a writer, and very happy."

"A writer. And happy. Now, that might be an oxymoron."

Despite herself, Helen laughed.

"What's this writer's name?" Edie asked.

"Laurence . . . I forget his last name. He writes science fiction or something. A lovely man."

Edie smiled. "Don't you remember how she loved *Little Women,* and how Ilsa used to tease her a little about having a crush on Laurie?" Helen nodded and felt surprised that Edie remembered such a detail. "Sounds like maybe Liane has her Laurie." Edie played with the stem of her glass. "And Fiona?" she finally asked.

"Wonderful. Great. Three boys, a big house in Rye—Ilsa lives near her, actually; their husbands are friends . . ." Helen breathed in. "We talked a lot this weekend, actually. More than we probably ever have. And she—" But the salad had arrived. The waiter asked if they wanted pepper. They both said no.

"Three boys," Edie said. "Wow, good for her."

"Yes." Now Helen worked up some nerve of her own. "You should tell Nate. Tell him he has three grandsons."

Edie sipped the prosecco, pursed her lips. "We never had children, you know," she said, ignoring Helen's entreaty. "I *did* want to." Helen wanted to hit her then, wanted to actually reach across the table and smack her, like they were two women in a daytime drama. "I tried, a little bit frantically, just after we got married. It was too late, though. I should have known that. I'm afraid my quest made the first few years of our marriage rather difficult. But he stuck with me."

Helen buttered a piece of bread and took a bite so she would have time to think before she spoke. She looked at Edie's hands as she chewed. They seemed much older than the rest of her, papery, several rings, nail polish over deep vertical ridges. When Helen finished chewing, she picked up her glass and drained half of it. This was not going as planned. Edie was too smooth. She'd spent too many years with Nate.

Finally, Helen was ready. She said, "Fiona was devastated that Nate rebuffed her when she tried to connect with him, and that you refused—*refused*—to help her. She's never gotten over it. It affects her, affects every part of her life, has the potential to ruin it right now. Maybe Nate thought it was nothing to turn her away, maybe you thought it was nothing to ultimately support him in it, but it *hurt* her. And for what reason? For you to keep him with you, back then, when you weren't sure you'd be able to pull it off? And him—I just never understood it. How many other musicians have *legions* of illegitimate children? Why was it so important to Nate to have no ties whatsoever? Until you, of course. I *do* have to hand it to you. Twenty years is impressive. But why didn't that change him, even a little? Why didn't you use your role as wife to help bring some healing into the life of the closest thing to a daughter you ever had, ever *will* have?" Edie flinched, and Helen felt glad. Old wounds, and now a new one. She felt her heart pounding, realized she was out of breath from her speech.

"Are we going to go back to this again, have the same old fight?" Edie's voice had turned cold. No more relaxed lilt. She was angry. "I told you years ago, the only reason Nate and I ever connected in the first place is because I approached him about Fiona."

"Yes, but how long did you hold out, five minutes? And this is *not* the same old fight. This is not about me being angry with you for taking up with an old lover who was off-limits. I'm over that, was over it practically before the ink was dry on your marriage certificate. Nate doesn't even go down as one of the great loves of my life. He just happened to get me pregnant. But what has always been difficult to get over is the fact that he hurt my daughter. That you *both* did. When Fiona and I talked this weekend, she told me she thought you and I ended our friendship because I was jealous about Nate. I imagine *you've* always thought that, too. But that wasn't it at all."

"Is this why you asked me to have lunch? So you could confront me, shame me into begging Nate to come to his senses, have a paternity test, to acknowledge these grandchildren?"

"A paternity test! Oh, please. We don't want him in our lives, no. Definitely not."

The platter had arrived, and the waiter was asking again if they wanted pepper.

"Not on a seafood platter," Edie snapped.

Helen stood. "I don't think I have much of an appetite now," she said, as the waiter backed away from them.

"I really don't understand what the point of all this was."

"My daughter asked me to do this," Helen said. "And I would do anything for her."

"So it's done. You obviously got some things off your chest about Nate. Now sit down."

Helen shook her head. "I never felt anything for him, Edie. It was *you* I wanted more from."

She paid the bill on her way out the door and finally felt like she had gotten the last word.

part three

What greater thing is there for two human souls than to feel that they are joined for life—to strengthen each other in all labour, to rest on each other in all sorrow, to minister to each other in all pain, to be one with each other in silent unspeakable memories at the moment of the last parting?

—GEORGE ELIOT, *ADAM BEDE*

11

Common Marmoset (*Callithrix jacchus*)

The mating patterns of wild common marmosets, most prevalent in Vienna, are exceptionally complex and vary over time. Parenting behaviors of marmosets often vary, too, especially in fathers. In studies, marmoset males who were already experienced fathers were more motivated to respond to infants and infant stimuli than adult males who had yet to become fathers.

Samira sat in the café and waited. What if he didn't come? *He might not come.* She told herself this, over and over. *And if he doesn't, I will not be disappointed. I didn't invite him here in the first place.* Well, technically, she *had* invited him, she supposed, by sending that letter, by then calling his house in a move that was impulsive and driven by grief—and this despite the fact that her roommate and friend Romy had insisted it had the potential to be a huge mistake. "I'm sorry, Sam," Romy had said. "I'm a Worst-Case Scenario kind of person." They lived together in a small room with a hot plate and a coffeemaker and attended the dance program at the Konservatorium Wien University. "But no matter what happens, I'm here for you."

What if it was a huge mistake? If my mother had wanted him to be in my life, wouldn't she have ensured that he was?

What Samira did know was that her mother hadn't done anything to *protect* her from the knowledge of her father's identity, and that had to mean something. In fact, Marta had purposely left his name for her in a letter she wrote to Samira just before her death, the summer before, of ovarian cancer. Too late, Samira had decided to ask her if she thought it was a good idea to get in touch with her father. She had always asked her mother everything. But when Marta had become sick, Samira had tried to pull away a little. She had decided it was time to start to train herself not to ask her mother about every little thing. Because it had been clear very early that Marta's time was limited and that Samira was going to have to figure it all out eventually by herself, with no mother.

So Samira had read the letter, and thanked her mother for it, and kept it tucked in a drawer. She had focused on other things, like being with her mother, trying not to fall apart in front of her, even comforting Marta's friends, who sometimes wept in front of Samira and said things like, "You poor little thing, now you'll have *no one*." She focused on trying to picture a world without her mother in it so that when the day came that the world actually *didn't* have her mother in it, she wouldn't be so shocked. But finally Samira decided she needed advice from her mother one more time.

Except by then she *was* too late. When she reached for her mother's hand in the hospital bed to ask her, it was already happening. She had started a descent that turned out to be meteoric. She only surfaced one more time, to say, "I love you, Samira, and you are going to be fine. Keep dancing." At which point, Samira buried her face in her mother's shoulder for the last time, hoping to catch her familiar scent but smelling nothing except illness and chemicals there.

Samira looked down at her half-finished cappuccino and thought that she was probably about to start crying, because she always cried when she thought about how her mother had said, "Keep dancing." She stood and walked out into the street. When she was no longer in the café, the feeling went away. She crossed the street and stood, watching the café entrance until a man who might have been him walked inside. She almost crossed the street, but instead she kept walking until she felt numb from the cold.

After a few blocks, Samira stopped and checked her phone. *Except I didn't even give him my cell phone number, did I?*

She walked until she was even colder and her feet were wet. Eventually she was standing in front of her apartment building. She went upstairs.

Romy was sitting cross-legged on the floor, reading a textbook and stretching her gorgeous limbs between paragraphs. "What happened?" Romy asked. "What's going on? He called here. Well, I assume it was him. A man with a deep voice. He said to say *Tim* called. That's his name, right? *Tim?*" Romy said "Tim" funny, trying to stretch it out into more than one syllable, give it more import.

Samira took the piece of paper upon which Romy had written the message—Romy was very conscientious about taking messages—and looked down at it. Then she looked up at Romy. "I couldn't," she said. Romy unwound herself and sat down on the bed beside Samira.

"Couldn't what? Couldn't . . . you mean you stood him up?"

"Yes. It suddenly seemed very wrong. It seemed . . . staged. Meeting him there, at Café Central. As though he is some *uncle* visiting from overseas, and it is my duty to show him the highlights of my city. *Café Central.* Ugh!"

"Why didn't you ask him to go to that place you usually go to?"

"I don't know. It seemed too personal."

"What are you going to do?"

"Nothing. He probably doesn't ever want to speak to me again."

"I doubt that. He came all the way here."

"He's probably really mad, though."

"He didn't sound mad. He actually sounded more worried. Very fatherlike, in fact. Like he thought maybe something had happened to you. I bet he's still sitting there. I know I was against this initially, but he really did sound nice. You should go meet him."

"I can't." And it was true. Samira knew she couldn't do it now. She wanted to, wanted to know if she had been right about who he was, about whether he was indeed the man in the dark trench coat with the gray hair and burgundy scarf who had paused outside the café and looked up at it for a moment, as if to make sure he was in the right place, before going inside. She had almost crossed the street and said, *Come, don't go in there. Let's go somewhere else,* and then taken him where she usually went, to Kaffee Alt Weine, at Bäckerstrasse 9.

Samira thought for several moments. Then she said, "I should call him, shouldn't I?" And she reached for the phone and dialed the number Romy had written down for her before she could think about it much more. A man answered, "Hello?" and Samira paused, but not for too long because she didn't want him to hang up.

"It's Samira," she said.

"Hi! I'm sorry, did I go to the wrong place? I'm here at the Café Central but I don't think I see you anywhere, although I *have* embarrassed myself by asking a few blond girls if they're named Samira. One of them was, actually, but not you. Isn't that funny? Maybe not." He seemed very nervous. Romy had backed discreetly away and was doing a downward dog in the corner of the room.

"I'm sorry," Samira said. "Something came up and I can't—I can't come."

"Oh." He was disappointed, she could tell. But not angry. Not at all.

"I can see you tomorrow." She glanced at Romy, at her upside-down face. "Tomorrow I'm going skating with my roommate." Romy's eyes widened and she fell into child's pose. "In front of city hall. You could come with us."

Romy rolled over. *Skating?* she mouthed.

"Skating," the man repeated, the man who was her father. "Well, I didn't bring my skates . . ."

"You can rent them at the rink. Unless you don't skate. In which case I suppose we could—" But she suddenly wanted to skate. It seemed like the perfect option. *Skating with my father.*

"No, I skate. My sons and I—" He stopped for a second and she found herself wincing. "We skate quite often. They like to play hockey."

My sons and I. "I, ah . . ." This was it. This was the problem. This was why she hadn't been able to walk into the coffee shop and why she now was telling him that he needed to meet her at the ice rink in front of city hall the next day, where they would skate together, the three of them, and she wouldn't have to sit and stare at him from across a table. Because he had a whole other life, and she wasn't a part of it. There were sons, half brothers who really weren't and never would be her family. "You poor little thing," her mother's friends had said. "Now you'll have no one." Or she wouldn't, and perhaps the knowing would be more painful.

Samira still remembered the moment in life when she realized she was supposed to have a father, that it wasn't *quite* normal that she and Marta were alone. She was in kindergarten, and it was her second day, and she and a group of girls were playing "family." "You have to be the papa, Samira," said a little girl named Pia, the leader of the small group of girls. "The papa?" Samira repeated. And it wasn't that she didn't know *what* a papa was. But at that moment she didn't know *who* a papa was, had no idea how a papa would behave, and she stood staring at Pia and wishing she could go home to her mother and ask her.

At the end of the day, she did. "Do I have a papa?" were the first words out of her mouth when Marta picked her up in the schoolyard. Marta frowned and looked around. "Did someone say something to you?" she asked. Samira shook her head. Marta took her hand and led her down the street. She was silent, and Samira waited, and several moments later Marta said, "You don't have a papa, Samira. You just have me, but it's all right. I'm your mama *and* your papa."

Then, when Samira was eleven, she said to Marta, "You told me once I had no father, but how can that be true?" She'd learned about it in school by now. And she didn't say *papa* anymore. She wasn't a *baby*. "Everyone has a father. It's not possible that I don't have one."

"You're right," Marta said. "You do have a father. But he lives far away and you'll probably never meet him." Perhaps an outsider would think Marta was being callous, but she was simply a frank and practical woman. Much later, when Samira was a teenager, she said to her, "I had never planned to hide it from you. But I suppose I never found a proper way to explain it, did I?"

"Who was he?" Samira had asked. She was fourteen and a half now. She remembered that her heart was pounding and her hands were sweating but she was trying hard to act like it was nothing.

"He was a young man I met when I was working at your aunt's hostel for the summer."

"You used to work there, too?"

Marta nodded. "Yes. I worked at the front desk, and I cleaned the kitchen twice a day. One afternoon, I went into the kitchen and he was there with a friend and they had some horrible chunk of beef they'd gotten from a butcher who should have given it to them for free, and they were trying to make *tafelspitz.*" She smiled at the memory and Samira's palms felt less sweaty. "I took pity on them and helped them, mostly because I had never seen any young men like that trying to make anything other than cheese sandwiches or pasta or maybe hamburgers. And they invited me to join them for dinner and I finished my shift and we sat on the back terrace and drank wine and . . ." She tucked her dark blond hair behind her ears. "And he stayed for a while. For that whole summer. His friend continued traveling, went to Hungary, I think, but Tim stayed."

"Tim?" She had said it the same way Romy had, drawing it out, making it significant.

Marta nodded.

"And then what?"

"And then he ran out of money, and he had to go home."

"Oh." Samira truly didn't know what to say. Finally: "Did he know you were pregnant?"

"*I* didn't even know at the time. Listen, he was nice. I really, really liked him. But I knew two things: When I did find out I was pregnant, I knew I wanted you. And I also knew I didn't want to be with him just because I was pregnant. So I let him be, and I never regretted it."

After that, there was really nothing else Samira could say. She pushed the idea of a father from her mind, and, most of the time, found it easy to do so. *I'm your mama* and *your papa.* It was true. Marta was.

Then finally, one day, when she was nearly sixteen and had had her heart broken for the first time, Samira asked Marta, as her mother gave her tea and rubbed her back, if she had loved her father. Marta looked mildly surprised. Then she said, "I never really got the chance to find out. One thing: I'll always be grateful to him. That I can tell you. I see some good things in you that don't come from me, like how driven you are, how ambitious and dependable, and I'm grateful to him for those things—and for you."

"What about when he left? When he ran out of money and had to go back. Were you sad?"

"Of course I was. I cried at the train station. I can still remember his face in the window."

For some reason, this made Samira feel exponentially better. She had wiped away her tears and finished her tea.

You did love him, in your way.

She had never asked any more questions about this Tim person.

Now Samira and Tim made arrangements and she gave him her cell phone number so there would be no backing out of her plan, then hung up the phone.

"Skating? In front of city hall? Really? And you thought *Café Central* was touristy?" Romy said.

"I know. I know. But can you come? Please?"

"Of course I can come." She shook her head. "But I warn you, Sam. This kind of stuff makes me nervous. I bet I'm going to start to babble. I'm going to be worse than you."

"It's fine, we'll be skating, how much can you possibly babble while we're skating?"

"A lot. How about this? If things seem to be going well, I'll pretend my skates don't fit or I'm hurt and I'll go sit on the sidelines?"

"Let's just wait and see what happens. Thank you for doing this with me. You're a good friend." And Samira stretched out on her single bed and soon fell asleep.

They skated in wide circles. Because she was beside him and because she had to watch where she was going, she couldn't look at him and study his face. Romy did indeed pretend to hurt her ankle, then sat on a bench and played with her phone, although Samira suspected she was trying to listen to what they were saying every time she and Tim skated past. They weren't saying much, though. Samira had dozens of questions—about what her mother was like when she was young, about what New York City was like, and about those boys he had mentioned, her half brothers—if they were any good at hockey, for example. She wanted to picture them. But how could she say any of this? She was too nervous. They both were. It felt strangely like a first date. When he had arrived at the rink, he had handed her a small wrapped gift. "Because Christmas is next week," he had said. She had wondered if she was supposed to open it. She didn't. She put it in her backpack.

Her toes started to get numb. Her skates were too small. They had belonged to her mother. "Your feet are bigger than mine," Marta would say. "That means you're going to be taller." But Samira had ended up about the same height and size, which meant that they had often traded clothes. Still, Samira had given most of her mother's clothes away to charity, even the ones she had coveted while her mother was still alive. She often regretted this. Once, she had seen a woman in a dark green peacoat similar to one her mother had owned and had imagined it really *was* her mother's jacket.

"How do you like Vienna?" she asked Tim, in an attempt to make conversation.

"Oh, it's gorgeous. Especially in winter. I've never seen it in winter."

"That's right, when you were here it was . . ."

"Summer," he said. "When I was here and I met your mother, it was summer." That was the closest they had come to talking about any of it. They skated around the rink one more time. She noticed that the spot on the bench where Romy had been sitting was empty, and she felt a little bit grateful and a little bit nervous. She opened her mouth, but Tim spoke first.

"I'm not going to lie to you and say that your mother was the great love of my life, Samira, but I did care for her. I have always had fond memories of her. She was a beautiful young woman, and you look just like her. She was beautiful on the inside, too. Smart. Kind. Practical. I want you to know that I have no excuse for the fact that I never sought you out. I wasn't sure what to do—it's not an excuse, and you probably know this: Marta was very strong and forthright and just . . . if I'd had any doubt that she'd be able to take care of you on her own . . ."

"She took great care of me," Samira said firmly. "We never needed anyone else."

"But still," said Tim. "I'm still sorry I wasn't around. I hope that maybe one day you can forgive me."

They skated twice more around the rink before Samira spoke again. "I'm not mad at you," she said. "I never was."

They both slowed until they were standing on the ice beside each other.

"I think I've had enough skating," Samira said.

He seemed not to want their outing to be over. "How about you go and open that present I brought you?" They went back to the bench and she reached into her backpack and unearthed the small parcel. Under the paper, she found a photograph of her mother in a small silver frame that felt heavy and expensive. The photo was sepia and her mother was young, looking away from the camera at someone else, her mouth open, talking or laughing, her hand up, moving through the air, a blur. She had always used her hands when she talked. Samira ran her cold finger over the glass. Then she put the framed photo in her bag and started to cry.

Tim hesitated. Then he reached across what seemed like a very large divide but was in fact only about a foot or so of space, and her face landed on his shoulder.

At one point he pulled a handkerchief from his pocket and gave it to her and she thought, *My father is the sort of man who has handkerchiefs on his person at all times.* At another point, she said to him, "I don't cry very often," and hoped that this provided some sort of explanation for why she had been crying into his shoulder for so long. Eventually she lifted her head and looked down at the shoulder of his jacket and saw the marks of her tears there and forced herself to stop. He looked down at the tear marks, too, and then at her. *This is your father,* she thought as she stared up at him. She realized she had hoped that if she found him, if he came, it might help to fill the hole her mother's death had left. *I'm your mama* and *your papa,* Marta had said.

But simply finding that long-lost papa didn't make the loss of Marta feel any smaller.

"I really miss her," she said to him.

"I'm sorry," he said. "Is there anything I can do?"

"I don't think so," she said.

"But you know that I would, right? If there was anything you needed, you know that I would do it, or at least try?"

And suddenly there it was. A very slight parting of the waves of her grief. *But you know that I would, right?*

"Thank you, Tim," she said.

12
Red-Tailed Hawk (*Buteo jamaicensis*)

The red-tailed hawk is generally a monogamous bird, often pairing for life or at least for many years. During courtship, the male and female fly in wide circles while uttering shrill cries. The male will dive steeply, then climb again, then repeat, showing off for his potential mate. He will sometimes also grasp her talons briefly with his own, as though trying to hold her hands.

iane was lying on the couch in the living room of Laurence's town house, looking up at the ceiling and around at the bookshelves, the colors—taupes and navies; the style was manly, and yet also there was a slight feminine touch: he *had* once lived here with his wife and daughters and she was okay with that, not being the jealous type. At least she hoped.

The stereo was on. The music, much like his reading taste, was mostly from the sixties and seventies: Arlo Guthrie, Neil Young, Bob Dylan. He had asked her what she liked and she had said, "I like listening to the music that makes *you* happy." She closed her eyes for a moment and then he was there, holding two glasses of wine. "What are you smiling about?" he said.

"I was smiling?"

"You were. You were lying there with your eyes closed, smiling."

"Then I must have been smiling about you," she said.

He smiled. "I'm smiling about you, too," he said.

"I love you," she said.

"I love you, too."

The song changed to "Sundown" by Gordon Lightfoot and he said, as she knew he would, "I *love* this song." She was growing to know the songs he would say he loved, growing to appreciate how important music was to him, growing to love the way he would always, always tell her *why* he liked a song. Mostly it was because of a line, a certain lyric that appealed to the writer in him. "This part, this part," he was saying now. "'*Sometimes I think it's a shame, when I get feeling better, when I'm feeling no pain.*' *That's* the line. It always used to make me think about how maybe you can't create something beautiful unless you're suffering." Now he put down the wineglasses, and ran his hand along the side of her body and up to her face. "I'll probably never write anything good ever again, because I'm so happy. And I'm fine with that."

"Have I destroyed your literary career?"

"Can you be happy being married to a librarian?"

Being married to. They hadn't actually talked about getting married—they'd only been together for five months—but sometimes it came up, casually, in moments like these. And Liane would thrill silently but try not to analyze it too much. Really, the only thing she cared about was being with him, and she *was* with him, right that very second, and she *would* be with him, for as long as they—

They were kissing, but the slamming of the front door, hard, twice, caused them to jump apart, and Laurence spilled one of the glasses of wine. "Shit."

Now, in all the commotion, they could hear Beatrice upstairs crying. "Shit," he said again. And then Isabel was in the kitchen, lifting the lid of the pasta sauce, sticking her finger in. "Ouch! That's hot."

"Iz, you've woken your sister," Laurence said. Liane was now sitting, then standing, not sure what to do with herself. Laurence returned to the living room with a bunch of paper towels, and Isabel followed him, approaching him and kissing him on the cheek. "Hi, Daddy," she said. "Sorry. I just didn't want to walk in on anything, so I decided to be as loud as possible." And she gave Liane a look. Or maybe she didn't. *Be nice, be nice.*

"Hi," Liane said, feeling awkward. Beatrice was now howling, "Moooommmmmy." It made Liane feel awful, out of place. Events like this were the chief reason she didn't truly like to come over during weeks that Laurence had the girls—but of course she never lasted in her resolve. Neither of them could stand to be apart for more than a day or two, so a week was unthinkable.

Laurence's hands were full of sopping paper towels. "Coming, Bea!" he shouted. "Daddy's here, coming!"

"I'll finish dinner," Liane said, wanting to feel useful.

"It's okay, it's done, we'll eat when I come back down. Just let me finish cleaning this up."

"I'll finish, you go."

"Really, I can do it."

"It smells good, Daddy," Isabel said.

Liane excused herself and went to the first-floor powder room, where she splashed cold water on her face because it had turned red.

Back in the living room, she found Isabel sitting on the couch. She'd turned off Gordon Lightfoot and was flicking aimlessly through the television channels. She was wearing a tight Decemberists T-shirt and low-slung jeans and she still had her shoes on and her feet were on the fabric.

"Hey," Liane said.

"Hey," Isabel replied, still staring at the television. It was an infomercial for a Shammy. "That would have cleaned up that wine my dad spilled pretty good. Look, they're even doing a demo with wine."

Liane nodded. "Yeah, for sure," she said, thinking that it was strange that whenever she tried to talk to Isabel she was reduced from being a PhD graduate to sounding like a monosyllabic teenager. "So, uh, what did you get up to tonight?" Isabel's eyebrows shot up and she looked at Liane sideways.

"I *told* my dad where I was," she said. "I was with Mykayla. We went to Starbucks. And now I'm here."

"Yeah, great, cool," Liane said, trying to indicate that she wasn't trying to grill her but knowing she just sounded dumb. She had the sudden urge to go home, make tea and toast, get into bed, and read magazines.

But then Laurence was at the bottom of the stairs and she looked over at him and experienced that shock of recognition that happened almost every time he entered a room. *You. There you are. The One.*

"There," he said. "She's back to sleep. Iz, maybe next time you come in the house, even if you're afraid you might interrupt something, you can be a little more quiet?"

And that was all it took to set her off. She rolled her eyes, tossed the remote to the floor, shouted, "Thanks a lot, blame it all on me!" and stomped up the stairs. When she reached her room, she slammed her door, and Beatrice, of course, began to cry again. For a moment Liane thought Laurence was going to cry, too, there was such despair on his face—and also anger; his jaw worked with it, she could tell he was holding it in. *But she deserves it,* she wanted to say. *You can't be the nice guy all the time. You're not doing her any favors.*

Liane wasn't the mother, though. What did she know? Gillian and Laurence had been talking a lot lately about how to handle Isabel, and apparently disciplining her, for anything, wasn't an option just then.

"I can go up," Liane offered, but they both knew Beatrice would just cry harder, probably start crying for her mother again if she saw Liane. So instead she sat back down on the couch and watched Laurence walk away, then turned her attention to the TV, where the man was wiping up spill after spill after spill.

Their beginning was now a story they passed back and forth when people asked. "I would check her out every day from the end of the dock," Laurence would say. "I lost my nerve several times as I drove," Liane would say. "Once, I stopped at a rest stop and almost decided to turn back—" "I actually thought for a moment I was dreaming, that it couldn't really be her . . ." Then Liane would start blushing and they would both falter. Really, it was almost too personal. She had stepped onto the dock, walked toward him. He was in a sweater, looking out at the lake. The sun was setting fast, because it was fall. He had heard the creaking of the dock and turned when he had seen her. She was holding the beat-up literary magazine in her hands, but of course it was practically mush at that point, so she had to explain what it was. She had faltered, thinking, *This is crazy, so she had red hair, maybe it wasn't me,* but he had stopped her and said, "It was you, I wrote that because of you. I know I don't know you, but I want to." It was the culmination of every single fantasy, every single make-believe crush she had ever had. But despite their relationship happening quickly, despite it feeling exactly right, they had agreed that they would wait before introducing Liane to the girls.

"Maybe we should even wait a year," Liane had suggested at the start. It seemed like a good time limit back then, mostly because she was a little intimidated, and also because she wanted her relationship with Laurence to remain insular, to be able to grow the way other relationships did without the pressure of a family. She wasn't sure if this was fair. She didn't say this to him.

But after just a few months it became clear that it didn't make sense to keep Liane and the girls in two different compartments. The first step had been to meet Gillian, Laurence's ex-wife, who had insisted that she meet anyone Laurence introduced the girls to. (There had not been anyone else.) Liane had dreaded this, but Gillian hadn't been as bad as she had thought she'd be. She seemed defensive, a bit jumpy, and very much like she didn't *want* to like Liane, but Liane could tell she didn't hate her. For Liane's part, she felt relieved. Gillian was pretty enough, almost frenetically skinny—Laurence had once mentioned that she ran obsessively—but she wasn't gorgeous, as Liane had dreaded. Not like Ilsa, for example. Not sexy, not namelessly alluring, not the kind of woman a man could never get over. Liane wouldn't have been able to handle an Ilsa. In some ways, she supposed, Gillian reminded Liane of Fiona, but she wasn't quite as together, not as solid. Plus, she'd cheated on Laurence. Fiona would never do that.

That night, after meeting Gillian, Liane lay beside Laurence on his bed and asked him questions she had been afraid to ask before, about his marriage, his relationship with Gillian, their parting. And he said things to her that she always carried with her. "Did you love her?" Liane had asked, hating herself as soon as she had said it. "Of course you did, sorry. She was your wife."

"I loved her at first more than I did later, and I loved her later because I felt like I had to try. But I didn't *know*, Liane. I didn't know what love could be. And now I do."

"Do you miss her?" she'd asked. "Like, when you're taking care of the girls, and you're tired, and maybe you . . . just feel alone. Do you miss her?"

"When I feel alone, it's because I miss *you*."

"But what about before me, before us?"

He had rolled over on his side to face her. "It feels like there was always you. You on the dock and then you not on the dock. That's all I remember about feeling loss and longing during that time. When you were gone, I missed *you*. I never missed her the way I missed you, and I didn't even know you. I only knew who I thought you might be."

They'd made love then, and the next day, barely four months in, Liane had met Isabel and Beatrice—and unfortunately, on nights like this one, Liane found herself wishing they'd waited.

"Maybe I should just go home," Liane ventured when he came back down.

"Do you *want* to go home?" He sounded hurt.

"Well, no, but . . . I can't help you. I mean, I can't go up there if she cries again, and Isabel clearly doesn't want me around, and—"

"Why would you say Isabel doesn't want you around?"

Liane's heart was pounding. They'd never had a fight. *Is this a fight? Or are we about to have one?* "Well, look at the way she behaves when I'm around. It's pretty clear she's not thrilled that I'm here. And sometimes I think . . . it's probably not fair to her for me to be here, kissing you on the couch, when she gets home . . ."

"You think that's because of you? She's thirteen, almost fourteen. Teenage girls are like that. And yes, the split hasn't helped but we're trying to keep things as stable as possible and work through this." Now he sounded exasperated. "Maybe if you'd actually talk to her, instead of acting like you didn't want her around—"

Liane gasped. "I don't act like I don't want her around. I do want her around!"

Another sob from Beatrice, above them. Laurence turned

and stomped up the stairs, much in the same manner his thirteen-year-old daughter had moments before.

Of course he knew the truth about how she was feeling. It was one of the reasons she loved him: because he knew her thoughts and feelings sometimes better than she did. Liane listened to his heavy footfalls and wondered for the first time, *Is this going to work?* Because what if her thoughts continued to go in this direction? How could a man love a woman who didn't truly accept his children? They had a connection, they loved each other deeply, this couldn't be denied. But they were his children. That was a different kind of connection. Liane could never compete, and if she started wanting to, if she started feeling envious, she knew she was probably going to have no choice but to end it, for all of their sakes.

She did go home, even though as soon as she walked through the door of her apartment, she knew she'd done the wrong thing. She had wanted to avoid a fight, but her departure had drawn a line in the sand she hadn't meant to draw. She felt panicked. What if she had ruined everything? She called him. "I'm so sorry," she said. "I shouldn't have left. I should have stayed and talked to you." "I'm sorry, too. It wasn't fair for me to say what I said. Parenting isn't always easy, and I shouldn't take it out on you." He lived in Riverdale and she lived on Queen Street West, but still, she said, "I could come back," and he said, "Part of me wants you to. But it's far and it's late and Bea is still out of sorts, and—well, Isabel and I are going to watch a movie." He sounded like he felt guilty to admit it, and this made her feel terrible. "You shouldn't have to sound like that. It's fine. It's good. She needs that time with you. It's your last night together for a week. Maybe we need to respect that a little—respect that during the weeks you have them, they might need a little space. With you." *And also, that I might be part of the problem.* "Please, try not to worry so much," he said. "Gillian is picking up the girls from school tomorrow. I'll come to you?"

After they talked, she tried to enjoy being home alone. Helen had always told her, told all of them, that being able to be alone was an important life skill. But it wasn't working now. She didn't want to read, she didn't want to watch television, she didn't want to take a bath, and she certainly couldn't sleep. She wanted to go back in time and not have left Laurence's. But she knew she probably shouldn't have been there in the first place, that she wasn't wrong: her presence really was throwing the girls off. She wasn't sure what to do about this.

She called Ilsa.

"You're a stepmom," she said when her sister answered. "How do you do it?"

"What do you mean? There's not much to do. They were practically grown when I came along, and Michael seems to only sire perfect children, so we've never had any problems."

"True," Liane said, feeling miserable.

"Trouble in paradise?"

"I don't know. Maybe not. I'm probably just overthinking it." She explained what had happened that night. "It's hard, because we're at that phase in the relationship where all we want to do is be together, and I don't want to overlook that, because it probably doesn't last forever, right?" Ilsa didn't respond. "But at the same time, I know I need to be fair to his daughters. It's just so hard. I feel resentful. Maybe even a little bit envious. And I *really* don't want to feel that."

"Don't beat yourself up. I'm sure it's completely normal. Back when Michael and I were in our first blush of passion, I probably would have been a bit annoyed if there was an almost three-year-old around. *And* a thirteen-year-old. Jesus. You do sort of have it bad, you know."

"Gee, thanks."

"Just being honest."

"You always are."

"It's funny you called, because I was thinking of you tonight. I was considering paying you a visit, but I didn't want to interrupt all the excitement. Sounds like you could use a visitor, though? A weekend to do your own thing, while he does his?"

"I would love that."

"Good."

"Are you bringing the kids? Maybe they and Bea can have a . . . what are they called, play appointments? And that will solve everything, because what can't your adorable kids solve?"

"They're called playdates. But no. I think maybe I'll just come on my own."

On the day of Ilsa's arrival, Liane ended up telling Laurence she would look after Beatrice alone for the first time. It was a Saturday morning and Gillian was away for the weekend with her boyfriend. Isabel had simply said no, that she had a school assignment to work on and had to go to the library for the entire day—which Liane didn't buy but Laurence clearly seemed to. "My sister is coming," Liane began, but then she stopped. Fear gripped her—*I can't be alone with Beatrice.* But she had to. Laurence needed her. He didn't have anyone else. And Ilsa would be there after the first few hours to help her.

She texted her sister. *I'm sorry, I can't pick you up at the airport, I'm babysitting Beatrice. Take a taxi to my apartment and I'll pay for it.*

This was how she ended up on the subway with Bea's stroller and all her stuff, which seemed an extreme amount for a person so small. The subway had been Liane's idea. She had imagined Bea would find it fun, that it would be a diversion for them—and, more important, that it would kill some time. And true, Bea was entranced with the movement, sound, and people on the train, chatting softly to Liane, making her feel like it was all going to work out. But then on the subway platform, Bea screamed in fear when the wind coming through the tunnel hit her in the face. On the escalator, juggling stroller and child, Liane nearly cried with exhaustion; how did people do this on a daily basis?

Finally, she made it outside, and with a diaper bag slung over the back handle of the stroller, a diaper bag that Laurence had packed, with Pull-Ups (Bea was in the process of being potty-trained) and wipes and snacks and toys and extra clothes and all sorts of things Liane never would have thought of, Liane plodded up Queen Street, trying to think of a way to shelter Bea from the cold February wind. "We'll be there soon. Five more minutes." But in truth, it was at least a ten-minute walk from the subway to her apartment. She longed to take the streetcar, but couldn't imagine how she'd manage to get the stroller up those stairs.

She continued to worry about the cold on Bea's face and leaned her head forward to make sure Bea's hat was still on and her blanket was still covering her legs. She felt like a mother, and knew she must look like one—except for the fact, of course, that Bea looked nothing like her, with her dark hair and dark eyes, and also for the fact that she had just started screaming, "I want my mommy!"

Liane continued to push resolutely, until Bea chucked her sippy cup and Liane had to brake the stroller and chase the cup as it rolled down an invisible hill. She gave the cup back to Bea without thinking. It was empty but Bea had been insisting on carrying it around for days, chewing on the spout. "It's BPA-free," Laurence had said. "It's probably fine."

Liane continued to push and Bea continued to cry and chuck her sippy cup. Liane would retrieve it and give it back, thinking each time that perhaps she needed to stop giving the sippy cup back, especially since it had fallen on the sidewalk so many times it was likely riddled with bacteria. But when she tried to withhold it, tucking it into the side pocket of the diaper bag, Bea screamed even louder.

Finally she was home. Her apartment. The stairs. "Shit," she said under her breath, parking the stroller just outside the door, grabbing the diaper bag—she could feel her shirt, underneath her jacket, soaked with sweat, despite the chilly temperature—and then picking up Bea. The child was quiet for a moment, but then she screamed, "No! I want my mommy. I don't want you!"

The taxi pulled up while Liane was still standing there. When Ilsa got out, she didn't say anything, just rolled her suitcase up to the curb, took the diaper bag, and somehow expertly folded the stroller and began to carry it, and everything else, up the stairs. When Ilsa was like this, it always surprised Liane. She was still Ilsa—unpredictable, lackadaisical—but when it came to being a mother, she was one of those women who was so relaxed she made it look easy.

Ilsa looked over her shoulder. "Come on, just walk. She'll keep screaming, but she'll get over it."

Liane carried the wailing Bea up the stairs, and managed to unlock the door and get them all inside. "See? I'm a terrible mother," she said.

"You're *not* her mother."

"I know that, but still. I'm a terrible whatever. Step-nothing."

"Step-something. You and Laurence are clearly going to get married, or at least be blissfully together forever."

"How do you know? You haven't even met him."

"Instinct. And I'll meet him this weekend, and it will just confirm it. Now put her down. Let her calm down for a second." Liane put Bea on the couch. "I'm Ilsa," Ilsa said to her, speaking to her the way Helen always had, like she wasn't a sobbing child but rather an adult. Bea gulped in air, but she didn't sob again. "I'm Liane's big sister. You have a big sister, too, don't you?"

Bea just sat silently, watching Ilsa and then glancing at Liane.

"What should we do?" Liane whispered.

"Take off her coat. Then pour a glass of wine for each of us. Quickly."

"But it's not even noon!"

"Oh, come on! We're babysitting."

"I'm going to try to pick her up again."

"I'd leave her for now," Ilsa warned. But Liane tried again, and again Bea wailed.

"Seriously. Wine. Do you have some?"

"Of course." Liane went to the kitchen and poured two glasses of white. Then she washed the sippy cup with hot, soapy water and filled it with milk, finishing the small carton she always kept on hand for coffee and the odd bowl of cereal. She brought the drinks out to the living room. She gave Bea the cup, fished some toys and books out of the diaper bag, and sat on the couch beside her sister. Bea continued to watch them silently, then picked up her cup and started to drink. She sighed contentedly after a moment, picked up a book, and began to study the pages intently.

"My best advice to you would be not to try," Ilsa said in a low voice.

"Not to *try*?"

"I don't mean don't try with her, I just mean don't try to be her mother. You're not. You never will be. Same with the other one, what's her name?"

"Isabel."

"You're not Isabel's mom, either. I did make the same mistake, when Michael and I were first together. I was certain Alexa and Shane were going to despise me, because I was so much younger than their father and they were already almost teenagers. so I tried to act like a second mom, draw a line, be . . . I don't know, kind of strict. I tried to force it, and that really didn't work. It didn't last long, I can tell you that. You just need to try to find another angle."

"Like . . . like what? I'm supposed to try to be their best friend?"

"No! Cool aunt. Trust me, it works."

"But I'm not cool at all. And anyway, I've been reading articles. I think I'm supposed to be trying to transition into the role of coparent."

"Is that what Laurence is asking you to do? Does he use that word, *co*parent?"

"He's not asking me to do anything. He's just asking me to be around, I guess."

"Then that's good. It's still up to you. Choose your role. And don't let it be *coparent* because that just sounds lame and clinical."

Liane sighed. "She won't even let me pick her up."

"A cool aunt wouldn't even *try* to pick her up. A cool aunt would sit on the couch drinking wine in the morning and ignoring her, which is exactly what you're doing."

Liane's mobile phone rang. It was Laurence.

"How are things going?"

Liane glanced at Ilsa. "Oh, they're going great."

"Well, my meeting is over already—not as many changes to this draft as I thought—so I can come get her if you want. You probably want to spend time with your sister."

Liane thought about the amount of time it had taken to get Bea across town and into her apartment and also about the fact that they were drinking. "No. Don't," she said. "We're planning a girls' afternoon. Go home, get some of those editorial changes done, and come get her later, maybe midafternoon." Ilsa nodded and smiled. *Perfect,* she mouthed, and Liane felt grateful to her for not feeling like having Bea around was ruining their time together.

"Don't forget about the potty, okay? Did she go when you got home?"

"Um, yes. It was no problem."

Liane hung up and approached Bea. "I think it's time to go potty," she said, trying to make her voice sound authoritative without sounding scary. Bea gave her a judgmental look, as if she knew Liane had just lied to her father. Liane opened the diaper bag, in search of the Dora the Explorer toilet seat, which, according to Laurence, was the only way she'd go to the bathroom. "I can't find the toilet seat. Maybe it fell out?"

"Hey, Bea, Liane has a big-girl toilet, for ladies only," Ilsa said. "It's really special. Want to try it?"

"Big-girl toilet!" Bea exclaimed. "Yesssss."

She didn't cry when Liane lifted her up and carried her to the bathroom. She did, however, fall directly into the water because her bottom was too small. Apparently there was a *good reason* for the Dora the Explorer toilet seat cover. But instead of crying, Bea laughed, and Liane started to run a bath and got some plastic cups and bowls and added bubbles.

Bea stayed in the bath for nearly an hour, until the skin around her fingers and toes puckered, while Ilsa and Liane perched on the edge of the tub with their wineglasses and added warm water every once in a while.

"I think this is probably her best play appointment ever," Liane said at one point.

"Playdate," Ilsa said. "It's called a play*date*. And usually, there needs to be at least one other kid invited. Anyway, listen. I have something momentous to tell you."

And Liane was sure, in that moment, that Ilsa was going to say she was leaving Michael. Which was why she was so shocked when Ilsa said, "Fiona and Tim . . . they're in serious trouble. As in potential divorce."

"*What?* How do you know this?"

"*Helen* told me. On the phone. Ever since that crazy spa weekend, and that fire ceremony thing, Fiona and Helen have bonded. Apparently they talk almost every day."

"Are you sure? Maybe Helen is mistaken. Fiona and I— well, we've talked on the phone a few times, too, and she's never said anything."

"Don't be hurt, Liane. It's probably really hard for her to talk about."

"I guess. Or maybe I just didn't ask. My own life seems to take up so much space that I haven't really been worrying about anyone else."

Ilsa put her hand on Liane's wrist. "Don't. Everyone is happy that you're happy. You deserve it. And you shouldn't feel guilty that Fiona and Tim *aren't* happy. But yeah, it's really serious." Now Ilsa started to explain about Samira. Bea was watching them wide-eyed, and for a moment Liane thought she understood. "Shhh," she said.

"Oh, please. Welcome to life, kid." Ilsa trailed a hand in the water. "It's lukewarm again. Do you want to get out or do you want me to warm it up for you?"

"Warm up, please," Bea said.

"Helen said Tim is asking for mediation," Ilsa continued as she ran the water. "And I think it's all really affecting the boys. I was out for a run last week and I saw Beck at the park near our house, sitting with a bunch of other kids, smoking a joint. Which is small-time, I get it, we did it, maybe not a big deal— but this is Fiona's kid, this isn't the kind of thing *her* kids are supposed to do. And also, he saw me. We made eye contact and he didn't even seem alarmed. He seemed almost . . . belligerent. And like he knew I wouldn't tell Fiona because I wouldn't want to upset her in her current state. Which is so true. But still, the little bastard. Oops, sorry."

"What should we do?"

"I don't think we can do anything right now. Except be there for her, I guess, when it all falls apart. That's what Helen said. I don't know if Fiona will even let us offer our support, but what else is there to offer her?"

"That sounds bleak."

"Yeah." Ilsa seemed distracted. "Things falling apart—it's scary, right? But I've been thinking lately . . . maybe you can try to put things back together eventually in a way that might make everything look more . . ." But she didn't finish her sentence. She looked back down into the water, at Bea. "She's pretty cute. Does she look like her dad?"

Liane wiped some bubbles away from Bea's left cheek. "Not at all. Like her mother. But she has his smile."

13

Raccoon *(Procyon lotor)*

*Raccoons used to live mostly in forests, but have now
adapted to urban life. During the mating season, males
restlessly roam in search of females and attempt to court
them during the three- to four-day period when conception
is possible. These encounters often occur at central meeting
places. Copulation, including foreplay, can last more than
an hour and is repeated over a few nights. According to
studies, about one-third of all female raccoons mate with
more than one male during this time.*

After Laurence came to pick up Beatrice—he was,
as Ilsa had expected, handsome and sweet and
kind and he and Liane were clearly madly in love,
but Ilsa still felt skeptical, and it made her feel sad that it appeared she simply didn't or couldn't believe in love anymore,
not even for her little sister, for whom she wanted it more
than anything—Liane suggested a nap before they went out
again, shopping and for dinner. Ilsa said she was fine, that
she wanted to go for a walk and get reacquainted with the
city and figured Liane was probably as acquainted with it as
she wanted to be at this point. They arranged to meet at their
favorite shop on Queen Street in an hour.

The sun had emerged and the biting wind had calmed, so

it was milder than it had been earlier. Ilsa thought perhaps she would get a tea and sit in the park, but she passed the tea shop, and the park, too. She realized she was walking toward a spire she could see in the distance. When she got to the church, she stopped in front of it. CONFESSION: SATURDAY AFTERNOON, the sign out front read. She wondered if there would be a line, if she would have to stand in a shuffling crowd with all the other sinners, like she and her father had had to do at the cathedral in Montreal.

But there was no one in there. She walked toward the confessional booth and opened the door, trying to act like she knew what she was doing. Strangely, she *did* feel like she knew, by some sort of instinct. "Come in, my child," said a male voice.

She hesitated, then entered the booth and made the sign of the cross, thinking she had probably gotten the order wrong. She stood for a moment, adjusting to the dim light. Then she knelt.

"Um . . . bless me, Father, for I have sinned. It has been . . . many years since my last confession. I'm sorry," she added.

"But you were baptized and confirmed into the Catholic Church, my child?" She nodded, then realized that because she was kneeling he couldn't see her.

"Yes," she said. "Yes, I was." *I have now lied to a priest.*

"Perhaps you should sit. You might be more comfortable."

She sat and could now see his eyes through the screen. She looked away from them.

"Have you performed an examination of conscience?"

"No."

"There are sheets by the door, you can get one on your way out. It will make it easier for next time."

Next time. "I . . . think I should just get started. I'm guilty of . . . I coveted, Father. I coveted my sister's husband, first of all, and I would have blown up her life if I could have, ruined it all just to make it my own. And knowing this makes me feel so horribly guilty, especially seeing her as she is now, so completely wrecked. I—*I* would have done that to her. I'm her sister, and I wanted to do that to her because I thought I wanted what she had. Except now I do have it, and I don't want it at all."

"My child—"

She ignored him and kept speaking. "And also, I committed adultery, Father. I committed adultery and I . . . and I lied. To my husband. To everyone. And I . . ." Her throat felt like it was closing. She wondered if this was what a panic attack felt like. "I became pregnant with another man's child, and I told my husband it was *his* child, and he was so happy, *so* happy . . . despite everything, he was happy. He said it was maybe what we needed, but I knew it wasn't. I knew a baby was never going to save our marriage, but still. I loved this baby because it was mine, and that's what you do. You love your babies. Because your mistakes aren't *their* fault. Right?" She was crying now. "Shit," she said. Then, "Sorry. Oh, God. Oh, *no*. Fuck." This was not going well. She swallowed hard.

"My child—" the priest began again, and Ilsa knew she was doing this all wrong, that the jig was up, that you probably weren't supposed to get into specifics, that this priest probably didn't want to know any of the sordid details of her life, and also that you were definitely not supposed to swear and take the Lord's name in vain while in a confessional booth. But she had gone too far now, so she pressed forward again. "I went to an appointment, to one of my prenatal appointments, and I found out, while my husband was sitting right there beside me, that the baby had a genetic defect. A serious one. They said that from the looks of things it wasn't meant to be, and that it would resolve itself on its own." Resolve itself. That's exactly what the doctor had said. And Ilsa had realized that maybe she was supposed to feel relieved.

She didn't. A few days later, the "resolution" came. Ilsa had thought she might die from the pain. Michael had banged on the door of the bathroom. "Let me in!" he had shouted. "Let me in! It's my baby, too. I need to be there for you." *No, it's not!* she had wanted to scream. *No, it's not, and I deserve to suffer alone!* She hadn't, though. She had stood, dripped blood across the bathroom floor, opened the door, and let him in. Later, he had asked Sylvie to stay for the weekend and he had taken care of her, made her tea and toast and held her while she cried, even though he had no idea why she was really crying.

Lincoln's child. Gone. And she shouldn't have been surprised because Lincoln had already had a severely disabled son. This was something Jane had told Ilsa, that night at the party. Apparently one of her acquaintances, someone in her book club or something, was close to Lincoln's wife and had told everyone about how the one child the couple had had was born with a rare defect that left him in pain for most of his life, and dead before he turned eight. It had all happened years before. "Sad," Ilsa had said, but she had been so detached from anything except her immediate need at the time that she had felt very little interest. Apparently Lincoln's wife, Rebecca, had wanted to try for more children, but Lincoln refused, Jane had told her. Ilsa now realized, of course, that maybe he'd known, instinctively, that the genetic variant was his and was destined to repeat itself.

"I am a flawed, horrible person," Ilsa said to the priest.

"My child, we are all flawed. We are all imperfect. We have all fallen from grace." There was something in his voice that was very tired, and very pitying, and she didn't like it.

"Some of us more spectacularly than others," she said. "Because even after all this, even after all I've been through and put other people through, I still can't stop thinking about . . . I still think about other men sometimes, I still think about betraying my husband again, I still feel like if I don't, I'll never be happy, like if I stay with him I'll die of starvation."

The priest was silent. She thought perhaps he might offer her advice, but he didn't. He said, "You should now make the Act of Contrition," and she said, "I don't know it," and he said, "Repeat after me."

> *O my God, I am heartily sorry*
> *for having offended you,*
> *and I detest all my sins*
> *because of your just punishment,*
> *but most of all because they offend you, my God,*
> *who are all good and deserving of my love.*
> *I firmly resolve, with the help of your grace,*
> *to sin no more and to avoid the near occasions of sin.*

"Have you ended this adulterous relationship?"

"Yes." *Did I have a choice? Was it even a relationship?*

"Have you considered the seriousness of your sin, the effect it might have on your husband, children if you have them?"

"Yes. I think about it every day."

"In order to truly achieve absolution, you need to tell your husband about your sins against your marriage. You need to ask for his forgiveness and you need to move forward, together. If he needs help accepting it, you can bring him to me. We can make an appointment for marital counseling through the church."

She was silent.

"Are you sorry for these sins, and all the sins of your life?"

She hesitated. *All the sins of your life.* "Yes, Father."

He gave her a prescribed number of Our Fathers and Hail Marys. He told her to attend daily mass. He said, "God, the Father of Mercies, through the death and resurrection of his

Son, has reconciled the world to himself, and sent the Holy Spirit among us for the forgiveness of sins. Through the ministry of the Church, may God grant you pardon and peace. And I absolve you of your sins, in the name of the Father, and of the Son, and of the Holy Spirit. Amen."

She said, "Amen." And then he slid the screen shut.

"It's that simple," her father had said.

It's not simple at all, Dad.

But at least she had told *someone*. And maybe, just maybe, she would never have to repeat this story again.

Ilsa and Liane went for dinner at a wine bar.

"Did things get better?" Liane asked her. "With you and Michael? After the summer, and . . . and everything?"

"Somewhat," Ilsa said. "I dealt with it, anyway. It's not going to happen again."

"You mean, something like what happened with Lincoln?"

"Yeah. That."

"And what is it that happened, exactly? You *can* tell me, you know. I'm sorry I was so judgmental at the cottage. I don't want you to think you can't talk to me. You can tell me anything."

"I know. I know that. But there's nothing to tell. It wasn't anything with Lincoln. Heavy petting. Some dirty texts." She tried to smile, then looked down into the red wine in her glass, part of a flight they'd ordered. She drank it all down in a large gulp.

"Since when do you text?" Liane asked.

"Yeah. I know. Since when? Since never. It wasn't worth changing who I was, so I ended it."

"And you're okay, you and Michael?"

"Sure. As okay as we can be maybe, at least for now. But yes. We are."

"Does it bother you that I'm always going on about how in love I am with Laurence, when you're . . ."

"When I'm what? When I'm seven years into a marriage, and not exactly thrilled with it? It's normal, Li. I'll get past it. We're in a slump. We'll survive. Marriages can have bad years, and then things turn around. It's the way it is."

Liane put down her fork. "Really? Do you think that's what happens to everyone? That they end up in slumps that last that long? I mean, even Fiona and Tim—look at *them*. Is it really just what happens?"

"I don't know, Liane. I can't speak for everyone. But our family doesn't seem to be doing so well with relationships right now. Maybe Helen was right."

"I don't want her to be right. I did think she might be, when I was with Adam, but then I met Laurence, and now I think if you just meet the right person—" She stopped. "I'm sorry. That's not fair, for me to insinuate that Michael isn't the right person."

"He isn't," Ilsa said. "The reality is, we're not perfect for each other, not like you and Laurence are. But we still got married, and we still had children, and so . . ." *We're obligated,* was what she had wanted to say, but it seemed too sad to say aloud.

"Can I ask you something? Do you think there's any hope at all that Laurence and I can stay like this forever? Deeply in love and happy with each other, even despite everything, the complications of his life, these *realities* you're talking about?"

"Do you want me to be honest?"

"Of course I want you to be honest!"

"No. I don't think you can stay happy *like this* forever. I think new relationships are happy, and then they change. I think you two are great together, but I also think no matter what, love's first blush is really mostly about hormones." Ilsa realized she sounded harsh. She realized she shouldn't have asked if her sister wanted her to be honest, that she should have just lied and said, *Yes, of course you're going to live happily ever after.* She should not have even hinted that there was a chance, years down the road, that Liane's eyes would have lost the light they had in them now, and that she could be sitting at another restaurant, saying something to Ilsa like, *I thought it would be different, I thought he was someone else, that I was someone else.*

You have to stop projecting onto her. You're not being fair, she told herself.

"Maybe we should go out dancing after this," Ilsa said. "Or listen to some live music. Or both. Have some *fun.* No more talk about love for a bit, okay?" Liane agreed, and they started talking about other things, and after dinner they took a taxi to the Dakota Tavern on Ossington, where a bluegrass band was playing. Liane found them a place to stand and Ilsa went to get drinks. She was feeling buzzed from the wine. As she walked through the room she experienced a familiar feeling. She knew her movements were followed by male stares. She knew there was possibility, that anything could happen. Her heart started to beat a little faster. *I just want to kiss someone,* she realized. *I don't want sex, I don't want to do what I did with Lincoln. But maybe just one little kiss, just a moment of feeling unknown and yet connected to someone who is completely new to me.* She had always loved that, the way it felt to kiss someone new. *Why?* Because, she realized. Because opening herself up in small ways had helped her make the space to create art. Because being with Michael had started to shrink her.

You should not be thinking this way. You should not be thinking about anything other than your marriage and your life at home. But instead, when a man in a flannel shirt at the bar looked at her she held his gaze for what she knew was an inappropriately long time. A moment later, she realized he was staring at her because they knew each other. "Johnny! What are you doing here?" She approached and hugged him, which she realized she had never done before, then led him back to where Liane was standing. Liane had her phone out. She looked up, embarrassed. "I'm drunk-texting Laurence," she said. "I'm sorry, I couldn't help myself." Then she saw Johnny. "Johnneeeee. Look, Ilsa. It's Johnny. From the marina."

"I know that, you goof," Ilsa said. "*I* brought him over here."

"Hey," Johnny said. "Hi." He seemed shy and very out of place.

"So," Ilsa said. "You never answered: What are you doing here? Of all the gin joints and all the towns in all the world, you had to walk into ours." Now he appeared confused, like he didn't get the reference. Or maybe he hadn't heard her properly. The music was loud. *And why did you say that, anyway? Are you flirting with him? If you are, you're getting rusty.*

"Oh, ah, just visiting someone in the city. What about you two?"

Liane wobbled a little on her high-heeled boots. "I live here," Liane said. "And oh, my goodness, I'm drunk, I think. Are you, Ils? How many glasses of wine did we have with dinner? Five? Twenty?" Then her phone lit up in her hand, and she looked down at it and smiled.

"Hey, maybe you should just go and see Laurence," Ilsa said.

"But the girls are there."

"So what? They won't know. You can sneak in and then out again before they wake up. It can be your little secret." She moved her lips closer to her sister's ear. "*That's* how you keep love new and exciting. *Frisson.* Go on, do it. Be happy."

"Are you *sure?* No. No, I shouldn't. We're having a sisters' night out."

"I'm sure. I won't stay much longer anyway. Just give me your keys so I can get into your apartment. I'll finish my drink with Johnny here, and then head back."

"And I'll come back early in the morning and later we'll go for brunch, just like we planned? Sneaky Dee's? *Huevos rancheros*?" She was texting again already.

When Liane was gone, Ilsa stood beside Johnny. The band was still playing. She wasn't sure what to say to him, and he wasn't saying anything to her, so she stayed silent.

"I'm going to the bar to get a drink," he finally said, turning away from the music. "I never did get one because . . . because then I saw you. Do you want anything?"

"I have a full beer." But she followed him to the bar.

"How about a shot?" he said.

She hesitated, then nodded. "But also a bottle of water, please."

He leaned across the bar top and ordered drinks for both of them while she watched his profile.

When he handed her the shot, the softness of his flannel shirt rubbed against her arm. "Ready?" he said.

"Aren't we supposed to have . . . accoutrements? Lemon, salt, something?"

"Look around you, Ilsa. This bar doesn't appear to have any accoutrements, whatever those are. Just drink up." He flashed her a white, even smile, and she thought, *He's so attractive.* She supposed she'd always known this, having seen him at least once every summer for more than half of her life, but now, out of context, slightly drunk, she noticed in a different way. *Bless me, Father, for I have sinned. I have had impure thoughts.*

Just a little kiss, she thought. *And I know him. Is this so bad?*

They moved to the back of the bar again to stand and watch the band.

Several moments passed before he leaned toward her.

"Do you come here a lot?"

"Never! I haven't lived in Toronto in years. I live in New York, in Rye. I'm just visiting Liane for the weekend."

"I can't remember the last time I came to the city. I'm

just . . . one of my sons moved here to go to school, and I visited him today."

"Your sons. How many do you actually *have*? I've always wondered."

Johnny chuckled. "Yeah, I heard about the rumors, that all I ever do is get women pregnant and then send them away but keep the sons. That's not what really happened. My first wife, the mother of my first two boys, she did leave me pretty much high and dry when they were just little guys." He was silent for a moment. "But Ben and Jesse's mom stuck around for longer. It didn't work out, either, though, but I raised them all up okay. Jesse's the one who got into school—my youngest."

"Which school?"

"He's taking some forest management program at U of T. Pretty cool, I guess." He sipped his beer. "Weird not having him around, though. So, what do you do out there in New York, Ilsa?"

"I'm . . . an artist," she said, feeling guilty. Should she have said, *I'm a wife*? Should she have said, *I'm a mother*? It wasn't like he hadn't seen her with Ani and Xavier—and Michael, when he had accompanied her to the cottage once or twice.

"An artist. Is that glamorous work?"

She laughed for some reason, and he laughed, too, and then they stopped laughing and just smiled at each other. She said, "It's not glamorous at all."

"It sounds like a cool job. Even if it's not glamorous."

"It's not even really a job." And she started to laugh again, and put her hand on his chest to steady herself. When she was steady, she kept her hand where it was, buried it in the softness and simplicity of his shirt. Then she drew her hand away. "Sorry," she said.

He took her hand and put it back on his chest, held it

there with his own. The band had stopped playing and now there was music on, the song "Heads Will Roll" by the Yeah Yeah Yeahs. People were starting to dance.

He continued to hold her hand against his chest. Then he leaned in and kissed her, and she opened her mouth and yielded to him completely, the way she knew how to do so well. A bell clanged and for a moment Ilsa thought she had imagined it, that the bell was clanging in her own head, reminding her that she was married, telling her to stop what she was doing immediately, that she had gone to confession just that day. But it was the bartender, ringing the bell for last call. "Want to get out of here?" Johnny asked her, pulling his mouth away from hers.

"Where would we go? I can't . . . I shouldn't ask you back to my sister's."

"To hang out with my dogs?"

"*What?*"

"They're in my truck. It's parked in a lot around the corner. I had to bring them because my other sons were away for the weekend, too, and there was no one else to take care of them. I was planning to drive back up north tonight after dinner with Jess, but . . . I just needed to go out somewhere. I didn't want to drive all that way just yet. So I decided I'd crash in the car with the dogs, and drive back home first thing in the morning, when I could, after the booze wore off. And before you start thinking I'm cruel to animals by leaving them in the car, my truck is giant and they have food and water and blankets. They love it in there. Their own condo."

"I never said you were cruel to animals." She was laughing again.

"What's so funny all the time, Ilsa?"

"I really don't know. Just you, I guess. You and your dog condo on wheels." He smiled, too, and she said, "Okay, sure. I *would* like to go to your truck and hang out with your dogs."

He was so familiar. It felt good to be with him. And she wanted to kiss him again.

When they got to the truck, he opened the back. And there indeed were the two dogs, dogs she recognized from the marina, big animals that would often greet her with barks that never seemed unfriendly. He explained their pedigree and she immediately forgot what he'd said. They were over-joyed to see Johnny, jumping up and licking him. "Hi, Marlin, hi, Bugsy," he crooned. The dogs turned their attentions on her. One of them pressed his nose against her crotch. "Get out of there," said Johnny, pushing the dog's head away. "I know she's pretty, but she's not yours." *I'm not yours, either,* Ilsa thought. "Come on, get back in." He closed the back of the truck again and led her around to the front, opening the door of the cab for her before he went around to the other side.

When he was in, he reached down and handed her a fresh bottle of water before turning on the heat and the stereo, something quiet and folky-sounding, with jangling guitars and a low male voice.

Ilsa drank more than half of the bottle of water. Johnny had pulled out a joint. "Want some?"

"I guess."

After, he put his arm around her, pulling her to him across the wide seat. Then he turned to her and touched her cheeks with both hands, ran his hands through her hair, pulled her bangs up and away from her face. "You're gorgeous, you know. Really gorgeous. Every summer when I see you coming, I think that. Always have."

Just kiss me. But when he did, there was something sour and wrong about the way he tasted, the beer and the pot combining in an unfortunate way. She imagined she prob-ably tasted the same. She began to grow self-conscious. She thought, as she kissed him, *Johnny isn't the answer, and kissing other people isn't the answer, and parceling small amounts of my-self out over the years to share, secretly, isn't the answer, either.* She pulled her head away.

"I'm married," she said.

"Well, I know that," he said. "I just got the impression you didn't . . ."

"Didn't care?"

"That's not what I was going to say."

"Well, I *do* care. I have two kids."

"Look, I didn't mean anything by this. I just . . . I was just feeling in need of a little companionship, that's all." He seemed suddenly sad. This surprised her a bit. She could tell it wasn't about her, that there was something else bothering him. She thought of the woman at the marina with the dark hair and mysterious eyes. Where was she?

The music was still playing. It was Townes Van Zandt, Ilsa realized. Helen used to listen to him, on quiet nights, when she was sad about some lost love or another. *In the night forlorn the morning's born, and the morning shines with the lights of love. You will miss sunrise if you close your eyes. That would break my heart in two.*

"I should go," Ilsa said. "Back to my sister's."

"You sure you're going to be okay? It's late, it's dark."

She reached for the door handle. "I'll get a cab." She stopped, leaned toward him, kissed him on the cheek, then got out of the truck.

"No harm done, right? See you next summer."

"None at all. See you."

She didn't hail a cab, though. She walked along Ossington until she got to Queen, and then turned left and kept walk-ing. When she was close to Liane's and hadn't seen a person in a block or two, she heard a crashing sound coming from the alley she was passing and felt momentarily startled. She thought of that night in the alley back home with Lincoln and how scared she had been when he left her alone. But this time she wasn't scared. The streetlamps were bright. She could see. And so she knew the crashing sound was just the raccoons, sifting through the waste with their strange little paws. She stopped and watched them, their bandit masks lifted toward her for just a second before they went back to what they were doing, guiltless, entitled. *The ultimate sinners.*

She kept walking.

In the morning, when Liane came home, Ilsa was sitting on the couch. She hadn't slept. She was still in the skirt and tights she had been wearing the night before. She poured her sister a coffee and she said, "I know I said a lot of stuff last night at dinner. Maybe I was just trying to justify myself, my actions. I don't want you to think I don't believe in love, or that it's not possible for you."

"Oh, Ilsa. I'm sorry I left you last night. You seem so sad. You shouldn't have been alone. And I left you with Johnny—oh, shit, did something happen? Did he try something? He seemed a little . . . smitten."

"He wasn't smitten. And no, nothing happened. Not really. But listen, just listen. I've been sitting here all night thinking, and I have to tell you." She felt a bit punch-drunk, crazy from the lack of sleep. But she still knew she was right, and that she had to tell Liane. "Here's the thing about love: It *can* last, but you have to be careful with it. You have to treat it like it's your most precious possession, you have to never, ever take it, or the person you love, for granted. Ever. Even just doing it once could spell the beginning of the end. Resentment, it's love's worst enemy. Don't forget that, Liane, okay? Don't forget that, and you'll be fine."

"Okay," Liane said. "But, Ilsa—"

"And also, don't be afraid. Helen said something to me

once, about the pain of love leaving behind a beautiful memory. Even if something doesn't work, maybe you don't have to let it scar you. Maybe it can be something other than a scar, something that makes you stronger."

Ilsa knew then that she needed to get home and jump off the ledge she'd been lingering on, even if she wasn't positive her parachute was going to open and allow her to soar. This was how Helen had intended to raise her, and all three of them: as women who could need and yearn but who could also walk away from a sense of obligation that wasn't rooted in anything they had ever wanted.

When Ilsa arrived home in the taxi, Michael was working in his office and barely looked up. He asked how her trip was at dinner, but then, when she started to tell him, his BlackBerry chimed and he reached for it and his eyes slid away from hers and she stopped talking.

The next morning, she went to her studio and she took out all the sketches she had been doing over the past few months, nudes, erotic paintings she had done because she was trying to do what Lincoln had said she should do. They were all sketches she hated. She knew this now. She began to cut them to shreds with scissors.

Eventually she got to the nudes on cardboard, some she had done recently and some that were older and that Lincoln had handled, the ones he had told her were so good. She hesitated, then got out a paper knife and began to slice them into long, stiff strips.

In the back of another cupboard she found a box. She lifted the lid. It was filled with letters, mostly in French, from when she had lived in Paris, letters from Eric, saying things to her like, *You are my queen,* and quoting Paul Verlaine poems ("*Votre âme est un paysage choisi*") and other such bullshit.

There were also letters from her father, mostly affectionately drunk ramblings because that was the only time he wrote. She put the letters from Michael aside. Perhaps she would show them to Ani someday, to prove that they really had been in love, once.

She ripped everything else up with her hands.

But she didn't throw any of the shreds away. She packed them into garbage bags and dragged them home with her, kept them with her as she began to pack her things. Ani was at school and Xavier was at the park with Sylvie and then Ilsa had arranged for her to take both kids out to dinner and a movie, even though she wondered if Xavier would be able to sit through it. But they had to be out of the house. "You can't bring them back until you call me first," she had said to Sylvie.

She called Michael. "You need to come home from work. I need to talk to you." She spoke quickly so she wouldn't lose her nerve and pretend she was calling about something else.

"Is it an emergency?" he asked.

"Yes. Come home."

14
Northern Cardinal (*Cardinalis cardinalis*)

Cardinal pairs mate for life, and they stay together year-round. Mated pairs sometimes sing together before nesting. During courtship they may also participate in a bonding behavior where the male collects food and brings it to the female, feeding her beak to beak. If the mating is successful, this mate-feeding may continue throughout the period of incubation.

The day before, when Myra had learned Johnny was coming to visit, she had tried to hide her agitation from Jesse. All the time, she had wanted Jesse to think it was fine, that Johnny had never become angry with her when she said she was going back to the city with Jesse, that their relationship was perfectly normal: friends who were once lovers (of course, she didn't use the word *lovers* when she discussed it with Jesse) and now were just people who had once known each other. "We're still connected through you," she had once said to him. "We're still friends." But it wasn't true. They weren't. They had barely spoken since she'd left, or only when they had to because of something to do with Johnny's son. They were like people who had gone through a divorce.

She missed him, though. It still felt acute. She had almost said to him, when he called and said he was coming, that he shouldn't come to the house, that he should meet Jesse at a neutral location so she wouldn't have to see him. It wasn't that she didn't *want* to see him. She just needed more time. Maybe another few months, and she would be over him and be able to be in his presence without worrying about the magnetic pull, painful to resist. But instead she had forced herself to say, "Okay, then, see you tomorrow," and she had hung up the phone.

"Your dad's coming for a visit," Myra had said to Jesse later, trying to sound casual. "Tomorrow afternoon. He's coming for dinner."

"Great," Jesse had said. "See you later, I have class."

"Got all your books?"

"Think so."

She had then gone shopping at St. Lawrence Market, and fretted about what to buy and what to make. She had returned empty-handed and texted Jesse: *Let's take him out. Let's show him around the city a little. Where do you think he'd like to go?*

And Jesse had replied, *Nowhere, or least not to any of the restaurants you like.*

But she had still taken them to Campagnolo, and had felt a little embarrassed when Johnny had said, "Damn, it's hot in here," and had taken off his flannel shirt and laid it across his chair, and had eaten his meal in his white T-shirt, essentially an undershirt, and then said, "Is that it? I'm still starving." He had summoned the waiter and ordered another dish, the tagliatelle, and she had fully felt the wrongness of the setting. She should have bought steaks and potatoes and vegetables at the market and made him the simple kind of meal he liked.

But why? Why should I have made him what he likes? What about what I like? Myra had barely been able to eat anything, and had left her meal mostly untouched before offering it to him. "I don't even know what that is," he had said.

"It's duck confit risotto."

"No, thank you." Meanwhile, Jesse sat silently, eating his spaghetti all'amatriciana, and Myra had, for just a moment, hated Johnny, and then hated herself. *We really shouldn't be here.*

She had invited him back to the house for coffee. The conversation had been stilted. At the door, later, Johnny had shaken Jesse's hand, then pulled him in for an awkward hug. "I'm proud of you, son," he had said. There were tears in Myra's eyes.

"Thanks, Dad." Jesse seemed genuinely happy. Perhaps he had missed it all, the subtext, the wrongness, the undercurrent of hurt feelings. Maybe he really had been simply eating his spaghetti at the restaurant. Because she *wasn't* his mother, was she? So what did Jesse care whether Myra and Johnny got along, whether they had anything to talk about, whether they were able to look each other in the eye, whether they had any sort of connection at all?

Then Johnny left, and Myra went upstairs to bed.

The next morning, the last person Myra expected to see at her back door was Johnny. But there he was. He looked tired and rumpled, his beard darker than the evening before, gone from five o'clock shadow to morning-after grizzle.

"What are you doing here?" she asked. "I thought you were driving back last night." She could see the dogs behind him running in the yard. "The gate's not closed."

"They won't run away."

"What's going on?"

"I didn't want to go back," he said. "But I didn't want to come back here, either." She stood still, not sure what to do. "So I . . . I slept in my truck."

"Oh."

"You going to let me come in, or what?"

Inside, he took off his boots and sat down at her table. "You know what?" he said, and he sounded angry. "Last night, when it was time for me to go home, all of the sudden I saw it. I realized it."

"Saw what? Realized what?"

"That's why I didn't go home."

"*What* are you talking about?"

"I saw what you hated about it, especially in the winter. What you didn't like about being at the marina. And then the idea of going back there alone, without you, without Jesse, with the other boys away and probably moving out soon, planning on living in town . . . there really didn't seem to be any point. And I realized . . . I realized that I miss you. I really miss you."

She stood staring at him. She was still in her pajamas, a long white T-shirt and purple shorts. She hadn't been able to sleep the night before, not even a little bit. She probably looked terrible, she probably looked old. She had cut her hair when she returned to the city, a bob that landed just below her jawline. Johnny hadn't said a word about it. Now she wished it was long enough to pull back into a proper bun. It was probably sticking up everywhere.

She turned away from him and put on the kettle, and thought of her mother, who had passed away a few years before. Her mother would turn on the kettle when things were being left unsaid. She would boil the water, and make the tea, and wait. And usually by the time the tea was finished the things that needed to be said would have been said.

Myra faced the stove. She looked out the window. She saw a cardinal, bright red, sitting on the neighbor's fence. In the city, these bird sightings mattered, these small brushes with nature. At the marina she wouldn't have noticed a lone cardinal.

Johnny came up behind her.

"I don't feel like tea," he said. He put his hand on her waist. "Turn off the stove." He kissed her neck. "I miss you so much, Myra."

"No," she said, pulling away but feeling the urge to push toward him, into him. "*I* want tea. *I* want to talk, *I* want to know what you're really doing here."

"I told you, I miss you."

"And *I* told you, it's not enough."

"Did you? I don't remember you saying that." She realized she hadn't, had only said it in her head, out of self-preservation. *Whatever he has to say, it's not enough.*

"I meant to."

He sat down at the table again and she stood, watching and waiting for the kettle to boil. "Myra, the truth? First of all, last night, I went to a bar, and I ran into one of the women who comes into the marina every summer, that Ilsa, the pretty one. And I thought maybe I'd find some comfort with her, so we . . ." Myra closed her eyes. "I'm sorry because I know it's probably not what you want to hear, but I want to be honest with you." No, it was definitely not what Myra wanted to hear. She waited for him to keep talking while hoping he wouldn't. "Anyway, nothing much happened. We kissed a little. It just made me feel lonely for you. I don't like that feeling at all, didn't like not being able to push it away." More silence.

What exactly am I supposed to say to that? Myra wondered.

He started to speak again. "I've never felt possessive of any woman, like I wanted her to be mine. And I certainly have never felt so upset about any woman leaving as I did when you left. At first I thought it was because you decided to take one of my boys with you, but I knew you were right to do it, I knew Jesse should be at school, and that just made it worse, that you cared so much about him you got him to the exact place he was supposed to be without even giving a rat's ass what I thought. You're not like anyone I've ever met before. You're not like anyone I've ever *been* with. You're so . . . you're so smart, you're so . . . I don't even know, just different. And *I'm* not smart at all, as you know. I've only ever read one book to the end, that I can remember."

"I know that, Johnny, I know. We've talked about this."

"For school, because I had to. I don't even know what it was called."

"It was called *No Great Mischief,* by Alistair MacLeod."

"See, you're so smart you even know the name of the only book I've ever read, and I don't even know the name of the fucking book!"

"Why are we talking about this?"

More silence. She turned the flame under the kettle down a little. "Most of the time, when you were around, I couldn't figure out what the hell you wanted with me, what you were doing, why you stayed," he said. "Honestly, right at the start, when you said you were staying, the first thing I thought was, *What would a woman like this want with a man like me?* And I figured it was maybe because you weren't so great after all since you wanted to stay, and I suppose I treated you as such. Less than what you are. But then I started to realize you were great. But then you left. I guess I wasn't surprised when you did. But it hurt. *That* surprised me."

She stood, still silent, watching him as he sat at her table. It was pine and long and pushed against the window. His shirt stood in contrast to the light flowing through the window, bright like the cardinal had been against the snow. Behind him, she could see the dogs playing in the yard.

"Do you remember *why,* even if you couldn't remember the title, you never forgot that one line from the book you read for school—that last line from it, the one you once told me about?"

"'We're all better when we're loved,'" he said automatically.

"*That's* why I stayed with you."

"You've got to be shitting me. You stayed with me because of a line at the end of a book I can't even remember the title of?"

"I stayed with you because I believed that *you* believed that, that you thought it was true that people were better when they were loved and that you, one day, were going to love *me* and we were both going to be better because of it. And I also . . . I also stayed with you because I wanted a baby."

"Come on, really? You never said."

"Yes. Always. The whole time. I bought the idea that you were this virile man who impregnated women at the drop of his hat, and I thought you were the answer to all my problems. I couldn't get pregnant, when I lived here, with my . . . ex-husband." Not technically a lie anymore; they had finalized things when she returned to the city. "When I lived here with him, I didn't have any luck. I'm barren, I think. Something is wrong."

"We could have tried. Maybe that's the problem. We didn't really try."

"Trust me, *I* tried."

"We should try harder. If that's what you want, well, that's fine with me. Let's keep trying."

The kettle had finally started to boil. She shut it off, turned, and got the kettle and two bags of Earl Grey. She stood waiting for it to steep.

"When you loved me, I *was* better," he said. "I know I didn't act like it, but I was better. And last night, I realized all that was going to happen if I went back alone was that I was going to get worse again. I sat awake all through the night thinking about how to get you back, what I needed to say. And all I can think to tell you is how much I've been missing you. How much I miss you. How much I . . ."

She waited. The tea was probably ready. Now it was probably too strong. Still she waited.

"I love you," he said.

It *was* enough. Of course it was. What she had always wanted to hear him say, more than anything, ever, was more than enough.

15

Black-Throated Loon (*Gavia arctica*)

It is widely believed that pairs of loons mate for life, but this is not true. A typical adult loon is likely to have several mates during its lifetime because of territorial takeover. Each breeding pair must frequently defend their territory against other adult loons trying to evict at least one owner and seize the breeding site. Territories that have produced chicks in the past year are especially prone to takeovers. One-third of all territorial evictions result in the death of one of the males; in contrast, female loons usually survive.

sabel hadn't wanted to go back to the cottage at first. "But we're not going to *that* cottage," her dad had said. "We're going to the cottage next door."

"Same difference," Isabel had replied. Then Liane had come into her room later that day and sat down on her bed.

"Hey," Liane had said, and Isabel had made an effort not to feel annoyed by her very presence.

Liane tried too hard, that was the thing. Isabel and her friend Mykayla, who also had a stepmother (they called her the step*monster*), had discussed it. Even though technically she was being nice, trying too hard was simply annoying. "Like a boy who likes you too much and, like, texts you every five minutes," Mykayla had said. "Ick." "Ick," Isabel had repeated, and they had laughed so hard Mykayla had snorted peppermint latte out her left nostril and then they had laughed harder, all the while glancing to the corner of the coffee shop, where Matt Tillson and his crowd were seated. Isabel had had a crush on Matt for as long as she could remember (in reality, for about a year) and he had never paid her any attention. But now he was watching Mykayla, with her long dark hair and the ability to somehow make mint-flavored milk coming out her nose look cute, and Isabel felt jealous. Boys always liked Mykayla. Mykayla knew what she was talking about when she said, "It's like when a boy likes you too much." Isabel could laugh along with her, but had never actually had the experience. Now she looked away from Matt, and from Mykayla now noticing Matt looking at her, and down at the coffee-spattered table.

"You know, though . . ." Mykayla had tossed a length of hair over her shoulder. "She's not a bitch. Not like the step-monster. That's the one thing she has going for her."

"True. She's not a bitch," Isabel had said.

"Let's say the jury's still out on this one. Maybe she'll start taking you out shopping and buying you great clothes and we can chalk it up as a victory."

"I think she's poor. She's, like, an assistant teacher at university."

"Oh. Bummer. It's too bad she's not a bitch. Then we could just hate her with impunity."

Now Isabel tried to smile at Liane. "Hey," she said back.

"I just wanted to tell you that I really think you're going to have fun at my mom's cottage. It's a really nice place. I mean, you know the lake, and it's a fantastic lake, and my mom, Helen, she's actually renting a boat, which may not seem like a big deal to you, but she's anti-watercraft, and my sisters and I always begged for a boat so we could go water-skiing, so . . . that'll be really fun."

"No one goes water-skiing anymore," Isabel said.

"Right. Oh. No. No one does?"

"No. People wakeboard. I've done it before, tons of times." This wasn't true; she'd done it once, at her friend Anna's cottage in the Kawarthas, and had been terrible at it, and had fallen off into a huge patch of seaweed, and Anna's brother, Chad, had shouted at her that she was probably going to be eaten by a muskie, and she had panicked and swum back to the boat, thinking of the photos on the wall of the cottage of Chad and Anna's father holding up impossibly enormous-looking fish, all caught in the lake she was swimming in.

"Well, I doubt Helen has a wakeboard. But I know she has old skis. And maybe the twins or Eliot will have one," Liane said.

Right, the twins or Eliot. Boys. There were going to be *boys* at the cottage. And this was the only reason Isabel wasn't flat-out refusing to go. "But what if they're total geeks?" she had said to Mykayla.

"They're from New York, right?"

"Well, outside of it."

"Hmm. I think there's still the possibility that they're totally hot. And if they're not, well, it's only a few days."

"Three days. Without cell phone reception."

"Yeah, you're totes going to die. Maybe send smoke signals?"

Isabel thought about asking Liane whether her nephews were cute. But she couldn't, there was no way. Then Liane would probably think they were best friends or something. So instead she said, "I'm going to start packing my bag." And Liane smiled at her so gratefully that Isabel felt the "ick" feeling again and turned away. Eventually Liane left the room.

"She's definitely coming," she heard Liane say to her dad in the hallway, as if *she* had had something to do with it. Isabel rolled her eyes but kept packing, carefully choosing her outfits and packing the bikini she knew her dad hated.

. . .

Now they were in the car, driving toward Muskoka. Isabel had her headphones in, mostly to drown out the sound of Beatrice, who was going through a very whiny stage—although, to be honest, every one of Bea's stages so far in her life had seemed like whiny ones to Isabel.

Her father reached back and touched her arm. She turned down the music. "It's too loud, Iz," he said. "You're going to damage your eardrums, and also, I can hear it. When someone else can hear the music from your personal listening device, it is no longer a personal listening device."

"It's not a personal listening device. Dad, this isn't 1982. It's an iPod, for Christ's sake."

"Isabel! Your language."

"What? It's not like we go to church or anything."

"But your sister. I don't want your sister walking around saying things like 'for Christ's sake,' all right?"

As if to prove this point, Bea said, "Chrissakes, chrissakes," and Isabel hid her smile with her hand.

"See!" Laurence said. "Thanks, Iz."

"Dad, *you're* the one who said it again, and then she said it—it wasn't *my* fault!"

Her dad opened his mouth to say something, but Liane put her hand on his leg and squeezed. "Don't," she said. "Bea will forget she even heard it."

Now Bea was whining again.

"I don't understand why I have to sit back here with the whiner and Liane gets to sit up there," Isabel said.

"Well, why don't we trade at the next rest stop?" Liane said. "And . . . why don't we listen to some music that we *all* like? And then you won't have to listen to your . . . personal listening device." She leaned back and tried to share a complicit smile with Isabel, but Isabel didn't smile back at her.

"We don't like the same music."

"I think we like some of the same music. You like Jake Bugg, and I have some of his music on my iPod. And we both like the Decemberists and Jack White."

Stop trying to be cool! Isabel wanted to shout. But instead she said nothing.

"We could play *your* iPod," Liane said.

"Don't you mean my personal listening device? Sure, fine," Isabel said, handing it forward and staring out the window at the familiar scenery that made her sad.

When they got to the marina, the woman, Helen, was waiting with the boat she had apparently rented from the owner of the marina, and a tanned blond man named Johnny was attempting to give her driving instructions and laughing at her.

"You, lady, are a prime example of why they really shouldn't give boating licenses out online," Isabel heard him saying to her as they approached. The woman looked like an old hippie, with long blond hair streaked with gray, a makeup-free face, and a long peasant skirt with a tan tank top that made her look topless from a distance. It was weird, the whole thing, Isabel decided. Beatrice was holding Isabel's hand and walking beside her.

"Aha! They've arrived. Laurence, darling, tell me you know how to drive a boat." Isabel was pretty sure this woman had maybe met her dad once before, but she was acting like they were old friends.

"I can probably drive it better than *you* can," her dad said, allowing the woman to embrace him and kiss him on both cheeks and say, "I'm so glad you're here."

"Me, too," Laurence said, then turned to Isabel. "And these are my daughters. Isabel and Beatrice."

"Gorgeous! Adorable! So wonderful to make your acquaintance. You're going to have loads of fun. The boys have already arrived. Cole and Beckett—who by the way are strapping and handsome youngsters who will doubtless be thrilled to meet you, Isabel—and their brother Eliot."

"Hel*en*," Liane murmured. "She's only fourteen . . ."

"And so are *they*," Helen said, smiling. "Now come, let's get your stuff loaded, let's get some firewood and eggs, and let's go."

Isabel realized she was blushing. She took out her phone and sent a final text to Mykayla while she still could. *About to head into the land of no cell phone reception, wish me luck. Some crazy old hippie lady just said the twins are "strapping and handsome youngsters." Feel like this is definite confirmation that they are losers. Help!*

Then she put her phone in her shoulder bag and went to get her overnight case.

Helen talked loudly over the motor as Isabel's father steered the boat toward the island. Beatrice sat in Liane's lap, sucking her thumb. Once the initial "you're not my mommy" shock had worn off, Bea, little traitor that she was, had warmed right up to Liane. Isabel's mom had even expressed concern about it. "What do you want me to do?" Isabel had overheard her dad ask, exasperated, one night when he was picking the girls up for his week with them. "Do you want me to encourage her *not* to like Liane?" "Well, I *am* her mother, not Liane," Gillian had said. "Liane's not trying to be her mother. She's just trying to be nice," Laurence had said, and Isabel had been tempted to poke her head in the kitchen door and say snidely, *Yeah, and she's trying pretty damn hard. Daniel could take some notes from her, in fact.* But she stayed silent. Daniel: there was a whole other story. He didn't try at all, either because he didn't want to, or because he was too boring to do anything but talk about the research he did with her mom or how smart he thought she was. It was beyond Isabel what her mom saw in him. "It's *because* he's the opposite of your father," Mykayla, who seemed to know everything about everything, had once explained. "Also, your mom is clearly impervious to the 'ick' factor."

"Ilsa's not coming," Helen said. "I told her she should, I told her she needs this, but she said she's trying to get settled. Maybe one year, *eventually*, we'll get us all back together here again."

"Yes, we talked the other day. She seems good, though. She seems . . . well, let's talk about it later." Liane glanced at Isabel, and Isabel realized that was because she considered what they were talking about too grown-up for Isabel to hear. Isabel remembered meeting Ilsa, months before, when she had come to visit in the winter, and being mildly fascinated by her. She was nothing like Liane. She was interesting. She was worldly. "And she's so sexy," Mykayla had said later, when they were in her room. "My *lord*. I didn't think it was possible for a woman over thirty to be that sexy." From what Isabel had already overheard her dad and Liane discussing, Ilsa had recently left her husband and was living in her art studio. And meanwhile, Liane's other sister, who also wasn't coming for the weekend, was apparently in the middle of some sort of desperate marriage situation, too. "These women don't have a very good track record," she had said to Mykayla, who had waved a hand. "Yeah, yeah. Who does, these days?"

They were approaching the island and Isabel reached into her bag for some lip gloss, put some on, saw Liane watching her, and felt embarrassed. She took out her phone to check if there was still service. There was: a text from Mykayla had come in. *OMG. MATT ASKED ME OUT.* Isabel felt her eyes blur with sudden tears. She turned the phone off and put it in her bag.

"This is a first: Isabel has turned off her phone," her dad, who had been slowing the boat down and glancing backward, announced. Isabel was grateful she was wearing sunglasses. She could see a person on the dock. A boy. But as they came closer she realized it had to be the younger one, Eliot. He was scrawny and definitely geeky, which did not bode well for his brothers.

The boat bumped into the dock and Isabel sat still.

Liane stood and passed Beatrice to Helen, who was already on the dock. Laurence got out and started tying the boat up.

"Coming, Iz?" Liane asked.

Ick, Isabel thought. *Please don't call me Iz. Only my dad calls me Iz.*

Helen introduced her to the boy, who was indeed Eliot, the youngest. "Where are your brothers?" Helen asked him.

"Inside, playing video games."

"Which is all they ever seem to do," she said. The group followed her up the stone steps.

"You and Beatrice are in Ilsa's room," Helen was saying as they walked toward the cottage. Isabel wrinkled her nose and glanced at her father, trying to indicate that she didn't want to bunk with Bea, but he was walking ahead, hand in hand with Liane.

The cottage was dark, dingy, and outdated. What the big deal about it had been, Isabel had no idea. Liane had talked about it like it was a palace. So what if it was the oldest cottage on the island? That was the operative word: *old.*

"Follow me," Helen said. "Let's put our bags upstairs. Then we'll all go sit outside." She said this loudly, presumably for the benefit of the unseen twins, playing video games in another room Isabel hadn't seen yet.

Upstairs, Isabel said, "I'm pretty tired from the ride up here. I might just take a nap."

"Oh," said Helen. "Okay, that's fine. You come down when you're ready." After Helen was gone, Isabel lay down on the bed, which was a nook in the wall (and, admittedly, slightly charming), closed her eyes, and tried not to think about Mykayla and Matt, the geeky twins, or the cottage next door she didn't even want to look at.

Later, Liane tapped on the door and Isabel wished it was her dad. She realized she missed him, that it had been better when he had been with her mom mostly because, since he had not been close to her mom at all, he had been closer to her. There had been a time during that awful summer when her parents had thought she was clueless (she wasn't) that she had felt closer to him than she had to anyone, ever. Like when he had given her that poem to read, or when they went for their morning canoe rides and he let her steer. But now, with Liane around, even if Liane was trying, even if she *was* nice, she was there, which meant Isabel had to share her dad, and that just wasn't an easy thing to do.

Isabel lay on the bed, thinking these things and looking at Liane. She wished she had pretended to be asleep.

"Dinner is ready," Liane said. "And Helen made your favorite. Fondue."

"How does Helen know what my favorite is?"

"I told her."

"It's too embarrassing to eat in front of a whole bunch of people I've just met. It's more like a private family favorite."

Liane smiled. "A private family favorite. I'm sorry, I didn't know. If you want, I can make you something else."

"Why do you have to be so nice?" Isabel snapped, swinging her legs from the bed to the floor. Liane stood, blinking at her, looking hurt.

"Well, because. Because I—"

"Because you love my dad, that's why. Because you love my dad, so you have to be nice to me."

"No. That's not true. I'm not just being nice to you because I have to be."

Isabel squeezed past Liane and went into the bathroom across the hall, where she wiped the tears that had formed beneath her eyes and put her hair into a messy topknot. It would have to do. What did she care anyway?

But when she walked into the kitchen, she wished she'd taken more care with her appearance. The twins were sitting at the table, looking dubiously at the two fondue pots and the dishes full of vegetables and chopped bread in the middle of the table. They both had yellow-blond hair and tanned skin, even though it was only late June. One of them had longer hair than the other. It was shaggy and fell in front of his face. He was wearing a Milk Music shirt and jeans. The other one had on a plain navy T-shirt and cargo shorts. "Boys, this is Isabel," said Helen. "Her dad calls her Iz." Isabel wanted to die, right then and there. *Die.*

"I'm Beck," said the one with the longer hair.

"I'm Cole," said the other one, and they resumed staring at the fondue pots.

"Got any burgers, Grandma?" the one in the Milk Music shirt asked.

"Give it a chance, Beck. Give it a chance."

Isabel sat in the empty seat beside her father before she realized it was probably Liane's seat. Thankfully, he didn't say anything. In fact, he smiled at her and said, "Did you have a good rest?"

"Yes," she said, looking down at her plate.

Liane arrived, her face blotchy, the way it got when she was upset.

"Wine?" Helen asked, standing behind Isabel with the bottle.

"Um."

"Helen," said Liane. "Laurence doesn't . . . we don't . . . she's *just* turned fourteen."

"Oh, please. You kids had wine with dinner when you were babies."

"Come on, no, we didn't really."

"Well, no, but almost."

"It's okay," said Laurence, and Isabel was surprised. *Wow, he must really be trying to impress Liane's mom.* "Let her have a little bit."

Helen poured a half glass of wine for Isabel, and Isabel looked down at it. "Thanks," she said. "And . . . thanks for making dinner."

Laurence smiled at her. She took some salad. She looked around the silent table. She thought, *This is the most awkward moment of my life.* But she forced herself to be the first one to spear a piece of bread and put it in the fondue pot. She dropped the bread.

"You know what that means?" Helen said, and Liane rolled her eyes. One of the twins caught her eye, the one with the shorter hair, and he smiled. She would have smiled back, but at this point she'd retrieved the cheese-soaked bread and shoved it in her mouth. "Mmm, delicious," she said with her mouth full.

"She's absolutely delightful," Helen said to Laurence.

I'm actually not having an awful time, Isabel realized the next afternoon. She was lying on the dock in her new bikini, reading a book, applying suntan lotion, and pretending not to be watching the twins, who were taking turns driving the boat and wakeboarding. They'd both asked her if she wanted to try, but she'd declined. "I'm pretty tired," she'd said, not wanting to admit that she didn't even know how to wakeboard, not really.

Isabel put down her book and closed her eyes. Helen and Liane were sitting in deck chairs a few feet away, and Laurence was in the water with Beatrice, who was wearing a life jacket and blowing happy bubbles.

"They look like they're having fun," Liane observed.

"They've barely gotten out of the boat all week. Well, except to play video games. And to ogle *this* one."

Isabel realized Helen was talking about her, and that she thought she was asleep. Or maybe she didn't. Helen didn't seem to be one of those adults who avoided saying things to protect young ears. She pretty much seemed to say whatever came to mind.

"Have you heard from Fiona?" Liane asked.

"No, which I take to mean things are going well. According to the boys, she texts every day to make sure they're all right."

Isabel made the mistake of shifting—a fly had landed on her knee—and the women stopped talking. *Too bad. This is actually quite an interesting family.* She reflexively thought about texting this to one of her friends, as she had about a hundred times since she'd arrived, but she couldn't, so she picked up her book.

"Sweetheart, those boys are going to exhaust themselves out there unless you sit up and at least pretend to be noticing them," Helen said to Isabel. Isabel obeyed, pulling herself into an upright position and putting her sunglasses on top of her head. She couldn't tell which twin was on the wakeboard and which one was driving the boat, but whoever it was did a complicated jump and then fell headfirst into the water.

"Oh, hey," Liane said to Helen. "I keep meaning to ask you, is that man around this summer, the one with the greens? What was his name?"

"Iain," Helen said, and there was something strange in her voice that made Isabel look at her, but Helen was wearing sunglasses so it was hard to read her expression.

"Is he here?"

"I don't know."

"I'd like to stop by and visit him. Thank him for the greens last year. And for, well, a few other things."

"Hmm. Okay. You do that."

"I might walk over later today. Should I invite him to dinner?"

"I don't know about that, Liane. I only bought a very specific amount of food." Isabel didn't know Helen that well, but had observed her for long enough to know that this statement was fairly out of character and that normally she was probably more likely to be the type of woman to invite the entire island over for dinner, regardless of how much food she had. *Everyone around here seems to have a drama,* she thought.

No, she wasn't having a terrible time at all.

Later, Isabel swam out to the floating dock and back. She tried not to look over at the other cottage as she swam. She was starting to feel better, sort of. She was trying to hold on to the I-am-not-having-a-terrible-time feeling she'd been having before, while lying on the dock, reading her book in the sunshine. She heard the roar of the boat's motor as the boys came flying around the corner. This time, she could see Beck was driving and Cole was on the wakeboard. Eliot was in the back. He had tried wakeboarding a few times, with fairly disastrous results.

They parked the boat and tied it up. Beck took off his shirt and dove in the water and started swimming lengths back and forth. Meanwhile, Cole was swimming toward the floating dock. Isabel sat, dipping in her toe and looking into the depths, pretending that she wasn't nervous that he was coming over. He climbed up on the dock and sat beside her.

"Hey," he said.

"Hey," she said, feeling herself start to blush. Why couldn't she be more like Mykayla always was around boys? She wasn't even sure she liked Cole, she hardly even knew him, but his very presence beside her was making her nervous.

"What are you reading?"

"Oh. Um. *The Hobbit.* I . . ." She trailed off. "My dad wants us to watch it together, but I really hate to watch a movie until I've read the book, so, uh." She felt embarrassed. But Cole said, "Me, too, totally. Meanwhile, Beck usually watches movies and then tries to write book reports on them."

"Hey, I heard that," came Beck's voice, and they realized he was swimming toward the floating dock. He reached it quickly and climbed up, dripping water on Isabel's book. "And I think *you're* the loser, not me, Cole. Why would I waste my time reading a book for days when I can watch a movie in a few hours and find out everything that happened?"

"Because most of the time the movie is way different than the book, so your teacher will know you took a shortcut."

"Whatever," Beck said.

"Also, um, the *Hobbit* movie is kind of in three parts, and . . . well, as you can see, the book is super-skinny, so in this case, you'd probably actually save time by reading the book," Isabel said.

"Yeah, well, I'm not really into *hobbits*," said Beck. And then he pushed his brother into the water and jumped in after him and Isabel sat watching them roughhouse and thought, *What strange creatures boys are.* Her friend Elise had once said to her, "Boys aren't mysterious at all, you know. They're dirty and disgusting and weird. I know this because I have two brothers." But Isabel didn't have any brothers, so she didn't understand boys at all. She continued to watch them until Beck dunked Cole under too many times and he sputtered out a mouthful of water and crawled back onto the dock.

"Seriously, man, leave me alone. Are you trying to kill me?"

Isabel realized they might really be showing off for her

and she wasn't sure how this made her feel. Good. Special. But also kind of weird. She stood and dove off the dock, leaving her book and towel, and the boys, behind.

Later, Beck came up to the cottage scratching his leg. His skin was covered in an angry-looking rash.

"Gross!" said Cole, who had been upstairs changing. "It looks like leg acne."

"Shut up! It's not leg acne."

"Well, what is it, then?"

"I don't know. Some kind of weird rash."

Helen approached. "Hmm, looks like swimmer's itch."

Isabel heard Cole mutter under his breath, "Looks more like scabies."

"Shut up, asshole."

"Beck," said Helen quietly. "Please. And, Cole, don't goad him. Now, Beck, upstairs in the medicine chest is a bottle of calamine lotion. You should put some on, and try your best not to scratch it. You also probably shouldn't go swimming any more today."

Isabel was fairly surprised when Beck came down a few moments later covered in pink lotion. He looked embarrassed, but he also must have been incredibly itchy. His leg really did look pretty disgusting. She was sitting at the table, shelling peas from the summer garden for Helen, and looked away, but she knew he had seen her looking. He scowled and left the room and she soon heard the sound of a video game in the living room. Helen sighed. "I suppose telling him not to swim any more is as good an excuse as any for him to plug himself back in. But I wish he wouldn't. I can't help but think those things simply soften the brain. Do you play video games, Isabel?"

Isabel shook her head. "No, not interested."

"That's right. I've noticed you like to read. Actual books.

I think that's wonderful. You know, there's a whole floor-to-ceiling shelf full of books in the living room."

"I noticed."

"You're welcome to borrow or take home any book you want."

"Thanks."

Helen went into the pantry and Cole came into the room.

"I was thinking of going for a kayak ride," he said to her quietly. Helen had bought two new kayaks, just for that weekend, apparently. "Do you . . . do you feel like coming?"

Isabel looked at him for a moment and thought that to her he was the cutest of the two brothers. "Sure. That would be fun."

"I always think of this place as my private beach," Cole said. "Even though I know someone owns it, obviously. It's just that hardly any of the people on this lake come up here. It's crazy. Look at these places. Huge! And they don't get used."

Together, they had taken the kayaks to another island, that one much smaller than the one they were on, and privately owned. There was only one massive cottage on it, and a boathouse that was the size of Helen's cottage, at least.

Cole steered his kayak directly toward the sand and she followed. With soft shushing sounds, they both landed their boats.

"Do you want to get out?" he asked.

"Sure," she said. He got out first and held her boat steady while she stepped onto the beach. They sat down beside each other in the sand. She took off her flip-flops and put her feet in the water. They were silent.

"Helen said your dad rented the cottage next door last summer, while your parents were still together. That must be kind of weird," he said.

"It really is," she said. "But you know what? I thought I was going to have an awful time when I came up here, and I'm not."

"I thought that, too," he said. "But . . . I'm not, either."

She wanted to ask, *Are you not having an awful time because of me?* but couldn't bring herself to. That would have sounded insecure and needy. That would have been the exact opposite of what Mykayla would have advised her to do.

Her feet were still in the water and a group of minnows had converged. When she moved her foot slightly they scattered, but returned right away.

"What do you think they think I am?" she said.

"Who?"

"The minnows."

He looked down at her foot. "I don't know," he said. "Maybe some kind of giant? Some kind of . . . really pretty giant?"

She glanced sideways at him and then looked back down into the water. The moment seemed to pass too quickly.

"I think my parents are getting a divorce, too," said Cole.

"Really? That sucks. I'm sorry."

"Yeah. I mean, I don't know. They haven't talked to us about it. But . . . well, it's like they think we're dumb, like they think we don't notice they basically never talk to each other anymore, or hear them arguing in their room at night."

"Yeah, but aren't they supposed to be spending the weekend together talking or something?" She hesitated. "Sorry. I've heard your aunt talk to my dad about it."

"Yeah. I guess. I really don't know. You probably know more than I do. They seem to think me and my brothers shouldn't be in the loop. *So* annoying."

"My parents were like that. We spent most of last summer up here, and they weren't together, they were just pretending. Obviously, Bea didn't notice much, but I could tell something was not right. It was pretty offensive, really."

"Yeah. That's the right word. *Offensive*."

"Are you mad at your parents?"

Cole sighed. "Sort of. Sometimes. You know, they're not bad, as far as parents go. My mom is pretty uptight, but she's also a good mom. She does a good job of putting up with Beck's shit, and he can be such a prick—but that's the problem, he's just turning into more of a prick, and it seems like for the past few months things are just getting worse. And she's checked out. And my dad . . . well, something is up with him. It seems like things used to be so good but I didn't really notice, because they were good. And now they're not, and that sucks, because I never appreciated it before."

She nodded. "Uh-huh. That's exactly it. When things start to go bad, you look back and think, *Wow, things were amazing and I didn't care.*"

"Because you didn't have to. Because you didn't know it was going to end."

"I really liked being an only child. I'm pretty sure my parents only had Bea to try to save their marriage, and things started to go way worse after she was born. Plus—well, I love her, but she's sort of a pain in the ass."

He laughed. "Yeah, she sort of is. Sorry."

"No offense taken at all."

"So, what's it like, you know . . . with Liane?"

She glanced at him.

"It's okay, I know she's my aunt, but you can say what you want to me."

"I don't have anything bad to say about her," said Isabel. "Really, she's super-nice. It's just . . . hard to share my dad, that's all. It's funny, because I guess most girls are closer to their moms, but it's really my dad and I . . . we're really close. I have no problem sharing my mom, for some reason. She's— kind of distant. She's a scientist," she concluded, hoping that explained things.

"I couldn't imagine having to do that, having to share either of my parents."

Isabel bit her lip. "Maybe it's okay, though," she said. "I mean, maybe it *will* be okay, one day. My dad at least seems happier with Liane. My mom—well, she's not the happiest person in general. I don't know if she'll ever be happy, and my dad at least seems to want to be happy. I think that's important."

"If only our parents understood how well we know them," Cole said.

"If only."

And then he reached for her hand and they sat on the beach and she looked at him and he looked at her. She wanted him to kiss her, but, because she'd never kissed a boy before, she had no idea how to convey this. Finally, she looked away from him. That was when she heard the sound of a boat motor, coming closer.

"Hey . . . is that . . . what are they *doing*?" Cole let go of her hand and stood. "That's Beck. And he's got Eliot driving the fucking boat." Cole started waving his arms. "He was trying to get Eliot to do it yesterday, and Eliot pretty much does everything Beck tells him to. But he has no clue what he's doing."

"Plus, don't you need a spotter if you're going to wakeboard? Wasn't that what Helen insisted on if she was going to let you guys go out in the boat?"

"Yes," Cole said. "Come on, let's go try to get their attention."

Another boat was coming around the island now. "Cole, Eliot's not watching where he's going," Isabel said.

"I know, I know, I—" Cole waved his arms again, and so did Isabel.

"Eliot, watch out!" she screamed.

Isabel was certain she would never forget what happened next.

16
Seagull (*Laridae*)

Gulls are monogamous and colonial breeders that display mate fidelity that usually lasts for the life of the pair. Divorce of mated pairs does occur, but it apparently has a social cost that persists for a number of years after the breakup. Gulls also display high levels of site fidelity, returning to the same colony after breeding there once and usually even breeding in the same location within that colony.

When Tim and Fiona married, they didn't write their own vows, but they did each choose a small reading to recite to one another during the ceremony. Fiona thought it would make the ceremony seem more personal (as if there were something *im*personal about standing in front of all your friends and family and declaring your intent to spend your lives together). Fiona still had Tim's reading, deep within her bedside table drawer. It was on a cue card, and it had been dog-eared and bent when he gave it to her, from carrying around all day in his tuxedo pocket. Now the paper had turned yellow and the ink had bled a little. *Not till the sun excludes you, do I exclude you; not till the waters refuse to glisten for you, and the leaves to rustle for you, do my words refuse to glisten, and rustle for you.* Walt Whitman. "I hope you know what I meant by that," he had said to her later.

"That I'll love you until the end of the world." Tim was not the type to make such sweeping romantic pronouncements, and Fiona was not the type to crave them. Which was why she *had* believed him. *Until the end of the world.*

And yet now, here they were, spending a weekend doing "intensive" couples therapy. It had been Fiona's idea—well, Helen's, actually; she had suggested it during one of the phone calls that had become so regular they were almost daily. Fiona still felt surprised by the way she felt when she hung up, like there was this person (person, not mother; it was one of the things Helen had asked of her during their talk in the labyrinth, to try to see that just as she, Fiona, was not *only* a mother, neither was Helen) she had neglected to get to know properly all these years. And while, yes, Helen and Fiona were still nothing alike, there wasn't as much threat in it anymore. When she stopped doing battle against Helen, stopped fearing being like her, she was able to really see her. And she realized that maybe, in some ways, being more like her wouldn't be so awful. So she had decided to try something different, to take her mother's advice and seek out the therapy.

She didn't hold out much hope, though. According to the research she had done, the main reason couples counseling so often failed was because couples mostly only sought therapy when things were already broken. Apparently, you were supposed to engage in couples therapy regularly, get monthly tune-ups to keep your marriage healthy. It amazed Fiona that she now wished she had done this. The old her would never have risked going to couples therapy even if presented with empirical data that it would help protect her marriage for the future. The old her would not have wanted to risk anyone finding out and thinking that her marriage was anything less than perfect.

The therapist's office was new. So new, in fact, that the wall-to-wall bookshelves in the office were empty. Fiona and

Tim had already been a few times, in the preceding weeks, and every time they arrived, Fiona wondered if there would be any books. The shelves always remained empty, though. It made Fiona feel as though perhaps it wasn't a real office, as though perhaps none of this was happening at all. They were always early for appointments that were always late to start, and they would sit and stare at those empty shelves and dread the moment when the doors opened and the couple came out. What if it was someone they knew?

The therapist, who was named Audrey Stevens and preferred to be called "Dr. Audrey" instead of "Dr. Stevens," employed a method called Imago Relationship Therapy. She had just moved to Rye from New York City and was supposed to be one of the best Imago therapists in the state. (Who had told Fiona about her? Jane, of course. "I credit her with saving my marriage, and I didn't think anything could," she had said to Fiona. *But you don't seem happy,* Fiona had wanted to say. She hadn't, though. Jane was still a new friend. She didn't want to risk offending her.)

Dr. Audrey had dark brown hair she always wore in a French twist, and reading glasses with tiny semicolons on the upper edge of each frame. Fiona thought she should be older, less pretty, less stylish. She wasn't threatened by her attractiveness. She just wasn't particularly comforted by her. Audrey used an iPad instead of a notepad, and this threw Fiona off, too. She suspected sometimes that maybe Dr. Audrey was just checking her email when she was tapping away at the screen as Fiona and Tim talked.

Tonight, for their second last-ditch session of the day, they sat on the brown leather couch and Fiona realized they were as far away from each other as they could possibly be. Fiona's legs and arms were crossed. *Judging from our body language alone, she probably doesn't have any hope for us at all,* Fiona thought.

Tim was talking. She had thought he'd be more reticent, but in her opinion he had been dominating the sessions. He had said so many things about her to a person they hardly knew. Things that made her feel excluded, diminished, and exposed. *How did it come to this?* It wasn't even about Samira anymore, either. They had barely even discussed her. Dr. Audrey had cautioned them to wait, to process and distill everything that had led up to the crisis first. *We were so, so broken and I didn't even know it.*

"It wasn't so bad when the kids were really little, when we were living in Toronto, but after we moved here, when it seemed like our lives really settled into a routine, she started to make me feel like I was irrelevant to the process," he was saying. "Like I was irrelevant in *general.* And also, to be completely honest, like she didn't really mind that I started having to go away so much. That she kind of liked it. That when I was around I was nothing but a nuisance. Just some guy who didn't know where anything was in the cupboards."

Fiona wanted to scream at him to stop. It was all true, of course. This was *exactly* how she had felt about him. She just couldn't believe Tim found it so easy to talk about her as though she weren't in the room. Meanwhile, she would either say nothing, or she would open her mouth and start to speak in an angry, irrational-sounding voice she didn't recognize. She had lost it once, completely lost it, and started shouting at him and crying, and then, when she had finished with her outburst, Dr. Audrey had shared a complicit glance with Tim and said, "Well, *that* was unpleasant."

"Whose side are you on?" Fiona had snapped.

"Fiona, I'm not on anyone's side. I'm just trying to help you."

Now, Fiona reached for a tissue and blew her nose loudly, hoping it would alert the other two people in the room to how wounded she was.

Dr. Audrey glanced at her and Fiona read only pity in her expression. "Time's up," she said. "Let's try again tomorrow."

The next morning, Fiona stood alone in her white, perfect kitchen. She made a caffè americano, then out of habit started making one for Tim. She stopped, stared at the two coffees, then dumped them both in the sink. She thought about something else Helen had said to her the day before, about Ilsa. "I realize you and Ilsa have never quite clicked—but she has always looked up to you. You never seemed to see that, but look at her. She tried too hard to emulate you, because she thought you were perfect, the ideal woman who could do everything. She's just a little sister who looks up to you."

Fiona left the two cups on the counter. She went into the basement to get her basket of cleaning supplies because, if she was going to do this, she wanted to arm herself with something. In the front foyer she picked up her purse and car keys and left the house.

At Ilsa's studio, she knocked. No answer. She knocked again. She thought for a moment that her sister probably had a man in there with her, and the familiar old resentments surfaced. *But even if she does, so what? She left Michael, didn't she? Why judge her, even now?*

"Ilsa? Hello?"

The door opened. Sun was streaming in through the window behind her and the flyaways rising up from her messy hair were illuminated. For a moment Ilsa looked angelic, as though she had a halo. Then she stepped into shadow and the halo disappeared.

"I thought I'd clean up in here," Fiona said, because she didn't know what else to say.

"Oh." Ilsa didn't sound especially surprised to be greeted

by her sister and a bucket of cleaning supplies so early in the morning.

"Do you have a mop?"

"In that closet, yeah. But, Fiona, you don't really have to . . ."

"Ilsa, this place is disgusting."

"Thanks."

"Well, it *is*. I'm guessing you think disorganization breeds creativity, and what do I know about creativity . . . but I want to help you." The words hung in the air. *I want to help you.* "You live here now," she continued. "This is your *home*. You need to make it feel like one." She was trying to say something else, but she couldn't put it into words. Dr. Audrey would probably say she was withholding. She was trying to say: *I forgive you. I'm not angry with you anymore. I understand.* And also she was trying to say: *I need you, too. I'm just as lost as you are.* But how did you just come right out and say something like that?

"What's that, Vim?" Ilsa asked. "I'm not sure it will work on the floors in here."

"It's not *Vim*," Fiona said. "It's biodegradable, plant-enzyme-based cream cleanser, and I'm not planning to use it on the floors." She lifted another bottle filled with yellow-tinged liquid. "I'm going to use *this* on the floors." Now she turned and started looking around the studio. "Wow. This place is *gross*," she said. "It's *really* disgusting in here. How do you live like this?"

"It's not gross. It's . . . *bohemian*." Ilsa attempted a smile.

Fiona moved to the windowsill, where a long-abandoned cup of tea had started to grow mold. She held the offending mug up in the dust-mote-studded light. "*Gross*."

"Yes, fine, that *is* gross." Ilsa walked over and took the mug from Liane and dumped it in the tiny sink, rinsing the horrid little chunks down the drain. Then she turned on the kettle and watched in silence as Fiona started to move chairs, pick up pieces of laundry. "Hey, I have Le Palais des Thés Imperial," Ilsa said. "I know how much you love it." The kettle was vibrating now, the water inside in controlled chaos. *Click.* Then it stopped. Only a small puff of steam betrayed the abandon of the moment before. "Do you want some?"

"Sure. Do you have milk? Wait. Never mind. Forget I asked." Fiona walked over to where her sister was making the tea. "Hey, is that a new tattoo?" Ilsa's other wrist was now encircled in a ribbon of ink, too.

"Yes."

"What is it this time?" Fiona hoped her voice conveyed interest, that she didn't sound judgmental. She was trying not to.

"A Cézanne quote. *Nous vivons dans un arc-en-ciel de chaos.* We live in a rainbow of chaos."

"It's . . . nice," Fiona said, feeling like she was being too careful with her sister. It wasn't natural. She wished there was something she could say to explain and then eradicate everything that had ever happened between them. But she couldn't, so she blew on her tea until it had cooled enough to drink. They made small talk, about the weather, about the kids, about what trip Helen was taking next, about Liane and her new almost-stepchildren. Then her cup was empty and she picked up a rag and started cleaning again.

At the drafting table Ilsa used as a desk, Fiona had to move a towering pile of mail.

"Oh," Ilsa said. "I can help with that, at least." Fiona was looking down. On top were four large envelopes, emblazoned with bold-font entreaties to please send letters. Ilsa had reached the table and made a move to hide the letters at the bottom of the pile.

"You don't need to hide them. I saw them already. Wow, how many of those foster children do you have?" she asked.

Ilsa sighed. "Four."

"*Four?* How can you afford that? You haven't . . . I mean, you haven't even tried to come up with any sort of a settlement with Michael, so how are you paying—"

Ilsa shook her head quickly. "I can't, I can't do that right now. The guilt will kill me."

"But, Ilsa . . ."

"But, what? I can't. I just have to wait. One day we'll figure it out. I don't deserve anything from him. I can't, I just can't."

"Of course you deserve something." Fiona felt surprised by her words. But she meant them, she realized.

"You don't think it's unfair? You and Tim wouldn't accuse me of trying to take him for all he's worth if I took him to divorce court now?"

"I can't speak for Tim at the moment. But *I* wouldn't accuse you of that."

Ilsa was silent. Then she reached forward and put her hand on top of her sister's. "We're a pair, aren't we?"

Fiona looked down at their hands. "We're a pair," she whispered. They stayed like that. She wasn't sure for how long.

"How are things going?" Ilsa finally asked. "The counseling."

"Terribly. It's absolutely awful." She laughed a dry laugh. "I don't think it's going to work. I might have to move in here with you." She tried to laugh again but couldn't manage it.

"You could never live in this filth."

"Maybe *you'd* have to move in with me then."

"Fiona," Ilsa began. She sighed and clasped her hands together, almost as though she were about to pray. "You and Tim . . . you *will* get through this." She closed her eyes now. "He's such a good man," she said. "I know he kept a huge secret from you, but I'm sure it was so hard for him. And also—and also, there's something I should tell you. Maybe it will help you understand just how loyal he is, how good he is. There was this one night—"

But Fiona interrupted her. "Don't, Ilsa. It was so long ago. Just leave it, okay?"

Ilsa opened her eyes wide. "*You knew?*"

"Of course I knew. Tim told me that very night. But his honesty with me, at least under some circumstances, is not really the point anymore. A good man he might be, but I'm not sure either of us is good enough to reconcile at this point."

"You have to do everything in your power, Fiona," Ilsa said, her voice very soft.

"But why me? Why do I have to be the champion of our marriage? Why can't it be *him?*"

Ilsa shook her head. "Because he's not as strong as you are. No one is."

Fiona looked back down at the stack of envelopes. She blinked quickly. She tried to be as strong as her sister thought she was. "You know, just because you feel guilty is no reason for you to be squatting in your studio—"

"I'm not squatting!" Ilsa interrupted.

"Whatever it is. I'm just saying, you really don't need to punish yourself anymore. You should get a place to live, a place for Ani and Xavier to visit."

Ilsa didn't say anything.

"I'm sure Tim would kill me for saying this, but—well, you really should be getting a lawyer. I can help you if you want. Because Michael might be my husband's best friend, but . . . you're my sister."

Ilsa touched Fiona's hand again, squeezing it quickly. Then they cleaned the studio together.

Later, Fiona would think that it always seemed to be when she was out gardening that the really awful calls came in. Although, so far in her life, she had only had one phone call she considered truly awful. After this afternoon, two.

"Hello?"

"Fiona. It's Liane. Something has happened. To Beck. A boating accident. He's hurt. They're airlifting him to Sick-Kids Hospital now. You and Tim need to—you need to come. Right away. I'm sorry. I'm sorry." Liane was crying.

How did they get to Toronto? There must have been planes and cars involved, but as Fiona walked toward the front entrance of the hospital, the logistics of how she got there were completely lost to her. She walked faster, ahead of Tim. She looked back at her husband and said, "Tim. I need to run. I need to see the boys, right now."

"Then run," Tim said, his voice weary. He was walking slowly, like the trip there had aged him, like he was the injured one. "I'll catch up."

She knew that what she should have done was walk into the hospital at her husband's side. She knew that her son was in surgery, that she wouldn't be able to see him, that there was absolutely nothing she could do, but she still ran. Cole needed her. Eliot needed her. *Eliot. Oh, Eliot. What will become of you now? What if Beck doesn't—* She silenced the thought by running faster.

She found them, eventually, in a waiting room on the sixth floor.

"Where's Tim?" someone asked, she wasn't sure who.

"He's coming," she said. "He's right behind me."

And then Helen stepped forward, stepped between her and her two boys, who were sitting, staring ahead, appearing to be in shock, which they probably were. *Oh, boys. Oh, my boys. Oh, my god.* The pain she felt nearly knocked her backward with its force. She now understood why people said they were brought to their knees by something.

"I'm sorry," Helen was saying. "Fiona, I'm so, so sorry."

"My god, is he . . . gone?" Pain, pain, pain everywhere. How was she still standing?

"No, *no*," Helen said. "That's not what I meant. I meant I'm sorry because it's my fault, all my fault. Getting the stupid boat, not watching them carefully enough. I'm so sorry."

Fiona stood staring at her mother, taking her in. *It's my fault.* And it was true, there was probably a time Fiona would have blamed Helen completely, for this, for everything. But now she said, "Of course it's not your fault, Mom. Please don't blame yourself." And she allowed her mother to hold her and hug her the way she desperately wanted to hug her sons, because she understood that that was what her mother needed. And also because this was what she needed from her mother. When she knew it was enough for both of them, she moved across the room to her boys.

"Boys," she whispered. "Boys. It's going to be okay. Mommy's here." And they both stood and pressed against her. "It's not your fault," she said to both of them. "It's not your fault, either. Got it?"

Tim arrived and they spoke with a nurse. Beck's doctor wasn't available, of course, because he was performing the surgery. The words Fiona remembered the nurse saying: *head injury, brain trauma, small hemorrhage. Small*, the nurse said again. Fiona had no concept of what the diameter meant. *Hopeful*, the nurse said. Well, she said something other than "hopeful," she must have put the word into a sentence, something like, "The doctors are very hopeful," but Fiona was having trouble processing the words the woman was saying because she knew that somewhere in the hospital her son was lying on a gurney, and his skull was open and vulnerable to the world instead of closed and protected the way it should be, and his brain was bleeding and they were trying to stop it. Small, big, it didn't matter, there was a hemorrhage, and they were trying to stop it, but they might not be able to, or they might do damage in the process, which meant she could lose her boy in other ways even if she didn't lose him completely.

What made it more painful was that everyone seemed to think it was his or her fault, and it wasn't. It wasn't Eliot's fault, even though he had been driving the boat. And it wasn't Cole's fault, even though he had been somewhere else, and had whispered to her that if only he had been with his brother, this wouldn't have happened. And it wasn't Helen's fault, for getting the boat in the first place.

It was Fiona's fault, because she had become so wrapped up in her own life she had forgotten about them, she had left them alone to make the bad choices that children, and teen-age boys especially, were wont to make.

She closed her eyes. She pressed her lips together. But she couldn't stop the tears, and realized she didn't want to. *If he survives, I'll do anything,* she said, and realized she was praying. She couldn't remember the last time she had prayed. *Dear God, please help me. Please help my son. Please be with those doctors, please guide their hands. Please be with us all. Please be with Tim. Please help me.* Funny, she thought to herself, her thoughts growing a little less blurry. *So many of us say we don't believe in God, but we do. When the chips are down, we do. We get right in the foxhole. Dear God, please be with my son. Please help him. Please save him. Please save all of us.*

The nurse had said the surgery was going to take another six hours at least. Six hours. Fiona didn't know if she could bear it, but what choice did she have?

They sat in the waiting room. They drank tea. They did not eat. The boys were silent, but every ten minutes or so she would reach for one of their hands. And then finally Cole said, "I need to go for a walk. Come on, Eliot, let's go." And he looked at Fiona, and then at Tim. "Is that okay?" her little boy said. "Of course," Tim said, and Fiona realized she had said "Of course" at the same time, and that Tim was reaching for his wallet and handing them both what seemed like way too much money. "Get yourselves some food, when was the last time you ate?" This was usually her department.

The nurse had suggested going for walks, even getting outside for air, but Fiona didn't see how she could possibly leave the hospital. What if something happened and she wasn't there?

Still, after twenty minutes with the boys still gone, she realized she needed to walk, too. "I think I need to get a little air as well," she said, and stood. No one offered to go with her, but she knew this wasn't because they didn't want to. They were waiting for her to ask for company. She didn't.

She took the elevator down and ended up in the main lobby, where she had been, hours that had felt like days, before. She saw the Starbucks and went to stand in the line.

Maybe I'll get a muffin.

But halfway through the lineup, she realized she didn't want a muffin. There was a lump in her throat she knew she would be unable to swallow over. And she didn't want to stand still.

She walked toward the front doors of the hospital and out into the sunlight. She continued to the street and stood on the sidewalk, looking up at the hospital. *Somewhere, in there, lies my son. Inside there is my family. Somewhere, my other two sons are walking, or sitting, or talking, or not talking. Somewhere in there, something small is bleeding, and they're trying to stop it.*

She turned away from the hospital. She looked at her watch. Three more hours. She started to walk. She was surprised by the fact that Toronto still felt like home, by the way the CN tower quickly became a landmark, a beacon, by the way the familiar buildings seemed to hold her, to keep her from stumbling or falling to the ground and screaming up at the sky. She passed the other hospitals, Mount Sinai, Women's College, and she thought, *There are other people in those hospitals, other families, other children, other people dying, or not dying, or being born, or not being born.*

She headed down University. She turned right on Queen. She walked past the stores, the bars, the restaurants, the street musicians. She did not process what had changed and what had not since the last time she had been in the city. She turned left on Spadina.

Eventually she got to the bridge. She stopped, stood at the edge, looked down at the train tracks, then across and toward the lake. A haze hung over it. A plane was descending to land on the airport on the island. For a moment she felt panicked that she was so far away from the hospital. She looked at her watch. Two and a half more hours. She kept watching the plane until it disappeared from sight. Then she watched the white shapes of the seagulls, feathers shining in the sun, flying up, down, around, over. They seemed beautiful from afar, even though she knew they weren't.

Finally, she called Tim. He answered right away. "Fiona. Where are you? Are you okay?"

"Has there been any word?"

"No. Nothing."

She swallowed over the lump. "Do you remember when we lived here, and do you remember when there was the blackout, when I still worked at the school and you worked on Bay Street, and . . . do you remember all the phones were out, and I didn't have a cell phone, and we had no way to reach each other?"

"Yes."

"Do you remember what we decided that night, by candlelight, when we finally did make it home to each other?

Remember what you told me? You said we needed to have a disaster plan, as a family. I think you were still thinking about 9/11. You said, 'If something bad ever happens, get the boys and go to the bridge at Spadina and Front.' Remember? And I said . . . I said, 'Something bad, like what, like the end of the world?' And you said, 'Yes, if it's the end of the world, go there, and I'll come find you.'"

Silence. And then Tim said, "Yes. I remember that."

"Well, I'm there. It's the end of the world, and I'm on that bridge. Will you please come find me?"

She waited. He did come, and when he did, they hesitated, but then they reached for each other. She started to sob, not caring what the people walking past them might think. *It's the end of the world,* she wanted to say to a girl who looked askance at them as she tapped at the screen of her cell phone. *It's the end of the world, you should go be with the person you love.* Instead, she buried her face in her husband's shoulder. When she didn't think she could cry anymore, she lifted her head.

"When all this is over, when Beck is recovering . . ." she said, keeping her voice firm, because he *would* recover, there was no other option. "When things have settled a little, we should sit the boys down and we should tell them everything together. We should even tell them who their asshole of a grandfather is. They might get a kick out of that, right?" She laughed in the way only a person who has just been sobbing can laugh. Tim laughed, too. She had told him about her father, during therapy, and he had marveled over how many of the band's albums were in the house, yet Fiona had never said anything. "And then . . . you should invite her to come stay with us for a while. Samira. Invite her here. It's the right thing to do. "

Tim reached for her again. The embrace was different this time. "Thank you," he whispered. She could still feel it between them, everything that had been said and done, all the ways in which they had taken each other for granted, all the hurt and resentment. But the flow had stopped. The hemorrhaging was over. Maybe they would never be the same again, but they would survive this. She would champion her marriage and she would succeed, because Fiona did not fail.

17

Black Vulture (*Coragyps atratus*)

Black vultures discourage infidelity. In fact, all nearby vultures attack any vulture caught philandering. These creatures do mate for life in the social sense of living together in pairs, but they rarely stay strictly faithful, and many males often end up raising offspring who are not their own, sometimes unwittingly.

H i, it's me! I have news," Liane said.

"You're getting married. You're pregnant."

"Nope. Laurence and I are *not* getting married. We're going to live in sin forever."

Ilsa laughed. "Well, then. Congratulations on your non-engagement."

"Thank you very much. Would you like to hear our reasons?"

"Of course."

"There's really only one main reason: because we want to wake up next to each other every day for the rest of our lives and know that we're there because we want to be, not because we have to be. And because we don't want the girls to think that marriage is the only option, that you have to do it out of duty, that you have to contractually tie yourself to someone in order for love to mean anything."

"Very progressive."

"Well, I do spend most of my time at a university. All those young minds must be rubbing off on me."

"You sound like Helen, by the way."

"Indeed. The waking up beside each other because we want to is a direct Helen quote. She's become very good at giving advice lately. Anyway, Fiona says you're having a show. At Patrick Francis's gallery in New York. And that it opens next Saturday. And I want you to know I'm coming. Me and Laurence, and Isabel, too, who is, apparently, sort of eager to see Cole. Isn't that cute? She'd also really like to see Beck, to make absolutely certain that he is, as Fiona and Tim say he is, making a full recovery. To be honest, I'd like to see that for myself as well."

"You should definitely come see Beck—he's doing great. But you don't have to go to the trouble of coming to my opening, it's just a small show at a gallery no one's ever heard of."

"It's *your* show. And I've heard of the gallery."

"That's because we went to school with Patrick."

"Ilsa, of course I'm going to come! I want to support you."

"Okay, but you should know, this isn't really like any art I've ever done before."

"Exciting! I can't wait to see it."

Later, Ilsa hung up the phone and stood in the middle of her studio, now her home. The room contained a single bed with a wrought-iron frame that she'd found at an antique store, and the furniture that had been at her studio before—two barstools, a shorter stool that she sat on in front of canvases, a drafting table. The armoire that had housed her old paintings and letters now housed her clothes and shoes; the shelves that had held painting supplies and detritus in general now housed books, necessities; and her art supplies lived on shelves she'd affixed to the walls and secretly believed would probably one day come crashing down because she had never had to install anything before.

Ilsa looked at her watch. She still had a few minutes before she had to leave to pick Ani up from school, as she did each day now. She'd take her home for lunch, where Xavier would be waiting with the nanny. Home as in her old home, but no longer her actual home. Some days she knew she had made the right decision, and other days she couldn't believe that she had done this terrible thing.

It's not forever. One day I'll have a home to share with my daughter and son. So far, Ani and Xavier seemed to be adjusting all right to the change. If anything, they saw Ilsa more. Ilsa painted— or attempted to paint; she was still having trouble and her latest show actually had nothing to do with painting—in the mornings and evenings, and spent her afternoons with Ani and Xavier. Sometimes she'd give the kids dinner and then leave when Michael got home. She and Michael were always cordial to each other. Sometimes she stayed and fell asleep on the couch if he was going to be late, or slept over when he was traveling on business.

It was a strange arrangement, but it was working. Or at least it wasn't spectacularly *not* working. And one day, things would change. She didn't know how, but they would. Didn't they always? It was the one thing you could count on in life.

I should probably clean up. The studio was messy again; when Fiona visited, she always brought her cleaning supplies. Ilsa crossed the room and picked up a stack of books. Old journals, things she had taken out of drawers, looked at, and never put back. Maybe, if she cleaned up more often, she'd be able to bring herself to show her children where she lived. But she grew distracted, as she did every time she tried to clean. She opened the cover of one of the journals. It was red leather with a fishnet pattern embossed on the front. The entry she glanced at was from the cottage, two summers before. She'd been reading a Violet Trefusis biography. She remembered she'd been struck by the lines she read, which she'd recorded in her journal:

> Heaven preserve us from all the sleek and dowdy virtues, such as punctuality, conscientiousness, fidelity and smugness! What great man was ever constant? What great queen was ever faithful? Novelty is the very essence of genius and will always be. If I were to die tomorrow, think how I should have lived!

She shook her head. She had indeed decided to *live*, to shirk all those "sleek and dowdy" virtues, and it had very nearly destroyed her. Did she regret it? She still wasn't sure. What surprised her was how lonely she felt sometimes, when all she had craved was the space to be who she was. It also surprised her that there were times when she thought of Lincoln and felt an ache that wasn't hatred or anger. She had practically sacrificed her marriage for him before deciding to sacrifice it simply for herself. She had carried and lost his child. It seemed strange to her that he was not in her life, not even on the periphery. She never saw him and Fiona never spoke of him. She supposed she could ask, but couldn't bring herself to do that. And what would Fiona say? *Yes, he still exists. Yes, he is still in this world. No, he has never asked about you.* Time would heal it. That was one thing you could be certain of in life. At least, she hoped.

"Hi, Ani!"

Ilsa looked up from lining up her purchases on the black conveyor belt at the organic supermarket close to the house: rice milk, elderflower water, arugula, mushrooms, berries, a maple-flavored candy for Ani, who was standing behind her and who had patiently endured her mother's wandering up and down the aisles and coming up nearly empty. Michael was working late that night and she was making dinner for the children.

Ani was looking at the woman shyly. "Hi," Ilsa said, a question in her voice. The woman had olive skin, aquiline features, and curly hair pulled back in a low ponytail. She was skinny and tall. Something about her lithe shape suggested boundless energy, even though she was standing still.

"I'm Tabitha," said the woman, smiling at Ilsa with closed lips.

"Ilsa," said Ilsa, not smiling at all even though she was certain she was supposed to.

"We did meet, back when you first moved into the neighborhood. I stopped by. We live on the corner of Oak Leaf and Elm." The woman said this proudly. Ilsa knew she was supposed to be impressed. Those were the two most desirable streets in the neighborhood, she had heard someone say once. Maybe *this* woman, when they had supposedly met.

"We had coffee. Your daughter had just been born. You kept her in her carrier the whole time." The woman let out a short laugh and Ilsa felt embarrassed. Those days had been a blur. She didn't remember Tabitha, but she did remember the carrier. It was a sling, actually, a complicated one that came with a DVD and made Ilsa cry several times, as she sat cross-legged on the floor in front of the television, searching for clues. Once she got it to work and tucked Ani into it and Ani stopped crying and settled her downy head on Ilsa's aching chest, Ilsa wouldn't take her out until she absolutely had to. And this woman said she had stopped by. Had coffee. Ilsa shook her head slightly. No. She didn't remember. "I'm sorry . . ."

"Hi, Ani," the woman said again, smiling and nodding encouragingly at Ani. Ani looked up at her mother. Ilsa didn't nod or encourage.

"My daughter, Georgie, is in Ani's class. They adore each other. Ani is all Georgie talks about."

"Right," Ilsa said. "Of course. Georgie."

"They're best friends," Tabitha said, talking to Ilsa but looking at Ani, still smiling and nodding. "She'll be so sad she wasn't with me today when we ran into you!" She turned to Ilsa. "She's at home with her father and brothers right now. Mommy's afternoon out!"

"Mmm, wow, grocery shopping," Ilsa said, and realized after she said it that she might have sounded sarcastic.

"We should plan a playdate," said the woman. She was pulling out her wallet. She handed Ilsa a card. "Here. Get in touch. Wednesdays are usually perfect for us. You?" Now Ilsa glanced at Ani and saw something like hope in her eyes. Ilsa took the card.

"Thank you," Ilsa said, looking down at the card. *Tabitha Woods,* the card read. *Rugrat Wrangler.*

Tabitha laughed that short laugh again. "Aren't they hilarious? One of my mom friends got them for me as a joke, but they're actually quite useful for setting up playdates."

Ilsa thought for a second about her own childhood, about all the traveling, the summers at the cottage. How, when they were home, Helen welcomed all the neighborhood children in and let her own children run house to house. It felt like they had complete freedom, that she and Liane could run all over the neighborhood if they wanted to, hide between the houses, come home when the streetlights came on. She suddenly hated the term *playdate.* But Ani. Ani wanted this. And it wasn't the kind of world anymore where you could just let your children run free.

The cashier had started ringing up her purchases. "Nice to meet you," Ilsa said, and pocketed the card, while Tabitha gave her a strange look. *Right. We already met.*

"Bye, Ani!" the woman said brightly.

Ani didn't say anything back and Ilsa thought maybe she was supposed to admonish her, say something like, *Say goodbye to the nice lady, Ani.* But she didn't, and Tabitha left and Ilsa paid for her purchases, took her daughter's hand, and walked home with her. "I love you, Ani," Ilsa said when they were halfway there.

"I love you, too," Ani said, and squeezed her hand. "Look!" She pointed up to the sky. "The pretty birds!" They were vultures, which Ilsa secretly always found slightly terrifying. But Ani always pointed them out and exclaimed over them when she saw them flying over a wooded area close to the house.

"Yes, the pretty birds. Do you want to have a playdate with Georgia?"

"Georgie. Yes."

"Okay."

"Mama?"

"Yes?"

"Are you going to sleep at our house again, every night, soon?"

What if I'm wrong? What if this is the wrong thing, not the right thing? What if she's not going to see this as me having integrity, but instead as me tearing her life apart when she was only four?

"No," Ilsa finally said. "No, I don't think I am." Saying it didn't hurt as much as the moment *before* saying it had. "But I'm always going to see you, every day, and I'm always going to love you, always, always, always . . . and one day soon I'll have my own house, and you can come there, and maybe sometimes . . ." She realized she was saying too much. She squeezed Ani's hand again and hoped she wouldn't ask more questions. She didn't. They walked in silence. But Ilsa thought maybe it wasn't a sad silence. She thought maybe it was a hopeful one.

• • •

Ilsa was surprised at how full the gallery was the night of her show's opening. She had been nervous, almost debilitatingly so, had imagined no one coming at all, an empty room, just her and Patrick, her sensing his disappointment and feeling it mix with her shame, not only at the poor showing, but at what she had tried to pawn off as art. *You didn't even pick up a brush. All you did was cut, paste, shellac. Ani could have done it.*

Her whole family was there: Fiona and Tim hand in hand, Tim smiling and kind, without any bitterness underlying his words, no accusation in his eyes indicating that he held it against her that she had left his best friend; Beck, looking almost healed, only with shorter hair, a scar you could see when he turned his head, and a slightly chastened expression; Cole, handsome and proud with young Isabel beside him; Samira, Tim's daughter; Ilsa was very nearly over saying it, but it still gave her a tiny little shock every time—with her long, caramel-colored hair and eyes that were like Tim's and mouth that was like someone else's; Laurence and Liane, Beatrice between them in a black and red dress with crinoline under the skirt, staring at the artwork, wide-eyed. ("Pretty," Ilsa had heard her say, and tried not to feel embarrassed that Beatrice was pointing to a small square of paper decoupaged to the page that was, in fact, Ilsa's breast.) But in addition to her family, there were also dozens and dozens of others, some friends, some fellow artists, and some people, many people, she didn't even know. She felt warmth in the buzz of conversation. Plus, Patrick had told her that one lone woman, slowly traversing the room with a thoughtful but not unimpressed expression, was an art critic for the *Village Voice.*

A few moments later, Helen arrived and began to walk around the room, stopping respectfully in front of each piece before approaching Ilsa with two glasses of champagne. "I already knew this, and I'm sure I've told you this before, but here it is again: you're brilliant."

"You're biased."

"I'm not. I tried to walk around the gallery pretending this was someone else's work. That's why I didn't greet you. I wanted to detach myself. It was impossible, though. You practically bleed off those canvases." Helen's eyes shone. "I wish it didn't all hurt you so much, my daughter. But I'm proud of you for making it all look so beautiful."

"It's getting better. I promise. I'm doing better."

"Listen, my friend Cameron, who lives about ten minutes outside of Rye, maybe you remember her, has decided to spend the next six months abroad visiting her son. She needs someone to look after her house, feed her cat, water her plants . . . I mentioned you and she said it was completely fine for you to stay there. Should I tell her you're interested? Ani and Xavier would love it there. The neighbor has a pony. They could stay with you on weekends. Sorry, I'm not trying to control your life, I just thought—"

"Thanks, Mom. I appreciate it. It seems like the perfect solution, maybe. I'll get in touch with her."

"I'll give her your number."

"How are *you* doing, Mom?"

"Me?" She seemed surprised that Ilsa would ask. Ilsa realized she hadn't in a while. And when someone asked how Helen was, she always told the truth. "Well, I'm actually . . . I'm lonely," she said. "I've been feeling a little lonely lately."

"Aw, Mom. No man on the horizon to distract you?"

To Ilsa's surprise, Helen didn't laugh. "Oh, there's a man on the horizon," she said. "But it's a distant horizon."

"You could come stay with me, too. At Cameron's. I mean, if I do decide to stay there, if it works out."

"Maybe. I think I might head up north, though." She hesitated. "Unless I'm needed here?"

"I'm pretty sure we're all fine. For the moment, at least."

Liane approached. "Oops. I have champagne for you, too,

but it looks like Mom already beat me to it. Ilsa, this is really exquisite work. *Really*. There's just something about these . . . I don't even know what to call them."

Ilsa laughed. "Me neither."

"They make me feel . . ." She tilted her head to one side. "Well, they make me feel sad, at first. They remind me of heartbreak and heartache. And yet, they also make me feel hopeful. They make me believe in love. Does that make any sense at all?"

Ilsa nodded. "It was the point. I was trying to prove that things that have been torn and ruined, things that have failed, can be put back together in other ways. Maybe even in beautiful ways, or at the very least in truer ways." She felt a hand on her arm. Fiona. All of them now, standing with their mother. She thought, *Maybe Helen was right. Maybe we never did* need *the men, the fathers. Maybe we just needed each other, and her.* But she also knew that wasn't necessarily a fair thought, that although the fathers weren't in the room, they were with them—*within* them—and always would be.

"You know, I always liked your paintings, but there's something about these that are better," Fiona said. "Different. Profound. Perfectly *you*. I know nothing about art, but I think these are really good." Liane handed Fiona the extra champagne glass and tapped hers against it.

"Hear, hear," she said.

Helen was smiling. "Girls," she said. "This is the first time we have all been standing together in the same room in a year. I think that calls for a *real* toast." She raised a glass. "To my daughters, my girls, my *people*." They raised their glasses in a perfect circle.

"To you, too, Mom," Fiona said, almost in a whisper. They drank. Then Helen looked across the room.

"How is the visit with Samira going, Fiona? She seems lovely."

Fiona thought for a moment. She, too, looked to where Samira was standing, talking to Cole and Isabel. "It's been strange," she said. "But not bad at all. I guess I was threatened in part because I thought she would be only Tim's and it was somehow going to distance him from all of us even more. When we went to get her at the airport, I was so afraid that everything Tim and I had been working toward would fall apart. I didn't know how I was going to feel, how I was going to deal with her, how I was going to manage to pretend I didn't feel as resentful toward her as I still did, that I wasn't as afraid of her as I felt that day. But then, when she got off the plane, when she came through arrivals, *I* was the one to spot her. I knew it was her immediately. She looks like Tim, a little, don't you think? Holds herself in the same way. And his mouth. And before I could stop myself, I waved. I'm not saying it's all been easy—but she doesn't feel like *just* his. She feels like ours."

Ilsa was listening to Fiona but movement at the door had caught her eye. Lincoln Porter had walked into the studio. He was wearing a dark gray fedora. Fiona trailed off and looked at Ilsa, wide-eyed, and Ilsa shook her head imperceptibly. *No, don't say anything. Don't tell them. And also, don't leave me. Stay with me. I'm scared.* Helen and Liane now started talking about how, if Helen was going to go up north for a few weeks, she and Laurence might bring the girls one weekend. Ilsa said quietly to Fiona: "Just talk to me, please, just talk to me. About anything."

So Fiona started telling her a story about how they had taken Samira sightseeing in the city that day and how fun it was to revisit spots you thought you already knew, to see them through fresh eyes. And then about how they had decided to separate from the boys and go shopping. "For, you know, *dresses* and stuff. It felt like having a daughter, at least I think. And I have to admit, I liked it." She paused. "Ilsa?"

"Please," Ilsa said. "Keep talking. I can't." When Lincoln was at the canvas beside them, Ilsa found she was having trouble breathing. She stared into her sister's eyes and focused on the sound of her voice. Fiona put her hand on her sister's forearm and held it there.

Then he moved around them and on to the next canvas. Only a few more and he was near the door. Fiona stopped talking. They were both watching him now. He was standing still. Ilsa thought he might take a glass of champagne and stay, and that eventually she would have to go over and greet him, thank him for coming. There was a part of her that wanted to know what he thought of her work. There was a part of her that was elated that he had come, even after everything. It meant something. It meant that it hadn't all been for nothing.

He didn't stay, though. He cast one more glance around the room. His dismissive gaze did not reach Ilsa or Fiona. It missed them just barely. Ilsa realized that she had been wrong, that his coming had not meant anything to him.

He left.

"I guess he didn't like what he saw," Ilsa said.

"He didn't *understand* what he saw," Fiona said. "It was above him. Leagues and leagues and leagues above him. Outside of the realm of anything a man like him could possibly understand."

"What are we talking about?" said Helen, leaning in.

"The past," said Ilsa.

Epilogue

ays into her time at the cottage, when Helen finally worked up the courage, he was in his garden, just as he had been the first time she walked alone up this same road.

But something *was* different. No apron, for one thing, and new bushel baskets that looked less worn than his old ones. Helen stood and watched him. Eventually he looked up, and she half expected him to say what he had said that first time, for her to realize she had fallen down some sort of rabbit hole and was being given the chance to do it all over again. *But that doesn't happen in real life, no matter how hard you wish for it. You don't get second chances.*

Instead, he looked up, and she couldn't read the expression on his face because he wasn't quite as familiar to her anymore. This made her sad.

"Hi," he said eventually.

"Hi," she said. She took a step closer, then a few more steps. Finally, she was close enough. "I'm a stubborn old woman," she said, and wished she had chosen to say anything but that as her opening line.

"That might have been one of the things I loved about you, the stubbornness," he said. "Old, though? Never. Not you. But listen, I think we'd better go inside now."

"Might have been? Loved?"

"Come here," he said. There was something in his voice that startled her. When she was beside him she turned and saw that across the road, standing in the trees, there was a coyote, thin and ragged, watching them.

"Oh, and here I thought you were inviting me in because you wanted to, not because we were in mortal danger."

"He's been coming around a lot lately," Iain said. "I should probably call someone in, but I don't have the stomach for it. He seems harmless, but still . . . a little too tame. Maybe he's just lonely."

"How do you know he's a *he*?"

"Something about him. Maybe I'm wrong. Did you know coyotes mate for life?"

Helen leaned against him and said, "I've always thought they were stupid animals." She didn't think he was going to laugh, but he did.

"They're smarter than you think," he said. "Now, please, come inside, Helen. I do want you to. Very much. I have so many things I want to say to you. I've even been making little notes. I have a notebook. Things to Tell Helen."

"Okay, but you're going to think this is weird."

"I bet I won't. I don't think you can surprise me at this point."

She spun around and walked backward toward his cottage. "Help me," she said. "Make sure I don't trip over anything and break a hip."

"*What* are you doing?" he asked.

"I'm rewinding," she said.

He smiled, turned around, took her hand, and started walking backward, too. "What if we both fall?"

"Then we both fall," she said. "But I think I know the way."

Acknowledgments

The following websites were useful when gathering information about the mating habits of the animals for use in the epigraphs at the beginning of each chapter: Wikipedia, eol.org (Encyclopedia of Life), hww.ca (Hinterland Who's Who), bear.org (North American Bear Center), defenders .org (Defenders of Wildlife), barnowltrust.org (The Barn Owl Trust), allaboutbirds.org (The Cornell Lab of Ornithology), northland.edu (Northland College). I also relied on research about swan "divorces" performed at the Slimbridge Wetland Centre in Gloucestershire, England.

Years ago, I was told that to find a home for a book a writer needed to find people who loved it, truly. I have been blessed with an entire team of people who love my book—and the perfect home for it. I am so grateful.

Thank you especially to Samantha Haywood, my passionate and instinctive agent (every nice thing my dad says about you is true); her assistant, Stephanie Sinclair, for a great first read; Sarah Cantin, my extraordinary editor at Atria Books, who has also proven herself to be a mama bear, cheerleader, and dear friend (and who sends the absolute best emails and notes on the planet); and Alison Clarke at Simon & Schuster Canada, for welcoming me warmly and offering wise insights. (Also, for oysters and cocktails.)

And special thanks to Judith Curr of Atria Books and Kevin Hanson at Simon & Schuster Canada, for captaining the ship and for making this publishing house a home.

Thank you to marketing mavens Felicia Quon (I'm still working on the accent) and Anneliese Grosfeld; my wonderful publicist, Amy Jacobson; the rest of the team at S&S Canada (with a particularly warm thank-you to Sarah Smith Eivemark for being my first actual fan); plus marketing pro Hillary Tisman and publicity guru Valerie Vennix at Atria Books.

Thank you to Kathleen Rizzo, Kimberly Goldstein, and Kristen Lemire for all of your hard work on the details and for shepherding my book along the path toward becoming "real"; and to Janet Perr for the beautiful cover.

I am also grateful for and to my friends. In particular, thank you to Chantel Guertin for early reads, literary dream sharing, and jokes only the two of us get; Nance Williams for reading *everything* I send you and for being a constant supporter; Asha Frost (you know why); Priya Karani Davies for keeping the faith (and for the pink champagne); Susan Robertson, Delphine Buglio, and Natalie Bordeau-Legris for the assistance with the French; Joni Serio for teaching me how to fish when it came to my website; and Leigh Fenwick, Michelle Schlag, and Amanda Watson—for being like sisters and for being great friends.

Many fellow writers have helped me out, including Moriah Cleveland, who read, believed, and gave me a much-needed mantra at exactly the right moment ("All shall be well, and all manner of things shall be well"; I suppose I should thank T. S. Eliot for that one, too); Jennifer Close, who offered so many kindnesses; Lauren Groff, who allowed her words to grace the pages of my book; and Grace O'Connell, who compared me to Wolitzer and Atwood, thus making my year, and possibly my life.

Finally, thank you to my family: Bruce Stapley, hands down the best dad ever, for being so proud of me, for passing down the writing gene, for all the cottages weeks and weekends over the course of a lifetime, and for being swell in general; my mom, Valerie Clubine, for standing beside me, behind me, in front of me, and all around me (it doesn't seem like enough, but I think you know how I feel); my stepfather, James Clubine, for the love, the prayers, and for always being in my corner; my brothers, Shane, Drew, and Griffin Stapley, for being untypical brothers (I love you all so much and am proud of each of you); my parents-in-law, Joyce and Joe, for the babysitting (there were times when I wouldn't have been able to write without you!) *and* for raising that Joe guy, of course; and the entire Ponikowski family, for making me feel like one of them, always; plus a special shout-out to my Stapley aunts and uncles: a zanier, prouder, more supportive bunch could not be found anywhere. Thank you also to my always encouraging grandparents: Ron Soper and, in loving memory, Jean Soper (who gave me the strength of character to see a book through to completion and whom I miss every day) and Margaret and Ray Stapley, both of whom were writers and would have loved to hold this book in their hands.

Thank you to my children, Joseph and Maia, for providing astonishing joy, giving me a reason to write, and offering unconditional love. You are my favorites. You are excellent little people.

And last but not least (most, definitely most), thank you to my husband, Joe, for patiently enduring the realities of being married to a writer, for holding my hand, for the bridge visits this past winter, and for loving me. I love you, too, until the end of the world.

Mating for Life

MARISSA STAPLEY

A Reading Group Guide

Questions for Discussion

1. How did the chapter epigraphs inform your experience of each chapter? Did the descriptions of the animal mating patterns make you think differently about monogamy?

2. How are Fiona's, Ilsa's, and Liane's personalities each shaped by their fathers? In contrast, how do you see Helen's influence illustrated in each of their personalities?

3. Turn to Chapter 7 and reread the scene in the faculty lounge in which Grace and Tansy discuss marriage. Why do you think people get married? Stay married? Remarry, even if they had a disastrous first marriage? Did this book affect your vision of marriage in general?

4. How integral is motherhood to Helen's overall identity, and does this change over the course of the novel? What is your perception of her as a maternal figure?

5. Consider the examples of female friendship that we see in the novel, particularly the dynamic between Helen and Edie. How are the relationships between friends different from those between sisters—both in the novel and in your own experience?

6. Discuss Liane and Laurence's justification of their decision not to get married. Is it possible that their vision of a

monogamous, committed relationship without marriage is as idealistic as the institution of marriage itself? Furthermore, in an era where marriage is less common, what do you think deciding to marry means?

7. Consider the evolution of the sisters' relationships with each other, as well as with their mother. Discuss the two scenes in which we see them all together—during the "spa" weekend at Crystal Springs and at Ilsa's art opening. Consider the significance of these two events, and compare and contrast the dynamics between the four of them in each setting. Can you chart any changes in them—as individuals, perhaps, but also as sisters, daughters, and mothers?

8. Discuss the types of secrets kept in the novel and the role these secrets play in the lives of these characters. Do good intentions justify keeping something hidden? If the truth will hurt someone, but discovering that a secret was kept will also hurt them, how can you determine which is the better alternative?

9. Consider the different relationships Liane, Ilsa, and Fiona have with their children and stepchildren. What does being responsible for children mean for each sister? How does it affect their relationships with their partners? What does motherhood mean to you, and has your understanding of it changed after reading this book?

10. We see each of the women in this book confront dissatisfaction in their relationships in a variety of ways. Who do you think handled their discomfort in the best way? What decisions would you have made differently, and how would they have been different?

An excerpt from Marissa Stapley's forthcoming novel

Things to Do When It's Raining

Coming to bookstores in 2017

Visit MarissaStapley.com

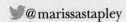@marissastapley

Virginia has always loved the rain. She never hides inside: she goes fishing or for a walk, and she doesn't mind getting wet. Even now, when she knows that rain means danger, she tilts her face up like always to meet the drops. The fear retreats for a moment. But then she lowers her head and keeps walking across the ice, faster now because she knows she must find her husband before it's too late to save him—again.

In the distance, she hears what sounds like a gunshot: it's the ice surrendering to the perfect storm of rising temperatures, melting snow, and precipitation. She wonders how long she has out here, how long he *has*, if he has any time left at all. If she had known it was going to rain she would have gone for help. And usually, she feels it coming. But this time the clouds gathered and she didn't notice. Now that she's already out on the river, she knows she can't turn back. She knows he needs her. Why is she so certain? Because the river, which tells her where the biggest fish are when she goes out in her boat, which tells her so many other things simply because she listens, is telling her now that Chase is in danger. She has known everything about Chase since the moment he stepped off his family's yacht and onto her dock six years ago. She helped him tie a proper sailor's knot and then he looked up at her and said, "Thank you," and the world stopped spinning for a moment, she's convinced. Later he told her he felt it, too: an axis tilt, a realignment of planets. It would be the same if Mae, her daughter, were in danger. Virginia would know. She would feel it. Everything around her would whisper the danger in her ear. But she is certain her little Mae is safe now, up in the attic of the inn playing with her friend Noah, oblivious to the ice that is shifting and about to crack her world.

There's another splintering sound in the distance just as Virginia approaches Island 51. She stands still, looking at the shack with its boarded-up windows. Pointless to even bother, Virginia knows, but maybe Jonah is her only hope now. There's a part of her that believes in this boy she once knew, who is now a broken man, so she climbs the slippery bank, scrambles up the stairs, and pounds on the door—but then doesn't bother to wait for an answer.

Inside it smells sour, like spilled liquor and dampness and failure to thrive.

"Jonah?" A groan. He's facedown on the couch, an empty bottle on the upended milk crate beside him. She shakes him hard and he groans again, so she slaps his face. He recoils, squeezes his eyes shut, emits a noise that sounds like a snore or a death rattle. "Jonah, I think something has happened to Chase. He took out our hovercraft and didn't come back, and now it's raining and the temperature is rising and the ice isn't safe and—oh, wake up, come on! I need you to take me out in your ice cutter to try to find him. Or give me the keys. Where are the keys, Jonah?"

She shakes him again and he mutters, "Tell the boy to stay away as long as he wants, I don't care, the little shit." And then she's crying, not just for herself but for his boy Noah, poor Noah. She's going to make sure, when this is all over, that Jonah starts treating his son better. And if he doesn't, she's going to adopt him, she's going to do something, she will, she will. But first— "Where are the keys to your cutter, Jonah?"

"Aw, fuck off, will you?"

She starts looking for the keys herself. Sticky patches on the counters, old newspapers, flyers, opened cans of stew, half of them still full and stinking. In the bedroom she tries to hold her breath against the stench of piss and vomit; she pulls out drawers, dumps them like she's a burglar, finds nothing but the flotsam and jetsam of a wasted life: matchbooks, ProLine bets, expired coupons. "Damn it! Damn you!"

Back in the kitchen she picks up the phone and hears only dead air. "Pay your goddamn phone bill! I hate you!" she shouts. But this isn't true: hating Jonah would be like hating a wounded animal. Still, she slams the door and the cabin shakes. She slides across the dock and looks for the keys in the cutter, but they aren't there. It's *raining harder than she can remember it raining, ever; she's soaked to her underwear and through her skin, soaked all the way down to her soul, it feels like.*

Back on the river, the ice beneath her feet feels soft but it still holds her. It's not too late, *she tells herself.* It's never going to be too late. As she runs, Virginia thinks of Mae, safe in the attic of the inn playing with Noah. She remembers the perplexed expression on her daughter's face that morning, what she said to Virginia about things she should never have known about. No more. *After this, everything will be different. Virginia runs because she desperately loves Chase, but also because she loves Mae, perhaps even more desperately. It is a love that surprises her, terrifies her, delights her, and has forever changed her, this love she feels for her child. Because of this love Virginia runs faster. Because of this love Virginia believes harder. Because of this love Virginia presses on toward her fate, determined that she will not give up, no matter how hard it rains.*

Chapter 1

Things to Do When It's Raining

A list by Virginia Summers, (self-proclaimed) Junior Proprietor of Summers' Inn, Alexandria Bay, New York

1. Is there someone at home you miss? Write her a letter and say it. Don't wait; tomorrow, it might not be raining.

Mae,

I'm sorry. And I want you to know you meant something to me. I won't forget you. And you won't be implicated. Cardiff had nothing to do with you. Everyone will know that, including the police.

P.S. Please destroy this.

Love, Peter

Mae studies the sentences scrawled on company letterhead like she's an anthropologist interpreting markings on a cave wall. She holds the paper close to her face and searches it for clues. But there's nothing there, just forty-three words that cease to have meaning if you read them too many times—which she has: twenty-seven times since the moment she found the note in her coffee cup, where Peter left it because he knew she would still make coffee even in the midst of crisis. She squeezes her eyes shut against the tears, wills them away, and succeeds but knows it's only a temporary victory. This man she was going to marry, this man who knew her morning habits and almost everything else, this man she thought *she* knew, gone. And he threw so much glitter at her that she missed the clues.

She crumples the note and puts it in her pocket. Then she

leaves her office and steps into Peter's. They have an adjoining door but she doesn't use it; it feels too intimate. She sits at his desk and looks out the window at Brooklyn Bridge Park.

In her mind, she lines up the events of the past twenty-four hours: first, the client calls ("Peter isn't answering his phone. Any idea where he is?"). Peter closing his door, something about a conference call, suggesting she go home because she has been so tired lately. ("Why don't you order dinner? I'll be there as soon as I can. I feel like sashimi.") She bought his favorite microbrew at the corner market and felt the pulse of wifely pleasure, that slightly smug joy one takes in being needed by another as they pass people on the sidewalk who are possibly not needed by anyone at all. She didn't forget the hot sauce and extra wasabi this time. She threw away the chopsticks in the paper sack and got out the mahogany ones she bought him for his birthday. She set it all up on the coffee table, then fell asleep watching Netflix and woke later to the smell of spoiled tuna and the silence that envelops a space when the person being waited for has not come home. (For Mae, such silences always bear the threat of accident and catastrophe; her life so far has given her no reason to believe that disaster is not lurking around every corner.)

She checked her phone: no missed calls. She called his cell phone: it went straight to voicemail. No answer at the office either. She checked the bedroom and the bathroom, the hall, the lobby. Raul, the doorman, said he hadn't seen him, *sorry, querida*; she tried to pretend she wasn't panicking when she asked. She pictured a rogue gypsy cab running him down. A mugging, maybe even a heart attack. His father had had one. Old feelings surfaced, childhood leftovers: heart-pounding fear, the sensation of spiraling down, of ice-cold water running through veins that aren't hers, the knowledge that anything could happen to anyone at any time, that no one is safe, ever.

She went to the office in a taxi. *Maybe he's fallen asleep at his desk.*

An empty office.

And the note. She felt a split second of relief because he was not dead, and then endless devastation after that. She was never confused, though. She knew right away what he had done. This disturbed her because it meant she had *always* known but had pretended not to. It meant she was culpable. It meant she was in trouble, even if he said she was not.

She looks away from the park and down at the yellow diamond on her left ring finger. It had belonged to his mother, he had told her, in a voice hoarse with heartbroken reverence. When Peter spoke of his family she had felt like she was listening to him read from a novel about the undoing of a prominent Southern family, all tragedy and romance, privilege gone sour, a murky history involving a plantation, slaves, family secrets, sex, lies, and a damaged boy. She would heal him with her love, she had decided. She would eradicate his grief over the course of a lifetime—and her own, too, by proxy. This time, with this man, she would succeed.

She bangs her fist against the desk. In response there is a soft *woof*, then a whimper, from the corner of Peter's office. *Bud.* "You bastard, you left your *dog* behind." The dog—named after Bud Fox in the movie *Wall Street*—is lying on a canine bed covered in toile-patterned fabric that Mae picked because it reminded her of the curtains in her childhood bedroom at the inn. There are other things, too, that she flecked her new life with to remind her of home: the painting of the St. Lawrence River that hangs in the firm's lobby; a vase in a fox hunt pattern that she uses as an umbrella stand, just like the one her grandmother keeps at the front door of the inn; the artist's rendering of Summers' Inn itself, hanging on her office wall, a halfhearted attempt to make up for the fact that she has the view of the alley, not the park; the photocopied list, tucked in her desk drawer, a replica of the "Things to Do When It's Raining List" that still hangs on a corkboard in the lobby of the inn. *What would my mother say to me if she were here? She wouldn't be proud of me, that's for sure.* Mae grinds at her eyes with the heels of her hands.

Bud woofs at her again, as if chastising her for not noticing him before now. Peter had said of the dog bed, "It's not very masculine," and Mae had said, "Come on, it's very classic. And it shows a certain security in one's masculinity, don't you think, not to be afraid of a little colonialism?" Who had she become, she now wonders, in the days, the months before this moment? A person who made jokes about colonialism. A person who carried fabric samples in her (obscenely expensive) handbag at all times. A person who had started taking a sommelier course for fun. (It was not fun. It was boring. And every time she spit out a perfectly good mouthful of wine she pictured her grandparents' incredulous faces, her grandparents who saved everything, even paper towels sometimes, rinsed and hanging on the line because, her grandfather George said, those new extra-absorbent ones were so thick they could be used several times.)

Mae stands. "Okay, Bud, let's go." She once found the name of the dog endearing but now she adds it to the list of things that should have alerted her to the fact that Peter was a criminal. Bud Fox, pure intentions or not, had ended up in jail. And how long had canine Bud been sitting there? Clearly, he had used his pee pad. She can smell it in the air now, the urine of a one-hundred-and-twenty-pound Irish wolfhound being a difficult thing to ignore.

"Come on, we'll go for a walk." Bud wags his tail and romps around her, knocking her back into the chair. He's not a city dog; he's a dog who should have many acres upon which to roam. But he's the same kind of dog Peter had on the ruined plantation as a child. Peter said the dog from his childhood—named Earl—was the one positive memory he had extracted from his youth. Until the dog had been hit by a train while out walking with Peter's suicidal brother, of course. Mae had rarely talked about her own childhood with him. She had decided at a certain point to allow him to be the one in the relationship with the tortured past. "You were so lucky," he had once said, "to have had such an idyllic upbringing at that inn, with grandparents who loved you so much." "But . . . my parents died." She thought maybe he'd forgotten somehow, but he'd waved a hand. "You were so young you can't remember them. How can you pine for something you never really had?" These words had hurt her, deeply and swiftly. What she had wanted to say was, "I was five, and I remember everything—and yet, I remember nothing. You can't imagine how much that hurts. Sometimes, I wake from a dream and I know it was a memory, but it slips away from me like a fish down an ice hole. And no matter how I try, I can't get it back. Except there is one memory that no matter what I can't shake: the last time I saw them. What I said, what I did, what I caused. I've never told anyone, but—" Except even when she's only imagining what she might say, she can't finish the sentence. So she buries it back in the place where it lives, deep inside.

Bud is nuzzling her hand, so she clips the leash onto his collar. He resembles an old man: gray, bedraggled, hair growing out of his ears. She suddenly imagines Peter leaving a note for Bud somewhere, maybe tucked into a corner of the dog bed. *You meant something to me, too, Bud. And I'm sorry. Please eat this note.* She shoves her own note deeper into the pocket of her jeans and thinks about what she's going to do with it. Burn it, maybe.

It's now past nine and the office is showing increasing signs of life. She peeks into the office of Gabe, the CFO, but it's as silent and empty as Peter's. He had a paperweight made of meteor rock. "It reminds me that the world could end at any second, so I might as well live it up," he said to her once, perhaps trying to explain why he was dating a twenty-five-year-old waitress he met at Hooters. Where is that rock? There's a dust-free circle where it used to sit, and she has the urge to sweep her arm across his desk and crash everything to the ground.

As she walks through the office, the phone at reception rings. Josh waves and says, "It's for you. Dale Best. He says it's important." She has a voicemail box full of messages from clients like Dale, clients who were hoping to get to Peter through her. She shakes her head and points down at Bud. "He has to go. Urgent."

"I can take him out."

Mae speeds up and pretends not to hear. The elevator opens as she pushes the Down button and Bridget, one of the account managers, steps off.

"Morning!" she says.

"Oh, hi!" It comes out as a shout.

"Hey, is Peter here?"

"Um, not yet."

"Can we chat? I got a strange call from Alex Moffatt last night. I tried to get in touch with Peter, but his phone is off—"

"Definitely!" Mae tugs Bud onto the elevator and feels like her shoulder is dislocating. "I'll be right back." She hits the Close Door button and keeps pressing until finally the doors shut. Outside, she shivers as she walks, rolling the sleeves of her sweater down over her hands and squinting against the winter sunlight. Bud leads her to the park. Once he's inside the fence she unclips his leash and he runs off, first lifting his leg against a fence post and then walking a few paces away to squat, lowering his head modestly. She sinks down onto a bench to wait.

"Mae?" She looks up. It's Jon Evans, a lawyer who works nearby and lives in Williamsburg, the same neighborhood as Mae and Peter do—*did?*—with his wife, Mattie. They have a baby named Jorja. Mae held her once at the office. "This is *my* wife," Peter had said to Jon. "Or—soon to be. She takes care of the marketing for us." How Mae had loved those two words: *my wife.* Jorja had reached her arms out and Mattie had laughed. "She loves meeting new people. She'd go off with anyone. We'll have to teach her about 'stranger danger.'" Mae had cooed as Jorja had pulled at her hair and tried to yank out one of her dangling earrings. ("Do you want kids?" she had asked Peter when they had been dating long enough, fearing the answer. So many men didn't, or said they didn't until it was too late and then had babies with women who had not been left on the shelf so long that they were reproductively challenged. "Of course I want kids," he had said. "That's a silly question.")

She had envisioned inviting Jon and Mattie to dinner parties.

She had imagined Jorja playing with their future babies.

Jon and Mattie had invested a huge amount of money in Cardiff Turbine.

"Mae? Are you all right?" She realizes she has been staring at Jon in a silence that has stretched too thin. Jon's dog, a Wheaton terrier, has wandered over to Bud, who is sniffing Myles's hindquarters with proprietary familiarity.

"You're a prosecutor, right?" she finds herself saying.

Jon frowns. "Ye-es. Mae, are you okay?"

Mae calls for Bud. "I'm sorry," she says to Jon. "Just . . . I'm not feeling well."

"Can I do anything?"

"No. Thanks. I need to get back to the office now, I think. Maybe head home and lie down . . ."

"That's probably a good idea; you look pale. Hey, but sorry, okay—can you have Peter call me when he gets a sec? I need to double check something with him."

Mae's hand trembles as she attaches the leash to Bud's collar. "Will do," she says without looking up. As she walks away, she realizes she's forgotten something. Let that be added to the catalog of her transgressions: *"And she walked away without even picking up her dog's shit."*

Back at the office, a knot of people have gathered. There is silence as she approaches, and accusation in their stares. "I'm surprised you came back," says Josh. "I thought *you'd* taken off, too." So he knows now. He's figured out that Peter is not coming back and he's duped everyone. Josh looks at her with revulsion and pity and something else. Because she was Peter's fiancée, which means she either knew about this—in which case she's a horrible person—or did not—in which case she's a fool. *I'm both,* she wants to say. *And I'm so sad, and I'm so sorry.*

The elevator doors open again. A man and a woman emerge. As their hands go into their jacket pockets, Mae knows they're reaching for police badges. She reaches into her own pocket and feels for the note. She crumples it tighter, makes it small enough not to exist.

"How long have you known Peter Greaves?"

"About a year." *A year next week.* Both detectives are taking notes.

"And you worked together, but you were romantically involved also?"

"Yes. We were engaged." She can picture Peter holding the ring out, six months before. In that moment she had felt like the pieces of her life were cascading into place—or, that her life was expanding to fit more pieces. They had been in Paris, at the top of the Ferris wheel at the Tuileries. On the way down, he had said, "Doesn't it feel like we're flying?" Everything with Peter felt spontaneous, even the proposal, even with the ring already in his pocket. *Let's take the ferry to Staten Island for lunch. Let's take a helicopter tour. Let's fly to Chicago, just to have dinner. Let's make love, right here, right now. No one can see.* She touches the diamond. "Maybe this sounds odd, or obvious, I guess, but I didn't know him as well as I . . . as I should have."

"Can you please explain that to us more clearly?"

"I extracted the pieces of him I needed for the life I wanted to lead, and I constructed a person who did not exist," she says. "I was in love with that person—"

"Ms. Summer—"

"—and I hoped he would eventually fall in love with me the way I had fallen in love with him. Or that maybe he, too, would construct a version of me that he could love." That Ferris wheel and flying through the Parisian dusk and feeling certain that she was not, as she had always feared, going to die alone, with no family left after her grandparents died, with no one left to care about what happened to her—that's what started the emotional landslide. "And then," she continues, feeling the tears making good on their threat, at last, "and then I could become that person. I wanted to become that person, whoever he wanted me to be, so that we could move forward and build our life. But it turns out all he wanted was a foil for his scam." In the awkward silence that follows, the female detective hands her a tissue. Mae blows her nose and wipes her eyes, then sits up straight, as if good posture might count for something here.

"Are you ready to continue?" the male asks.

"Yes."

"Mae, what we need is for you to stick to the facts alone." His tone is paternal. This strikes a chord deep inside her but she doesn't start to cry again. She won't.

"I know. I'm really sorry."

"We do realize that this is difficult. It's just that right now it's crucial we act if we're going to find him before he disappears completely."

"I get it. It's fine." *Before he disappears completely.* As though

Peter was a magician and all this time she had no idea that she was simply the assistant, about to be sawed in half.

"Did you have any reason to believe that something wasn't right about Cardiff Turbine?"

"Yes. No. Not exactly. I mean . . ." She wipes her sweaty palms on her pants. *I really should get a lawyer. Why did I say no?* "I had a feeling, I think. But I—I was too afraid to say anything to Peter."

"Afraid why? Afraid that he might harm you in some way?"

She shakes her head. "Afraid, I guess, that he would leave," she says in a voice that sounds too childlike. "Afraid to make him angry or unhappy. Because it was very important to me to make . . . to make him happy."

A look Mae can't decipher passes between the two officers.

"When was the last time you were in contact with him?"

"Last night, around six o'clock. He said he would meet me at home. He said, 'I feel like sashimi.' I was tired, and I fell asleep waiting, and then came straight here when I woke up, around five in the morning."

"And he wasn't here?"

"No."

"Did he leave anything behind, any sort of message for you?"

"Nothing." She can no longer feel her legs. She thinks she's having a panic attack. *Please destroy this.*

"And he didn't ask you to meet him anywhere?"

"He didn't, no."

"Recently, your name was removed from a significant loan that was cosigned by you and Gabe Marchant, around the time the company was started."

Here, she feels a glimmer of something. He hadn't acted like it at the time, when she told him about the island, but she sees now that he did understand, that he did see her parents' legacy as meaningful. But what does that matter now?

"Yes. It was refinanced in Gabe's name only."

"Do you know why?"

"We recently visited my hometown together. Alexandria Bay. And we discussed . . ." She clears her throat. "There's an island that I own, on the St. Lawrence, near the bay. I told him about it." *I've never told anyone about it. I almost told him more. I might have told it all, except . . . he didn't ask. But it mattered to him. He heard me, and he cared.* She is clinging to this fact like a drowning person. She hates herself for it.

"And so he was protecting your assets? Is that what he said to you?"

"I . . . he didn't really put it that way. But I guess." Should she be grateful for this small mercy? She is, she realizes, even if the island exists only as a dark, distant memory at the edge of her life. She hasn't been out there for years.

"Did you ever wonder why Peter never cosigned on the loan for the business?"

"He said he had a problem with his credit rating because of a company he tried to start when he first graduated from college."

"Earlier, you said you had a feeling something was amiss, but nothing you could formalize. Was this just a *sense* he was keeping secrets from you?"

"He would often tell me that there were parts of the business I didn't need to worry about, that he was the one with the business sense. That sounds awful said out loud, doesn't it? Because I have business sense, too. I received a merit-based fellowship at Columbia Business School, every year. I made the dean's list every year, too. I'm sorry, I know maybe that doesn't matter, but—Peter used to tell me that wasn't the 'real world,' the world of academia. I always found his disdain for higher education strange, given that he was a Harvard grad."

At this, the female detective raises an eyebrow and Mae

"I'm not alone, I have *you*. My hundred-and-twenty-pound millstone."

She turns out the light and leaves him in the dark, feels mean, but is incapable of extending kindness to anyone, even a dog. He doesn't take it personally. She hears him pad into the bedroom and jump onto the bed to join her where she is lying, fully clothed. He weighs down the side of the bed that used to be Peter's, and when she reaches out, he licks her hand in the darkness. She wishes, for just a moment, that Peter really did have a dog named Earl, that maybe that one thing was true. That, for what it was worth, he really was once just a boy with a dog.

The next morning at the police station, Detective Baker says, "Mae, we have confirmation that Bradley was on a flight to Cape Town Tuesday night. But the South African authorities have already lost track of him." In the distance, Mae hears a phone ring, car horns honking outside, someone coughing.

"It's where he said he wanted to go on our honeymoon," she says. "South Africa—or close. He was doing a lot of research on it. He said he wanted to find somewhere very remote. Somewhere we could hide away. God." She grips the table with both hands. "He talked about an island near South Africa with a really small population. I can't remember what it was called now. Tristan something?"

Detective Baker grabs a pen. "Tristan da Cunha?"

"Yes. That's it."

"This sort of thing happens," Detective Galati says, and Mae knows he's trying to comfort her because she can't imagine what her face looks like right now. "This sort of thing happens all the time." And Mae knows this, of course. She's read the articles, heard the names: Bernie Madoff. Jeff Skilling and Ken Lay. Dennis Kozlowski and Mark Swartz. "It blew up in their faces too soon," he adds. "They all had to run before they were prepared to. And we're confident many of them will be apprehended."

"What's going to happen now?" she asks.

"We're handing the case over to the FBI. This should happen within the next twelve hours."

"Are they going to need to talk to me?" She's relieved when both detectives shake their heads.

"We'll pass our file on you along. But the investigation is going to become an international one. You'll be expected to be a witness if Bradley and company are ever found and charged, but you shouldn't hear anything before that. We're certain there isn't any more information you can provide."

"Can I leave the city? Once the case is handed over? Because the thing is, I'm getting evicted from the apartment. And I'm pretty sure I have no choice but to go home."

"Where's home?"

Bud, at her feet, rolls over, his way of requesting a tummy rub. She complies. "Upstate. Alexandria Bay. It's beside the St. Lawrence River. It's where they invented Thousand Island dressing." She doesn't know why she has offered this piece of information, but it feels good to give them something so inconsequential in contrast to all the things of great consequence she has said to them over the past week. Perhaps she'll tell them the legend of Pirate Bill, or the heartbreaking tale of Boldt Castle. "Also—"

But Detective Galati hands her a notepad before she can say anything more. "Could you put your contact information here? Address, phone number?"

As Mae writes "Summers' Inn," she pictures it, perched at the edge of the place where the St. Lawrence River flows into the bay. She sees the yellow-gray stone walls, the navy blue shutters on every window, the red roof, the weathervane in the shape of a sturgeon. She sees the guest cabins and the dock and the white-painted boathouse and the old gas pump that's no longer in use. She sees the trees lined up along the bank, their leaves and needles the color of army fatigues in peacetime; she sees the old oak tree with the rope hanging from its thick branch; and she sees herself and Noah as children, swinging and splashing, over and over. She sees his little boat with the outboard motor. She sees the islands, the white chalk on the rocks, the numbers, and the names: Blueberry. Rachel's. Half Moon, and Island 51. She puts the pen down.

"Good luck, Mae," Detective Galati says to her, and he sounds so sincere and she doesn't know how to reply so she tries to smile instead, but doesn't quite succeed.

**Look for *Things to Do When It's Raining*
in bookstores in 2017**

Visit MarissaStapley.com

 **@marissastapley**